LEABHARLANNA CHONTAE FHINE GALL
FINGAL COUNTY LIBRARIES

Items should be returned on or before the last date shown below. Items may be renewed by personal application, by writing or by telephone. To renew give the date due and the number on the barcode label. Fines are charged on overdue items and will include postage incurred in recovery. Damage to, or loss of items will be charged to the borrower.

Date Due	Date Due	Date Due

The
COLLECTED SHORT STORIES
of
ROLAND MATHIAS

Edited, with an Introduction and Notes
by
SAM ADAMS

UNIVERSITY OF WALES PRESS
CARDIFF
2001

British Library Cataloguing-in-Publication Data.
A catalogue record for this book is available from the British Library.

ISBN 0–7083–1660–3

Published with the financial support of the Arts Council of Wales

THE ASSOCIATION FOR
WELSH WRITING IN ENGLISH
CYMDEITHAS LLÊN SAESNEG CYMRU

Typeset at University of Wales Press
Printed in Great Britain by Dinefwr Press, Llandybïe

Contents

෨

Foreword

❧

This edition is part of a series of publications, sponsored by the Universities of Wales Association for the Study of Welsh Writing in English, bringing together collected editions of Welsh authors writing in English. The field has received relatively little attention in the past and it is hoped that, with the re-publication of major literary works from earlier this century and before, critical interest will be stimulated in writers who will handsomely repay such attention. The editions are conceived of on scholarly lines and are intended to give a rounded impression of the author's work, with introductions, bibliographical information and notes.

JOHN PIKOULIS
General Editor

Acknowledgements

ॐ

The making of this book has been greatly assisted by the cooperation of others. In the first place, I am deeply indebted to the University of Wales Association for the Study of Welsh Writing in English for accepting my proposal that to gather together Roland Mathias's short fiction, all of it many years out of print, was a worthwhile project. More especially, I am grateful to the Association's series editor, Dr John Pikoulis, who put me firmly on the right track, read the typescript, and made many helpful suggestions. As ever, the editorial department of the University of Wales Press has been meticulously supportive in the task of preparing the text for publication. Most of all I offer my thanks to Roland Mathias for his readiness to discuss any issue related to the project, and for giving me access to a wide range of documents and books that have helped to increase my understanding, appreciation and enjoyment of stories that I have always admired. My best hope is that the book succeeds in doing the same for the wider readership the stories deserve.

Editorial Note

ॐ

The first four, previously unpublished, stories are printed from typescripts supplied by Roland Mathias. Acknowledgement is gratefully made to the editors and publishers of *The Anglo-Welsh Review* and *Planet*, where the final three stories first appeared. The text of the latter and of the remaining stories which were gathered in *The Eleven Men of Eppynt* follows that of the published versions, except that inconsistencies in punctuation have been removed and the very few typographical errors amended silently.

INTRODUCTION

Roland Mathias was born at Ffynnon Fawr, a farm in the valley known as Glyn Collwn, near Talybont-on-Usk, Breconshire, on 4 September 1915. His father, an army chaplain, was with the forces in the Dardanelles and later on the Western Front. His mother, who had been for a while a pupil-teacher at the elementary school in Talybont-on-Usk, remained with her parents. They had married in the December following the outbreak of the First World War, but did not set up home together until early in 1920, when they moved into a top-floor apartment in what had been an elegant mansion on the bank of the Rhine at Riehl, a suburb of Cologne. The writer's earliest memories, later incorporated into one of his short stories, are of watching from a high window the passage of shipping on the broad waterway below. In 1923, the family returned to Britain and a succession of temporary homes in or close to army camps, at Bulford on Salisbury Plain, Aldershot, Catterick and Aldershot again, before Evan Mathias, by this time a colonel and the longest-serving chaplain of the United Board (the combined Free Churches), retired and brought them back to Wales. They settled in a town he and his wife knew well – Brecon.

Evan Mathias had been born in a humble roadside cottage at Gât Bwlch-Clawdd, Rhos Llangeler, Carmarthenshire, though the family soon moved to Llanelli, where the father's skills as carpenter, builder and wheelwright were better rewarded. Evan was one of nine children and throughout his life kept in touch with the extensive network of his family relations. This close-knit group sacrificed much to enable him to proceed to University College, Cardiff and subsequently to theological college in Brecon.

The father of Muriel Morgan, who would become the writer's mother, had been obliged by ill health to give up his share in a family building concern in Cardiff for the purer air of Breconshire. He communicated to his daughter his distrust of their Welsh-speaking neighbours who, he thought, had conspired to cheat him when he was taking up his first farm tenancy. This did not prevent her being bowled over by the darkly handsome student of Brecon's Coleg Coffa, who preached in both Welsh and English and was steeped in the culture of his native land. They continued unalike in the measure of their regard for their Welsh heritage, and this was not the only source of tension between them. He was sociable and outgoing, she retiring and truly happy only at home with her children. Above all, he committed himself to participation in the war effort, albeit as a chaplain, and made a career in the army. For her, the usual round of peace-time army life went against the grain. He soldiered on, while she developed, through the 1930s, a radically puritan faith and an extreme pacifism that brooked no qualification or equivocation.

Until he retired in 1940, Evan Mathias had little time to spare for his family. It was predictable in the circumstances that his wife's particular brand of religious conviction and her pacifism would have a strong influence on their children. As he grew older, however, and began to make his way in the world, Roland Mathias found he had more in common with his father, and more to discuss with him. They became interested in each other in a way that the circumstances of an army childhood and a boarding school education had not permitted. Above all, the writer's realization of his Welsh roots and commitment to Wales has everything to do with Evan Mathias and the Welsh-speaking cousinhood who had their humble origins on 'the Rhos', the moorland of Rhos Llangeler. Their stories, their constant familial warmth, their natural worthiness, and the distance the writer perceives between his worldly status and comfort and their unconsidered, harsher lives, have a profound influence on his creative output in poetry and prose.

Roland Mathias overcame childhood diffidence, a stammer and lack of inches by the exercise of a formidable intellect and his father's attributes of sociability, energy and vigorous application to tasks. In 1926, he entered Caterham School, Surrey, a notable independent school with a strong Christian tradition, as a 'ministerial', one of that large group of boys whose fathers were ministers of religion. He also found there a substantial number who shared with him a strong Welsh connection. He survived initial homesickness to become academically successful and a keen participant in the many cultural and sporting activities the school offered. Barely eighteen when he went up to Jesus College in 1932, he continued much as at Caterham, gaining a First in history, and a B.Litt. for his research on 'The economic policy of the Board of Trade 1696–1714'. Reading among primary sources for this topic made him familiar with actual events that would provide the basis for his short story, 'The Neutral Shore'.

At the beginning of the Second World War, he was teaching at Cowley School, St Helens. As a conscientious objector he resisted conscription and, with a strength of religious conviction and doggedness that echoed his mother's, refused to be registered for non-combatant duties, since in his view that too would support the war effort. He was sentenced to three months with hard labour. When he left prison in November 1941, he ignored the direction to civil work that would allow another man to serve in the forces and found a teaching post at the Blue Coat School in Reading. The authorities continued to demand compliance with the original court ruling and again in December 1942 he was sent to gaol. Within a week or so, staff colleagues and pupils raised the sum necessary to pay a fine and obtain his release. That he was a conscientious objector was never a secret and it is significant that, at this most difficult period of the war, he won the support of many fellow teachers, pupils and, at St Helens, players and officials of the rugby union club for which he played.

In Reading, he married Molly Hawes, daughter of a farming family from Enstone in Oxfordshire, and his other career, as writer and editor, began. His first book of poems, *Days Enduring*, came out in 1942 (finding its best sales at the Blue Coat School), and in 1944–5, while still living in Reading, he helped to found and co-edited *Here Today*, an ambitious, if short-lived, literary magazine. The three numbers include several contributions by Mathias, three poems, a short story and two articles, one on Robert Frost, the other on trends he disapproved of in the modern novel. Also in 1944 his work appeared in Keidrych Rhys's *Modern Welsh Poetry*. There he found himself in the company of Idris Davies, Vernon Watkins, Dylan Thomas, R. S. Thomas and others, but since infancy he had only holidayed in Wales and they were unknown to him.

Towards the end of the 1930s, the aspiring author might have found a number of potential models in the catalogue of practising short story writers from Wales: Caradoc Evans's literary fame, or notoriety, in the genre dated from 1915; Rhys Davies had already published six collections of stories, commencing with *The Song of Songs* in 1927; Glyn Jones's *The Blue Bed* and Geraint Goodwin's *The White Farm* had come out in 1937; and Dylan Thomas's *Portrait of the Artist as a Young Dog* created a stir in 1940. There is no sign of indebtedness to any of these in Mathias's story writing, nor should there be, since he knew nothing of most of them.

By his own account, it was not until the mid-1940s that he learned about Dylan Thomas as a poet, and his interest in Thomas's prose began in the 1970s. He did not read Caradoc Evans until the 1960s, and then he did not like what he read, for understandable reasons: Rhos Llangeler is but a short distance from Caradoc's Rhydlewis, and Roland Mathias's view of impoverished, chapel-centred, rural communities, derived from knowledge of his father's kin, is diametrically opposed to that presented in *My People* and *Capel Sion*. He began reading Rhys Davies, a writer for whom he feels greater artistic sympathy, only in the 1960s.

His acquaintance with Gwyn Jones and Glyn Jones is of earlier date. In 1944, he sent copies of *Here Today* to both. From the former, whom he knew only as editor of *The Welsh Review*, he received an encouraging, if ultimately unhelpful, response: '. . . we of the provinces should help ourselves in these matters [that is, lack of interest among metropolitan critics] and breathe through other than London lungs. More power to you.' The latter he admired as the short story writer whose book *The Water Music and Other Stories* was published in 1944 – by Routledge, the company that, not long after, would bring out his own second volume of poems. Glyn Jones replied with a critical observation – 'I enjoyed your article more, much more, than your story' – which did not prevent Mathias re-publishing 'Block-System', the fictionalizing of a piece of family history, in the first number of *Dock Leaves*.

Correspondence continued and the writers met while both were on holiday in Pembrokeshire in 1946, but the indelible characteristics of Glyn Jones's highly imaginative art have left no mark on the short stories of Roland Mathias. Nor do we see signs of the influence of Geraint Goodwin, another writer whose work, published in London, he noticed in the 1940s, and sought out because Goodwin's subject was the border country between England and Wales, for which he too felt a strong affinity. Their routes to writing could not have been more different. Goodwin, a successful newspaper reporter, had clear ideas about what was needed to transform his journalistic skills into those of a creative writer. He resigned his Fleet Street job and asked Edward Garnett, that remarkable literary adviser, who had nurtured the talents of Conrad, Lawrence and E. M. Forster among others, to be his mentor. Garnett agreed and it was under his tutelage that Goodwin produced his best work, including the short stories in the *White Farm* collection.

Mathias, as we have seen, went from Caterham and Oxford into a succession of demanding teaching jobs, and did what he could to develop his writing in his spare time. The notebooks (actually standard school exercise books) in which he wrote or fair-copied several of the stories and many poems of the 1940s, the latter usually with the date and place of composition, reveal that his literary efforts were largely confined to school holidays. There was no one to suggest he delve in this corner or that of his experience and emotional life, as Garnett had advised Goodwin. The stories simply came as and when they would, and time allowed.

Teaching took him briefly to Carlisle in 1945, and then south again to London, where in 1946 his second collection of poems, *Break in Harvest*, was published. In 1948, at the age of thirty-three, he became headmaster at Pembroke Dock Grammar School. When, soon after, he appointed Raymond Garlick as a member of staff, the stage was set for one of the most important post-war literary developments in Wales. Roland Mathias was a prime mover in the founding of *Dock Leaves*, invented its punning title and was its most prolific contributor. The magazine displayed the scope of his talent, not only as a poet of recognized achievement and still-growing strength, but as a skilled and versatile short story writer and a gifted scholar and critic. Mathias's familiarity with, and championing of, Welsh writing in English began with *Dock Leaves* and has much to do with the cultured and historical perspective of literature in Wales of the magazine's editor, Raymond Garlick. Eventually, with number 27 (and by this time renamed *The Anglo-Welsh Review*), the editorship passed to Mathias. The breadth of interests represented in the magazine, the service it performed as a showcase for writers, the standards it set in literary criticism and reviewing, made it uniquely valuable at a time when writing from Wales received scant attention, even in the University of Wales.

Unusually for a headteacher, he led by both inspiration and example, taking an active part in the school's burgeoning cultural life. Outside, he was constantly in demand and constantly busy in the artistic and religious affairs of the community. During this period, he produced his third book of poems, *The Roses of Tretower* (1952), and his only collection of short stories, *The Eleven Men of Eppynt* (1956). After a decade in Pembrokeshire, he moved on, first to the Herbert Strutt School, Belper (1958–64), and then to King Edward VI Five Ways School, Birmingham (1964–9), maintaining in both a regime hardly less vigorous and culturally enlightened than that he had instituted at Pembroke Dock.

A further collection of poems, *The Flooded Valley*, was published in 1960. That it contained only eight new poems to represent the years 1952–9 is an indication of his industry in the field of education and a preoccupation with prose writing of various kinds. Election to a schoolmaster studentship at Balliol College, Oxford, in 1961 gave him a term's respite from Belper, which he used to complete a research project upon which he had been engaged intermittently for twenty years. The outcome, *Whitsun Riot: An Account of a Commotion amongst Catholics in Herefordshire and Monmouthshire in 1605*, a remarkable work of historical detection, was published in 1963. The influence of his studies into this upsurge of protest among recusants in that part of the borderland known as Archenfield is apparent in several poems and, inasmuch as it involves certain friends and supporters of the Devereux, the Earl of Essex, fleetingly in one of his short stories, 'The Palace'.

In the summer of 1969, he quitted the education service to become a full-time writer, and moved with Molly to a bungalow in Brecon. The monumental task of editing *The Anglo-Welsh Review* continued to absorb much of his time until he finally relinquished it in 1976, but he still found the intellectual and creative energy to publish a number of articles on aspects of literature and historical topics, notably the history of the English language in Wales, a key study of the life and work of Vernon Watkins (1973), and perhaps his finest book of poems, *Absalom in the Tree* (1974). A book-length study, *The Hollowed-out Elder Stalk*: *John Cowper Powys as Poet*, followed in 1979, the year that also saw his sixth volume of poetry, *Snipe's Castle*. His selected poems, *Burning Brambles*, was published in 1983, and a collection of his major essays on Anglo-Welsh literature, *A Ride through the Wood*, in 1985.

In May 1986 he suffered a stroke, which brought to an end his remarkably rich and diverse labours as critic, editor, scholar, historian, preacher and lecturer. The loss to life and letters in Wales has been incalculable. He has, nevertheless, continued to write poetry and to prepare for the press work that was on the stocks when he fell ill. Yet another volume of poetry, *A Field at Vallorcines*, was published in 1996. In 1999 his contributions were still appearing in magazines.

The range of Mathias's published prose, of which there is a very great deal, is impressively wide. A large tranche is securely founded on his scholarship as a historian. He wrote the chapters on the Civil War period in the Pembrokeshire County History, and if we judge by public lending rights remuneration, *Whitsun Riot* is his most popular book. As noted above, he has also written magisterially on the shifting language frontiers of Wales, and on the story of Anglo-Welsh literature: his *Illustrated History* appeared in 1987. An important study of Henry Vaughan, based in large measure on fresh historical research, was unfinished at the onset of his illness in 1986 and is unlikely now to be completed.

In addition to history and historical studies in language and literature, there is a great deal of literary criticism. He set standards in rigorous textual analysis that remain a touchstone for all who have aspirations in this field. Then there are the reviews, which were drafted with the same meticulous care he gave to his creative writing. For *The Anglo-Welsh Review* alone he wrote 124 reviews in which he dealt with more than 160 books in considerable detail, as well as brief notes on dozens of magazines, tracts, pamphlets and spoken-word recordings.

Roland Mathias began writing short stories in the early 1940s, at a high-water mark for the genre. Stories found a ready response in a population that had needed to become used to reading in snatches. Numerous small magazines came briefly into existence to cater for the habit and they attracted a host of would-be authors. The seriousness of Mathias's ambition to supplement his income (he taught at the Blue Coat School for a pittance), and to make his name as a writer, is borne out by a diary for 1941 in which he listed the addresses of some 260 magazines, editors and publishers. Later in the same diary, over a period of several years, he also recorded the fifty-three publications to which he submitted stories or poems and, with a cross or a tick, whether or not successfully. Unfortunately none of the entries is dated, but the ticked stories include 'Joking with Arthur', which appeared in *Seven Magazine for Popular Writing,* 'Digression into Miracle' and 'One Bell Tolling' in Keidrych Rhys's *Wales,* and 'The Rhine Tugs' in *Adelphi.* 'Cassie Thomas' was promised to an anthology, 'Stories in Transition', to be edited by Lionel Montieth, which never appeared, and lastly 'A Night for the Curing' came out in a special 'Welsh Writers' number of *Life and Letters To-day* in 1949. 'Incident in Majorca', published in *Penguin New Writing* number 20, 1944, is an absentee, presumably because it was taken by John Lehmann, editor of the Penguin series, before the list was started.

During the period 1944–8 the writer's creative energies were chiefly expended on poetry – or teaching – but a revival of interest in story writing followed his move to Pembroke Dock. 'A Night for the Curing' was the first product, and, in addition to 'Block-System', four new stories were published in *Dock Leaves* in fairly quick succession: 'The Palace' (1950), 'The Eleven Men of Eppynt' (1951), 'Ffynnon Fawr' (1953) and 'Match' (1956). All, with the exception of 'Joking with Arthur', were gathered into Mathias's only collection, *The Eleven Men of Eppynt and Other Stories,* where they were joined by two stories making their first appearance in print, 'The Neutral Shore' and 'Agger Makes Christmas'. Only three stories were written in more than twenty years following the publication of *The Eleven Men of Eppynt,* and they complete the present volume: 'The Only Road Open' and 'Siams', published in *The Anglo-Welsh Review* in 1964 and 1978 respectively, and 'A View of the Estuary' in *Planet* in 1973.

The 'Author's Note' to *The Eleven Men of Eppynt* asserts that the contents appear 'for better or worse', in strict chronological order – of composition rather than publication, since 'One Bell Tolling', which appeared in *Wales* in 1945, precedes in the book 'Digression into Miracle', also first published in *Wales,* but in 1944. It is clear nonetheless that the first seven stories in the book were written between 1941 and 1943, since they all appear in draft in a notebook the writer began using while he was teaching at Cowley

School, St Helens (referred to elsewhere in this introduction and in the notes as the 1941–3 Notebook). The earliest dated entry in the book, a poem, 'Nepotism', subsequently published in *Days Enduring*, was written or transcribed on 5 February 1941 at St Helens; the last, also a poem, 'Credo', which remained unpublished, on 5 January 1943. The 1941–3 Notebook contains drafts of two more stories – 'The Roses of Cwmdu' (in a later typescript retitled 'The Roses of Tretower') and 'Joking with Arthur', which, as noted above, was published in *Seven*, in 1944. Neither found a place in *The Eleven Men of Eppynt*, presumably because they were considered too slight, though the former was later re-worked metrically to become the narrative title-poem of Mathias's third volume of poetry. The contents list of *The Eleven Men of Eppynt* tells us that 'The Neutral Shore' was written next, but it failed to find a publisher, or was simply put aside, until gathered into the book.

Considered overall, the eighteen published stories are interestingly disparate, thematically and stylistically, and for the most part their origins can be traced to a known range of sources. 'Digression into Miracle' and 'The Neutral Shore' are the by-products of historical research, but above all Mathias exploited personal experience. This is chiefly the basis of 'Take Hold on Hell', 'Incident in Majorca', 'One Bell Tolling', 'The Rhine Tugs', 'The Palace', 'Agger Makes Christmas', 'Match' and 'The Only Road Open'. A combination of personal experience and tales about his father's family lies behind 'Block-System', 'Ffynnon Fawr', 'A View of the Estuary' and 'Siams'. Anecdotes the writer had heard are the source of 'Joking with Arthur', 'Cassie Thomas' and 'A Night for the Curing'. They came in the main from his father, from a favourite uncle, one of his father's brothers (memorialized in the poem 'For an Unmarked Grave'), and from a cousin of his father's, a gifted and indefatigable story-teller, who is fictionalized as the eponymous character in the story 'Siams'. Only 'The Eleven Men of Eppynt' does not fit conveniently into one or other of these categories; it is simply a piece of narrative invention.

The organization of the stories in this book and in the discussion of them that follows takes account of the writer's chronological scheme in *The Eleven Men of Eppynt*. It is a simple matter to follow the pattern with the three stories published after

1956, but less easy to fit into it 'Joking with Arthur' and four unpublished stories – 'Saturday Night', 'A Duty to the Community', 'Jonesy and the Duke' and 'The Roses of Tretower', the first three of which exist only as dog-eared typescripts. It is certain they all belong early in the 1941–3 period, though the order in which they were written is unknown. Not entirely arbitrarily, therefore, they have been placed at the beginning of the book.

Like 'Joking with Arthur', they are lightweight. They range in length from under a thousand words to about fifteen hundred and, with the exception of 'Saturday Night', are not far removed from their anecdotal sources. Characterization and the use of imagery are far less developed in them than in the published stories. Nevertheless, they offer a useful introduction to the short story *œuvre* of Roland Mathias, not least because they foreshadow certain developments and characteristic features in his writing. 'Saturday Night', for example, begins without explanatory preamble. As with 'The Neutral Shore' (discussed below), the reader may well be unable to grasp what is happening. The sense of uncertainty is compounded in this case by biblical language and rhythms, and a mock-heroic tone. The effect is surrealistic, and there is something of this in the intention of the writer. A similar sense of disorientation is produced by the poem 'Judas Maccabeus', published in *The Roses of Tretower* (1952), which begins in similar tone:

> The gallery of faces is a cloud
> Hiding a thunderbolt. Below stairs feet are loud
> In the aisle . . .
>   . . . Shortly is heard the roll
> Of despair, the Israelitish women crying at the wall
> Dragging their sorrow like hair . . .

The mock heroic comes easily to Mathias who sees, beneath the vain pose, the frailty of man. To understand both the poem and the story, the reader needs to be familiar with the long tradition of religious oratorios (vocal music being another of Mathias's many interests and accomplishments), for the former describes a production of Handel's *Judas Maccabaeus*, and the latter a rehearsal of Mendelssohn's *Elijah*, at 'The Plough', a chapel of the

United Reformed Church in Brecon. Both exploit the incongruity in amateur performance between powerful biblical language (the text incorporates recitatives and choruses from the oratorios) and commonplace settings: 'the prophet slept under a juniper tree and the angels of the Lord were camped round about him. Their gymshoes were light on the boards and their breathing tight out of uniform collars. "Arise, Elijah, for thou hast a journey before thee".' In its approach to the theme, though not in particulars, the story is a lively sketch for the poem, which was written and first published (in *The Welsh Review*) in 1946.

'The Roses of Tretower' bears a similar relationship to the far more complex poem of the same name, in which the roses become symbols of Christian love and sacrifice and there is no room for the link made in the story between their miraculous transplant-ation and ancient family ties with the Vaughans of Tretower. The framing of the story, however, provides a more or less authentic explanation of how it came to the writer's ears. As a tale about farming life in the Brecon area, an authoritarian father and a beautiful, disobedient daughter, it may have had a particular appeal for Mathias, who would return to the same theme (in 1945) in 'The Ballad of Barroll's Daughter', a narrative poem about similar events two generations back in his mother's family.

'Jonesy and the Duke' is a sketch (one that was not elaborated subsequently), incorporating three anecdotes about Jonesy, the town clerk of Cwmwd Coch, hearty drinker and prankster. Its source is again gossip from the Brecon area, a familiar patch to Mathias's parents, especially his father who, after his retirement there, got about in the community a good deal. 'Joking with Arthur', though a published story, is best considered here with the unpublished stories. Like 'Jonesy and the Duke', it is a light-hearted anecdote from the Brecon area told in language that imitates colloquial Anglo-Welsh rhythms, word order and diction. The description of Arthur, 'like one of them big old ewes that look over the wall at you', anticipates that of Morgan Williams in 'One Bell Tolling', who is 'big-boned, almost sheeplike', but there the resemblance ends. The location of the action in 'A Duty to the Community' is 'the Rhos', for Mathias heard the tale from his father's Carmarthenshire relations. The writer's intention and approach are identical to those in 'Joking with Arthur' and a sad fate for ducks becomes a laughing matter in both stories.

Whatever the writer's intention, 'Saturday Night' and 'The Roses of Tretower' turned out to be preliminary sketches for more finished work, but 'Jonesy and the Duke' and 'A Duty to the Community' seem to have been designed to appeal to the editor of *Seven*, as 'Joking with Arthur' had done.

It was from *Seven* that Mathias earned his first fee as a writer, for 'Study in Hate' (later renamed 'Take Hold on Hell'), in the autumn of 1942. The narrative of the claustrophobic prisoner, driven to a crazed murder by the casual brutality of a warder, retains considerable power even now, but the story is memorable for the first-hand observations of life in gaol. Mathias drew upon the same experience in a handful of poems in his first book, *Days Enduring*: 'Inter Tenebros (Even Here)', 'Vista', 'Bars', 'Wishes from Walton', 'Cries in the Night' and 'Fagenbaum'. The last named, a portrait poem, clearly relates to the story, which briefly identifies 'Fagenbaum, the Hoxton fence, with the perpetual pitted sneer'. Visual imagery of prison bars and windows has an impact in both the poems and the story, but the latter contains striking images of its own, many of which carry an emotional charge. As well as visualizing him, for example, we sense the discarded hopelessness of the sleeping prisoner 'humped in a curious swept-up heap'. Above all, and unexpectedly, the story's description of the sounds of prison lingers:

> The dusk would deepen. In the right-hand block the rows of bars, gripped here and there by the clenched fists of longing, would darken imperceptibly into lines of menace. And after sunset an eerie Ben Gunn who was never seen called softly for Bartholomew. 'Barth-ol-om-ew' – the name echoed urgently around the stack. No answer broke the stillness.

During the 1940s, *Penguin New Writing* was a popular and influential pocket-sized journal. It published, among many others, Saul Bellow, William Sansom, Graham Greene, Frank O'Connor, Tennessee Williams and Boris Pasternak. Roland Mathias achieved a significant breakthrough, and all the encouragement he needed to go on writing, when its editor, John Lehmann, took 'Incident in Majorca'. The story displays for the first time Mathias's skill in portraying schoolboys. They are the dominant characters here and in 'Agger Makes Christmas', and they steal a good deal of the limelight from the theme of conflicting adult relationships in 'Match'. Experience as a boarder at an independent school, and as a teacher, gave the writer many models for his characters and an unusual depth of insight into juvenile attitudes and behaviour. Theo Littlejohn, the boy around whom the 'Incident in Majorca' revolves, is a particularly interesting creation.

As we have seen, Mathias made the most of his opportunities at Caterham and Oxford. Yet, with the self-critical honesty that distinguishes much of his mature poetry, he believes he sees in himself as a child a capacity for mischief. That it ever found expression outside this story is hard to believe. Dr Mallinson, the headmaster accompanying a group of his pupils on expedition to the island's Torrente del Pareys, is fully aware of mankind's potential for sin. No one among the school's four hundred boys, he knew, 'could contend with the fiend. They were all souls like his, helpless, weak, mischievously wicked, often kindly or cruel in a small way', but in his stepson, Littlejohn, who has insisted on joining the party, he believes he has glimpsed the very devil. The story shows how the melancholy foreboding that afflicts Mallinson is borne out by events. In the 'small tubby goat' who 'grinned reminiscently with a semblance of frog' is a very unflattering self-portrait of the author, and in Littlejohn's insubordinate (if agile) clambering descent into the gorge a kind of fictional wish-fulfilment. At one point fact and fiction merge. In the story, a dislodged step that could have crushed his skull brushes Littlejohn in its descent and, without breaking the skin, leaves his forehead 'swelling so fast he could not hold it in'. We know from the 'Mallorcan Notebook', published in *Dock Leaves* (no. 21), that it was Roland Mathias, as a member of a school party from Caterham, whose 'temple was nicked by death' in the gorge of Torrente del Pareys. With its deft characterization, particularly of the boys, evocative description of scenery and the almost occult strangeness of the opposition of stepfather and stepson, 'Incident in Majorca' is a remarkable story, worthy of the distinction conferred on it by publication in *Penguin New Writing*.

Among the stories which have their source in Mathias's family, 'One Bell Tolling' is an oddity inasmuch as it is a fictionalized account of events based upon relations on his *mother's* side. For

Morgan, the farmer whom the young man Hedley accompanies on a delivery round, home is a mountain farm above a mining valley (accurately located in the 1941–3 Notebook draft at Beaufort, above Ebbw Vale). Thought of it makes him smile, and he becomes 'almost animated'. He has not set down roots in 'the dull fields of his Vale of Glamorgan farm'. Morgan is an early illustration of that sense of deracination that is a common thread in several stories in *The Eleven Men of Eppynt*, and in those published subsequently. In the young man, Hedley, we have another unflattering self-portrait: the ample buttocks, the smart thoughts kept to himself, the desire to make an impression, the failure to lift cleanly the sacks of potatoes, are a sample of the faults exposed by his scrutiny. Those interpolations of educated, even *affected*, language – 'the veracity of nature', 'little frivols', 'not infrangible' and so on – though applied to Morgan's perception of the world, are of a piece with Hedley's supercilious attitude to the expedition before he is gripped by panic in a small, dark room. The story memorably mingles humour and self-deprecation with confusion, fear and, ultimately, sad reflections on age, decrepitude and the inevitability of death. In the darkened house, the slow revelation of objects and the ancient inhabitants establishes Mathias's skill with chiaroscuro (which we see again in 'The Neutral Shore'), and prepares the reader for Hedley's ignominious panic and flight.

'Cassie Thomas' is the second of the four school stories in the book. Like 'Incident in Majorca' it centres on a 'difficult' pupil, who brings chaos to the classroom, or the school expedition. Roland Mathias knew a great deal about the subject. When he began teaching, recruitment to the forces was progressively stripping boys' grammar schools of the more vigorous, and often the more competent, of their masters. Not a few of the classes in the schools at Carlisle, and at St Clement Danes, were out of control and, as a naturally gifted teacher, he soon found himself bringing order to the classrooms of colleagues. He did not need to stretch his imagination to portray that kind of malignancy among the young that, like an upsurge of original sin, subverts normal behaviour. The story is loosely based on gossip about a teacher heard from members of his father's family who had settled in the Rhondda – hence Cassie's south Wales valleys upbringing. It offers an interesting examination of personality. Cassie, one of that first educated generation born of mining families, has to reconcile home, where her father 'still sat in the kitchen in his shirt-sleeves, with the coal dust deep under the rims of his nails', with the culture of her school, 'Trebanog County', and in due course her role as a teacher. She develops a persona and a 'face . . . made by her own efforts' to match. This disciplined and efficient 'dummy', which has nothing to do with the 'Silly, soft things . . . out of place in the life of an educated woman', enables her to rise in the profession until she achieves the ambition of headship, at a small country school. There she meets her nemesis, in the shape of an evacuee from London, an overgrown, malevolent bully, who sees through the shield of the dummy to the weak woman behind. The psychological analysis of Cassie, laying bare the duality in her nature, may seem over-simplified, or odd (though this is not the only story in which events seem to split a character, so that one half observes the other), but the depiction of the teacher's breakdown before pupils and colleagues has a powerful impact.

For the next story he wrote, Mathias turned for the first time to the fictionalizing of characters and events in his father's family history – a source he would frequently revisit in his prose and his poetry. In the hope of making his way in the world, poor Ben Davies in 'Block-System', a simple carpenter from the Rhos, has borrowed heavily to buy a London milk round. The work is uncongenial, but that is not all; he is browbeaten and cheated by local officials determined to get rid of the small operators, to the anger and despair of his wife and daughter. Despite prostrating himself with effort, Ben will never be able to repay the loan and obtain their release from a downhill grind to penury. Thus far the story is representative of those small family tragedies that must have occurred frequently enough among the London Welsh. It is, however, chiefly concerned with the terrible wrench of leaving Wales ('The tree had been pulled up somewhere and in the new soil only a few roots had contrived to find cover'), and Ben's imaginative escape to an idyllic past on the Rhos as he washes milk bottles for the next delivery. These lovingly preserved memories are preferable to the reality of returning, with the need that would entail explaining his failure to others. As a defining characteristic, Ben has an unusual sensitivity to words, which is perhaps the writer's own, though the memory of the 'little black horse' and the first learned English word that named it is that of Evan Mathias, the writer's father.

Although the text does not betray it, the first of the historical stories, 'Digression into Miracle', has a strong personal dimension. Roland Mathias has albums containing many hundreds of family photographs, all carefully mounted and captioned. One such, for the 1940s, records among other events holidays in Aberystwyth when he was pursuing a research project on mining in the locality. On its inside front cover he pasted a typed extract from a letter sent by 'Tho. Brodway. 4 July 1641' to Thomas Bushell:

> I have no more, but to signifie my confidence, that as your desires are set on the materiall Rocks of Wales and Enstone, so will your better affections be firmly grounded upon the Rock Christ Jesus, that no tempest may be able to shake you, when the sandy projects of others will be laved to nothing by the floods they are built upon.

The quotation must have leapt from the manuscript page as he studied it. The writer had learned about Bushell in the course of his Oxford research. His interest in this page and protégé of Francis Bacon and, in later life, engineer, entrepreneur and loyal supporter of Charles I, was strengthened by his wife's connection with Enstone, where Bushell had designed spectacular water displays. The epigraph to the photograph album, with its references to desires and affections, Wales and Enstone (where 'the Rock' exists now only as the name of a spring), and strong Christian belief, was peculiarly apposite. Broadway's words reinforced that sense of happy coincidence that appealed to him as poet and historian, alert to evidence of links across time. The same heightened sensibility of the past gave rise to poetic celebration in 'For M.A.H.', a poem addressed to Molly Hawes before their marriage:

> Walls cannot hold the wind against me now:
> I am the one to walk the rows at Tew
> Believing jasmine breathes the shape of you
> And Lucius Cary makes you his first bow.
>
> I am with Hampden in his ragged charge
> Hoping for Chiselhampton held or down:
> I ride with Bushell into Oxford town
> To mint the college loyalty in large.

As 'Digression into Miracle' begins, we discover Bushell at a London inn. He has recently arrived from Aberystwyth in the hope of putting a petition to the king. This is not the first time that he has sought to catch the king's eye, but his past success in obtaining the right not only to mine for silver but to mint the ore at Aberystwyth is unlikely to be repeated. However, finding his plans frustrated by a local landowner who resorts to sabotage to prevent him mining, all he can do is seek again royal intercession on his own behalf. The scene changes to the mountains north of Aberystwyth, overlooking the village of Talybont. It is the evening of 27 June 1641. As the sun sets, four miners are enjoying a smoke. The events that propel them into the story have clearly been described by 'the reverend Thomas Broadway, chaplain to the mines' in his correspondence with the absent Bushell, for he is quoted – 'three of them had come back from the face for their "smoakie banquet" . . . afraid that if they stayed in the forefield the air would get damp'. The 'damp' is, of course, fire damp, which the story subsequently shows they are right to be wary of. Brief descriptions of these men allow the interpolation of further historical detail, including reference to earlier, successful mining in the same place, which had brought Hugh Myddleton great wealth, and Bushell's belief that extensive reserves remained in Myddleton's drowned level. The invented gossip of the four men, largely about the ghastly effects of the waste and water from the mine on vegetation and livestock, is interrupted by a rumble. The pent-up water in Myddleton's old workings bursts out and, as they run clear from the mine entrance, sweeps down the mountainside to flood the houses of Talybont. The four men take their candles to inspect the mine and are met by the second shock of explosion. They survive, just, and the story ends with Thomas Broadway writing to Bushell to congratulate him on being so favoured: 'Behold, sir, how deare you are to providence, which for your sake hath vouchsafed to digress into a miracle.'

There is a great deal more to the story of Thomas Bushell and the mint he established in the castle at Aberystwyth. During the 1950s Mathias lacked the time to write about it as he intended, and when, having left teaching, he might have returned to the subject, he found the work had already been done by another researcher.

Personal history is much to the fore in 'The Rhine Tugs', which draws extensively on the writer's childhood memory of life in

Cologne after the First World War. There, from a high apartment window, he watched the shipping on the Rhine and, with special interest, the tugs. The story allows us to apprehend other well-remembered experiences through the senses of an imaginative and rather lonely child – a toy in a shop window, learning to read with his mother, having his finger lanced by a doctor, visiting his father's office, getting lost and being found again. To provide a frame for this graphic return to childhood, Mathias gives his memories to a forlorn figure, though one familiar enough at the time, a refugee from the war in Europe. Unkempt, ill-clothed and alienated from the 'phlegmatic British public' he is driven to meditate upon the cost of war, the moral degeneracy of victors and vanquished and, in the newsreel image of the spires of the cathedral, still standing amidst the rubble of bombed Cologne, a symbol of the persistence of religion. Even as he angrily leaves the crowded cinema, we see a strange duality in the character of the man, rather like that portrayed in 'Cassie Thomas': he contains both a morally righteous, alienated persona and 'his romantic uncritical self' that would wish to be like other men. The characterization is perhaps a projection of the writer's watchful weighing of his thoughts, motives and actions, his public and his private personae.

A good deal of the critical comment in reviews of *The Elēven Men of Eppynt* was directed, explicitly or implicitly, at the perceived obscurity of the second historical story, 'The Neutral Shore'. This was largely a matter of the writer's choice of a mode of expression in keeping with his dark subject. The action takes place at night. It is lit by draught-blown and guttering candles and a feeble, cloud-obscured moon. In the darkness the glint of teeth or the white edge of foam on the shore catch the eye. Characters and motives emerge gradually and uncertainly out of a prevailing gloom, through which the reader must pick a way slowly.

No date is given, but it is the year 1696. The plot is simple: two men, Captain John Ellesdon, the local customs officer, and Isaac Manley, a man with a record of success against smugglers, dispatched from London by the Commissioners for Trade to tackle a gang of 'owlers' engaged in the illegal export of wool to France, meet at an inn on the Kent coast to complete their plans for the night. They receive intelligence that the English organizer of the trade will land from a French boat to settle accounts with his suppliers. Manley has made his dispositions secretly, to the discomfiture of Ellesdon, but the game's afoot and the latter has little option but to go along with it. Too late for the course of the affair to be altered, Manley divulges how the trap will be sprung: he has involved the militia. His companions know this is a fatal error. The militia, who are also in the pay of the smugglers, kill the one honest man in their midst, while the renegades and the French get clean away. The events of the night show that, for all his crisp assumption of command and strutting, Manley is 'a fool like all these metropolitans'. This, Ellesdon's first intuition, allows the writer a sideswipe at London critics and reviewers.

The historical accuracy of 'The Neutral Shore' is as secure as Mathias's Oxford research can make it. The key issue, however, is whether a knowledge of history is a prerequisite to the enjoyment, or even the understanding, of the story. While it requires careful reading, and acceptance of a mode of expression freighted with imagery to an unusual degree, especially for the contemporary reader, the answer must be no. Behind this lie further questions: why was the subject, at its simplest level a boys' adventure, chosen? And why was it so ornately dressed?

The appeal of the historical events is easy to understand. Discovery of the reports of Manley, Ellesdon and the rest among the original Board of Trade papers was immensely interesting to the researcher. A great deal is added in the interpretation of their evidence and the telling of the tale. Allusion distorts and slows apprehension, so that, like Ellesdon and Manley, the reader peers into the darkness and sees imperfectly. The narrative point of view shifts restlessly; we do not know until the end which of these two has the better grasp of the affair, which is to be trusted, as the story twists suddenly between the perceptions and thoughts of first one then the other. The quality of the language, the density of the imagery, the extended images, associated more often with poetry than prose, should alert us to the seriousness of the writer's intention. He saw it as more than a yarn about smugglers and excisemen. It concerns the triumph of venality over morality, integrity and trust: at the end the 'one true Englishman' is left dead 'for very honesty' on the road, and the malefactors flourish. A similar sober message is reiterated from time to time in Mathias's poetry.

Two stories are based on tales from the Rhos that the writer had heard from his father's family. It is interesting to compare

'A Night for the Curing' with 'A Duty to the Community', written
a few years earlier. Both have a simple anecdotal basis, and the
latter retains the brevity and colloquial expression of anecdote.
The former, however, was conceived on a larger scale and written
in a different register, the Welshness in the telling being largely
confined to the dialogue, some of which is in Welsh. Its language
and imagery have a power, both muscular and richly allusive,
characteristic of Mathias's poetry and prose:

> His head sank like a stone on his breast and lolled sideways a little,
> oddly. The chance sun of the moor struck him below the cheek-
> bone, brimming in through the doorway, filling the charlatan's tale
> with passion. For a moment the cheek was a pool of pig's blood with
> poor men swimming in it. Then the shaft shut off as suddenly as it
> had come. The shed seemed cold. The tale of the moor was close to
> the telling and the question struggled for lips to speak it.

The story begins with a careful description of peasant poverty,
the high value placed on the seasonal killing of the pig that will
feed the family through the winter months, and the friendly and
sensible sharing of a portion of the pig meat with neighbours. This
explanatory mode, not a regular feature of Mathias's story-telling,
should have pleased some of his critics. Here, too, characters are
delineated in considerable detail. That of Methy, in particular, is
presented in a way that will expose his selfishness and greed, and
justify his bitter come-uppance. The description of his changing
demeanour as he runs through a gamut of emotions is
psychologically acute, and includes in the final sentence one of
those sudden variations of linguistic register, or metaphorical
leaps, characteristic of the writer:

> He sagged and stiffened, circled and deployed, crooked his neck and
> reached bolt upright, all in the space of one normal emotion.
> Execration, anxiety and cunning followed each other over his face
> like shadows over the stubble. His eyes ran shallow and deep by
> turns. Within the shed and the narrower limits of the bone he pulled
> the nerve-ends of tension to him.

For his next story, after 'A Night for the Curing', Mathias
exploited his growing familiarity with the landscape and history of

his new home, south Pembrokeshire – one of the gems of which is Lamphey Palace, a great house built by the bishops of St Davids in the thirteenth and fourteenth centuries. However history, in the foreground of 'Digression into Miracle' and 'The Neutral Shore', is in the background of 'The Palace'. Here, character is the inspiration, although the climax introduces a ghostly presence from earlier in the seventeenth century. Just as Mr Burstow, humble gatekeeper to tourists, has found wife-free contentment among the chimneys and broken roof walks of ruined Lamphey Palace, and has uncharacteristically grown into the true spirit of wardenship, an outrider of the Devereux, the second earl of Essex, suddenly materializes to demand preparations be made for his lord's arrival. With the promptness of an inferior lackey, he hastens to obey – as would a gateward in the Elizabethan past, when walls and stairways stood complete. Alas for Burstow, they are no longer and he falls to a present death. Details of the ruin are exquisitely drawn, but 'The Palace' says little about past events, although it refers to a historical figure, on whom, with his supporters and rivals, Mathias had lavished much time. It is principally intended as a humorous portrait (drawn with a hint of mischief) of the caretaker at Pembroke Dock Grammar School.

It is well to remember that, though they have sources for characterization or plot, the stories considered above are essentially fictions, but the title story, 'The Eleven Men of Eppynt', is pure and joyful invention. Its inspiration was the great snowfall of 1947 that left many south Wales communities isolated. Out of that, and his fine sense of the mock heroic, Roland Mathias created an engaging and memorable tale. After nine days cut off by snow in their mountain village, eleven men set out from Upper Chapel for Brecon, to buy bread. There are elements of traditional folk tale in Maggie's recruitment of the expedition's heroes, especially the reiteration of names and dwelling places as the list grows. The journey downhill to the town is hard, and once there the weak-willed succumb to the temptation of strong drink. Having bought the bread, they turn again to the mountain, but the familiar way is obliterated by darkness and snow. They struggle through a minor epic of difficulties and danger, guided at the last by the light gleaming from the window in Matti's cottage. It is a tale that glitters like the lamplit snow with allusion and imagery and deserves to stand alongside famous others, like Geraint

Goodwin's 'Janet Ifans' Donkey', among the archetypal Anglo-Welsh short stories.

The writer's experience of Caterham in the 1920s appears in the characterization in 'Incident in Majorca', and in elements of the diction – in phrases such as 'young blister', 'high-hat stuff', 'one irrepressible wisp', which one might as readily associate with P. G. Wodehouse. The apotheosis of this influence is seen in 'Agger Makes Christmas'. If the development of the plot is fictional, the motivation is entirely believable, and the boys' characters are psychologically plausible. The original of Agger (whose name may have been borrowed from a river in Germany to the east of Cologne) was a friend of the writer's who had a reputation as a joker. Boot is based on another friend, from Aberdare, who had a strange proficiency with the musical saw. The boys' uniform of morning coat and striped trousers, the language they speak and the institutions they have (like 'Hell', the cubbyhole under the stairs to which miscreants are half-humorously banished), the end-of-term exuberance and anticipation of holidays are all Caterham. Agger is the odd-boy-out as the others pack for the Christmas break. Because his father is ministering far off among the Papuans, he has to remain at school and somehow to come to terms with his loneliness. There is more than a hint of snobbishness in his ironic contemplation of the 'delightful detached semi-Tudor' houses springing up in the nearby residential area, but it is clear that, at the end of the story, they represent an ordinary homeliness that he cannot enter: 'Of souls outside and their methods of contact he knew little. It sometimes seemed to him that a deal of organisation was necessary to get people in touch at any point.' For all his assumption of 'an acid dignity', he is to be pitied, an outsider to human warmth 'practising for his future wounds'. A practical joke at the expense of the sober commuters entrained for London succeeds to his satisfaction, allowing him the momentary celebration of 'the best Christmas yet'. A parody of idol worship, it also carries a message for his absent father, whose belief 'in the oneness of man' means no more to Agger than the 'roar of roller skates under a glass dome, cold and thunderous in its beginning, eerie and repetitive and menacing in the upper reaches of its imperfect sky'. The story has pace and humour, and a great deal of subtlety in the development of the character of Agger.

It makes better sense at this point to depart from the chronological order of the contents list of *The Eleven Men of Eppynt* in order to allow 'Ffynnon Fawr', the penultimate, to be considered last, alongside the three stories based on family history that were published after 1956 and complete Mathias's contribution to the genre. The final story in the collection, 'Match', takes the details of its setting and the portraits of minor characters, rugby players and spectators, from Pembroke Dock Grammar School. Mathias thought the account of the rugby match itself so close to actuality that he sought permission of the headmaster of Gwendraeth Grammar, the other school involved, before publishing it. The skill with which the rugby action is described is testimony to Mathias's long experience as a player. While at Pembroke Dock, he still regularly coached the school team. Soon after his arrival he had taken the controversial step of changing the school's winter game from association to rugby football (and introducing Welsh into the curriculum, a development alluded to in the story). The drawn match against Gwendraeth was the team's first taste of something like success. The main character, Wynford, is in the toils of an emotional crisis, suspecting that his wife is involved in an affair with Iorwerth, a colleague on the staff, whom 'in the cause of kindness' they have taken in as lodger. The task for the writer was to interweave the true story of a game of rugby with the fiction of the triangular relationship of Wynford, his wife Kathy, and Iorwerth. The match unfolds in parallel with the revelation of Wynford's inner turmoil, the struggle on the field becoming emblematic of his emotional response to the 'damned dirty intrigue' he believes is already happening. The story is rare among those in *The Eleven Men of Eppynt* for its contemporaneity, and unique in its 'love' interest. With its poetic description of landscape, its sense of historic continuity in the references to Monkton Cave, and unexpected variations in diction (in his 'trance of vengeance' Wynford uses biblical language), 'Match' is a characteristically multi-layered and intriguing story.

The ruins of Ffynnon Fawr, the farm where Mathias was born, were pulled down in the 1960s, but the site is still recognizable by the cypress tree that his grandfather planted to mark the birth. He has revisited his birthplace in poetry as well as prose. 'On Newport Reservoir' in his first book, *Days Enduring*, invokes familiar features of the past. It begins with the train, 'the sluggard puffing up' the opposite valley side and the '[signal] box at Pentir Rhiw', which in the final stanza conjures up a more intimate reflection:

> I pray no pardon then to mourn
> The muted line of rubble mounds beneath
> The water's level flooring, think
> Of infant journeyings by Tyle's fields . . .
>   and how . . .
> My father leapt the train beside that box
> And downward falling to the farm's dull life
> Was happier in that force, that stain, than we
> Who silent, numerous, watch beauty's face.

'The Tyle' (literally 'the hill', the name of the farm his mother's parents first occupied) in *The Roses of Tretower* also represents the lost link with infancy, and 'The Flooded Valley' in the same book calls upon the familiar streams of childhood, Caerfanell, Grwyney and Senni, to remember him. The opening images of the latter closely resemble the story:

> My house is empty but for a pair of boots:
> The reservoir slaps at the privet hedge and uncovers the roots
> And afterwards pats them up with a slack good will . . .
> I am no waterman, and who of the others will live
> Here, feeling the ripple spreading, hearing the timbers grieve?

The story describes the house tumbling towards destruction and, with quite wonderful imagery, the watery element by which it is besieged: a reservoir laps at the edge of what had once been lawn and rain teems. With her dying breath, Rendel's mother has exacted from him the promise that he will go back to his father's home, his own home for the first four and a half years of his life, in Caerfanell. The imagery of the oppressive heat of Australia, where his father had brought them, himself to fail and to die seven years before, is strikingly contrasted with the pervading wateriness of the place he comes to find. Although he has taken on the mission, there are signs that Rendel, 'slight and unremarked', is not up to it. His queasiness at the sight of the hooks in the kitchen ceiling of the old

farm tend to confirm the suspicion – and so it proves. In a dream
or ghostly vision (reminiscent of the conclusion of 'The Palace'),
presences of the farming past of the area and, importantly, the
voice of his father authoritatively in control of affairs, finally betray
him. He cannot stay. Ultimately, 'Ffynnon Fawr' is about being
called and being found – or finding oneself – unworthy.

The word 'road' occurs twice in the last few paragraphs of
'Ffynnon Fawr', on the second occasion with an extra burden of
significance. After the eerie disturbance of the previous night,
Rendel finds by daylight that there is no longer a road serving the
house by which noisy travellers might have come. A little later,
with a decisiveness born of the realization that he was 'too timid
for Ffynnon Fawr, too timid to make a future where the
generations cried out on him in their sleep', he gets in his hired car
and begins his journey back to Australia, which 'was all one road'.
The colloquial expression, 'any road', expressed with a shrug of
resignation, is in part what is meant here, but it also carries a sense
of the inevitability of the road of life leading us away from our
roots. A decade after the publication of 'Ffynnon Fawr' (in *Dock
Leaves*, 1953), when Mathias turned again to the short story genre
with 'The Only Road Open', it was that sad view of life's road he
had in mind.

The Reverend Evan Mathias, the writer's father and the conduit
to the whole 'cousinhood' of the Rhos, who had come to have as
profound an influence on his adult life as his mother had had on
his childhood, died in 1962. His death and funeral are the
inspiration of 'The Only Road Open' and the remarkable poem 'A
Last Respect' (in *Absalom in the Tree*). In the latter, a sudden gust
of wind striking the cortège as it winds its slow way to the chapel
graveyard seems to be a sign: 'all/ But the elm and the brass
handles had air/ About it and petals flying, impassioned as/Wings',
and the question that ends the poem is not an expression of doubt
but an invitation to the reader to share in an affirmation of faith:

> Who are you to say that my father, wily
> And old in the faith, had not in that windflash abandoned
> His fallen minister's face?

The story returns to the melancholy resignation of the conclusion
of 'Ffynnon Fawr', and its strong undertones of self-accusation
and self-criticism. Alun's initial contempt for the 'townee' bus

driver 'playing pioneer' on the icy road is eventually seen to be ironic, for he too can no longer claim to belong to the place: 'Still in the land of his birth and his remembering, he was shut out from the secret centre of being. He was outside, outside for ever and rapidly moving away.' Glyn Collwn, where he had been born and his father buried, depopulated, its railway line closed, has changed irrevocably, and the yearning to stop and turn back, familiar from many previous journeys along that route, does not come to him. Along with the truth of early photographs of his father, 'the young dark italianate face . . . the streets of Llanelly etched in behind . . . the tricky, tireless out-half, tasselled cap on one finger; the veteran student, still young but bulging learnedly over his butterfly collar', this fiction offers us an insight into the depth of the exiled writer's emotional response to home. It is only at the end that Alun realizes the final severance that came with his father's death. With the curious splitting of the personality into observer and observed that has been noted in other stories, he sees 'That other self of mine, that man I am but for age . . . up there, caught . . . when they sprinkled earth on his coffin I never knew it . . . But now I know it. I am there and here, trapped and yet free, if only to ride away'.

When, nearing the end of the journey, a minister climbs aboard the bus, he has a sensation of recognition as the images of his father and of this stranger merge momentarily, but he knows it is 'The merest nonsense'. What has gone cannot be recovered. There is only one road and that leads away.

The last two stories Mathias wrote are about withering branches of his father's family tree. They are fictionalized accounts of actual visits to aged relatives. In contrast to them, the narrator in both is comfortably off. The stories, especially 'A View of the Estuary', have the same strand of bitter self-deprecation that runs through some of the most important later poems. The old men share a strong family resemblance. Uncle Ben in the 'A View of the Estuary' has a 'dark face . . . fronted by a great nose that looked as though it had grown too ambitious for its station'; Uncle Aaron in 'Siams' is 'Dark, long-nosed like all my father's people'. Connections with the Mathias family history do not end there, as references to 'old Carmarthenshire' and 'the Rhos' show.

The title 'A View of the Estuary' might alert the reader to a special significance in the opening paragraphs, where the narrator describes the grey and dismal scene of the river 'broadening indistinguishably into sea'. That this symbolizes the merging of all things into ordinariness and mediocrity soon becomes clear: 'It was a scene not meant to charm. It was full of the commonness of man, rugged, makeshift, tricky, work-stained, attaining any sort of peace only insofar as it avoided self-justification.' The symbolic force of the scene is re-emphasized a few lines later when he realizes that what holds him briefly in contemplation of it is 'The pull . . . of verity, of life lived'. Within the general allegory of the undifferentiated tide of life, there is the particular relevance for him of the tributary of his own family. This story (like 'Siams') is about the way in which the distinctive and memorable character-istics of a close-knit clan dwindle and become lost in that sea 'into which rivers poured themselves and were forgotten'. The writer's art alone will survive as their memorial.

The Uncle Ben, who bought 'a dairy business in Cricklewood at a price that crippled him financially', is not the Ben Davies of the much earlier story 'Block-System', although they have a great deal in common. (A family history would show that one brother followed the other hopefully into the dairy business in London, and neither prospered.) 'Uncle Ben' is the last survivor of the 'six brothers and three sisters' of the narrator's father's generation. 'A View of the Estuary' concentrates upon the narrator's relationship with Ben and his wife, and with their son, Idwal. The narrator preserves these memories, is indeed the living repository of them. His daughter Mair, who has accompanied him, was 'born away and outside the generations of rigour' and cannot possess them as he does. The story also exposes the fragility of the links of kinship that he embodies. Ben's family line is petering out, as dead Idwal's only child, a daughter, will grow to adulthood in Australia.

How time and wayward fortune can unravel family until little of the memory and blood remain is also the theme of Mathias's last story, 'Siams'. Aaron Aaron insists on accounting for all surviving members of the clan and exacts a promise that the narrator will pass on to Siams a secret that reveals his own line has come to a halt. He and Siams are identified as not strictly uncles but cousins of the narrator's father, the former a sometime exciseman, newspaper reporter and Plaid supporter, the latter a secondary headmaster who derived a Pumblechookian pleasure from pursuing him, when he was a child, with abstruse mathematical problems. Two bright young men, 'come out of the customs of poverty with an inbred suspicion of the world outside', they or their loved ones had nevertheless been undone by sex. Aaron recalls Siams admonishing him, 'Women . . . [are] too smart for the likes of you, boy. Too smart by half. You want to watch who you go with. Or one of them'll make a fool of you, sure enough.' Wariness and cleverness had not prevented Siams's son from marrying and then leaving a 'coarse, unbearable' woman, and Aaron knows he was 'diddled' by his wife and that the 'daughter' who looks after him is not his child: 'A is for Aaron, W for Wales. Very nearly Z.'

No sympathy is enlisted for the narrator in either story. He visits out of a sense of duty and observes dispassionately, or with distaste. No matter how warm the welcome and anxious the communication of the old people, he is glad to leave. Yet he cannot free himself of his obligations to that 'poverty stricken cousinage' that came from Rhos Llangeler, not least because fate has dealt differently with him. His guilt on this account is compounded by his failure to cultivate family ties as assiduously as his father, 'a great caller-in on his relatives', and by his relief at getting away. As a writer, Mathias has sought to secure the family memory in all its mundane history of ambition, honest effort, modest and usually short-lived successes, failed relationships, loss and sickness – in these stories and in poems like 'They Have Not Survived':

> They have not survived,
> That swarthy cenedl, struggling out
> Of the candled tallut, cousins to
> Generations of sour hay, evil-looking
> Apples and oatmeal porringers . . .
> Cousins like bloodspots in the wasted
> Grass . . .
>
> For this dark cousinhood only I
> Can speak. Why am I unlike
> Them, alive and jack in office,
> Shrewd among the plunderers?

The last four lines are not merely rhetoric. With the moral serious-ness he brings to all considerations, he has taken on the remem-brancer's task partly in the mood of Grey, honouring the 'rude forefathers of the hamlet' whose 'lot forbade' them access to wealth and influence, but also guiltily, because of the contrasting comfort of his own life, his lack of Welsh, unlike the *cenedl* of his relatives and, ultimately, his inability to relate to them as he would wish. These final family histories, redrawn as fiction, needed to be written, not only for the usual creative reasons: they were the artistic means of achieving a temporary catharsis, and a partial expiation of that scourge of the puritan soul, the taint of worldly success.

The Eleven Men of Eppynt was quite widely reviewed. In the *Manchester Guardian*, Vernon Johnson declared it 'something of a literary ragbag, but . . . put together by an acutely intelligent, acutely senstive writer'. In a broadcast, Glyn Jones said the stories bore 'the unmistakable stamp of the devoted and self-conscious craftsman'. He was critical of the historical stories which 'blur and becloud [the reader] with an excess of care and labour', and concluded that Mathias 'lacks . . . artistic abandon. He keeps too tight a rein on himself, and on his words, so that they can do anything except soar. But he is at the same time a writer of integrity and courage . . . originality and . . . a steady personal vision.' The *TLS* review considered the book exemplified 'amateur writing in the proper and better sense of the word'. While disparaging with the words 'general water-colour effect' and 'slight', it acknowledged that the book had 'compensating virtues . . . There are no tricks and no slickness; the eye keeps its sharpness of vision and the pen its freshness; everything is first hand.' Geoffrey Nicholson in *The Spectator* thought the stories 'would be at home in such good company as Alun Lewis and B. L. Coombes. They . . . manage to be sympathetic without being patronising or sentimental', and added, 'I would personally prefer it if Mr Mathias didn't pile image upon image, search quite so inexorably for the striking adjective, and, as he sometimes does, keep vital information to himself. I would sometimes just like to be told exactly what is happening. The stories in which the pace is quickened – the title story, "Cassie Thomas", "Match" – are excellent.'

Notwithstanding the critical observations, this would surely be accounted a favourable reception for a first book of short stories, one that might be expected to encourage the writer to continue working steadily in the genre. As we have seen, he did not. The sheer busyness of life as headteacher, combined with the many chapel and community responsibilities, which he never shirked, and, from 1960, his editorship of *The Anglo-Welsh Review*, might well have left him less time than the broader expanses of prose fiction demanded. Yet he wrote copiously on history, literature and language in the various ways described above, and he consolidated his position as a poet. Furthermore, any preliminary reading or research completed, Roland Mathias is a writer of unusual fluency. Whatever planning was involved in story-writing was not committed to paper: examination of his manuscripts shows, in a very few cases, a short jotted list. Thereafter, all the evidence suggests that most of the stories were written at a sitting and with little subsequent amendment. The failure, if there was one, was not in the ability to write prose that was elegant, exciting, impassioned, penetrating, as occasion demanded, but perhaps in commitment to the genre.

All the published stories, and certainly 'Saturday Night' among the previously unpublished, are readily identifiable as the work of Roland Mathias by their use of language. Yet, they do not have a pervasive, common style: rather the writer speaks in an array of voices in each of which we apprehend a constant poetic sensibility. Similarly, Mathias's mature poetry has a distinctive voice, which is cultured, authoritative, at times even pedantic, often profound, melancholy and questioning, and almost as frequently witty. Several poems show how readily and completely he can adopt the voices of others:

> Eight years ago come Tuesday now I walked
> Big as a brown wind angry from your door.
> Mad you had made me, Ellen Skone . . .
>
> ('A Letter')

> You are a debtor three
> Times over, a turbulent
> Fellow whose affrays have given cause
> For the judges of Assize
> Long to take bond of you.
>
> ('Indictment')

Some have thought these 'found' poems. They are not. It was inevitable that, in the course of long study of primary sources from his specialist periods, the writer should absorb into his own expression diction, structures and rhythms that are archaic. Further, he possesses an actorly panache for taking on the personality of another in his writing. In the poems this is a product of painstaking composition and, indeed, a delight in theatrical performance that he demonstrated from his school days.

Similar skills are displayed in the stories. Ellesdon and Manley and their men in 'The Neutral Shore' and the four miners in 'Digression into Miracle' have carefully differentiated characters who present an interesting array of speech patterns. The demotic of the lower ranks is spelled phonetically, while Manley's speech has seventeenth-century diction and word order – 'Whistle the catch Lillibullero as you come to the ford: they will start forth at the hearing . . . Press on, all three, to the Warren and succour Underwood . . . I fear me what may befall him and you come not.' It is hardly surprising that the predominant voice of several of the short stories is that of public school and Oxford, larded with their peculiar slang, but more generally cultivated, erudite, often syntactically complex. In its purest form it is heard in 'Agger Makes Christmas' and 'Incident in Majorca', where it is the register of the dialogue as well as the narrative. Elsewhere, it becomes a constant underlying tone, varied as chronology, locale and characters, most obviously in their mode of speech, demand.

The internal monologue of the self-pitying, claustrophobic prisoner in his first published story, 'Take Hold on Hell', reveals some characteristic Welsh markers: 'Duw, he couldn't stand this. Bobol annwyl, he had stood a lot, but he couldn't stand this.' A more thorough appreciation of Welsh speech-rhythms and word order is observable in the later stories, 'Block-System', 'The Eleven Men of Eppynt' and, above all, 'A Night for the Curing'. In the last named, sowing the seeds of his own undoing, the conniving Methy tries to involve the butcher in a plot:

> 'Un bach yw e,' he said. 'He's a very little one.'
> The butcher looked up surprised. 'Nage, Mr Morris, not at all. He'll keep you in pigmeat a supper or two and in bacon a good bit of the winter, if you will be careful.'
> Methy did not move. 'From by here he do look a very little one, anyway,' he persisted.

This may appear derivative, but, as we have seen, it is not a product of Mathias's reading of Anglo-Welsh literature. He has said (in his *Artists of Wales* essay) that his father's attempts to teach him Welsh as a child were 'desultory and short-lived'. Intermittently over the years he attempted to repair the deficit. He worked at it on coming down from Oxford and, though he could not maintain momentum once he began teaching, some knowledge of Welsh came from this effort. Above all, however, the Welsh vocabulary, structures and turns of phrase, wherever they occur, come, like several of the stories themselves, directly from those relatives already mentioned whose peasant roots lay deep in Gât Bwlch-clawdd, or as the text has it, 'the moor by Y Gât'.

Roland Mathias is primarily a poet: his stories are the stories of a poet. Most are driven by the same head of creative pressure that found expression more frequently in his poems. The imagery and symbolism he employs have their parallels in the poetry, as do those unusual expressions which leap from the page in almost every story ('the dignity of man took another bounce'; 'Hurrying to shift the lodgement of the conversation'; 'Gethin was passing, overhung with Ceffyl and the gamut of words'; 'she was beginning [to speak] again . . . when the crouch of her tongue was overwhelmed with sound'; 'peering over the welter in his mind's front was the head of another question'; 'the calm envelope of morning seemed at pressure', and so on). These are not contrived formulations, worked up for effect. They are manifestations of his distinctive rhetoric, itself a product of his immensely wide reading, and arise freshly minted from the poet's creative intuition for language.

After the 1950s, he needed a special reason for writing short stories rather than poems, or perhaps something to write about. As his relatives gradually loosed their hold and slipped away, he lost his suppliers of gossip and tales, though not one of the constant motives in his work – the sense of debt to his kinfolk that, no matter how many times he bore witness to them, remained unpaid. We are left with a corpus of twenty-two short stories – not a large number, though not many less either than, for example, fellow-poets Alun Lewis, Glyn Jones and Dylan Thomas. For the energy and variety of the writing, for impressive experiments in mood and the consistent power of language and imagery, and for the overarching integrity of his art, Roland Mathias's short stories deserve to be reread alongside theirs.

Saturday Night

~

'Call him louder,' sang the prophet, contemptuously. 'He heareth not. With knives and lancets cut yourselves after your manner.' He sawed at his arm with an exaggerated biceps. One eye looked to an inward kingdom and one held hard after the prophets of Baal. Around him in dim postures they had life, his voice darting like a snake's tongue, licking the altars like a threatening fire. As always, it was Saturday night.

The windows were open, but there was not a breath of wind. Not the least hope that any wish of Baal's could blast this overwhelming prophet. In the forecourts even the faintest cadence of the crowd, their 'Hear and answer, Baal' was bullied into silence. Elijah, who troubled Israel, moved a little closer, and the grey figures retired before him. His saturnine face was fixed in a grim slant where beyond his will, but not his purpose, began a distant heaven. He sang like an angel draggled by Lucifer, black and parched with the desert, starved like a crow in the high lands, with hands cunning as claws. Parched he was and terrible, yet full of liquid sound like the twisted water of a mill-race, dipping ominously and foaming with triumphant reappearance. His eye gleamed and terrible the voice came on, out of the spectre of days, out of the dust and the nights in the desert, out of the stained blanket and the arms tossed like thorn-trees against the evening. Out of it, single and unafraid, came the voice calling on God for vengeance. Vengeance on Ahab, vengeance on the priests of Baal. Redress that the kingdom was so walled and small to the spirit, that of the singers of God none but he was left.

The room trembled with his contempt and the walls gave back. The cornices crawled with flame, descending like a tongue, joining with his which set it on, demanding sacrifice. 'Is not His word like

1

a fire,' he sang, 'and like a hammer that breaketh the rock?' Again and again he sang it, his thin chest like an anvil and the voice beating it out stroke after stroke. The room was like an oven. Over the singing was a sound as of the basting of meat, the golden flow-back of juice from an enormous sacrifice. Elijah snuffed it and stood stronger. His nostrils wide like finger-stalls, he stood uplifted against a ceiling of brass, powerful with God and waiting. Waiting for a cloud like a man's hand. And it came. Behold, it came. Over his eyes it passed, making shadows in the stubble like a windy day. The crow took wing and circled the field once, shaking the dust off silently. And the air was wide with voices, clamorous and thankful in the ears of the prophet, who entered into his kingdom cold again and powerful with men.

Silence fell. Beyond the bars of the window the air darkened. The distant thumping of a dance hall added a congruous, primitive note. In the centre of the stage the prophet slept under a juniper tree and the angels of the Lord were camped round about him. Their gymshoes were light on the boards and their breathing tight out of uniform collars. 'Arise, Elijah, for thou hast a journey before thee.' The heap moved, the blanket was flung like a fountain. The prophet who was like to die rose like a lamp against the backcloth. Again his words were like flaming torches, tossing from hand to hand nearer, nearer. He heard the judgments of the future and in Horeb its vengeance. Out of the mount of providence came a fiery chariot with fiery horses. The whirlwind began and he was lifted up.

'Take him gently, boys. Great he was in Carmel in the days that are gone. Have reverence now.'

Wrapped in his whirlwind struggled the prophet, rejecting his translation from one glory to another. The collars of his horses pulled tighter yet as the skinny arms sought to flail and gesticulate. The memory of Elijah was now an unavailing gasp. He was no more remembered, no not in Carmel nor in the mount. And there was no more reverence.

Haled from high land to higher, cast like a broken crow upon the darkness, the prophet with a final twist of desperation loosened the blanket from around him, and it fell slowly, almost laughably, upon the head of a bystander in the dark night near. Saving it very barely from unbalance and a sheer drop to the floor, the man below juggled with it awhile and at the last pulled it eagerly around his shoulders, clutching it for great heart against the winter and the favour of the Lord in a place where the minds of the people were turned away. He rose in his place, stained and confident, his head bald as a toadstool in the glimmering of light. There was a sudden titter from the other inmates and the man's eyes gloomed like a she-bear's coming out of a wood. The sound ceased as suddenly as it had begun and nothing remained but the thump of the distant dancing.

So was Elijah lifted up and Israel was no more troubled in his name. As always, it was Saturday night.

A Duty to the Community

~

A good old trick there was played up on the Rhos this morning, though it's not me's the one to be telling it really, Dafi Morris being a sort of relation through my uncle Luke Rees the Waun that's dead and him very good too with the eggs for my sister-in-law Rachel Jenkins. If you are telling things, back to you they get somehow, whatever. That's what I say. But Dafi Big will be telling it all round the next couple of days and what for should he get all the laughing? What lives in the river will never be walking to the table, mun. Still, not much dragging this one'll need. Listen you.

Dafi Rees, you'll be knowing him? Dafi Big they are calling him, the butter merchant up on the Rhos. Though why they are calling you a merchant when you do nothing all day I don't know. Anyway, Dafi Big, a bit of a wag he is, with the sides of his face looking different at different people and a wink in his eyes that the chap it's not meant for don't see. Ah, you know him? That's right, mun. That's the chap. A big purple spotty sort of face he has and little tight trousers. Looking as if he was lowered into them a good while back and never found the way out. Topheavy he is, that's the word I am wanting, topheavy. Well, Dafi Rees and Dafi Morris are butties. Or I should say, Dafi Morris is butty to Dafi Rees, as Dafi Rees will be telling you in case you get it wrong now. Poor old Dafi Morris. Dafi Morris Glaspant he is proper, him being the tailor hereabouts. But there is no sense of humour with the little man. No indeed, none at all, and not much sense of any sort except for the tailoring. The perky look of a cock-sparrow he have and quick little hands that are running about all the time even when the work is not in the house. Stitching and turning, stitching and turning, but not a laugh in him. I don't know; indeed I think the poor chap is knowing it himself and that is why he is sticking to Dafi Big.

Proper follower he is and laughing regular. A wag is Dafi Big and everybody is saying it. So Dafi Bach, he is laughing too. There's a wag is that Dafi Bach Glaspant, people will be saying. Indeed that is what I am thinking.

Well, Dafi Rees the butter is often up to Glaspant in the mornings. For a conference, he is saying. And Dafi Bach sitting there sewing away, getting into tucks with the hemming and the ha-ing. The order is all wrong with him, but he have tried fit to bust. This morning now, of all things, Dafi Bach takes him out the back to show him the ducklings he have got there. Hens he have had this long time but ducklings no. There are great ideas with Dafi Bach, ideas of giving up the tailoring and starting as a farmer. That is the meaning of these ducklings then, only he is wanting Dafi Big to look them over. Give them the O.K. as Dafi Bach is saying before the next laugh.

Dafi Big looks at the brood. He is saying nothing. There is a hen there, up just from sitting on them. Bustling around now it is, terrible anxious. 'Ah,' says Dafi Big, meaning he is thinking up something. On the other side he is making a laugh with the corner of his mouth. But next to Dafi Bach he is solemn as solemn. 'Ah,' he says again. 'Ah,' says Dafi Bach. Not going to be outdone he is. Dafi Big still says nothing. Thinking up is a slow business with him and he is often lying in bed getting ready a couple of jokes for the morning. It's a full time job being a wag hereabouts. It is indeed, as I do know. Well, Dafi Big is holding one of the ducklings upside down now. A little yellow ball it is, not more than a couple of days old. 'Nothing wrong with them, is there?' says Dafi Bach, a bit anxious with all this quiet. 'I don't know mun,' says Dafi Big. 'I don't know indeed.' Waiting a bit now will bring it out. Patience it needs and Dafi Bach is knowing this. Though he is worried, he have tied his tongue at the back. Dafi Big thumbs the bristles on his chin once or twice. 'This is what I am thinking, Dafi Bach. You have brought up these ducklings with a hen. Now is that sense? There's heredity to be thinking of. Heredity. You have heard of heredity. Course you have, mun. Shinkin Morris Glaspant, he was a tailor. You are a tailor. You are son to Shinkin, dead now, God rest him. There is heredity for you. But with these ducklings now it is split. O Dafi Bach, shame on you. Ducks they are trying to be and a hen it is you put to bring them up. You should know better than that. Indeed you should.'

'But Mari Penfforddnewydd is using a hen,' says Dafi Bach, hopping about now, with the words of Dafi Big wise in his ears and coming up thump under his heart.

'Mari Penfforddnewydd and old rope. It is in them both to hang a man.' There is scorn in the voice of Dafi Big. 'Pay you attention. Can they swim?'

'Indeed Dafi Rees, I don't know. I suppose they can. Ducklings they are. From Sara Pwllgloyw I had the eggs.'

'Dafi Glaspant, the more shame on you for not knowing. Get me a tub, mun. A tub, I am saying. And fill the thing with water. You – don't – know.' Dafi Big is squeaking in his throat a bit now just like Dafi Bach. 'You – don't – know. Then we will be finding out for you.'

In a minute in comes Dafi Bach staggering with his hands half-way round the wash-tub. Back and fore to the pump he goes. Three, no four buckets of water. That's the boy. 'Now,' says Dafi Big. 'Put the ducklings in. One by one. Go on, mun. Put the little blighters in.'

Dafi Bach is not the man to refuse on the point just. He is putting one in. Out come the little yellow feathers and fill with water. Under the surface goes the duckling, down to the browny bottom. 'Gone down he is, Dafi, done down mun,' mutters Dafi Bach, with another in his hand.

'Only diving he is, Dafi Bach. Go on you.'

Down goes the next. And another. In a minute the bit of ground is empty and the top of the water too.

'What is it is at the bottom of this old tub that they are all diving?' says Dafi Bach having a good look down into the tub. Trusting Dafi Big he is, but a bit anxious too.

'Something to hold them up, Dafi Glaspant,' says Dafi Big, trying to look as though the joke is just coming to him then. 'Looking for a bit of wood they are but they are not seeing you in time.'

It takes a minute for Dafi Bach to be considering this. Then he gasps in his teeth. 'You mean they're drowning. O Mawredd, o my ducklings, come you up.' With that he dives both his arms up to the elbow, sleeve or no sleeve, and lays them in a small wet heap on the grass. 'All dead,' he moans, 'all dead,' turning them over one by one. Up he stands after a bit, straight up off his knees. 'I do not take this kindly, Dafi Rees. Clever you are, is it?' On he goes on the top storey for a while, turning them over between times and sniffing. Pretty good list of words he has for a chapel man too, they are saying.

But with Dafi Big there is no move. The spotty face on him is calm as water in a ditch. More than Dafi Bach it would take to stir up his mud proper. 'No, no,' he says in a patient way of speaking, 'no, no Dafi Bach. It's the bad heredity it is.' The word is slipping off his tongue now like peas off a knife. 'Bringing them up with a hen, it is no good, bachan. In the river those ducklings would be drowning soon and you none the wiser. Then all over the Rhos the laugh would be on Dafi Glaspant. Better it is this way, I am saying. Come you in and stick to your tailoring. No farmer are you yet. Wait a bit now. Practising you are really.'

On the road by Blaenllain Dafi Big was first in my sight. Narrow on his legs he was as usual, picking his way on the back of the road and a bit more purple even in the distance. It was the laughing in him. And I am feeling now like I have eaten a pound of plums twice. All bottled up it is and not meant to last the week. Well, Dafi Big shouts out at me a tidy way off. 'From Farmer Morris's I am just. Ducklings he had, but he will be sticking to his goose a year or so yet.' He have thought that one up since leaving Glaspant, I was thinking.

A bit of a cruel trick it was really. But Dafi Big is saying any twp from Pwllgloyw would know ducklings keep out of the water till the feathers grow proper. There is a duty to the community we have. More bad farmers we shall be having hereabouts. That is if Dafi Big is not watching.

Jonesy and the Duke

~

Y ou all know the Duke. Iron he is in history, but stone we have him in these parts. I ought perhaps to say that stone he is standing in the square at Cwmmwd Coch, facing that hostelry of ill repute, the Griffin. For some funny reason he has on his back side the name of another man, but no matter of that. He is glaring at the Griffin without the need of any moral support.

Jonesy you will not know. He may not be anything at all in history, but in Cwmmwd Coch he's a good deal bigger than pint-size. Bigger in stowage, I should say, for it's in that that the bobtail go about spreading his fame. After all, it's quite something to those who don't know any better to stand a drink to the town clerk. No question of him standing you one: that would be a blot on bureaucracy, not playing the game by the town. But the town clerk – are you surprised? Mawredd, so is Bill Gittins when he sees him in the court-room of a Monday morning. He may be a bit thick after a spell in those holes they call the police-cells, but it always seems to him as though Jonesy is away up there lost in a blue cloud, winking with both eyes at once at a barmaid that's back behind, near that patch on the wall where old Sergeant Rosser sits. And every time he shuffles his papers his fingers go curling round a little brown pot that nobody but him can see. Bit of a shock to a tidy man, Bill Gittins always says.

A little man, Jonesy, and lined in the face. Twinkling little eyes he has when he's only midway through the morning. And Jonesy he is to everybody, though Jones-Evans he is by rights. It's the hyphen that makes him feel he's doing the town more of an honour by being its chief legal adviser than he is to Bill Gittins when he has a pint off him any night of the week. And if business takes him to the Mandrill Arms of a Sunday, well, that's bona-fide travelling and two miles is enough to make anyone thirsty. That's what you get legal knowledge for boys.

The way I'm going on talking about Jonesy anybody would think he was more important than the Duke. Jonesy would never make that mistake. Battles he's fought over again for the Duke, but no disrespect intended, of course. Always back of his mind was a suspicion that men were not pint-pots and you couldn't move them about so easy. Men weren't pint-pots on cold nights either, more's the pity. That was what made Jonesy think of the Duke with a sort of consideration. Poor old chap! Always outside the Griffin he was. Wind outside and nothing in. It would be kind of nice to do something for him. One Sunday morning his blue woollen scarf was knotted tight about the Duke's neck.

People were a bit late into Bethel that morning for staring. Jonesy had some youngster who did the climbing for him, they do say. Well, well. What next?

This story lasted a long time. It even got about that it was Jonesy's wife's fur coat that the Duke was wearing. But that was a silly story anyway. What would the Duke be doing in a fur coat? No, a muffler now, there was some sense in that.

But Jonesy was not content to remain on swopping terms with the Duke. There were things between them too sacred for the public ignorance of some of the corporation's mistakes. That was why Sid Griffiths the Labour Officer caught it badly over Quarter Brass and the thin red line. Mind you, Sid was bound to catch it anyway. Jonesy spent a lot of time explaining to his pals just what Sid could do with himself, even when he hadn't seen him for quite a while. A wonder it was that the Griffin held them both during hours.

Jonathan Edwards, of all people, was the first to notice this little bit of work. Now Jonathan being one of the mainstays of Bethel thought of Jonesy as the back end of the beast in any case. Still, he was a bit surprised, he said, at what he saw in the Griffin yard. The gate was open and it was half-past one in the afternoon. Half-past one, mind you! And there were Jonesy and Sid Griffiths shaping up to one another and fairly choking with rage. At least, Jonathan thought it was rage. But then he's never been in the Griffin.

Anyhow, it was a great sight this. Sid Griffiths is a bullock of a man with curling grey hair and bumps on his forehead that reflect bits of light. He should have tried dazzling Jonesy with them. But it wouldn't be much good because whatever he punched a hole in, it wouldn't likely be Jonesy. Sid is three parts blind and he began by shining all over his glasses. Still, he kept on looking a bit surprised when the tail end of most of his thumps landed long afterwards on unexpected parts of his own anatomy. Jonesy by this time was all fire and method. He hopped up and down, he side-stepped, he feinted, but all out of reach of Sid's flailing arms. His load of ale began to wash about and be awkward like. This wasn't strategic. The Duke would have finished the man off. A quick thrust, that was it. Done. Jonesy stepped into one of Sid's lengthening gaps and cracked his fist home on his spectacles.

That finished it. Jonathan didn't see any more because there was quite a crowd there by this time, and several ran in. And anyway he'd had no lunch yet. Half-past one, and the town clerk. Well, well! The man wasn't only bad, he was mad.

But for all that Jonesy began to choose better company for his exploits. What was a Labour Officer after all? They grew on the trees in government forests. Bah! Give him a minister any day. Now he didn't mind arguing theology with any minister you'd like to mention. That is, he wouldn't have minded if they'd have given him the chance. But they were shy birds. Never came in the Griffin at all.

There was a shock coming to the Baptist Minister, D. O. Williams, all the same. A shock he couldn't have foreseen. In hospital he was. The Memorial Hospital, Cwmmwd Coch. Dr Benjamin had advised him complete quiet for a couple of months at least. Hospital wasn't the place for quiet, not that day anyhow, and perhaps D.O. wasn't sorry in the end. Many a laugh he had about it afterwards.

The ward sister was away for the moment. It was afternoon and there were only two other chaps in the ward. Slack time it was, just before Christmas. Suddenly the door opened. One of Jonesy's winking eyes looked round. 'Hallo, Mr Williams,' he said to D.O. 'What you doin' here, mun?' 'The doctor said I needed rest,' said D.O. Jonesy opened the door wider. Both his eyes came in sight. Thinking he was, it seemed. 'Well, well,' he said, 'that's funny. Just what I need too. Extraordinary. Dr Benjamin say that? He's my doctor, he is. Rest, eh?' With that he moved in and round to the bed next to D.O. 'I'll join you,' he said. 'I need rest too!' And off he starts, undressing. Mind you, he'd had a drop. But I don't need to tell you that by this time, do I? Well, D.O. did his best. Not much he could do, of course, and him on his back. But he tried arguing. When Jonesy was half undressed, though, he shut up, because the ward sister might come back any minute and Jonesy would look better in bed. If there was any choice, that is.

Believe you me, nobody, not the nurses, the matron nor the porter could get him out that night. A rest was what he needed. Dr Benjamin had said so. And the doctor being out on a call they had to leave him.

The last weapon of guile was with D.O. 'The Duke never took a rest,' said he. 'He kept right on standing up to the end.'

'When I've been dead a hundred years I'll be able to stand outside the Griffin too and see you carried out first,' said Jonesy, turning over.

The Roses of Tretower

~

I think the name of the family was Isaacs. It was old John Price the Cross Keys was telling me and he's eighty-three now and not as good in his memory as he was. But it's a funny thing all the same because though he often forgets where he put his pipe last night and when exactly his old woman died and so on, he's as clear as a bell about things that happened when he was a boy. That's why it's funny he can't be sure of this name. I've seen him sometimes muttering to himself that maybe it was the folk up to Parcylan and then again maybe not. If I took a day off from the sawpit now and went up Bwlch and down along the line of the poplars into Cwmdu I might be able to find out for you. But indeed, I'm not so sure. Folk don't remember like they used to. The country's changed a good bit in these days, you know.

I'd as soon take old John Price's memory for it indeed, though it's nearly sixty years since he packed a few things and came over Bwlch. It's funny really he hasn't been back since. But then, he's a deacon in Benaiah and there's some things you can't ask.

Anyway, up on the hill farm where old Isaacs kept an odd cow or two there was a son, a tidy fellow too, a bit too handy with a gun on dark nights perhaps, but a pleasant way with him of colouring up the neck when he spoke to strangers. This chap, at the time old John heard about it, had been some months after Marged Lewis, Cynghordy, the biggish farm down by the poplars, about a hundred yards from The Sun. Thought well of himself, did Tom Lewis her father. His sheep were always fetching a good price in the marts at Talgarth and Crickhowell and Brecon. He had some queer notion too about being descended from the Tretower folk, you know the Vaughans who used to live at the court down the valley hundreds of years ago and were famous in the wars in

France. I don't know about that: old John says he never told anybody just what the connection was and perhaps it didn't amount to much anyway. He thought it a mighty smart bit of work, did Tom Lewis. I wouldn't be surprised if we would call it differently these days. All the same he was deucedly proud. This was sixty years ago, you see, when folk were more stuck-up than they are now, and heaven knows there's too few plain chaps around the district as it is.

This young Isaacs, he was in the habit of coming up the dingle at the back of Cynghordy, up the steep bit where the garden ends, close to the river. Just after dark he'd come. He'd made quite a thing of it with Marged and I'm not surprised really. There weren't many boys in the valley then who looked as well as he did. In fact, there weren't so many boys in the valley at all. Well, Marged thought it fine and romantic to be courted in this way and him whistling for her every time from the top of the dingle bank. Night after night it went on and young Isaacs was in a good way to persuading the girl to chance her father – Tom Lewis knew nothing about it so far, you see – when the night I'm going to tell you about came around.

It was a Sunday, old John Price says, and the boy came up the dingle with a bunch of crimson roses in his hand. Been down to the garden by the side of Tretower he had, the side away from the gatehouse, and picked them quietly after dark. It was Marged's birthday too, you see, besides being a Sunday. Well, he whistled in the usual way, but this time Tom Lewis was just by the cwtch at the back of the barn and heard something unusual going on. The boy had only just given Marged her roses and a hearty kiss on the lips before the old man came round the house. Marged ran in by the bakehouse door she had come from and up to her bedroom like the wind, the boy the other way down the dingle bank. Tom Lewis pursed his lips and went slowly up the stairs looking like thunder: Marged, hearing him coming, looked all round the room in plain fright and then threw the bunch of roses out of the window at the back.

I'm not going to tell you what Tom Lewis said to his daughter. For one thing nobody knows exactly, but they do say his language was no better than old Twm Channey's, and the upshot of it all was that Marged was never to see young Isaacs again or any other sweepings that didn't know what was too good for them.

Now everybody had forgotten about the roses. They fell behind a bush at the side of the flower-bed and were kept from lying on the ground by the cut edge of the lawn. I don't pretend to say how it happened, and it doesn't sound sense to me now, but nobody found those roses for a fortnight and when they did they were growing. It was Marged found them, Marged who looked thin and unhappy because her boy was from her now: and indeed it looked as if the roses had been feeding on the colours in Marged's cheek. Not a bit faded they were, as crimson as the day they were picked in Tretower garden. She ran and told the housekeeper and the housekeeper told Tom Lewis.

He went dead silent when he heard. The light went out in his face that had always looked like a keen old hawk's and he said very quietly. 'They haven't forgotten then. A hundred and twenty years and they haven't forgotten. What was it possessed the lad to go down there?' And after that nothing else. He scarcely spoke for weeks afterwards and never mentioned young Isaacs when he did. Marged and the boy were married some months later and I do hear an Isaacs is farming Cynghordy now. Tom Lewis died in the night a few days after the marriage.

As I say, it was old John Price was telling me, and old John is eighty-three this week. I'm thinking I'll miss him when he goes. They don't remember things in the country any more.

Joking with Arthur

~

There's no telling what some chaps will think funny. No indeed there isn't. Whenever I come to think of Arthur Vaughan I get sort of hopeless and turn my hands up. But there's no sense, whatever, in walking round a thing: I'd better tell you the tale, same as Tom Morgan my father-in-law was telling me, after he'd been up to Tredomen doing a job.

Tom, you see, is a bit of a mason and though he's getting on now he's still a handy man to have about the place. On the day I'm telling you he was up to Tredomen patching up the pantry wall that had been in a terrible state for years almost. Arthur was in and out there then, staring at him and getting in his way. Since his father died close on two years ago he sort of feels he's in charge of the farm. Not that his brothers take much notice, but he's no ordinary chap just the same. A white, long-boned look he has, like one of them big old ewes that look over the wall at you, and little reddish hairs running all along his jaw. He never opens his mouth but to put some food in it or to have a bit of a row with somebody, and as for smiling, he'd as soon to give maldod to Mari Bettws's kids. And that's saying something, they being the dirtiest for miles. Anyway, the great thing about Arthur is that he's got no sense of humour at all. Not to my way of thinking at least. Sense of humour? – Always offing with his coat he is down in the field, during dinner-time I mean. He's not so ready other times. Some of the men do go on at him a lot, I dare say, but let anyone say a word, he bristles all along his jaw and up with his fists in a second.

I mean, just to show you, he was on Newport station the other day, working his short bit of temper up and down with every turn he took back and fore, when up comes a porter. Well, Arthur he collars him and says, 'How long is the Brecon train going to be?'

impatient like. This Shoni looks him up and round and back again with a cracked sort of a smile and says, 'Two carriages, a van, a tender and an engine.' Well now, an ordinary chap would have laughed his head off and been glad for something to laugh about down by there in all that heat and smoke. But not Arthur. No, he had this chap by the front of his coat in no time and was threatening him something awful. Going to knock his block off, report him to the stationmaster and heaven knows what. And all with that long white look about him that I've seen on him often enough to know what I'm talking about. Oh, there's no sense to Arthur: I don't know how he's lasted so long. Indeed I don't. But I'd better be getting back to what old Tom was telling me.

When tea-time came around Tom was invited to the table, same as everybody is on the farms out Tredomen way. About seven there were of them all told: three sons younger than Arthur, Joyce the little girl Mrs Vaughan was fond of saying was the maid, Arthur, Tom and Mrs Vaughan herself. Always beaten me it has how Mrs Vaughan, with her poor worried little look and her hair always in her eyes, ever got a son like Arthur. Something like a miracle it was. Makes me think she must have scuttered around once too often. But no matter of that now. Leaving out of account the awful eyes that Joyce was making at Howel, the youngest of the sons, keep you watching Arthur's jaws clamping up and down in a straight line. Eyes on his plate he had, except when he wanted to grab something. And not the least little whisper of talk. Well, Tom not being much of a one for farmhouse bread or bara ceirch either for that matter, he'd soon got to the cake stage, and there was but the one cake there, a big uncut golden thing that looked sort of promising, Tom thought. Never the one to push himself is Tom: anyone who's seen him turning his hat round in his hands like a windmill when Mr Evans the Mansion stops to talk to him sometimes of a Sunday knows that well enough. It was some minutes then before Mrs Vaughan finished scuttering around with her eyes and seen that his plate was empty. Tom was a bit shy: he didn't think it was right for her to cut the cake for him, and him only a workman come in, but come along, says Mrs Vaughan, come along, and Tom reaches out his plate at last.

The first bit he had stopped him dead. Not since he swallowed that soap by mistake when he was a boy had anything tasted quite like this. It was plain awful. A sort of sick taste like as if he was

giving the soda a turn round his mouth. Trying to avoid Mrs
Vaughan's eye now he started again in a hurry, champing a bit like
Arthur. He daren't say anything. Not up to him it was whatever.
He kept on hoping as one of the sons would try it and say
something. Then he could stop this go-slow policy. And in a
minute who should stick his plate out but Arthur.

Well, it wasn't long then before the explosion. 'Darro,' says he
suddenly, and 'Pfff!' – and most of his mouthful went all over the
floor. 'Another blinkin funny joke, is it,' and out he goes, with his
white face longer than ever, straight out of the door. Poor Mrs
Vaughan looked fit to cry. She brushed her hair up out of her eyes
and daren't look at Tom. And Tom was very interested in his plate
that hadn't got a pattern on at all. Presently she cut herself a little
thin bit and her eyes nearly popped out of her head. 'Do you know
what I've done?' she says at last, rather louder than need be, 'I've
put saltpetre in it instead of sugar. Oh my goodness!' and off she
was apologising and scuttering round the kitchen like a scalded
hen. Farmers do keep saltpetre in the pantry often enough in these
parts, you see, for putting on their hams. Round the bone they put
it where the meat needs a bit of hardening. Anyway, she crumpled
nearly all the golden lump that did look so good before, crumpled
it in her two hands and threw it over the wall for the ducks.

Tom didn't hear the rest till later. It was Howel was telling him,
as a matter of fact. The pantry wall was finished and Tom wouldn't
hang it on to the next day, like some of these modern chaps. But
the next morning five of them ducks were dead, flat out in the
yard. And there was Arthur leaning up against the bakehouse
door, champing up and down and laughing his head off. 'That'll
teach you, mam,' says he, with a bit of a crease in his whiteness.
And off to laughing again.

Him and me, we don't see the same things, I do believe.
Anybody'd have thought as they weren't his ducks at all.

Take Hold on Hell

~

He stirred uneasily, seeking to move the ache from one thigh to the other. The pupils of his eyes, contracted by the darkness, continued awhile their endless hover from the dim realisation of the walls to the heaviness of his simple furniture. Then they focussed suddenly and anxiously upon the twelve little grey squares high up in the dark that were his window. Grey, grey, grey, white . . . Yes, surely. That square at the bottom right-hand corner was whiter than the rest. Was it a light? . . . or the dawn . . .? or . . . The straining eyes drew the body upright for a moment, fighting the blackness. But only for a moment: presently the shoulders sagged and the whole frame slumped back, regardless of the boards beneath.

It was a mirage, deadliest of all midnight hopes. A hundred times had he teased himself into thinking one square whiter than the rest; first it had been the top left, then the left again but lower down, always an outer square that glimmered upon the edge of a new world. The whole persuasion was symbolic. Outside, beyond those edges, events did move unexpectedly, the illimitable ball of existence did present some new face as hour followed hour. Each startled hope of his cried for a hand to slide those twelve grey shapes away, to proffer him the moving blank of an unparcelled existence. From time to time he was convinced the slide had begun. But even night could not rid him of an inconvenient reasoning power. He could never completely forget that outside the twelve shades of his life nothing could be seen but the prison stack, the outer wall, a railway cutting along which great curveting clouds of smoke periodically rode, and a few rows of dingy houses. There were never any people. In the evenings he sometimes heard the cries of unseen children. And when the sun shone, out of the brown blot of distance came a church spire. A human building, a church, much more human than divine. He could think about churches, of his father in the big seat . . . and the people streaming out . . . But it only appeared occasionally. And there were never any people. None of that earlier, kindlier generation that had remembered his father and patted him hopefully on the head. Only as the sky grew darker, and clouds of smoke swirled viciously from the stack crossing the silent space like an old tramp beating through a waste of sea, would he see a working-party officer, a dim foreshortened figure, move soundlessly across the yard below and disappear. Then his toes would grow weary of bracing the body on the table drawn up to the wall. The dusk would deepen. In the right-hand block the rows of bars, gripped here and there by the clenched fists of longing, would darken imperceptibly into lines of menace. And after sunset an eerie Ben Gunn who was never seen called softly for Bartholomew. 'Barth-ol-om-ew' – the name echoed urgently around the stack. No answer broke the stillness. It was always the same. The voice always called after sunset, high-pitched and soft at first, then urgently, repeatedly. But Bartholomew never answered. He had the feeling that it was a voice from an older age, that Bartholomew lived on in the timelessness of misery but would never answer in this world.

But then he ought to, he ought to. Nothing was altered here. The prisoner turned almost frantically to his left, feeling the cold wall upon his forehead. Even Bartholomew got no ticket of leave from this place, no remission for the endlessness of age. Tears of self-pity sprang to his eyes and swam in the darkness. He would never go on tirelessly sitting down the years. He would die first. Old Summers would see to that. Summers with his heavy red face and jutting triangular lower lip following him everywhere, coming between him and every lighter picture of the past . . . A tide of heavy hatred lapped into his being so that he could not think . . . The sun was going down into the sea, a red sun with a jutting lip that cast the waves back and back to thud against the tautness of his skull. A bottomless sea and the sun riding it . . . He almost screamed out loud. That sun wasn't going down. It would never go down. That horrible red level gaze would burn him for ever and for ever and his world would go on dying in a thousand evenings. He struggled up involuntarily, mouthing. For a moment his arms belaboured the void . . .

Duw! he must get a grip on himself. Near to slipping that time he had been. He must watch for it, watch for it. All the same, Summers was more than man could bear. From the first day (his mind was back in its groove now) there had been no mercy for him. When the heavy door of his cell swung open that first grey morning, out he had stepped with his slops, just as the printed instructions told him. But on the long landing there was no one in sight. Nothing save the wide-hipped, lumbering retreat of old Summers. The door of the cell next to his own was open, but its occupant was nowhere to be seen. For a while he had stood hesitant, holding his pot like a sinner uncertain of the reception of his offering. Then Summers turned on him, snarling and threatening. What the hell? Hadn't he ever emptied slops before? Fouler and fouler words had tumbled from the man, blasting his bewildered brain. How, he had thought to himself miserably afterwards, was he to know where the recess was? You couldn't see it from the door. Was he Solomon then?

Early pain and humiliation had turned to a sickening dead fear in face of the utter lack of discrimination shown by Summers and the other landing-officers. Summers most of all, of course. He cursed the prisoners if they asked for a letter; he cursed them if they asked for anything else (and then never brought it); he cursed them on exercise. No time of day or place was free from his pestilent jutting curse. He would walk up and down landing G4, shouting and bellowing, insisting with a horrible foul-mouthed sarcasm that everyone got back off his doorstep and waited for his dinner out of sight. Then with the heavy door swung to, they were expected to know by instinct the precise moment to appear with ready hands stretched forth for their tins, and to retire obediently at the double. Even the orderlies never knew from day to day what new whim he might not be fattening; obedience to another officer's orders was all the same as mutiny to him. Round every corner jutted his red jowl; every corridor resounded to his rolling tread.

All that might be all right for some people. But couldn't they see that he wasn't like the rest? Kearney across the landing now, he looked like an animal. So did that foxy Hilberson. And Fagenbaum, the Hoxton fence with the perpetual pitted sneer, and even young Wood next door, sullen young lout that he was. But hell! Anybody with half an eye ought to be able to see that he wasn't like them. He came from a good home. Oh darro! – and the tears sprang to his eyes again – look at his pale face and thin shoulders mun: wasn't it plain as a pikestaff how poor and ill he'd been ever since he was a kid going to school at the Pentre and his mam not letting him play in the back lane with the other boys? . . . He sniffed a little. You might as well swing your arms in the wind as try to explain anything to Summers. He opened his mouth and the stream knocked you flat.

Yesterday he had noticed in his little glass how flat and lustreless his hair was. Lying flat along his head it was, the same as if he'd had the 'flu'. Didn't that show he was ill? He would have thought any fool knew about hair like that. But not Summers. He was a stone lighter, more than a stone lighter, than when he'd left home, and oh darro! Wasn't he ill then? What for did they think he'd stayed away from the factory? Wasn't it the need for life itself that had made him take the bus to the seashore those days, and his mam not knowing? But no, there was no justice in the world: from Isaac Williams the Bryn, who called himself a J.P., to that blasted Summers here in this corner of hell, there was no justice. Everyone was against him, always had been. Lot of mean, despicable curs they were. All of them . . . No, no, there was his mother. He'd nearly forgotten her. With misty eye he saw his mam standing in her kitchen in the Watton, red-eyed and heavy, not willing to come to the door to see him go, fearing the sight of his back growing smaller and more stooping in the hostile distance. His mam . . . the world was against her too, against her grey hair and her heavy hands . . . A spasm of crying overtook him, and with the release the pull went out of his pains. Presently he sighed more regularly on his bed-board.

So the minutes passed. There was no change in the grey monotone of the window. Suddenly the prisoner leapt to a sitting position. The bell. That must have been the bell. Quick, to get washed and dressed and have the bed made before Summers opened the door. He couldn't stand any more years of scorching from that angry red shape. That animal voice, with its barbarous half-hidden burr, its sliding nasal sequences . . . Duw! it made him shiver. No more of it. No more. Take it away . . . Heavens, he was falling asleep again. Quick . . . But wait a minute. It couldn't be six-thirty. It wasn't light. Wasn't that the bell then that he had heard? He could swear he'd heard something. Listen . . . Then he heard it again. From somewhere in that shell of darkness came a muffled howl. There was no other word for it. A howl. Like a wolf baying the void. The sound rose and fell in the silence of that great black hollow building. The hair stood up at his nape, his flesh crept. Like a spirit in the charnel-house it was, crying for an end . . . Silence . . . Then the howling again, and moans and a rattling sound. Duw, he couldn't stand this. Bobol annwyl, he had stood a lot, but he couldn't stand this. It was that scarecrow John Arthur Jones, he knew it was, that tall dim figure in for cruelty to his child. The man's soul was half out of his body, crying, crying. But only the hollow arch hanging over the sound made any reply. The inhuman sound was clearer now, not so far away. John Arthur Jones was in the cell right beneath him. He felt that that muddied outwelling of a spirit was carrying him away too, with a sick dizzy reaching for the marks of humanity, for the pillars of the world he had never known. His clutching hand slipped off the smooth, turning, unrelenting wall of the cell . . . But suddenly a tintinnabulation of bells broke out all over the landings and steadied him. The men couldn't sleep. They wanted the man Jones taken away. And presently the officers came, very surly and ungracious. He could detect Summers's animal snarl and for an instant his face blenched. Then he could feel the tide of hatred setting strong within him. It moved sullenly and slowly, as though it were dragging great rocks from the illimitable fastnesses beneath. It seeped slowly, curling white and vicious round that hot, grating voice and lapping ominously about the promontory of the lips. That ball of fire would go down. It must go down. Already the leaden waters had covered that venomous, jutting voice. The tide swept on, over his heart and on into the distance.

He lay like the dead.

Slowly the grey whitened. An ashen glimmer began to play farther and farther from the window, bravely striking along the bare wall of the cell. The table and chair, hung with the grey shapeless coat and bagging trousers of the prisoner, stood in a dull group midway between shade and light. Farther back the heavy steel door, painted a brazen yellow that made unbroken the rectangle of the room, began to point its lines. Along the left wall lay the sleeper, humped in a curious swept-up heap. The face seemed very white.

From downstairs came a shuffling of feet, a coarse laugh and the sound of voices, and then, with the final whitening, the bell. Its first clang beat the sleeper bolt upright. In a sort of strained haste he washed, dressed, lifted his bed-board against the wall and folded his blankets automatically in the order stipulated by the regulations. Overhead another man let fall his board with a thud. Through the stone and plaster came the muffled pokings of some apprehensive prisoner already at the feverish dusting of the walls expected of every inmate on every morning of his dwindling life.

But none of these sounds meant anything to the young man gazing at his drawn face in the glass. He saw nothing beyond a white blur. He was not really looking. Through his mind coursed a hundred hares of thought, crossing and recrossing a path . . . a path across the mountains . . . yes, that was it. Duw, that was it. Why hadn't it come to him before? That would get him out, sure. Mr Roderick the Vro had been willing to stand surety for his brother Ianto about the shop: he was an influential man, very important in the chapel he was, went to the undeb and everything. If he would write to the governor . . . that would get him out. Yes, it would, it would. But first a special letter. Special letter. Must see the governor for a special letter. The words ran round and round in his brain. Special letter . . .

A footstep sounded. The key grated in the lock and the heavy door swung slowly open. Summers, true to his practice of avoiding the early morning demands of prisoners, was nowhere to be seen. A man carrying his chamber like an acolyte passed the opening. Then another. Blue-jowled, heavy-eyed, they crowded to the recess. In the cell the pale slight figure stood unseeing for a moment or two, then stiffened into consciousness, lurched out and began to thread a course against the stream. He must find Summers. There he was. Over there. Opening the doors on the other side of the landing. His hurrying thoughts filliped behind the blue stooping back, anxiously jostling the rolling method of the man. At last the bull-neck stopped by the roll-board and growled at the crowd in the recess . . . 'Turn that damn tap off there. How long . . . What the hell do you want? Governor, governor – no, you can't see the governor.' His voice grated. 'He isn't here today. In any case you're too late. D'ye think I've nothing better to do than wait till rats like you choose their own time to ask me about seeing the governor? Get to hell out of it!'

For a moment the pale face blenched and into the eyes came a beaten shuddering look. Then he turned his back and stumbled away. He would die. Die. Another day, no, another day and he would be dead. Dead . . . A black ball of fury hit him between the eyes. Summers. That red grating animal Summers . . . Killing him by days and by inches . . . The thought rattled in his throat. In front of him an angry rolling sun blew boiling waves across the sea. Wind, wind come up, he would swim. He would sink that mad crimson cruelty and cram the salt back into its own mouth. Then they'd have to let him go. He'd be free . . . free . . .

Some sixth sense made Summers turn his head as he jutted his words at the recess across the landing. But he was too late. A pallid, murderous figure leapt upon his back, sobbing through parted teeth. For a second he fought to save himself, one hand seeking to press the white venom away. Then the roll-board snapped off short.

The men across the landing turned in time to see a heavy body jerk over the rail, rebound partly from the netting spread from floor to floor of the next landing, and fall again through an un-mended loop to hit the stones of G2 with a sickening thud. High over the sudden clatter of feet came a hideous triumphant howl. 'Free, free' echoed around the hollow walls and fell back from the roof. The men never moved. Their eyes were fixed on the white wolf's face, the bared gums and clawlike hands.

Incident in Majorca

~

The last piece of chaff made McAllister look up wearily from the guide-book in which he had dutifully kept his finger for an hour or more. He was faintly annoyed. It had not been easy to conceal from the boys that he had been lost for some time. Now this confounded plateau had finished it. In front lay a wilderness of honeycombed rock, falling in steep terraces near at hand and rising again into interminable coruscations against the sky farther off. Somewhere in the sponge-like basin was hidden the sheer gorge of the Torrente del Pareys which was their supposed destination.

The numerous and not always inaudible suggestions of the boys whetted the edge of McAllister's temper very fast. He felt particularly aggrieved at the behaviour of the Headmaster, who was in nominal charge of the expedition. There he was, mooning up and down the verge, probably not even conscious yet, despite the stoppage of the last ten minutes, that there was any difficulty to be overcome. Ever since leaving the farm called Escorca he had splayed aimlessly over the harsh dry grass of the plateau, plainly following more by sound than attention. Even the dispirited wanderings of the boys along to left and right in search of the mythical steps provided by the peerless Baedeker had not so far drawn his mind to the need for his assistance. McAllister was getting thoroughly fed up. He slammed the book shut and sat down. No suicidal descent for him if he could help it. Much better go back to the monastery and play cards. Yes, even if it meant having the miserable Simmons close down on his one-no-trump again.

A shout roused him. 'Hey, Littlejohn. Littlejohn's gone over the edge, sir. He's going down.' McAllister stiffened to his feet in alarm. 'What? Gone over the edge? Has he fallen down or something?' – 'Oh no sir, he's jumping down. There he is, down there.' Beating back a sudden horrible preview of the national headlines, the master craned his head in the direction indicated. Away down, bounding with all the agility of a small tubby goat, went the form of Theodore Hallworthy Littlejohn, rapidly foreshortening into the spongy grey. 'What in heaven's name did he do that for? Go after him and get him back. You, Lister and Evans, you go, both of you. Go on, put a shake in it. Can't think what you chaps are doing standing around letting the little poop do a thing like that. Move, Lister.' Thus adjured, first Evans and then Lister dropped over the edge with some deliberation, bridging the points of rock in slow and gingerly fashion. The fugitive had already disappeared. In exasperation McAllister hallooed after them more than once but they did not seem to hear. A minute later Lister turned and remarked with devastating clarity of tone that Littlejohn had stopped and was waiting. Then he disappeared behind a pinnacle bordering the next rough terrace level. For a moment there was a relieved silence.

With one accord the boys, suddenly aware of the Head's presence, split into two groups. Down the lane so formed he came, a moistness plainly visible above his bushy eyebrows. 'Get Lister and Evans back,' he said with unusual intensity. 'Stop them. If my stepson wants to kill himself, we can't have other people getting into danger too.' This rectitude impressed the company into immobility. 'Go after them, Sampson and you, Page. For pity's sake get a move on. Get 'em all back. Only be quick.' Not content with this and without waiting for Sampson, the senior boy of the party, to jump down, the Headmaster lowered his stocky form till his head alone was showing, and working his way diagonally to the left disappeared for all his bulk quicker than did the two boys.

What should he do now, McAllister wondered. Organise the rest of the gang and follow? Or wait? This responsibility was hell. Just the sort of thing that would happen, with the Boss going off like that without saying anything. He had had visions a moment before of frantic mothers in England . . . No, dammit, no – he must cut that out. No point in making things seem worse than they were. Bad enough, though. If only he'd gone down instead of old Mallinson, that would have been easy. Still . . . Might help to see what the boys thought about it. Should they go down? To the master's surprise the remainder of the party maintained a glum silence, save for one irrepressible wisp who wanted to follow the Head. But there were no backers. It soon appeared that the others did not like the look of the place at all. At any rate, whatever it was, they wouldn't go down. McAllister caught himself reflecting, even in an inconvenient moment, how often he seemed to misjudge people and things. To him there was nothing especially forbidding about these honeycombed terraces. A tricky descent, he did not doubt. And one he would not care to take the whole party down, whippers-in and all. But he was surprised at the oppression in the faces around him. It was as though beneath that glancing sunlight there was a shadow he could not see.

Half an hour passed. Not one of the six absentees put so much as a head in sight. And not a sound came from the gorge. McAllister decided unhappily that the Head must have found a way down. Best get the rest back to Escorca anyway, he thought, back to the outpost of life. From there it wouldn't be so far to the monastery. But there would be no cards now.

Almost three-quarters of a mile away as the stone drops, down where the massive honeycombs all but touched one another in a rock of stiffer sort, the feet of Theodore Hallworthy Littlejohn sank with a crash into the bed of pebbles flooring the gorge. He grinned reminiscently, with a semblance of frog. Those twirps Lister and Evans, how he had baited them! Now teasing them almost into reach, now scuttling off at double their speed, old slow-coaches that they were. Hadn't half made the Old Man mad too, because the silly asses kept thinking they were going to catch up and so wouldn't stop for him. What did it matter anyway? All this fuss and bother. Anybody'd think the cliff was difficult, the way they were all yelling about it. And he was in the gorge they were looking for, wasn't he? What if the Old Man did storm and rave, what could he do? Beat him in the monastery? – Not bloomin' likely! Besides, Mum would take care of any delayed action. She had Dr Thomas Mallison, the miserable old sourpuss, pretty well under control in the two years or so she'd been married to him. And he needn't think just because he was in short pants and a sombrero that he was out of her reach. Oh golly no! Littlejohn grinned again in the unpleasant way he had. Headmaster old Tommy might be, but he was tied to an apron-string like a bit of

elastic. Let him try any high-hat stuff and see what happened to
him.

Absorbed in these satisfying reflections he did not at first hear a
persistent scraping sound. But in due course the perspiring and
assiduous countenance of Evans appeared beside a rock some fifty
feet up. Further away still could be heard voices, at least one of
them very wrathful. Mockingly docile now, Littlejohn let Evans
come up with him and stood aimlessly banking the stones before
him with one foot, the picture of mild apprehension. 'Ol' Moke is
thirsting for your blood somethin' terrible,' said Evans. 'I should go
slow with him if I were you.' Littlejohn eyed him tartly. 'Well you
needn't talk, you fat speedy ass, he isn't exactly patting you on the
back for catching me and all that, is he? You watch out yourself.'
Littlejohn smirked a little as he eyed the other four toilers pressed
against the rocks above in varied and ludicrous attitudes. He had
an odd feeling of pride that it was he who had drawn these silly
muddlers along a road they could never have followed if left to
themselves. What a set they were! There was Evans and that fat oily
face of his. Good job he had it hidden under his broad-brimmed
straw sombrero. Imagined himself a daredevil gaucho, presumably.
Fat ass. Then Lister, snaky and stammering and nervous. What was
he good for, anyway? Sampson, he supposed, thought himself no
end of a nut just because he was a prefect and could wear the
foulest plus-fours. Everybody knew really he was the biggest
dumbell old Chuffy had ever taught. He'd heard Chuffy say so
himself, in the sixth room before break one day. And Page. Well,
Page wasn't worth talking about. He was just a mess. There wasn't
a decent chap in the whole gang. No wonder this tour was like a
Sunday School walk . . .

Safe in this spiritual fastness he gazed brightly at the Doctor as
he staggered in. The latter seemed suddenly to blanch even
through the turkey-red of his complexion and avoided the boy's
eye. Muttering something about later developments in a thick
voice, he shuffled on. The boys, after a curious look at one
another, shrugged their shoulders and moved off without more
ado.

Dr Mallinson had had good cause to reflect. He was not by
nature an unkindly man, but an hour before he had had the
strongest impulse to leave his stepson in the lurch. Only when he
realised the crowd listening had he stopped short. Even then it

had been a hard job. It was almost as though he had had to break through a thin transparent barrier before he could remember and warm his wits at the likely reactions of an objective party and the unpleasant bruit it would make in a corpse-warming world.

Somehow all this had been outside his contemplation two years ago. Emily Littlejohn had seemed to him then a plump and matronly presence, no more, with dark inviting eyes beckoning him to the delights Ted Littlejohn had had to leave almost un-tasted. Poor old Ted, he had thought then, always the first to be called over the coals! Poor old Ted. Emily's little villa in Oxted had been then a lighted haven into which his tired mind could sail for evenings together without taking thought or caring for the next world. The whole air was one of unforced domesticity, of years devoted to the ethic of the slippers by the fireside, the pipe after supper in the garden. Bachelor existence seemed plainly a poor shift. Peace was more than a promise; peace, just what he needed. Then too, Theodore had been a myth. He spent most of his time with an aunt in Cumberland whose home was in convenient proximity to the miserable forcing-house where he was being prepared for Duncumb. His frog-like look had penetrated only very occasionally into the consciousness in those days and then to be thrust away again up the backstairs by conspiratorial hands. The cosseting had continued.

At last he had married her. But not hastily. He consoled himself with that. He had taken his precautions. None the less, in a matter of months the warm matronly shape he pursued appeared rarely and then only before the most tender concern. In its place he found an uncertain-tempered, dark-eyed dominance that man-aged his domestic affairs with the utmost efficiency and sought new social worlds to conquer. He was never a social man himself. But the worst had come when Emily became convinced that Theodore would do infinitely better at Cullingham under the eye of his stepfather. That was the beginning of the end. The pleasant house above Halewood's had, so to speak, had its doors blown in. Or that was what it felt like. True, they didn't have the boy up often. And it wasn't that Theo was abnormally mischievous or disobedient. It was something else. He felt – there was no way of putting this properly – that with him there came in a wind of raw indecency that blew every finer feeling like stubble before it. A ridiculous idea, of course. Mallinson had tried, goodness knows how he had tried, to laugh himself out of it. But it was no good. It always crept back. Once or twice of late he had believed that the devil stared solemnly round the flowers at Sunday supper when he had the boy in. He had felt him, too, looking over the shoulder of his brood by the pillar in morning prayers, when the shafts of sunlight crossed the dais and opened his eyes.

But in school it was not so bad somehow. He had a thousand times rather take a form as he occasionally did than sit alone, toying with business in that study of his, where the black nakedness of the spirit waited outside, waited for the door to open. In school there was no help, but the warmth and weakness of others held him for a while. Not one in all those four hundred souls, he knew, could contend with the fiend. They were all souls like his, helpless, weak, mischievously wicked, often kindly or cruel in a small way, but not like Theo. A door had opened somewhere. The wind was blowing and he could not shut it. A black wind.

He had not dared to mention his feelings to anyone. It would be awkward enough to have to do so, admitted. But that wasn't all. Propitiation of this stark power demanded the abandonment of all alliances against it. He had felt it rise to towering heights at the mere suggestion that he should speak. And without foreseeing it he had known all at once that Theo would insist on coming to Majorca with the party. Left to himself he might have had the courage to tell McAllister, idiotic though the confession would seem. Theo intended to prevent that. There was to be no escape. None at all.

Back in the fixed groove of melancholy Mallinson's mind found an unhappy satisfaction in the fitness of the scene. It saw each ridge of round pebbles surmounted only for the next clashing hollow to ensue. Undoubtedly there was something horrible about the place, the whitish interminable walls always threatening to meet overhead, the crack of sky far away, narrow as the thread of existence. But what did it matter? – existence? It was here, the fear of all the ages and here he must face it if he would. He was suddenly sure of that.

'There's the sea.' It was Sampson's voice. Gorge met gorge and into the new width swept an arm of the sea sparkling with a thousand lights. Mallinson felt a surge of new heart, as though an arm had reached him out of the voyaging of friends. He was in touch at last with the circle of good.

For more than an hour this strength continued. It was as though his eyes had never seen at all. Theo was once again an ordinary unpleasant little boy, not even a popular one, as he could tell from Evans's shoulders hunched in his direction. There did not seem to be any particular animus in the boy's gaze. In fact, he wasn't even looking. Mallinson fell into happier reverie, in which his new penetration notably failed to detect the silent agonies of Lister in dropping a surreptitious cigarette-case into the blue measureless depths. The Doctor was benevolently at sea once more. For him an ordinary set of boys were going through the ordinary motions of their kind. He had not felt so free for months.

Time passed. The word to start back was given. Common discretion could disregard no longer the warning path of red across the watered blue of the horizon. They must be back at Escorca before dark. Suddenly a chill struck the Doctor's heart. Dark. Out of the light, back to the dark, away from the warm sea back across the dead plateau, the dead plateau with the drying grass – and Theo dogging at his heels. He almost cried out. Could not he settle with the thing here? Now? He looked at the sea with a last intensity.

The sun had already cut a glowing shaft into the right-hand cliff wall when Sampson shouted that he had found some steps. Obviously they constituted the lower end of the guide path, coming down in wide spirals almost to the point of the Y where the two gorges met. Twenty yards' climbing, however, brought the party to a dead stop. The steps came suddenly to an end. Twenty feet above they went on again. The interval was covered by nothing more than sheer rock wall, smooth to the touch, without hand or foothold. The trailing wire looping from the first sound post above was worse than useless. All six stood for a moment nonplussed, scattered at intervals along the spiral below the gap.

To scramble up the way they had come down was anything but a happy prospect. Even Sampson's usual optimism drew the line at that. But what else was there for it? – unless they could cut into this path higher up. He pondered. With odd irrelevancy the boy found himself noticing how the least exertion made little beads appear on the broad lipline of Evans just in front. He shivered. It was suddenly cold. Someone was looking at him from behind, of that he was sure. He felt a slight pricking of the hairs along his neck. Turning round, he saw the headmaster planted on the spiral below, his face tense, two prominent canines fast in his upper lip and his whole form braced for some invisible effort. The Old Man must be pretty well done in, he thought.

'Look out!' – it was a sharp cry from Lister. Sampson shot round to see him pawing at the topmost step. At the same instant something plunged past him and crunched solidly upon the stones below. Then he noticed Page and Evans crowding with every appearance of concern round Littlejohn, who had been standing directly below Lister. Littlejohn murmured exaltedly that he had not known whether he was dreaming, not till he felt his forehead swelling so fast he could not hold it in. The skin was not broken. The step had barely touched him. Another inch and the skull would have been like egg-shell. Trying to keep his hand steady Sampson offered Littlejohn a bismuth tablet he happened to have in his shirt pocket. 'Make you feel better, clear the head, ol' man,' he urged. Accepted without alacrity, the tablet ultimately disappeared. Littlejohn, waving away any further appearances of solicitude, scrambled down and presently was heard from the forefront complaining of wind, the particular product of that ass Sampson.

The latter could not help casting another glance at the Head. He had never moved. Funny way to act when your own stepson was hurt, thought the boy. For that matter, a funny way to act when anybody in your charge was hurt. Just standing there like that. No interest at all. Even when the others moved on up the gorge, it was some time before he stirred. Sampson could not understand it. They hadn't come so jolly far as all that. Yet here was the Old Man stumbling over the stones with unseeing eyes, for all the world like a sleepwalker. He must keep an eye on him, the boy decided.

After a few minutes Page, who was in the lead, struck up a slope on the right that was not too sharp at first and offered a handhold of occasional sparse tufts of grass. Dusk was falling very fast. Nothing could be heard but Evans sniffing the sweat off the end of his nose and the roaring of the shale sent flying down. The steps behind seemed heedless and unutterably weary. There was no panting at all.

Presently Page cut into a stony path that was plainly the ascendant of the cliff steps. The rock gave way here to bare patches of earth and beds of stiff green flags. The going was easier. But the pace of those at the rear grew correspondingly slower. Whatever it was in the Old Man that had made him come so far was flagging now. It was not spirit, for he had none. There was a blank look in his eyes and his face had grown grey in the twilight. Every few yards he halted with a sort of irresolution. But for the droop of his shoulders one would not have thought him tired at all. His breathing was quiet, irregular.

In the gathering darkness Sampson and Evans had lost touch with the others. They took the Head by the arm, one on either side, and encouraged him as far as the next ragged array of green flags. The man between them took not the least notice of their exhortations that they could see. He stumbled brokenly as far as he was led and never said a word. Away ahead Page could be heard calling the rest to hurry, and just faintly audible to those who knew what it was, a low growling note that was the regulation grumble of that young blister Littlejohn. But behind there was nothing for it. The pace got slower and slower. Presently the Old Man sank down upon a boulder and, a few yards farther on, another. From each sitting he was slower to rise, or be assisted up. On his chin a light foam was sprinkled.

Night had now fallen complete and black about the three. They had no idea how far they were from the top of the cliff and from Escorca. Nothing could be heard but the rustle of a faint breeze moving the sharp green tips.

At Escorca McAllister uneasily surveyed the void before him. Away to the right stood two big cars with headlights shining out across the plateau, but there was no one to be seen. Through the half-open door of the farmhouse young Littlejohn could be heard telling the tale of the day in a cocky, superior little voice. He was certainly making the most of that swollen forehead of his to the couple of boys McAllister had allowed to accompany him from the monastery. He had even got to the stage when he was prepared to regard it as a triumph of personal aplomb that the rock had missed him at all. Extraordinary the lengths to which conceit could go, mused McAllister. Not a sign of penitence, either. It was not for him, the master thought, to say anything to the boy about the day's outing in general. Undoubtedly the Head had dealt or would deal with him. He had a private hope that the Old Man would be stiff on him, but didn't quite see what he could do. Yes, the difference between youngsters was amazing. There was Lister now, absolutely overcome by his share in the disasters of the day. For all his nervousness he had insisted on accompanying the guides back along the path he had come. Page had vowed that they couldn't be more than a mile off at most. That had decided McAllister to stay at the farm, but he wished the business were over. The silence got on his nerves.

At length shuffling footfalls could be heard. Someone stepped for a moment into the direct beam but he couldn't see who it was. Good God, weren't they carrying something? The bearers stopped just a few paces away, by the footboard of the car, and Sampson, his pug face oddly strained, detached himself from the group and approached the master. He stood a moment, balancing on his feet with an incredulous air. 'What is it, man, what is it?' snapped McAllister. 'Say something. Don't stand there like that. Who's hurt?' – 'The Old Man's dead, sir,' said the boy slowly. McAllister let out his breath in a long hiss. He stared at Sampson dully. 'He died a mile back, from exhaustion, I think. He said something queer about the sea, that he shouldn't have left it or something. He said it several times and that was all. Then he just passed out on us. We couldn't make head nor tail of it. Was it – do you think he was ever a sailor, sir?'

McAllister did not reply. The horror of the measures he must take, his new and unpleasant responsibility, were just breaking in on his mind. This was no time for speculation upon the almost posthumous wanderings of the individual dead.

One Bell Tolling

~

Hedley Williams leaned forward a bit to take the weight off his buttocks. He never had been one to ride far, even on posh upholstery, without having a dull feeling spread along his thighs from the back and peg his feet miserably to the floor. Strange, that was, and he so well developed in the portions named. But there it is, he reflected, if you will ride in old farm vans that the motor firms turned out when they still thought farmers ran on solid rims like Boadicea, the only thing to do is to prop your heart up a bit higher and ride on what you've got. Hedley often had long humorous thoughts like this. They were made like sandwiches of strange content and he kept the glass cover between him and the other side of the bar. Often he filled them with long slices off the meanness of Morgan Williams, his employer. No relation either, though they had the same name. But Morgan and his dirty old van without so much as a bit of lettering on the outside were good for a meal of laughing. If you had to have a meal, that is, and you were hungry enough for anything. Hedley, whenever he was almost empty enough to think, could always fall back on the joke of being on the farm at all and on Morgan's farm at that. Perhaps he'd better himself yet. Travel in silk stockings or something. After the war that'd be, of course.

But for the present his bottom was sore. For one thing he wasn't driving. And on his lap was John Elias, Morgan's eldest son. The boy was quiet as kids went, but he was heavy and he spoilt the view. What chance had Hedley to cut a bit of a figure driving through the valleys, even if it was in Morgan's dirty old van, when there was no more to be seen from the outside than the crane of his neck at the shops flashing past? He shifted the boy's weight with difficulty to his other thigh, and cut himself a thick slice of wit for the part of him that was still alive. When he laughed under glass like this, it came to him sometimes that life was a stodge after all. He began to feel like that now. Back it came at him with unsweet breath and he was suddenly sick of its everlasting savour. Before long a dull feeling crept from both ends. The chuckle that he didn't remember starting was as indigestible as anything.

At his side Morgan Williams swung the wheel slowly from hand to hand. Always a bit late with it he seemed, always driving on the last inch of road. His hands, in any case, did not seem made to contain the wheel. They had a crude, unfinished look, not thick and stiffly-jointed like a countryman's, but long and slivered, slipping without warning from skin to nail. They hung on the wheel like the rudimentary claws of a great bird. He said no word to Hedley. Upper Boat, potatoes; Llanbradach, potatoes; Sirhowy, potatoes – what was there to say? One part of his brain went on recording names. The Rhiw, potatoes, yes. No! Some other reaction was struggling through and the brief tussle brought him to concentration again. Potatoes for Cathy, yes. But this was home. Home. The word almost stung him with its onset. Nothing to do with potatoes, no nothing. Home was a swathe cut through his conscious mind, straight from the dull fields of his Vale of Glamorgan farm up to the hill of his first recollections. A brief smile rested on Morgan's lank look a moment, and his high cheek-bones were not just then the tightest features of his face. Some of the blankness had gone out of him as he strained for the hard back of land supporting his home. In front the ribbon of road dipped and rose; the last garage in the valley flashed past, a blob of red and grey. The engine began to falter upon the back of the great comb of mountains whose black teeth stretched south-eastwards to the sea. The land was hard and featureless as vulcanite. It tried perpetually to cast back its invaders into normality, to let them slip and forget them. But the van clung obstinately to the camber of the road. Morgan's hands gripped tighter now.

Soon the houses of the village came into precarious sight. None of the veracity of nature had gone to their building. Two careful lines tightened along the neck of the ridge and dwindled against the skyline. Every variant roof was grey with determination to regain its place in the narrow lines. The van came at them from the angle of the dislodged and in it was the same determination. The hands on the wheel were almost human now, the fingers tensed with an emotion that even the long bones could not smother. The engine swooped for the last dip.

Morgan was coming home. Home to the high silence he understood. Other men might raise laughter as perverse and unnatural as their lives themselves: they might fight in their little frivols for the dust of the valleys, for the song of tips and chapels. But Morgan was older than that. He came of the stock of the mountain itself. The mountain before the molehills grew on it. His people came there from Blaen Onneu, over the top, where the ash trees grew in a solemn line, one by one, as befitted old men. Lower down the narrow cwm there was only English; but the Williamses had kept the Welsh. Where they had it from, nobody could then say. Nor indeed how long they had been there. They grew at Blaen Onneu with the ash trees and the centuries had passed on either side.

When Morgan's father died, they had moved to the Rhiw. Only a step in distance, but the district never understood. It had ceased long since perhaps to recognise either life itself or the need for it at Blaen Onneu. But when they moved, the silence was not infrangible any more. It perched unwitting above the coal-dust and the singers. The colliers felt it and were moved, though it meant nothing in terms of the pit, the pub and the chapel. The incessant intake and regurgitation of life made occasional forays now into that silent orbit, seeking for the motions common to living. But there were no more than the bare elements of reconciliation there.

All Morgan's people were big-boned, almost sheeplike in appearance. All of them had been old before they were young. Only Morgan was under six feet and he looked smaller, maybe, because of the irregular hump behind his shoulders. Not a handsome man, at the best, even with the new look on his face. But he was not, all the same, the mean man they took him for down in Glamorgan. How old were they there, with their hundred and fifty years?

He peered ahead, almost animated. The centuries made perilous progress on either side.

'I'll take the old van up by Curry's and turn 'er,' he said. 'You an' me'll drop the potatoes at Cathy's, Hedley.'

Hedley awoke from what was almost a stupor and began to take an interest. They couldn't be all like Morgan in these parts, anyway. Might be an odd daughter or two worth looking at when they'd got the sacks out. A first look at the street round John's neck helped this new optimism to last more than the one chew over. Not a classy place, it seemed, but clean with the incredible white doorsteps of the collier's pride. And people about. Quite a few. He had time to note a strapping girl at the counter of the grocer's nearly opposite as Morgan was putting on the brake.

The more shame that he made such a mess of the blessed sacks. There was a knack to it, that was all. Just a knack. Morgan just twitched them on to his shoulder and they lay along the hump safe and steady-looking. But with Hedley they beat his wrists to the fall. Once down it was the devil's own job to get them up again. He could have kicked himself. While Morgan was taking in three . . . But it was only a knack. That was all. In the open street, though . . . Stumbling over the step up into the whitewashed passageway at the side of the shop, he did kick himself. The side of the ankle it was. He plunged into a hobnailed purgatory where was none of the thin skin of wit. Dam, O dammo. Let him only dump this sack. He leant against the wall, gingerly fingering the ankle. Taken the skin off, the blasted business had. Dam, dam, dam. Wear boots the next time on a ruddy ride like this. And smarty nothing.

Morgan broke in. 'Hedley mun, take John down the road to see Mamgu. John'll show you. I'll be down after, when I'm finished by here.'

Hedley had no thought for the instinctive courtesy of Morgan's action. Back in the street now, there were other things to be concerned about. He knew he was breathing too heavily to cut any figure. People would think he was an ordinary vanman. Much better go while the going was good. He turned on his heel. John got out of the van and came quietly with him. The boy had not said much all day.

Barely a minute's walk from Cathy's shop lay a short cobbled alley, up a steep slope. The stones were grey and dry. Water would never rest there longer than a ball of wool. Up this John turned. Hedley hung back a little. He didn't like these swift transitions. He would have liked the walk to be longer, so that he could straighten up a bit and take a look at the possibilities. No day had so taxed the lightness of his digestion as this one. Before he had time even for a tasty little bit of street-walking, he was pulled in through a low doorway and down a step into what seemed total darkness.

At first he could not distinguish that John stood just ahead, although their hands still touched. In this lower world they were yet higher than the street, and the harsh scrape of footsteps, the bang of van doors and the momentum of conversation came from below, indescribably confusing the rightness of light and dark. For the first time since he was little his glib system of colours was being challenged. There was no time to assimilate the challenge or compose the counter in the fantasy of seconds that followed. Silence was the more immediate opponent and that lingered, inexorable. Slowly the line of a heavy dresser became visible to the right. To the left, a faint gleam from a cold fireplace.

'Oh John bach, it's you. Come on in,' said a weary voice from the corner beyond the hearth. The searching eyes turned in that direction with an almost audible click. In the farther twilight half-sat, half-lay what, standing up, would have been a very big man. The first glance, though, showed that he had trouble. The left hip lay exposed by the uneasy posture and one long hand hung awkwardly between the chair arm and the unhealthy thigh.

'Hallo, Uncle Jack,' said the boy, not moving.

'Who is this then, John? Who is this you have with you?' Hedley moved up a bit, noticing that he was blocking what little light crept through the low door. He gathered round him the little confident noises of the street below. 'My name's Williams,' he began, 'Hedley Williams. I work for your brother down at Tyisha.'

'Pleased to meet you, Mister Williams. Sit you down a moment.'

Silence intercepted again with audible success, but was checked for a brief space by the voice from the corner. Its pitch was higher, wavering uncertainly with the ebb and flow of effort.

'Well John bach, what have you been doing in school this term?'

'Noth . . . Nothing much, Uncle Jack.' The boy sounded ungracious, but was too embarrassed to drag on what he knew was intended only as a formal answer. 'How's your leg?' he added, hurrying to shift the lodgement of the conversation.

'Better, boy, better.' The man moved uneasily, as though in half-hearted demonstration of this. 'Be down for the shooting now in a week or two.'

This was always the high flame-mark of hope. Once, three years before, Jack Williams had been well enough to go down with two other men from the Rhiw to shoot over Morgan's land. Not that the bag had ever been much. But shooting over Morgan's land was the symbol of fitness just within sight of his flickering hope. It was a symbol too that was accepted by the neighbours, glad of something they could understand. He was always on the verge of another visit.

The voice flattened. The demands of courtesy had been met. The man rose, the pallor of his face showing even in the curtained light, and turned the whole of his body towards an ill-defined passageway opposite the door.

'Mam,' he called. 'Mam. Here's John bach come to see you.'

The effort over, he stood a moment erect as might be, the shortened leg, bootless, barely touching the floor, and then resettled himself deliberately in the chair, grimacing. Presently his eyes closed.

The attention of Hedley and John had died almost before the man's trying. John had not moved from the middle of the floor where he had stood when he first came in. Both he and Hedley peered now in the direction of the passageway. Beyond, the eyes could faintly distinguish a widening of the walls and, at the end, a small smudged window giving on to the coalyard. Below was the rim of what looked like a deep sink. No sound came from the semi-darkness save an occasional clink, not readily identified. No immediate answer came to the call of the man in the corner.

After an interval there was a dull and persistent scratching. What it was Hedley could not tell. Old fingers on ankle boots perhaps: there was no means of knowing. There was no means of knowing anything. Suddenly a fit of cold horror took him, smooth and spinal in its reachings. The room slipped to one side and an inescapable surface of bone, malignantly extending farther and farther as he clutched at it, fronted his eyes. He could not remember, no, he could not remember any way round. In a cold sweat he gripped at himself desperately, racking his brains for anything he knew and could recognise. Gradually the fit passed. In a few seconds he had made contact with the outlines of the room again and understood that they were walls after the pattern he knew. He warmed himself at the memory a little and grappled hurriedly with something to say to Jack Williams, anything to cover the seeping minutes and silence the gnawing of sound. But the eyes of the man in the corner were still closed and Hedley no longer had the confidence to disturb him when his bolt was shot. Instead he twisted his stomach tighter and watched the passage.

Slowly there crossed the threshold an old woman. When she came into sight Hedley could not have said. One moment it was dark and moveless; then she was there, advancing with incredible slowness. In her two hands she carried a cup, saucer and plate, in a tidy pile before her.

John still stood in the middle of the room, his cap rolled in his hands. 'Hallo, Mamgu,' was all he said.

The old woman made no direct reply. She made past the boy towards the dresser. Her words came from her one by one as she went. 'John – bach – here's – something – for – you.' Her breath gave out in a wheeze and she leaned on the dresser. The walls began trembling again in Hedley's ears. The air was warm. Full of the smell of something he did not recognise. Little drops of cold sweat fell panicking from the hairs under his armpit and rolled one by one towards his hips. With all his heart he wished Morgan would come. Unlikely he would ever wish for that, he would have said, recognising his other life a long way off. In the glimpse he had of it, there was not much to be got for comfort. That was the worst: you never knew till you were up against it.

The old woman had drawn some keys from her side now. With painful slowness she fitted one into a drawer. John moved nearer. Jack Williams did not open his eyes. One by one the old woman took her breaths. Grasping after them she was, as though they were coming in too slow from behind the curtains. In the intervals of this preoccupation she lifted out a long box and raised the lid with trembling fingers. Then on the withered palm lay a shilling, dull and remote. It moved towards John, unshining.

'For you, John bach. For - you - good - boy.' The words came painfully over the intervening air, back from the head of the queue.

The moment took Hedley by sleight once more. His half-arranged words began to wheel within the walls he had managed to recognise. The drops fell from his arms now in an unregulated stream. He knew. That was the trouble. He did know. His swimming ignorance before had been half-pretence. He couldn't make new marks of recognition. He just couldn't. And so he had pretended. But it was no good any more. There was no way back now. A cup, a saucer and a plate, what were they? A lifetime's washing up. That's what they were. He had seen it and known it. And the coin for payment that there was no keeping. The air . . .

the air wasn't warm, it was foetid. Heavy with breath waiting to be clutched, to be pressed into a last service. But there must be an end. There was always an end. He looked wildly about. It was a small room and there were curtains. Behind the warm there was the cold. Behind the stone the bare hill. Behind . . . Duw no! Out, out, must get out. Must get out. All at once he was on his feet.

'John, John, come on quick. Come on. Mus' go.' The words died away in a mumble. The lighted alleyway was all round him and John on his heels. Then came the street, grey and large as the expanse of life. He gave no explanation. John seemed to need none. The shilling was not in his hand and its clink in the box still rang in his ears.

The half-enclosed slope of the hill, as they swung up it at unnatural speed, restored Hedley's balance of light and dark. Over the way hung the sign of the Newton Arms, green and gold. The other houses looked dull and ordinary. He was conscious of rich brown paint on a baker's shop. But hot and cold would not so easily come to an understanding. Under the shirt his side was uncomfortably wet.

A moment later John and he were sitting in the van, leaving the driver's seat free.

Presently Morgan came out of the shop unseeing and went down the road. Minutes passed. As he returned the high cheekbones showed up candid over the face that was as slow as ever. The blank wall of the eyes was gone. In its place looked out the silent understanding of the hill.

'Well John boy, did you see Mamgu?' he said. 'Great she was, didn't you think? And Uncle Jack, looking better than ever. Not be long now before he'll be down for the shooting.'

His long hands moved the gears. The van rode off, in fresh ballast, down the hill.

Cassie Thomas

~

Cassie Thomas was past her forty-third birthday and looking a little faded. At least, that was the face that most people saw. It was not so much that the hair was grey in streaks over the ears as that there was a hard, compressed look about the mouth that you often notice in women teachers. You could not see the eyes really, unless you looked very closely, because they were a long way away through thick glasses.

This face was one she had made by her own efforts. Discipline was part of it and another part was efficiency. When she was making it she had found there was no room for a lot of things she had had when she was a girl, but after all they had not been things worth keeping. Silly, soft things most of them that were out of place in the life of an educated woman. Like many of her friends she had had to make her dummy carefully, because there was no one at home who could show her how. None of her family had ever been educated, you see, and so she had to watch her friends and her tutors with an extra bit of attention, just to make sure that she had the shape and expression right. When it was finished, her dummy began the day by carrying her little brown case to school and sat at the back of the class, watching, fitting on the expression and watching. Later on it sometimes forgot itself and answered with her voice when some little round-faced child caught it unawares. But on the whole it was a good dummy and made very few mistakes.

Cassie could not remember quite when she first had the dummy. But she could remember the first time she brought it home to Trebanog. Her mother had been a bit surprised at seeing it the day Aunt Maria came up with Arthur and the boys, but she had been pleased too. Yes, pleased and proud. It was a wonderful thing her daughter had brought home, the sign and token of an education paid for, stamped and delivered. Better than the old certificate it was. You could see this meant something, an authority, a position you carried about with you wherever you were. Even in 27 Albion Street there was all the difference in the world. Cassie wasn't just merch Tom Thomas now: she was a schoolteacher. And the neighbours were always asking how she was getting on.

Of course, her father would never learn. He still sat in the kitchen in his shirt-sleeves, with the coal-dust deep under the rims of his nails, and sniffed and read the newspaper. But men couldn't be expected to understand, at the best. All they thought of was beer and international matches and the miners' lodge, in that order. It was nothing to them that dignity, poise and learning could be had all at the one shop. With hard work, that is. But every year since she had gone to coll her father had groused about the money and even now he didn't seem any too pleased with the result. Well, it might not be glamorous or beautiful or even pretty, or any of those things men made such a fuss of, but at any rate her father could take more than half the blame for that. She had done the best she could with herself, anyway, and it was up to him to look pleased when she put her glasses on and brought her prize out for inspection.

It wasn't as though she hadn't done well since too. After one post at Trefriw in north Wales she had come nearer home to Pont-lottyn, to a bigger school there. After some years in Pontlottyn she had risen to be chief assistant, which was more than any of the old girls of Trebanog County had done since 1907 or some time like that. But that wasn't the best yet. She had always hoped and hoped to be a headmistress, and now she was one. Out in the country she had gone for this. A better type of children you had there usually. Of course Peterchurch-on-Arrow wasn't a big place. And the school wasn't a big school. Only about eighty children and there was just Miss Bufton, and Mrs Maidment who did the handicraft work, and herself. Neither of these others was much use as a teacher, because Mrs Maidment's idea of discipline seemed to be to keep up a lot of old fussy farmhouse backchat. But they didn't appear to resent her coming. It was a quiet school and it was nice to be on her own. The country children were much quieter than the Pontlottyn boys, you see, and her dummy looked after them all very efficiently. In fact, she'd been able mostly to sit back in her chair and think about other things. Many days she never bothered to come to school at all. Though there were still times when she found herself at her desk when she hadn't expected to be, and that always gave her a bit of a turn then, with the big crowded room right in front of her. It was just that it was unexpected, you see. But she had only to draw back and take a peep at her dummy carrying on so calmly and she was clear away and herself again. Really there was nothing she could reasonably complain of.

Nothing until a week or so ago, that is. Then her quiet little school had been invaded. The county authority had informed her that she would have to take in five boys from the Woolwich district of London. There were many more of these evacuees, she understood, but only these five were billeted on farms in her school area. The rest would be going to Cwrt y Cadno.

Naturally she took a good look at them the first morning they came and tried them over for standard. One of them she didn't fancy at all. The name on the list was Alfred Dannett. He was big for his age and a nasty look about him. He seemed to know more than he pretended to, more about something anyway, though he wiped it off his face when he saw her looking. A pity she had to take in these town boys, but there was no need to worry. The dummy never asked for trouble. It waited for the move and blocked it adroitly when it came. And it knew all the moves. It had not been fourteen years in Pontlottyn for nothing.

That had been over a week ago. Now things were very different. Miss Bufton and Mrs Maidment had made a poor showing with the new boys, which was just the sort of thing she had expected really. The climax had come when Alf was found cutting the V sign out of the back hem of Mrs M's dress as she was bending down to attend to the boy in front. This Alf, he was a gang leader: there was no doubt of it. Already a whole alphabet of mysterious signs and responses went out like waves from his corner. Obviously he must be taken in hand. Nothing would meet Alf's case but personal supervision of the most rigorous kind.

Bit by bit, however, even this was not enough. Alf grew familiar with the dummy. He did not seem as impressed with it as he ought to be. Once or twice she caught him studying it narrowly and his search came right through the glasses and twisted in past the eyeballs and caught her unawares. Uneasily she noticed that she was in the schoolroom almost all the time now, watching. Watching the struggle. It was beginning, she was sure. Yes, it was. Bits of chalk it was first, thrown at the children at the back with a show of furtiveness. One eye always on the dummy. Then it was the window. Now he wanted it up, now down. There was a draught, there wasn't a draught. He was out of his seat. No he wasn't. Throwing chalk again. Now he was out of his seat. He . . . She pulled herself together. The dummy had seen all this too, of course. She had almost forgotten that. The inevitable counter-attack was beginning. She breathed more freely. In the dummy's hand was the cane and Alf was coming forward to the desk. On he came, with that narrow, watching expression on his face. Her breath caught. Alf was standing now, watching. Nothing happened. She looked sharply at the dummy. Her heart pumped violently. The dummy was motionless. It was not working. It was not working. It was not working . . . Desperately she shook the mechanism, working over all the control positions in turn. Nothing moved. Again, again. Nothing. Nothing. Nothing. The schoolroom sounded the word excitedly with a border of red and stopped suddenly . . .

Cassie knew that Miss Bufton was looking at her strangely from the other end of the room. Staring at her, yes. Staring, that's it. By her side the dummy moved into position and the red flowed back. The air grew clearer. To her amazement Alf was half out of his seat again, testing the cane in the space between the desks. That was awful. Awful. No wonder Miss Bufton was staring. Still, it would be all right now. The dummy was working again.

The cane was recovered from Alf by stratagem before many minutes were up. Miss Bufton did that. Cassie was always behind the dummy now, one hand on the mechanism. Just in case, you see. It had stopped before, remember. She swung it round by main force to face Alf wherever he was. It was a shield, anyway. Wherever Alf was it faced that way. It was a shield, you see. But it stopped every time Alf came near. Every time. She couldn't understand what had gone wrong. Every time. Her breath was too short to work it now. She was tired. That must be it. She was tired. And though she glued her eyes to the holes in the dummy's face she couldn't seem to see properly any more.

The end came very quickly. Alf was wandering about the place now, interfering with every class. The room was in an uproar. The dummy was stiff, almost too stiff to move. It was a shield, it was. But it didn't keep off the noise. The noise, the awful noise. A shield that didn't keep off the noise. Behind that noise there was the face. That's what it was, a shield against the face, a narrow face. But it didn't keep off the noise and the bits of chalk. No, the bits of chalk and the noise and that cheering . . .

She realised with a feeling of dim curiosity that the noise had stopped. Alf was dragging the dummy around the room by its hair. Was it Alf? Yes . . . That screaming. That was Miss Bufton and Mrs M. both together. Where were they? Ah, over there. Both together, screaming. And the children between . . . Was it Alf? Somehow she had to twist her neck to look up at him and it was rather a job. The screaming went on. It was a nightmare. It must be. It was a nightmare. All that screaming. She felt like screaming too. She did scream. And as the sound left her throat she saw the dummy had fallen to the floor in the middle of a ring of children. Miss Bufton was elbowing her way to reach it. Miss Bufton . . .

When they got her home to Trebanog, she could not remember what she had done with the dummy. After they got it up from the floor the mechanism had never worked since. She had sat for hours with it and tried. Oh but she was so weak, she simply had to give up. It was colder this winter than last. That was why she wanted to cry all the time. It was cold in Trebanog always. She didn't know really where they had taken her dummy now, the dummy she had had so long. It was cold, and her mother just looked at her and said nothing, not like when the dummy was with her at Trebanog. She supposed sadly that it wasn't much use her going to coll again and trying to get another one. All the other girls would have got all the best ones by this time. There was always a rush for the best ones.

Block-System

~

Mr Hetherington, the Milk Officer, raised his voice a little higher.

'You must understand,' he said with asperity, 'that the committee has no desire to do anything that is in the least degree unfair. If you suggest that, you are raising a very dangerous issue and I promise you that the authority concerned will not treat the suggestion lightly. I have told you before, and I tell you again, that your gallonage has been made up, in the same way as the rest, by a system of compensation approved in principle by all the interests represented on the committee.' He shuffled the papers on the desk a moment and knit his brows, a parting concession of official good nature. It was best to admit that there might be some small difficulty. It was a cover for the future.

The old man across the room was already making for the door, the thin panel of authority clicking back into place behind him. He looked dully for a second or two at the denial as it came smoothly in his direction, then dropped his head. 'Thank you sir,' he said 'Good morning.' The door closed slowly with the indifference of wood.

'The sooner we can get rid of these blessed fiddling little retailers the better,' said Hetherington, more gustily now that the need was gone. 'Don't you think so, Browning? Day after day they come along here mumbling and muttering, knowing next to nothing about accurate book-keeping and trying to confute us by some wonderful system of their own. Instinct and a permanent sense of grievance, that's all they've got. It'll be a mercy when Mobile buy the old fool out, in my opinion.'

'I hear he's got no good customers as it is,' said Browning, scrawling his initials on the dotted line.

Ben Davies would not have heard them had he been on the near side of the glass panel instead of at the bottom of the broad staircase of the Town Hall. His mind was shut like a fist and in it anger lay screwed away, forgotten, like a coin too small any longer to buy him satisfaction. In the droop of his shoulders was the cost of living.

To the passer-by he would have been only a red-faced old man, with no gentility in his shabbiness. His suit had never fitted, because it had never been his until it was past hope. Only his son had bought suits and the Army had cured even him of late. Occasional photos from Paiforce, compact of brown in knees and face and sand, had not really cheered Ben much: he wore the suit to keep its memory warm in the family more than to cover his own needs. Round his neck straggled a thick flannel collar, uneasily projecting its heavy black stripes into the undiscerning city air. He had kept his shirt and boots from an earlier age, one to which his son and his son's suit would have been strangers. These were the only unchanging things about him. His face was an odd fusion of new and old, in which the new sought desperately for perman-ence. Conceived on broad lines, with high cheek-bones, broad forehead and stubborn chin, it had suffered the disuse of much of its surface working, which had slowly subsided and settled back on the essential bone. Countryman's red was mottled with a rash of anxiety, and the bushy moustache seemed intended as much as the last hold of a pitiful bluffness as any sort of living functionary. Ben Davies was white, and so he might well be at seventy. But no observant judge could think it likely that the broad head and slow stiff hands had met with age alone. The tree had been pulled up somewhere and in the new soil only a few of the roots had contrived to find cover.

Back in Drayton Street the old man pushed open the little curtained door leading rearwards from the shop. The living room was empty. A flame moved feebly in the grate. The table was strewn with cups, most of them used. He shut the door behind him with exaggerated caution, hoping to get out to the yard unobserved. But the stiffness in his fingers clutched unwillingly at the knob seconds after his mind had released it silently into posi-tion. He withdrew his hand, suddenly conscious of the lag. The knob creaked slightly, and the tale was more than half told. Up came Mari his wife in an instant, up from the basement kitchen where she scuttered unavailingly when the shop bell was silent for a moment. Her hurrying feet brought the anxiety he feared. The tilt of her peaked face was a question.

He shook his head. 'Cornell Mansions it is,' he said flatly. His mind swerved from further explanation.

'But machgeni . . .' Her voice of protest was only a reflex now, deprived of the anger of her husband: it registered no more than the two words. She knew the thing was an injustice and her fear had prepared her to say more. But the moment, as always, broke her thought and left her empty, waiting. Her *but* faced up to the future with the wounded venom of an instinct that had never been idle enough to grow claws and go hunting. It was at bay, silent, intent on preventing the kill.

'But . . .' she was beginning again, with as little of hope to follow, when the crouch of her tongue was overwhelmed with sound. The passage suddenly filled with it. Ben's daughter Beryl cracked back the door from the yard and penetrated like an auger of aggression into the unvociferous room. London had taught her words and noises even for feelings she did not know. Her accent stepped in readily from the pavement beyond. Drayton Street had not pinned anything on her. And indeed it had given up trying long since.

'Dad,' she shouted, 'you back? Who did you see? Did you swop Cornell Mansions?' Her voice came before like a gale. In the room she stopped suddenly. 'Come on Dad. Get it off your chest. Is anything the matter?'

Her words ringed him round. He slowly faced up to them, letting go the wretchedness that was their quarry and looking at it as it lay cumbering his feet. It already seemed small and muddy and far away, a torn semblance of the fear that he in his turn had pursued. 'I don't know who it was I saw,' he began. 'A tall man, bit big round the neck. May have been the Milk Officer himself, because when I was down the Town Hall Saturday week there were a lot of people in the office and . . .' 'Oh Dad, get on. Don't make a great song about it. What does it matter who it was? What did he say?'

Beryl was always impatient with her father. He never understood the real question behind what was actually said, she thought. With the characteristic unfairness of the quick-witted she gave no credit to those who were slow of speech, least of all when they revealed a dumb sense of exactitude. And slow of speech old

Ben certainly was. He would have stuttered a little if he had got the words out quicker. But until recently they had come up out of him with dignity, as they had done down the years, stopping a moment or two in bewilderment, Welsh and countrified, on the threshold of existence. He could remember them still as he had seen them when he was as bewildered as they, lost in the little school on Rhos Meurig. Some of them then were odd and pointed at one end like the pears he used to find in the grass under the wall of the Star. Smooth they were and chill to hold against one's face. Now and again he had chewed one over, and always it had seemed different then, different from the look it had when first he picked it up. The word that he remembered always from the first touch onwards, with no hope of forgetting, came to him with the little black horse he was holding to his cheek in school. He had been given the horse because he shouted so in the classroom, shouted loudly, with no words, for the joy of shouting. It was his first day in school. Then the shaggy feel of the black horse took him. He held it to his cheek, rough and satisfying. One eye held the word in place, the English word, along with it. And so he fell silent. The same rough Horsa had fallen on Kent hundreds of years before and won the silence of his fathers. Ben never knew this, but he turned the word over and felt its strength go through him.

One word at a time then had been enough. And almost all his life he had been slow, because he cared for what he said and at times forgot to even say it. Until lately, that was. Now the sentences were rattled out of him, hot and unwilling. There was no joy in them. Indeed, people were always pulling them out of him when he was not attending properly, and they never knew the words he was really keeping for their delight.

Of late there was no delight that he could make, in any case, for Mari and Beryl his daughter. They were his only audience. Even the hot unwilling words for them came past a contraction of will, a closed-in muscular debasement of feeling that was not their source nor their reason. They could not describe it nor dwell upon it. They just came past it on their way out. Ben was helpless against this separation of feeling from words. Dimly he realised that the rotten cores of the fruit of his childhood had been thrown to waste by circumstance, in a place he did not know. The feel of the words had gone long since and the heart in them had died for the lack of it.

Communication now was part of the constant pressure of hostile circumstance. The memory of a natural love seemed to make it necessary, but not easier. He felt a vague irritation at the need for questions, at the urgency of any occasion.

'Dad, for pity's sake, don't stand there saying nothing and staring at me like that. What did the Milk Officer tell you?'

'I told him,' said Ben, remembering the occasion far back in history, 'that the committee had gone and taken away forty gallons a day from me and that it was up to them to give me back the same gallonage as I had. That was only fair, block-system or no block-system, I said. Not for me to tell him, of course, that what he calls his committee is made up from the Mobile people, the Mercury and the other big combines, with the small dairymen spoken for by Harry Twiston down in Breakwell Street. Sold out he has, to Mobile, Dick Thomas was telling me last week on the quiet, and going to be a manager for them in the West End. But where is the use of me saying that, without I can prove it? They would have the law on me in no time.' Ben was finding his words keeping closer under the lump of his feeling now. But he was not telling his hearers anything new.

'Oh Dad, don't string it out. We know . . .'

'All right, my girl, all right. I am coming. Well, this Milk Officer said I had the same gallonage, didn't I? Still polite he was then. Yes, I said, I have my gallonage but part of it is in Cornell Mansions. There were no customers there with me before. On paper, I said, there are hundreds of people for milk in the Mansions, but there are not fifty of them taking it. And not thirty paying for it, anyway. I know, I said, because we are living just down the road from them. You have taken away all my best customers, I told him, the ones I had in Malimwood Road and Spray Street, and left me with a lot of bad debtors. Every week they are doing the flit with their things in a barrow, because I have seen them.' To Ben his own shabby figure and that of his opponent had already taken on some of the heroic cast of history. The past grew beautiful even in its shadows. Only the present was insipid and importunate, a horrible mockery of remembered challenge.

'Well, you put it pretty straight, Dad.'

'Too straight, my girl, by half. He got on the high horse and used a lot of Town Hall words. The committee and the committee's honour it was all about. And was I making an accusation?

I could see he would be having the law on me in no time and me with no money by to fight them all. So out I went and not a word more.'

'Better you had stayed carpenter in Pontwillim, Ben bach, instead of coming up to old London this time ten years.' There was no spring now in Mari's voice.

'No, no, Mari fach, London it is.'

'London. Bah!' Beryl broke in with the ferocity of the child who has seen through her teacher. 'London. Fine old place, I must say.' The words began to beat savagely out of the squared corners of her mouth, driving a wedge through the threatened ruin of tears.

'You keep the ruddy shop open for twelve hours a day and then they come round after eight o'clock at night, hammering on the side door and crawling all over you. Can I have a small loaf, please?' Her mimicry grew sharper and more hysterical. 'My old man's come in and I haven't a bit of food in the house. Any old tale and the dirtier the better. Think they'll get round me any time with the latest from the Havelock or the chip-shop. I'm sick of it, I tell you. For Christ's sake let's sell up and go back to Pontwillim or anywhere, I don't care. Anywhere out of here, that's all I want. Oh Dad, come on. Let's get out, quick.'

Ben watched her vehemence from a great way off, recognising it as the past in himself but not seeking to recover it. Anger was till too near in time and too shoddy for him. It offered no escape from the blank peeled wall in front of him. His mind peered at it a moment and put it patiently aside. When he answered he followed explicitly in the train of the last words spoken, because it was easier so to skirt the mountain of feeling which his memory could not mistake.

'I borrowed twelve hundred pounds from Fulford's to buy this place, my girl. Have you forgotten that? Since 1940 there has been nothing paid back, and six hundred pounds still to go. Stick it out is all we can do, Beryl fach. Mobile would buy the place willing enough, I dare say, if I would be settling for three hundred. They know the small men are right in the corner like rats now. Three hundred is all it's worth to them for the trouble of letting us out. No, no, stay it is for us, my girl, and keep hoping.'

'But Dad, what's the use? We're not making enough on the milk to keep going as it is. You know that as well as I do. And with Cornell Mansions we'll be done for. Done for, Dad, yes . . . O and it fair breaks my heart to see you near seventy like this, and up at four in the morning, washing the bottles and then doing the longer round. Never finished till after tea, and no rest, never. You can't keep it up, you . . . Oh Dad, Dad, what can we do?' The wedge of words gave way, and the tears sprang into the gap, filling it loudly, unavailingly.

Neither of the others moved. The sun rose reluctantly over the smoke-blackened parapet of the yard wall and shot an uneasy glance through the half-curtained window. The thin ray swam with motes of dust, broken off from the silence of the room and hanging there, uncertain of the end.

'Mus' go out on second round in a bit. Barrow's half-full now. Only a few more bottles needed.' Ben got up stiffly and went out to the back. He proffered this explanation to the room hurriedly: it hung in the air behind the closing door like a jumbled overtone, the conviction in it hollowed out by the words. The women neither moved nor looked at one another. To them it was nothing. It had no beginning and no end.

Out in the shed Ben was already plunging the mop automatic-ally into the bottles, submerging them first in the hot tank and then ripping them quickly through the cold. Already the sense of guilt was gone, the guilt at having a place to go to, a place out of that room of end and no beginning. Already he had forgotten the memory of the ill that was his and Mari's and Beryl's. He had forgotten Mari and Beryl too. For he had a place of seeking. He had joy. In the shed he had it, a long way from the words that were only questions knocking, knocking.

Misery they were now, the English words, once round and skinned with beauty. Once he had seized them and driven them with the driving of his plane across the stern grain of the wood. That was in his workshop on the Plasdu Estate, twenty years ago, before the questions started. But the words were knotted now, knotted in his throat, and he was too old to work at them again. He had known that a long time.

But something different there was behind. He had been seeking it and had found it for a bit. He would find it again. It was the quiet, the eager quiet of the time before words. You would not think he would remember, but he did. They always remembered up there on the Rhos. The coughing of the wind in the clotted chimney at night, the clacking of branches against a winter sky, and first of all, the blue crackle of the saw as Jack Saer bit the blade into a log. Nobody had explained then, and he had not wanted an explanation. The steel of the saw was his own shining sword, and the words ran wondering a long way behind, neither known as yet nor cared for.

The Rhos had been the beginning and was now the end. Not that he sought to go back there. Some crabbing consciousness of arms stiff from icy water and tongue loose with disappointment told him that it could not be the same again. Young men and children would laugh at him. The machined logs from the sawmill would be strange to his heart. People would talk to him, inquire of his doings, make much of his life away there in London. And he would have to reply. To speak, in words. Words that shredded all the misery through his mind over and over again. No, he would not go back. Here in London nobody cared. Nobody asked him anything or thought twice that he was a stranger. Nobody except the weeping women in there, and they had nothing to ask.

No, he would not go. He had already forgotten that he could not. Little Ben Davies, Cefen, who spoke so slowly, was home already and would not go to school any more. As he fitted the last bottle into the tray on top of the barrow, he ran out of the cottage door into the evening sun. The thick scarred bark of the plum-tree was under his hand and the grass of the garden rose in little hills to his feet. There was no sound in the air. The stick he had pointed yesterday stuck in the ground a few paces off. He went up to it gladly and took up the trail where he had left off.

London with its million tongues said not a word against the wonder.

Digression into Miracle

~

Thomas Bushell sat in his rooms at the sign of the Bear not a little disillusioned. He had posted up to London from Cardiganshire a few days before to expedite his petition before the House. Too well he knew that nothing was accomplished either at Court or at St Stephen's Chapel save by lobbying of the most untiring sort. From Aberystwyth or from Enstone he might petition for ever, only to have his travel-stained plea lose its way at last in the everlasting dust of anterooms. As it was, Milord the Secretary of State Windebank had been short enough with him. Plainly he was becoming weary of his virtuosity. Nor could he hope more from the King himself. No longer dare he catch the royal eye by outdoing every page in Lord Bacon's service. These were no days of flesh-coloured satins and buttons of gold. All his world rested upon the dull strokes of silver drawn heavily through the Welsh hills.

Of what use, he reflected wearily, was the grant of the mines, and the unprecedented right too of minting himself at Aberystwyth the silver he won, when every day brought, not success, but fresh expense? He trembled at the intelligence he had by every post. No word came of his new working above Talybont. But of the malice of Sir Richard Pryse of Gogerddan his correspondents had much to say. Every day, it seemed, Pryse and his fellow landowners sent their tenants up to block up his levels, fling rubbish into his pumps and discourage the miners who, heaven knew, needed no such discouragement. Even his discoveries were rendered of little or no value. Turf would serve for charke for smelting as well as wood. But Pryse would not let him cut turf. Already he had laboured for upwards of four years with small result. Already he was laughed at by his enemies and pitied

by his friends. Bushell shivered greyly. The injunction against
Pryse must go through or ruin as stark as the hills faced him.
What was new from the House? And what from Talybont? He
shivered again and settled back in his chair to wait for patience.

That evening in Talybont the sun set as dully as ever it did on an
evening in June. The air scarcely moved. A deadness was on the
hills. The steep converging slopes were pitted with shafts, mostly
fallen in and unfenced. Bushell had not bothered to stake them
and keep them clear of rubble because he favoured the new
German method of Agricola, so far not used in England, of
pumping air along pipes to the face by means of bellows at the adit
mouth. The narrow floor of the valley was littered with tumbled
heaps of ore, many of them of long enough lying to be the
remnant of the divinations of Myddleton's men. The little feeder
that fell uneasily out of the grasses above twisted back and fore
among the sliding hillocks and was grey before it disappeared.
There was no sign of habitation. Out of sight at the foot of the
cwm lay the village of Talybont itself, but no sound or smoke rose
from it to the slopes where the mine was. Away to the right was a
backcloth of sea, a wash of grey behind the misery of the hills.
Nearer at hand there was blackness. The rocky deads cast out
from the workings, the strange bare shapes where turf had been
cut away, and the unaltering shadow of the peaks above looked on.
The spirit of the place had been lost for a long time and the
mountain had changed its heart for a black invention.

As night came down comfortless, four men sat taking tobacco
about ten fathoms from the adit mouth. Three of them had come
back from the face for their 'smoakie banquet', as the reverend
Thomas Broadway, chaplain to the mines, had once pompously
called it; they were afraid that if they stayed in the forefield the air
would get damp. The fourth was the man on the bellows. Most of
the talk came from old Bartholomew Clocker, a Derbyshire man
who had come to Wales years before at the summons of Hugh
Myddleton. There was no level south to Strata Florida he did not
know and no trick he had not tried to entice silver from the
unwilling lead. When he worked, which was not often, it was with
the wariness of long experience. Next to him sat James Fisher,
longer of face and younger. He had come out of Gloucestershire
with high hopes seven years before. Even now he was eager, but it
was after some new things. On his left again hunched Edward

George, whose home no one knew. Rumour had it that his coming to Cardiganshire had saved him from deportation. Bushell was generous like that. He had told the Secretary of State he was sure a man would sooner make his own country rich than endure slavery in foreign parts. Edward George had been brought up to the level one day about noon by Lewis Morris the agent. No one knew more than that.

The only Welshman in the group went properly by the name of Rees ap Lliky, but by old Bart he was never called anything but Jacko. He had not been long in the mines, and from what he said he did not intend to make his stay much longer. Welshmen did not take to the mines at all. There was too much feeling in the district that the spirit of the mountain was injured and resentful. It had not deserted the place. It was holding back. But one day, come soon come late, it would overwhelm all within its borders.

Bushell, in despair at the unwillingness of the natives and the lack of industry of his shaven recruits, had the year previous written a prayer entitled 'The Miner's Contemplative Prayer in his solitary Delves, imploring Heaven for his mineral increase'. This had been read to the assembled men at each level by the puffy-faced chaplain, still in a perspiration after his climb, and had been received in an unenthusiastic silence. Jonathan Best, the dullest of all the scratchers above Goginan, had forgotten to take his cap off, it was said. But no one had nudged him at the time. It had not seemed important enough.

Four years the men had been pushing this great drift above Talybont. It was now two hundred fathoms deep and creeping slowly on, with much rattling of the whimsy at the mouth and much guttering of candles, on to meet the great drowned work that Hugh Myddleton had abandoned in despair. Beneath the waters of the old shaft of thirty-eight fathoms lay a fortune, Bushell believed. Certainly Myddleton had dragged enough wealth out of Cwmsymlog, Talybont and Cwmystwyth to enable his generosity to provide London with an unfailing water supply and to permit his name thereafter to drop silently into poverty. Bushell yearned to do something like that. Not to be poor and forgotten, but to engineer some magnificent work that men would see and remember. In later years he was to raise a regiment of Derbyshire miners for the King at his own charge and hold Lundy Island for the royal cause: but that was not the same thing. He wanted his name remembered as the name of an engineer, the name of a disciple of the great Lord Bacon who had raised him and for whom he must startle the world.

But on this night of June 27, 1641, nothing of this could be seen or heard. Talybont had none of the noise of science. Around it were jeers and disappointment and sullenness. It was a place of pressed men.

In the cave the four spoke little at first. Now and again their faces glimmered whitely when a shifty moon looked across the lead-heaps, caught their eye and looked away into a cloud. Edward George, for all the tobacco which he alone was chewing, was almost asleep. Yet it would be as well to be awake. Perhaps Pryse's clods would come over the hill from Gogerddan and wreck the pumps again. 'Bad 'cess to 'em,' muttered old Bart. 'Dunna see why Big Tom don' give ol' ferrety Pryse some fifty shares an' keep t'long nose of 'un out o't. Clods'll do what they'm told. Cud cut turf too nor see yon Powell t'bailey hallooin' lak an ol' cuckold across t'hill.'

'Aw, dang 'em all. Dang Big Tom too, whatever.' This from Jacko. 'Gwely for me every night then an' a good ol' supper too.'

'Blasted country, blasted ol' muckheap,' muttered Edward George. 'Nuthin'll grow hereabouts. Blasted . . .' Fisher cut in quickly. 'They'm sayin' as there be no fish in yon Rheidol river an' none in Ystwyth neither. An' all t'green plants runs back from t'water lak childer from a snake. Well mun, 'ee seen yon bit o'water down to Tallybont. Do 'un look black an' mucky or do 'un not? No fish in there, nor none for miles, I'll warrant. I do believe as there be a gurt black ring i't sea as grows wider an' wider. One day 'ee'll catch t'sun, 'ee will, an' drag 'un down.'

'Don' 'ee chaffer lak a toddlepate, Jamsie. List 'ee here to me as knows.' And old Bart emphasised the attention due with a series of vigorous nods. 'I do be talkin' wi' Lewis Morris t'agent often enough, see. Years I bin an' 'e no more'n a five year man. 'E do show respec' an' yon hat o'hisn wi't black crape . . . Crape 'un calls 'un, I'm thinking . . .'

'Jawch, mun, be getting' along an' no more o' this upstickery,' said Jacko. Old Bart ignored him and took a puff or two at his clay pipe before continuing. 'Hanna 'ee heerd tell o't bellon? Corse 'ee 'ave. T'mountain's full of 'un. They'm saying as none but black cattle an' sheep'll live long hereabouts. None beast but they wi' tallow, howsomedever. Horses an' fowl is worser'n any in dyin' o't poyson. All of 'ee knows well enough down to Tallybont there be neither fowl nor feather, nay none for miles. All us do see be a few o' they long-horned blacks up above Rees Pentwyn's house there.'

'Eh but, Bart . . .' began Fisher.

'Wait 'ee now, Jamsie. Wait 'ee now. I do be comin' to't. 'Ee knows all yon, but I be at summut else. This Lewis Morris now, ol' saltspot 'e be, but none sich a dullard. Horse 'e 'ad, ten year old, as were dyin'. Turrible soft of 'un 'e were. An' 'e do say as how when yon beast were tooken ill 'e turned 'un out on t'hill, thinkin' 'un too hard rid or worked. Sweet drenches 'e gave 'un, bled 'un an coddled 'un wi' gunpowder an' soot. But none effect. T'beast 'gan for to pine, bein' took wi' convulsions i't hind-parts. Morris do say t'colic'll take 'em quicker if they be mares, an' t'only road for savin' 'em be to work 'em an' stir 'em about an' about so quick howsoever, if so be as they'll sweat 'un out.'

Bart paused. 'Go on, mun, finish 'im off,' urged Jacko.

'Struth, yon beast 'gan for to swell i't thighs an' legs come August an' for to break out on t'feet, lak t'fallin' o't grease. Morris gave 'un all 'e cud, nobbut salves for to dry t'feet. An' by t'seven devils all, t'swellin' abated. Next 'e went for to cut a rowell under t'belly of 'un, for t'bring down a swellin' 'un had in t'yard, and look 'ee, yon abated likewise. But t'horse, 'un grew excessive lean. 'Un nobbut grazed quietly, 'a couldna stir. At t'last, come September, a night o' hoar-frost followin' all but a fortnight's rain an' bad weather, 'un died.'

'Eh well,' Fisher and Jacko brought out together.

'Wait 'ee, mates.' Old Bart held up a grimy hand. 'Morris done more'n I'm told 'ee yet. 'E opened 'un. All was sound enough, t'entrails, guts an' sichlike. But t'chest an' lungs was rotted away. In threads 'un were. An' in t'space o' yon there were a gallon or two o' yellow liquor.'

Fisher sucked in his breath audibly.

'Morris do say 'e be cursin' 'isself for none tappin' 'un afore. If so be 'e do find how t'poyson in t'grass do be makin' yon yellow water, there's none i't country as'll forget 'un.'

'But that be not t'bellon, dang me,' expostulated Fisher. 'Summut' . . . 'Oh yes 'un be,' said Bart. 'There be a hen as Morris 'a cut up when 'un died o' swallowin' t'ore. Fast i't'backbone, 'e do say, were an oblong bladder very full an' containin' near a teacupful o' clear liquor, saltish. 'E tasted 'un – plain daft, thinks I – an' 'un made 'e spit excessive for several hours.'

Edward George sent a long column of tobacco-juice spurting suggestively into the darkness. It was unusual that he was still awake.

'Morris do tell,' Bart went on, 'as how fowl as died o't'bellon be full o' water an' t'flesh of 'un be bitter to t'taste.'

'Dang Morris, dang t'fowl, dang t'bellon.' Edward George's voice died away into a mumble.

'Dai John as do devil up to Goginan' . . . 'Hist, Jamsie,' suddenly said old Bart. 'Dang me,' began Fisher, 'I do' . . . 'Hist, mun,' whispered old Bart fiercely. 'I do hear summut.'

All four strained their ears. The night was now very dark. The moon was gone. In the distance a faint rumbling could be heard. 'Storm be comin,' said Jamsie. 'Ay' . . . 'Hist,' said Bart again. 'Aw, be stoppin' they ol' hen tricks,' muttered Jacko, irritated. But he fell silent none the less.

The rumble was louder now, perceptibly. It grew, it became a roar. It pulsed, it drummed with thunderous fists, as though unwilling clouds were being forced with irresistible strength through a narrow collar of sky. The beat grew faster and louder yet. The storm was racing towards them. The earth began to shake.

'Get 'ee out,' suddenly yelled old Clocker. 'She'm holed. Get 'ee out.' He stumbled blindly to the opening and disappeared to the left. Jacko and Fisher dashed after him. Above the roar sounded a shout of 'Move 'ee Groggo' and for an instant there was a wash of white about the roof of the tunnel some yards away. The next second Edward George flattened himself with unwonted speed against the outside wall of rock, and a great deluge of water burst into the air a full yard from the mouth of the adit and hung there, pouring and shouting down into the valley below. 'Myddleton's ol' drowned work,' muttered Bart in Fisher's ear. 'They'm done for down to Tallybont.'

The darkness was impenetrable. The shouting of the water went on. Presently a grating, rolling sound diverged insistently from the roar and reached the ears of the men. A hundred tons of rocky deads were washing down the slope.

In Talybont householders awoke to the pouring of water under their doors and the straining of great shoulders against their walls.

They could not reach their candles in the darkness. Furniture was afloat. Holes were gouged in the stonework of the cottages. The black tide foamed in and swirled about the stairs. Shriek upon shriek split the gloom. This was the judgment, the judgment so few were ready to meet. The judgment by water. Utter darkness and the roaring of hell. Not fire, but water.

For four hours it lasted. At its height the torrent lashed Rees Pentwyn's windows up on the slope. In the last hour or two, however, the violence abated and after four hours it ceased altogether. Nothing was heard then but the sad droppings of the streamlet men had known, apologising wearily over the uneasy washing to and fro of the tide indoors.

When the last spittle fell away from the adit mouth, Fisher rose from his cwtch by the side of the rock. 'I be goin' in,' he said. 'Dang fule 'ee be, dunna go,' expostulated old Bart. 'I be goin', Bart,' persisted Fisher. 'We'm all goin' then,' said Bart, accepting the inevitable. Presently four candles crept along the adit that was shining now like the silver it led to and sending heavy drops to plop in the deep pools left along the level.

'Diallin' be none so good,' began Fisher. A drop extinguished one candle. Feet squelched steadily. Little rivers ran gladly over the uneven walls. The grey of the adit mouth was hidden beyond the humping floor.

Suddenly the tunnel was alight. For a second four heads showed up black like beavers in line. The momentary glow was followed by three flashes in quick succession. Then came a heavy report like that of a piece. All the candles went out with the wind. One pair of feet turned and stumbled madly out towards the air. The splash of their going slopped on into the distance. Then there was silence. 'Dang 'ee, Groggo.' It was old Bart's voice, husky but audible. 'Come 'ee here, Jacko. Jamsie be done for.'

When the two men finally dragged out of the adit the wet smoking lump between them, they found that it still stirred feebly. The hair was burned down to the darkness of the scalp, the jerkin in holes, and the two eyes were ringed with black as though they had seen over the gate of hell and would never rest again.

Three days later the Reverend Thomas Broadway pursed his lips and paused before writing to Bushell at the sign of the Bear. 'Suffer my congratulations of your late Successe at Tallibont,' he began. 'Thus happy are you here when least you think it, for I finde the subterranean spirits, the supposed guardians of concealed treasure, as officious for you as if they were in pay with you. Behold, sir, how deare you are to providence, which for your sake hath vouchsafed to digresse into a miracle.'

The Rhine Tugs

~

The plane flew straight in, devouring the entrails of building and the interminable gut of road. It skimmed without check or shame over the pitiful eviscerations of pots and furniture puddling the way of ground traffic. There was no need of shroud for this death. Who lived that cared? Or who had not the smell in his nostrils now? Shame would have been less direct and ultimately more intolerable. The main impression to make was one of efficiency. Any other issue would be merely confusing.

But after a moment there was something. The plane seemed to shy a little, like a horse with a hard eye. A shadow first, felt before seen, it pressed on the back-leaf of consciousness. And then there it was, a head with two monstrous towers climbing, lifting, shaking off the rubble like the ears of an animal emerging from an earth the hunters had not drawn. There was no time to appraise them. Only the points scored the sky as the plane shied and the engine resumed again after the missed beat. The most sensitive observer could have made no more of it, without the eyes of a child. And only one child there could have seen in the platz the taut skins of the drums and the flaunted drumsticks of the hunters. That child was become a man and the screen was shaken with the shame it had suppressed.

The newsreel switched, and the audience, released from the joystick's crouch, leaned back more calmly for the next shot. Idly the great Hohenzollern bridge hung in the water, broken off short by the near bank. Then the camera, content with this visual underscoring of the motif, passed without comment up into the stifling air.

The young man who alone of any present had been much moved glanced hurriedly around, hoping he had not been observed, trying faithfully to simulate the tolerant blur of face that the one-and-ninepennies usually affected towards newsreels. It was no difficult task. In the haze of smoke the ranked heads were already lifting, the suppressed expectation of many eyes piercing the credit titles of the next film, ready for romance even in a name. He need not have worried: he had given no cause for remark. The grey check overcoat, several sizes too big for his rather puny frame, had hidden untoward movement, and untidy hair masked much of his face. But still the little puce feelers of the seat stroked the palm of his hand, weak airs and sentiments paltered in his ears, and for release there was only the stripped half of the ticket torn at entrance. It was unbearable, this forbidden martyrdom, and yet it was borne. The moment passed. He was still in his seat, picking with his hands and checking the feeble to-fro of his mind. The one-and-ninepennies had it. Trust the phlegmatic British public to sit through anything. There they were, conquering still, victors over half Europe and his stormy nerves. He slewed round more naturally, with a sort of wilful admiration, and forgot the screen. His eyes fixed diagonally across the auditorium where the yellow dusk hung timelessly from the clock.

Those towers. He saw them again, over a shoulder at breakfast, cold and flat on a page of newsprint. The same surrounding desolation, the same unimpaired animal resolve reaching up in those points, quivering as he watched. Slowly the buildings flowed back and the dust settled under the replaced pavements. Mulheim on the far bank, the hostel of the clicked heels and the cold morning bugle, the giant bridge with the black engines stealing surreptitiously into the hidden bag of the main station, they drifted slowly into his eyes like a mute exhalation from his lost teens, like an adolescent vapour from off the idle water. He was suddenly conscious of the picture he was trying to create. The wrong picture, he knew all the time at the back of his mind, and seen with the wrong eyes. The Dom was so watchful, so persistent, her ears so attuned to centuries of change that a thousand days in her sight altered little, and yet meant much. It was easy to be deceived.

He began again, shutting his ears obstinately as a New World trumpet reached up for the plaster orbs of the ceiling and fell at last, snubbed by the functional severity of the amusement palace. Patiently he built up his concentration, without perhaps hoping so high. The blue and white tram – yes, he was on the way now – the blue and white tram with the real bell that he had seen in the shop in the Blindgasse. Did he ever possess it? He could not remember. There it was in the window still, just round the corner from Tietz's. Tietz brothers, Jews. Dead in the pogroms long since, he supposed. The terrible sign of the Judenhetze had appeared even in the tiny villages by the old Austrian border next to the tolerant maypoles of a forgotten age. There was no corner left, no pavement, no green foot of mountain for them, even now. Yes, Tietz brothers were dead. And the tram too. Did the bell really ring? He was no nearer saying.

He got up. Without a glance at the screen he sidled past the ranks of white upturned faces, conforming even in the moment of his contempt lest his gingerly tread disturb the reverence of the place. In the aisle a white shaft of anger pushed them all aside. Plushed and darkened, poorer by paying a price for the sight of a life that never existed, there they were, the ranked automatons of the new age, intent on what? Intent and bulging over a poker-faced band-leader trying vainly to reduce the squeals of his boys to the length of an American short. God! perhaps those damned heel-clickers were right. Which was the more degenerate? He remembered the Munich cabaret compère who blew cigarette-smoke dutifully into the microphone for a second or two before whispering huskily, 'This is London.' Which was the more degenerate? He stopped at the exit, for the second time entirely conscious of his separateness, of the voice that called him out from amongst them. And yet, before the brusque step could carry him out, he felt that his seat was occupied again, that he could not be utterly angry with the scraggy weakling in the grey overcoat several sizes too large for him. For his sake he went out quietly and without malice, letting the swing door back into place reverently.

Outside the stars were a cool shock. A fresh wind from the turning world tangled the last conventions in his unruly hair, which covered his face and made him less and less recognisable in terms of the screen he had left. The way he went was nothing to him. He made for the only lodging-place he knew, following the turns and slopes of the pavement without engaging his mind in the matter in the smallest degree. Along the rough shaft of darkness went the solitary steps, quickening now and then as the sudden hollows attracted the fixed pace of legs from which will was equably separated. The street lamps were shaded crosses on tall curved standards, austere relics that allowed a faint martyred light to hover over the drab upper storeys of the flanking houses. There were no haloes in the lower reaches and in the unfeeling darkness he was beginning again that struggle with his remembering which was also the conviction of his romantic uncritical self. Out of the interested light it was easier to forget the generation and the gulf. The ground teeth in his gaze, the symbol of his own desperate integration, gradually dropped apart and he was one with the man who had gone to the pictures and with the man who had come away. His arms dropped loosely by his side, abandoning the instinctive gesture of defence he had been making. The coolness of the wind suffered everything, and his pace slackened. Soon foot followed dawdling foot, and what was left of his resentment ran out to the extremities of gesture and hung there. The street was very still.

Presently, however, he stepped off the pavement, cutting off the corner as he always did, with the faint hurry of a field mouse crossing from one cover to another. In front of him all at once were the penetrating orbs of a trolley-bus coming up with the silent prowling stride of a hunting leopard. The round lidless eyes seemed to fix relentlessly on his. Down the dusty tracery of his brain they swept like the beam of a torch in a disused shed. Webs of dust showed up and the lumber of years, pile upon pile. Nowhere was there a switch, not the right switch, no light of his that would turn this forgotten world into a factory of order and progress. It was urgent, he knew it was urgent, though not quite why. He began to panic. Then as suddenly the desperate fear broke in action. He stepped back, springing the last yard or so to the curb, one foot failing completely to achieve the elevation of safety and slipping sharply into the gutter. He fell on one knee and as the pain cut a line across his shinbone, the yellow eyes and heavy prowling head rushed past him, the more fearful for their disregard, and plunged down the slope.

He was more annoyed than hurt and allowed his fear a cheap revenge. What was the good, he began angrily, of instant reaction to every crisis? Could this strain be kept up much longer, could the wheels be set in motion by minds at fever pitch of concentration and still be controlled by others tired, lazy, worn out and abstracted? No, a few years more and man would be extinct, prehistoric, unadapted, or else a soulless driven mechanic. A few years more for the head in the air, for the carefully marked curb and safe walking, and then those fever-haunted eyes and that unpredictable strength would run down everything in their path. Not long, he thought, not long now. All will be twisted steel and concrete and broken integrity like Cologne, another and last feast for the dung-scattering Harpies. His diving, devouring thought shied suddenly and failed to recover; there were those ears again, strained and volcanic, sticking out of the rubble. Standing right up in the wide air, not a mere foot or two off the crawling ground, but hundreds of feet clear. What could they mean? Older, more spiritual man perhaps, thirteenth-century man who had fought with the devil for his building and knew him when he came again? Did he live on? Could he? Was Master Gerhardt dashed in pieces for ever?

Perplexed by a question which he felt to be important and yet at the moment unconnected with the memory he was really seeking, he allowed himself to revert temporarily to the corner site of waste ground his steps had now reached. On an impulse he turned into the unlighted path by the canal bank, soft underfoot and sticky with mud from the recent rains. After a few steps he was conscious of the smell of sawdust: piles of planking to his left rose in a hierarchy of shadow. The timber yard, barred with moonlight along one side where the overhanging roof failed to reach the outermost piles, held the corner of his eye long after his feet had sucked their way past its confine. The planks, machined and mechanically dumped as they were, kept for him an odour nostalgic and remedial: they belonged to an age of less accuracy and more spirit than this, when life was less exhausting if only because of the roughness and unimportance of its mistakes. In that barred shadow was benison, and his brain moved in slower tempo, unconsciously bringing him nearer to what he sought.

The surface of the canal lay half in moonlight, half in the shadow of the low fence which projected indefinitely beyond the timber-yard, giving some cover to the depressed allotments which succeeded it. The line between staring light and darkness was clear-cut, unembarrassed. Right down the middle of the canal it ran, each leg of water separate and yet complementary like the parti-coloured costume of a fool. For a dancing second he saw the ears again, oblique and distant, but this time he was not sure where or how they cast their shadow. As he strained after them, one foot slipped sideways into an unnoticed depression and when the shoe came up with the sucked mud clinging to it, the water was calm and divided as before.

None the less, the very smallness of that last image and his own unsteadiness of foot brought in a second or two a curious change to his body. He was cold now and small, cold as a bee kept in a tin, and the ears that were two towers in his eyes stood over him, challenging. He saw the marching troops in the platz and would have liked to watch them, keeping his eyes down, steadfastly down on the cobbled lines of the great platz, away from that challenging tallness. Yet in some sort of way he knew that the challenge was not directed at him. But he was down there and was enveloped by it. Soon, too soon, he was caught up and carried in paternal arms up thousands of steps ascending crookedly, like the whim of man, towards the bosom of God. And at the last there was a vision of still greater heights, black smoke-grimed foliage of stone, and then a deadly sickness. Down he went, casting himself in a kind of madness of nausea, spinning down to the littleness of the platz where the drums beat obstinately, minutely.

Which was the wiser, the child or the man? Had the world, too, fallen those thousands of steps in so few years? He did not know, but the muted throbbing of the platz was with him again and this time he looked up desperately to the height from whence he had come.

The parti-coloured water seemed to dance and gesticulate, unconcerned at the division of life. For an instant he had the urge, like Wordsworth almost cursing his memories of Arras for the sake of Robespierre, to cut from himself the part that could not forget . . . The legs of the water danced with glee. He stopped, impotent, knowing as he thought it that his was not the power to mar the pattern, to cut the fool from his folly. As he looked at the water he was small again, a child in a high window. Capitalism, cried his nearer, louder voice, Nazism, filthy domination. You remember Hugo Stinnes and are doomed. Cast yourself down, come down for ever. No, cried his small voice desperately, I will not, I will not. He was a king with eight ships and he honoured me. I will remember. Slowly he approached the window and looked down.

The water was calm, spread wide now in one interminable neck to right and left. The farther bank was a prodigious distance off and lined with factory chimneys, some of them squat and puffing smoke like bottles with brushes in them standing on a low shelf. The window from which he looked down had a wide stone sill, warm to the sun and inviting to bare legs. You got up to it ever so easily – one, two, the couch was there to help, and you could crawl on without so much as a heave. From there you could see to the bend away northwards, a couple of miles at least, and all the space between was like a great moving band, dotted with important little figures waving their shawls in the wind. Tugs with trains of barges trailing across the stream like tails they couldn't wag properly, and sometimes great rafts, filling the river from shore to shore, with little huts like dog-kennels on them and men paddling out of them across the patterned logs. On these rafts in winter there were fires lit and it made him wonder why the king up the river was not angry when his logs were burned in black circles and why the men steering were not more careful when there were ice-blocks in the water and the wind made the waves stretch up big arms and push the rafts threateningly.

But the fussy little tugs interested him most as he looked down on the weight of water flowing beyond the trees. They insisted so on telling everybody – everybody who wanted to listen, that is – that they were on an errand for the king and that they must hurry back in time for the next job. They all had bands round their funnels and flags and numbers, though all they had to do was just to go round the corner to Rotterdam and turn their barges upside down and come back again. But it was often days and days before he saw them again, long days during which the water moved on out of sight and yet was always there, green and untiring, running past the squat chimneys on the farther bank. He went on looking out of the window, with all the time in the world, waiting. Then they came back one by one very slowly, making a great deal of smoke against the stream and always cutting out into the middle just below the window. That was because they knew he was there. They knew it was no good trying to sneak past under the trees so that he couldn't see their names and numbers. Far, far down the stream he could see their funnels and tell just exactly who they were. So, you see, they might as well be proper and friendly about it and go out into midstream so that he could wave to them as they went up.

But they were none of them so quick and quiet as Hugo Stinnes VIII, who had two funnels and three bands on each. It was easy to see that he was rather a special person. He came and went, cutting round the corner to Rotterdam with a thick brush of foam at his bow. From the window he looked very important indeed. Perhaps it was not right to wave. You were never sure till it was too late.

Sometimes, when the warm stone of the window and the green river had become part of him so that he could not remember when he had not run from breakfast to jump one – two on the couch and up to his seat over the world, his mother would call him to read. But the words were lost in his mouth and he could not find them for thinking of the little tugs below, puffing along and fussing because he wasn't in the window to wave. How many might pass while he was searching for a word? Impatiently he began to jig in his place, imagining an open funnel smoking by out of the water with every ten jigs. It was a way of counting your losses and keeping a tally at the day's end. Sometimes Maria, the German maid, would call him to his bath in the evening much too early, just when he was expecting Brunhilde back from Rotterdam or when Albert Ballin was a whole day late and he was worried. Then it was that he was rude and deaf and would not answer and had to be carried kicking out of sight of the darkening neck of water that would not wait until tomorrow.

Once or twice too Herr Faulhaber, the rich cable director who owned the schloss with the high tower where he had his window, lent them his red open tourer and his chauffeur to drive and they would go away, away on the white roads, stopping to pick the yellow flowers in the fields whenever they were tired. Once, car and all, they crossed on the ferry at Andernach. But there was Hugo Grotius waiting to pass, a bit dirtier than usual and pulling four barges, and it made him worry. Worry that there was more work to do than usual and the little tugs could not manage now that he was away. It was not worthwhile going for rides really because you always felt something awful might have happened while you were away. Later they told him that Herr Faulhaber had got into trouble at the works and had been taken off in a car by the police. There was no red car then any more and the only fields would be the green tossing one he saw every day. He was sorry. Herr Faulhaber had been kind. But it did not make any difference. There was another day and he would be in the window.

It was after this, long after this, when he did not have to ask someone to spell out the names of the tugs to him any more, and he could call out to them properly and not just know them inside himself, so to speak, that he paid them his only real visit. He had not meant to, but he supposed somebody knew about it before he did and made it very like the dream he had the night after Dr Koch had lanced his finger. Only, as in the dream, he awoke too soon and felt the hurt. But this time it was the middle of the afternoon.

Now and again he went with his father to the office with the dusty steps, in the narrow little street off the Domplatz. Not often, because there was nothing to do there except watch old Corporal Lemon stick his teeth out when his typewriter bell rang and pull them in again with a jerk as the roller went back. You soon got tired of that and there was no window to look out of except the one over the dark little street that twisted down and round as though it didn't want the sky to see where it was going. It was not a very interesting room and Corporal Lemon was not allowed to play even if he wasn't very busy. So usually he would not come with his father unless there were only letters to be fetched. Then it was just in and out, and he needn't bother to climb up the stairs.

But this day it was different. It was a holiday, mother said, and they all walked up from Riehl together because it saved twenty-five pfennigs on the tram and the cigar-smoke didn't get all over your clothes. Along the embankment they came, with the leaves freckling the floor like a lace tea-cloth and the sun stepping across the water to them because he always had to come the shortest way. Mother did not often come out with them, but today she had on a big fur coat that looked as though it was climbing up to her ears. A tiny claw, all that was left of a different animal, kept a hold on her bunchy cap, though there was only just enough wind to make the yellow leaves hop along the embankment a little way or drag with a rustle into the shelter of a tree-trunk. Now and again one of them made a mistake and fell through the railings on to the cobbled quay by the water's edge. It was quiet down there and safe for them, so he did not worry.

In the little street off the Domplatz it was all as secret as ever. There was no one about. Run in, said his father, and see if there are any letters. And don't say I'm out here. Run in, run in, up the stairs come on. It's only Corporal Lemon with a cup in his hand, looking a bit angry and surprised. And there are no letters. No letters, said Corporal Lemon without showing his teeth at all. He doesn't play even on holiday, the funny old man. Down again quickly. The door shut softly and the treads of the dusty stairs creaked ever so little as though a field mouse had plucked up courage and come solemnly into town on a visit.

The street was still empty and some of the shops had their blinds drawn. A few yards up father and mother were hidden in the shadow of a projecting sign, momentarily engrossed in a toyshop. They did not turn round and he did not see them. Funny, he thought, and turned back down. I expect they're round the corner waiting. The little street twisted expectantly. A few of the blinds of the shops jumped out on him and tried to pretend they were hiding somebody. But they weren't. Well, he did not worry. He knew the way home, under the trees by the dancing water. Funny, he thought again and forgot on the instant. The corner turned quicker than thought. Straight in front was the green water, flecked with the sun, hurrying, hurrying. There was no time to lose.

In less than a minute his hand was going bump, bump on the knobs of the lead railings lining the embankment. The cold rail slid along the curve of his fingers and at each swollen joint his clasp opened regularly and rhythmically into a pat that left a harsh singing sound in the hollow tubes. Out to the right was the smooth band of water, its edges lifting against the quay and the heavy breath of winter hidden in the swell. Under the great Hohenzollern bridge he could see, as he looked back, the black and white rings of Hugo Grotius coming down. He stood stock-still to watch the tug pass, the barges heavy with coal and a man jumping forward from the bow of one to the stern of another. He saw the little dinghy swinging to and fro, last of all in the string, and the dark triangle widening behind it in the water. Poor old Hugo Grotius, he always had a heavy load.

A slight bend of the tree-lined embankment showed him the powerful flick of the swell against the quay wall and, what caught his breath for a second, a tug at anchor close inshore. Oh and another. They had not been there on the way up. One had a gangway down to the cobbles. He must go and have a closer look. The cobbles were quite safe and there were many sets of steps from the embankment to the quay. He had never been allowed to go down before, but it was quite safe. There was no need to worry. Oh Brunhilde. And Ehrenbreitstein. In his excitement he had not really noticed which tugs they were tied up by the side so unexpectedly. Down on the quay he stopped, moved a little nearer and stopped again. The water flicked against the side of the cemented cobbles and found a way out between the bows and the anchor of Brunhilde. The trees nodded encouragingly overhead.

In that hub of the underworld of Europe, hatch down which disappeared inopportune children and desperadoes alike, a distracted father and mother scoured the streets. Lower than they could see with any ease their child stood stock-still, lost as a dream, watching the wasting smoke that was all of Brunhilde's hair and listening to the chink of the lifting anchor chain.

The scream that followed was buried deep in a dream and it was a second or two before it rose to the top and screamed as a separate sound. Hearing it he was frightened for the first time. There it was again, behind, up, up the steps. Calling attention to his lostness. He turned. In the confusion of sounds his delight, his vision vanished. Only the lostness stayed. A yellow car screamed, braking at speed, but this was not like the first screams. There were men in it, police. But nearer, faster, a fur coat was coming down the steps, sudden with tears, and he was crying when his face was buried in it. When he looked up at last the tiny claw was reaching down tenderly and almost touching his hair.

The trees went into furious debate and Brunhilde and Ehrenbreitstein were alone with the stream arguing by their bows.

But they did not forget. Days afterwards, when he understood that the window had brought to him the very last light on the tossing green field below and that Maria, his father and mother and he were all to go on the following day to Marienburg to a house without a window, they came to him again. Many of them together. Downstream they came, twenty or thirty in a group, fat little tugs with coloured bands and smoke flying, puffing all over the place with excitement because for once they had no barges with them. And some came up alone from the windy distance, round the corner from Rotterdam. These too had no barges with them and on the little stepping masts appeared flags.

He was entranced. They had come to say goodbye. Slowly the procession formed, a little downstream from the window, with a deal of pushing and arguing as to who should go first. One by one they began to move, not across the river nearer the other bank as they usually did, but straight up underneath the window, just over the tops of the trees. They pushed and fumed, treading on each other's heels, moving up ever so slowly and fussing all the time.

Opposite the window they let off their sirens, irregularly in a piercing line, and the water went dark beyond the trees.

Goodbye, O goodbye, he cried with face streaming. I shan't forget you. Goodbye. He gave a little wave of the hand that was pitifully like a gesture of drowning. A door opened behind him and silence came to his farewell. He kept his face looking steadily out of the window, swallowing what was left of tears. They would not know it was for him and he could not bear to explain. Dear window, he thought, and pressed his fingers hard into the stone.

But the ceremony was not yet over. One messenger was still to come. Hugo Stinnes VIII it was who came dropping down with the stream, down from the haze of the great bridge, swinging his sharp nose round into the wake of the fat, black little ships who made up the bulk of the procession. Then came his siren, deep, strident, the voice of a great count in his own country. The boy in the window was quiet, loaded with honours. The king had spoken, the king with the eight ships. This was his doing, this last duty to the watcher who had pleased him. Goodbye, O goodbye.

The forest of masts, funnels and flags was dipping now, slowly falling out of sight beyond the converging trees. He strained after them with his eyes, staring at them churning, churning with studied slowness, like children near the end of a slow-bike race. Little by little they appeared again farther off as the river shook its great back, piling up against the loops of the Hohenzollern bridge, mingling with the shadow of the stanchions. Back on the air came the hoarse cries of the sirens, the waving farewells of the flags. In another minute the river was covered in a mist and all across it were lashes of sudden furious rain.

He got down from the window, too sad to look further, experiencing no surprise that it was but the shortest step to the ground. He could see only a few yards again, only as far as the other side of the canal, which he accepted unmoving as the natural bound of his vision. The moon had disappeared and the water was no longer divided. The mud of the pool in which he had been standing sucked at his feet reluctantly as he changed position, uncertain whether to go forward or return the way he had come. In the end he went on, not caring greatly, and as he reached the main road crossing the canal he had an odd illusion that the bridge was drooping idly in the water and that all traffic had stopped.

The Neutral Shore

~

At first sight there was no one in the room. The two candles leaped uncertainly from the battered branching stick towards the heavy curtains beyond, falling back again before the first depth of shadow. There was only a play of courage there, braving it in brocade for a moment but coming shortly for confidence to the closed door and the twice-turned lock. It was no strange thing at the Spyglass for council thus to be expected behind curtains. The landlord, in keeping a council-chamber, did not feel called upon to explain the ponderous lock he provided or to enquire very closely into the business of the gentlemen who turned it. It was enough ado to keep an inn and broach ale to drown the bitterness of the times. Locks and laws there were, but a man was wise in the marshes who knew enough to be ignorant of the twists of either.

In the leaping twilight the candles fled nervously before every enquiring breeze lifting the twitch of linen off the secondary casement over the yard. The highbacked settle was a half-feared solidity, like the hidden minds at work. The man pressed against the wall by the casement was so much a part of the anxious neutrality of the inn that the partisan eye would not at once discern him. But time would give him up where sight failed and mark his step out of that flitting neutrality. The linen beside him blew out and dropped to the pane again. The candles advanced up the farther wall and changed front nervously. From the taproom the side-talk swelled and receded as the evening went. Only the man was rigid, unmoving, one finger boring away the light shift of linen from the window and both eyes fixedly upon the yard. In time he became a sentinel element of blacker sort, sharp on the neutral background of the room and stiff out of the frightened crowd below. Only his pressure on the wall and a crumpled cap showed that he, like the rest, was afraid.

The little half-cocked glances of the room ran about catching the tail of half-seen things in corners. Minutes passed up and down on the stairway, creaking as they met. Once the handle of the door turned noiselessly and fell back again before the ponderous lock. The watcher, eyes strained towards the yard, heard nothing but the beat of life in himself and shivered, finite and unprofitable. The hours were stretching out with the dreadful prolongation of misunderstanding. Still they did not come. Hope had its measure by the clock and the weights were long on the chain already. He was trembling involuntarily at last, cursing his forwardness. The crowd were afraid but at least they clung together in their fear and would not own to each other who hurt them. He alone must remember what was inconvenient and elect to right himself. In this hour his blood began to thump madly and the shortest straw was in his hand.

Suddenly his knees tensed. His heart dropped down, far down, for a second and then was hoisted up higher than usual, working like thunder in his ears. A horseman rode into the yard. Two, three horsemen. Torches flared in the stable doorway and the talk in the taproom died stone-dead as footsteps came up the passage. Fear had come to the crowd, but it was hope to him mounting, mounting with the three turns of the stair. The indissoluble fear of the coming was slowing, was splitting into separate footsteps. The beat was broken: there were six dogging feet on the worn treads and the bridge of his blood steadied.

Up they tramped, with no secrecy in it. One solemn little minute passed them on the way down. A thumb-nail scratched down the door. The watcher, confirmed, threw over the double lock with all his strength and stood back. A new candle flared in, casting streamers away on the bare walls of the passage. In the immediate wedge of shadow stood the three men, square and expected, assured of the neutrality of the heavy curtains and the long conciliatory table. The fears of the room were pressed back into place with the new arrivals. The last in threw over the lock and stood by it listening.

The second man went over to the window and narrowly surveyed the yard. No other lattice commanded even a glimpse of the room and anyone in the yard or beyond the gate must be visible to its occupants. Then he turned, appraising the stiff figure waiting for him. 'Ah, Hudson,' he said, smiling with his teeth but making no other gesture, 'I am the happier for seeing you whole and unspitted. You have been circumspect. The buttery door was unlocked, I trust?'

The old man nodded and turned his sea-cap in his hands. The moment had overrun him and his tongue was lost in the sudden light of the room. Candle watched candle now and each made little comforting runs out of its own circle into the other. Some of the farther shadows were intersected, and everywhere there was a faint overlay of light.

Only the man by the window was obscure and impenetrable. His still forehead and hooded eyes resisted friendship, whether of light or talk, and the showy teeth were a reflex, superficial, almost a shell protruding against the pressure of sound. The smile came and went on wires. In the plain black suit, splashed thigh boots and rolling walk were the marks of incessant activity, but the motive was not to the first looker.

The reassurance of the room, none the less, was for the time sufficient. The eyes of the man in black rested calmly on Hudson, without hurry or reservation.

'Tell me,' he said, 'what you have. A minute or more must pass before they can mount the stair and that time is freely in our hand.'

The old man met his expectant look like a bombardier with a lighted fuse waiting for the word of command. He stood poised on some invisible line while the other spoke, eager to run a race with his burning tongue to the touch-hole in view.

'T'name of 'un be Burnfield, zur. They dogs o' Frenchies had me into Calliss on't wool-boat an' kept me strict confined on account that I did open mouth agin the dirty rummagin crew of 'un. No more was to see thereafter, zur, and little enow before. But Will Cherry now, as were pilot on t'Portuguese – ah! God's pity on t'man, 'a wouldna come for fear. A coward is yon Will bydam, grey as colour o't guts on 'un an' clingin' to 'un grandam on't settle-end.'

'Burnfield . . .' mused the other hooding his eyes. 'What more?' He waved a hand, hinting impatience more in the tone than the gesture.

'I have no more, zur, but t'one thing: yon Burnfield hath a son, and they do come fro' Calliss, both of 'un, once a month to

England for to cast up accounts. So much I ha' taken fro' t' tongue o' poor Will Cherry, as were abroad t'Portuguese. 'A said but one word at parting, 'a did, an' besought me most earnestly to mark it. They would ha' wool, 'a said, do what we could, for they had friends here which we didna dream of. This twice, an' shaking every limb.'

'Which we did not dream of . . .' repeated the other, giving each word weight. His eyelids went up suddenly on wires and a flash ran from the train of thought out into the room, seeking to illuminate the triangle of faces and as suddenly disappearing. The man at the table moved uneasily, aware of the implication, but said no word. There was an interval, only a second or two in time but crooked with the mark of many questions still without an answer, and the white smile of the interrogator was a cover for the prepared confidence to follow.

'Suppose we fall out with the fainthearts?' . . . His laugh was jarring. 'Who knows what our net will trammel?' There was an air about him as though he had stopped the holes in Providence with his own fists. His eyes moved in starts over the room, too quick for the direct glance. The candles followed, nervously conciliatory.

The man by the door lifted a finger silently. He had missed what went before with his friends, but he heard the march of the enemy. The finger threw a leaping shadow on the panel of the door like the threatened death of the knife.

The man in black turned and observed the signal. Without a word he stepped towards Hudson and covered his mouth with his right hand, half-turning the old man by the shoulders with the other before extracting from his own doublet a small roll of paper. This he held presently at arm's length before Hudson. But some seconds passed before it could be read. Fumbling at first for his knife, eyes clouded with the secretion of sudden excitement, the old man saw nothing but the lost trace of what he thought was about to happen. Then he brushed his forehead impatiently of all but the pride of accomplishment. He could read as few could on that shore and had not forgotten to let himself be known by that fact to the landguard. 'Hudson,' ran the script, 'say no word. Avoid the line of the door. Betake yourself as softly as may be to the wood bunker under the window facing east and lie concealed for a space. Await the departure of our enterprise and go not thence until the hour of eleven by the village clock. Be sure that the stairs are clear. Leave by the way you came. Accept your country's thanks and whatever promise of future reward my sworn word may procure. Farewell. Isaac Manley.'

The old man read to the end before stretching out to take the paper from the other's fingers. For some seconds longer there remained on his face a numbed look, as though he had been overtaken by the quickness of the candles and the glances and the sudden rush of silence to the door. It needed a pluck or two at the shoulder before he began to move as instructed. Three faces shadowed like clocks counted the motions until the lid of the bunker closed and the faded drape was pulled across its opening.

Manley made a covering pace towards the candles as the lid creaked. His smile was determined. More quickly then he rounded the table, balancing on his toes with the action of a swordsman, though he carried no blade. The man at the table watched him narrowly, seeking a clue. The ear of the third was again to the door.

'We'll play these fellows for the thieves they are.' Manley's tone pressed the unseen enemy like a sword on a narrow stair. Round the table he went, swart and pressing, chest puffed and hand ahead. 'We'll show them who is for the wall, or Isaac Manley is with the worms already. Who broke the Isle of Man trade? Let them tell us that. Who caught the Lancashiremen snivelling a second time for the export bounty? Let them tell us that. These shall learn, these rogues of the fist, that the game is not played so easily. Owlers forsooth! – they shall find that a still tongue is not the only thing in the head worth having. What say you, Thomas Lee?'

The man by the door laughed. He was simple enough to be glad of the bold tongue, without enquiring what it meant. 'They s'all have shorter wool for your coming. I'se warrant me,' he said, winking ingenuously at his fellow by the table.

But this last face gave no answer. It hung above a bent forearm like the head of a weary question, eyeing the processional victory of the present and feeling even the anxious table ring with the replies of the muffled future. In front of the face, within the pool of light, lay a document, closely-written with the same whorls and flourishes as that held before Hudson a moment since. But the gaze of the eyes was fixedly at the door, lifting only from time to time to take in the nearer of Manley's extravagances and conscious of Lee as one may be of a child whose simple antics are sometimes intrusive.

Manley continued up and down the room in heavy strutting fashion. He was short enough for there to be something faintly ridiculous in his bounding solidity, practising with every step or two a sudden dash of footwork for a fight against odds. Despite the quick teeth, however, there was more to be feared than laughed at in the face. A smile there was, a sharp mannerism, athletic in its physical relief. No attentive observer could for long be assured that he understood the passage of emotion or thought under this scrutiny. There was an odd colouring about the eyes, tighter than the braggadocio of words, though they were laboured out in short swaggering periods. With every moment the owlers grew more besotted and traitorous: theirs was no easy listening. Words hung thickly in the room, clotting its shadows with hatred, gathering in the exile of the curtains. The candles streamed hopelessly into new spaces and the neutral pool of the table was broken into innumerable fleeing ripples as the words fell inexorably into it, overwhelming the timid recovery of time.

'God's truth, an' the clock strike soon, there will be one glad o' the greeting.' The ripples had reached Lee's corner at last, washing back and fore on the shale of his nerves. Every second a desperate remnant of light found refuge in his face, only to lose hold and slip and be endlessly replaced. He had given up any pretence of alertness at the door. There was, in any case, nothing he could do.

Manley stopped his parade. 'Underwood yet lacks the time. The appointed place is distant one mile only from the Folkestone Warren. It will serve us little to beat the covert too early. And this night we must not fail.' The peculiar emphasis with which this was said seemed to arise less from a natural desire to reassure Lee in his unnerving than from some deliberate purpose of the speaker's. The man had held above the pool a larger rock, balanced it and pushed it calculatingly in. The former pebbles were forgotten in the splash and uproar. Amid the flying darkness it seemed momentarily as though the effort had taxed even Manley's strength. His teeth were fast in a white smile.

Captain John Ellesdon half rose in sudden stupefaction. The whole room was lost, out of alignment, unrelated. The locked door was a myth and the inn and the whole purport of their coming. Only words were real and they whirled madly round his head, spinning farther and farther from the fixity of that smile. Nothing was as he had calculated. Nothing had the meaning he had given it. His mind made a few pitiful motions like a child and came back again to its sheltering amazement.

When it ventured again out into the cold of surmise the overwhelming giddiness was past. Silence was coming back and slowly light to the pool, like the vexed water from the top of the scar. There was rest in that silent return, if no answer. Presently he dared to look round, to face again the prospect that was and the jar of the necessary question. Was Manley a fool like all these metropolitans and an overbearing fool to boot? Or a jaded mountebank flogging his chance? He had uneasy recollections of other strutting fellows who had kept the confidence of the Commissioners of Customs longer even than rank inattention should allow. But Manley, in his plain black suit, had not seemed a natural addition to the roll. For a little while, he had to confess, he had been impressed. But now it was inevitable that he should return to the irritation and pessimism he had felt on that day, that first day no more than a week ago and yet years away, when the dusty messenger had delivered the letter from London stamped with the seal of his masters, signed by the indefatigable John Sansom, and consigned to himself at Lydd. Overseers from London, he supposed, were everlastingly to be deemed cleverer and more diligent than regular officers and confidence and lack of breeding be mistaken for ability. So it had been. And so it was.

The name of Underwood, in the first place, had caused his waiting hand to tremble. It was not in his power to question Manley's dispositions, but he could not help knowing that Robert Underwood was not the man for a mission of this sort. Only two weeks past, at Manley's request, he had handed over a confidential statement on the preventive officers as he knew them. Clearer than day, without equivocation or flourish, under the head of New Rumney appeared the man's description: 'Robert Underwood, a diligent officer, but disabled by girth and limitation of mind from rendering excellent service. His credulity is useful to the owlers: they outwit him in talk and use him as a check on other officers.' The more he thought of this the more sinister seemed the disregard with which his knowledge, indeed all previous knowledge of the situation on that coast, was treated by this metropolitan play-actor. Half-memories jumped out of the last week, single stifled instances of suggestions ignored, of ideas received with an air of tolerant amusement. Cumulatively they began to press on him, a weight on the edge of anger.

He looked up with hot distaste, not bilking the straight stare. But there was little to meet his eyes direct. The candles were at their evasion again. In and out of the dodging light moved Manley, an occasional frightened sheen on his curling hair and his teeth fast clenched on whatever purpose was in the room. In the steadier shadow of the curtain was the massing of the enemy and counsel ran round and round the table, desperate in the little light.

Ellesdon stared hard at Lee, hoping for another anger to rise with his. The strained darkness by the door showed little of him. What could be interpreted from his posture was only diligence and tension. The fool! – had he not stirred even at Manley's unwarranted disclosure of the time and place of the assault? In God's name was he, were they all mad? Were they to ride once more on a lost errand? Manley knew, had been warned, that their every action would be marked and known, that from their rendezvous on the Dymchurch road they had been watched over sedge and dyke to this room in the Spyglass: that Underwood, filling his fat belly in the ale-room, would blab all that was worth knowing of their plan that night: that on the very landing outside the door was the nearest carrier of news. Manley had been told of all this as often as his attention would permit. What could this idiotic tap-talk mean?

Ellesdon clenched his fist loudly on the table.

Manley turned towards him. 'Good heart, Captain Ellesdon, what ails you?' he smiled. 'Like you not the night's work?'

'The less for that I hear who are our other undertakers.' There was no affability in Ellesdon's voice.

'Haply, sir, Underwood will block a road as well as another. On what principle do you propose to proceed?' The smile had died on Manley's face and only the teeth marked were it had been.

Ellesdon stared at him unwinkingly for some seconds and shook his head. It was too late for proposals now. Plainer it could hardly be, in any case, that the distrust confronting him would confound more than his present hopes. Beyond the darkness and this desperate enterprise stretched the uncut thread of suspicion, taut around every endeavour and knotted securely away there in Sansom's files in London. Manley did believe it, after all. O generation of vipers, well sheltered from any wrath of his! O wise in their generation! Richard King and he, the only two officers of whom the marshmen were afraid, so to be accused of harbouring Godfrey Cross. It cut him deep at last, worse than the first hearing. He knew, without speculation, that insubordination had begun the tale, that the black tongue of underling Harrison had licked Manley's ear and the air of New Rumney and Lydd had made it smart. No warrant out for Cross, he heard them mock. You hoped to use him, small fry for bait. A likely tale! God's truth no, a tale like a taut thread to hang him in the owler's place and Richard King in a spare noose by his side! Why was King tied to the wool-seizure barn at such a time? Why was he himself here in the Spyglass, like a dog on Manley's chain? There was only one answer. He sucked at his lips and found dryness.

Nothing moved in the room now except Manley. Ellesdon sat as though tethered, turning dismay over and finding despair. God save us all, was his thought, God save us all. Officers had been shot at in Folkestone Warren and Shorncliffe already. Tonight was the night for the cutting of a few throats in Lydd. There was no end to Manley but that, and no end now for those he had kept with him that was of their choosing. How shall fools be led? Faintly he wished for the two menservants that he alone of all the landguard possessed. Weakly he built his money up like a barrier behind which he was safe, with men to his back and a pistol for guard. But he knew as he wished it that this thinking was far-off and feeble. The room was the reality, the trap with four uncertain walls and three allies at secret odds. This was the bound of life, the circle of light and the long leagues of shadow. He moved a little and courage came back into his hands. The candles were low, but the flames were steadier on the shorter wicks. It was not time yet.

Manley stopped short in front of him as though determined to parley. 'The tale of the night will bear tomorrow's telling, captain,' he said. 'Think no more of Underwood. He will discharge his part.'

'I should be the more certain of that if I knew what ours may be,' replied Ellesdon drily.

The muscles of Manley's face twitched before the point and steel dropped from his eyes downwards like a visor. The echo of the clash ran fainter from corner to corner of the shadow, and the shuffling intermediary moments backed slowly towards the door.

Lee was no more than a steward in these lists, shouldered out by the onset of the circling courages and pressed with the weakling candles against the wall. Outside the insatiate enemy gathered a sheaf of minutes and got no further harvest. Inside was the cockpit, cleared of almost everything but courage.

The move was Manley's. He felt the antagonism of his opponent and the urge was strong on him to close with it. Yet he had meant that the actions of this night should save him the trouble and he remembered, after the brace of the first shock, that courage could be quick on this field and outrun all his other dispositions. It was a sword but a simplification too. The room was not all. A stride in it might be only the little step of irresolution on a wider field.

He let the challenge die as the echoes died. Anxiously he fronted all ways, examining the genesis of his plan.

Doubt ran back along the line of preparation, back to the boot-slapping of William Carter, the little lawyer with the badger's eyes who had preceded him at this task. In his present anxiety he was kinder to him than he had ever been. The man had had experience, after all. What if he were right? But no, no. His brag about Admiral Allen was climbing talk, no more. His system of off-shore signalling so that ships of the line could ·intercept the shallops would not work, had not worked. No amount of significant nose-tapping and boot-slapping and heavy testimonials from the wights of Exeter and Devon had convinced him then that the way to get at the owlers was by sea. And he saw no reason to change his opinion now. If the wool was to be taken it must be taken far from the coast, while it was on the move. Only so would conviction be certain. These marshmen must be taught willy-nilly that to export wool to feed the manufactories of Lille and Tournay, rivals of their own countrymen's works, was the rankest treason. A sardonic smile curved his train of thought. Could a Kentishman be persuaded that to obtain the best price for his goods was treason? A penny out of pocket was worse to many than a fill-dyke month in the fields of Folkestone.

The smile ran out and about and came round to the same point like Badger's Eyes at the Board. He could almost be sorry for Carter now. But the man was a fool to think he could do it by sea. Mounseer Colbert, he had said with a worn air, had complained that ships of the line interfered with the French fishing-boats, and

His Majesty had withdrawn the commission from Admiral Allen. Fishing-boats, forsooth! The smile was a little wry then. His Majesty had had enough wool to spare for the eyes of his Privy Council.

But times were changed. There were Commissioners for Trade and Plantations now, not above a wry smile in their turn. The Court was a Whig and the rest beardless. John Sansom set no guard on his tongue. Messengers came and went, sped by his invective. His Majesty's Commissioners for Customs were better served.

One scene was firm in Manley's mind, fixed like the plan he had formed. In the middle was Carter, crouching under his final examination by the Commissioners for Trade, badger's eyes stubbornly giving ground before the terrier work of John Pollexfen, himself in the corner quietly triumphing. He had had no pity then. At the head of the table the noble earls leant towards each other: old Sir Philip Meadows's beard wagged in earnest palliation: Pollexfen knew more names for the French than Mounseer Colbert dreamed. His Papistical Majesty was dead in England, not a doubt of it, and Master' John Locke was away. Not a doubt of that either, when there was so much of Master Pollexfen. Badger's Eyes bore it well, even slapping his boot desperately from time to time. But the man was a fool to think he could do it by sea, where the French could outwit him. A fool, yes, what else? And yet it was well to be sorry for him, to remember his effort gone sour and thrown away. The more so now that his own strength had come to the turn and was doubtful. There was always pity in doubt, he supposed, in the moment of self-trial. In that scene at the Board he had been silent, withdrawn in his confident corner. Now he was more disposed to go out with Carter, linking arms with his folly.

The candle on the nearer branch began to gutter piteously, feeling no more future than he. He braced his chest. There was nothing to fear except treachery, nothing except a composition with the owlers, nothing except the wretched few pounds made over as pay to the landguard, nothing except a disinclination to starve. Private means alone could be trusted, or integrity, whichever should persist the longer. He looked round. The faces of Ellesdon and Lee wavered with the guttering light.

The nearer flame swam desperately in its molten sea. Time to be gone.

'God send our enterprise success, gentlemen,' he said, back in the grand manner again, and struck his fist on the table. The flame drowned and his doubts were only a vague reminiscent smoke leaving the dead stick. 'We must ride.' Neither of the others made any reply. Ellesdon took up the candle they had brought. Lee whipped back the bolt of the door, as though to run the enemy through.

But there was no one there. Nothing but the wet gleam of the passage wall and the sudden louder roar of the ale-room that told the lower door had been opened and shut. The neutrality of the council-chamber reached after them as they began to descend and the drape of the wood-bunker lifted a moment in farewell.

Twenty minutes later three horsemen passed the end of the old sea-wall where the track for Dymchurch crossed and recrossed the dyke. The stones jumped back stricken and fast, planted like trefoils of sound by the fiery hooves. The darkness eyed them impenetrably.

Manley twisted in his stirrups and peered on either side. Suddenly he raised his hand and reined in on the quieter verge. The others followed suit. There was no sound, nothing that could be distinguished above the caught breath of men and horses and the creaking of saddle girths as flanks thudded unwittingly in and out. Manley leaned over his nearer companion, clipping the words with his teeth into a whisper. There was an unnecessary haste about all he did, and the jut of his head alarmed Ellesdon into clapping hands to his holster. There was a laugh but no prologue. 'Lee,' urged Manley, 'at the first creek yonder you will come upon Captain Ellesdon's two servants, whom I have taken the liberty to bend to this service. Their master will permit me so far, I'll aver.' He went on quickly, ignoring the perplexed anger barely a yard away. 'Whistle the catch Lillibullero as you come to the ford: they will start forth at the hearing. See that you draw not rein. Much depends on your swift riding. Press on, all three, to the Warren and succour Underwood at the turn by the three-mile stone. I fear me what may befall him and you come not. Once met, ride as you may to Hythe and alight at "The Quiet Woman". Mark well the name of every man who shall enter the house after your coming there. Am I well understood?'

'Yes indeed, sir, but . . .'

'Let there be no argument, I pray. We leave you here. It is important that you ride at our former pace, steadily. Above all the catch, forget not the catch.'

Lee nodded. His horse lurched and he was gone. Only the promontory of sound stretched back out of the darkness, the silent tide narrowing its sides.

'S'blood, Mr Manley' . . . 'Silence, man.' It was a rap, cold as a knife on a nerve. 'Come.'

Manley's mount swerved suddenly through a break in the wall on the left. Ellesdon, caught unawares, over-ran the gap in his first essay and bungled it badly at his second. Manley had already dismounted. Both men felt their way forward until the shelf of ground broke off short and the forelegs of Manley's horse struggled back from the sharp declivity. Gradually they faced round. 'Hist,' said Manley. Ellesdon stood, hand on bridle, listening. His head was cocked so for thirty seconds at least. 'I hear nothing,' he whispered, suspecting more than ever the shifts his companion had made. Almost at that instant he sensed rather than heard the passage of horsemen by the gap in the wall. The nerve went cold again. He recognised the first step.

'Three, I'll swear,' said Manley.

'The cunning dogs ride into an east wind and make no sound ahead,' added Ellesdon, amending his calculation again.

'In that they use good fortune, captain, and trust all but the heels of her. The horses are flannel shod.'

A shifty ray began to play along the marsh seawards and edge craftily in the direction of the dyke on which they stood. The moon sidled out of cover and looked at them, temporising and oblique. Nothing was certain yet, save that the dyke was untenable, like the old defences. One trick would not serve, without movement and a new front.

Ellesdon recognised this and abandoned his own calculation. The data changed every moment and the labour was useless. 'Whither now?' was all he said. Manley was already in the saddle. The new light struck oddly upon the cape of his jaw, as though making up its mind to retreat and advance elsewhere. Ellesdon too began to feel himself part of the perpetual ebb, of the ineffectual water headed off by the broad thrust of that jaw. He stopped the struggle to make up his mind, finding a comfort in uncertainty, an elemental drift that was at one with the weakness of the universe, with the swell and fall of the water and the oblique, anxious face of the moon. In this second he escaped the crushing jar of the prow's impact on the farther beach, the pressure between the black certainty of the owlers and the gritting metropolitan will. In this second, unstable as water, he was the slip of the earth, the heave of the crowd, he was fear and still found comfort. The turn of the world was his, and life. In that second he thought no more.

Manley was waiting with impatience, his horse manoeuvring among the tussocks. 'Make haste, captain, we ride for Denge Marsh,' he muttered.

'Denge Marsh?' echoed Ellesdon.

'Ay, Denge Marsh. In an hour's time, by God's grace and our own cunning, I purpose to take one Burnfield, the owlers' factor at Calais, as he comes to cast up accounts.'

'God's truth, I feared we were for the Warren. But wither goes he?'

'To East Guldeford, as I surmise. Sir Robert Guilford will give him cover. You know him for an owling man. But Burnfield must be taken by us at the Midrips.'

Ellesdon allowed the words to halt wonderingly in the front of his consciousness. The action of the horse numbed his intelligence and he no more than picked at their significance. He was still easy and without choice. Talking was difficult across the wind. They had turned sharp right by this time, along a track leading southwards towards the shore. A few minutes' riding brought the glint of black water ahead and they swerved again to the right. The lights of New Rumney rode like pursuit behind them and the scrape and thud of hooves came with them, threatening the secrecy of their plan and crying out discovery. Ellesdon lost his ease. He was caught up in the conflict, no matter how, and his breath came shorter.

It was as though Manley sensed something of this. He leaned slightly out of the saddle to collect his allegiance again. 'Mr King and Thomas Chidwick await us a mile from here,' he said.

'Mr King?' the echo was sent forward on the wind and came curving back, surprised and overtaken. 'Then . . .'

'There is no more to say, captain. And the saying would be our danger henceforward. We reach the owlers' cover hereabouts. I fear the wind will carry news of us as it is.'

The horses fell into a walk. The sea had gone peering off to the left, exploring the shingle banks of the point, pretending it had given no ground save by design. Now it was muttering far away, a sound on the edge of conspiracy. This was a spot where plans

might be made and victories won without them, where the land
arched its back and threatened to intervene. The sedge-grass
seemed to hustle them in an ominous manner, getting higher like
a hostile crowd in a dream. There was a flurry in the shaggy tops.

Suddenly a man started up on the right of the path. Manley's
horse reared up and plunged twice.

'God's truth, Chidwick, a second more and I had brained you.
Why showed you not yourself sooner?'

'The surer to tell 'ee were no Frenchy, master.' The voice was
husky and ingratiating, like the rubbed pebbles on the shore.

Manley looked at him like the halting tide. 'What salary have
you from the Commissioners, Chidwick?'

'Twenty pound, Master Manley sir. Every year come Lady Day
when the Dover men be in.'

'And how much did the owlers give you three years agone?'

'As much ale as a man could drink and a pound for misen what
time the shallops were safe away, master.' The pebbles had been
washed and whitened and felt no shame at the turning. The tide
would go in and out again, and had done unmeasured and endless, claiming and disclaiming its natural shore.

'But I be true man now as swore to Captain Ellesdon. Indeed,
master.'

'Ah. Mr King.'

'Sir?'

'Do the Frenchmen show a light?'

'Not yet, Mr Manley.' The answer came from the grasses deeper
to the right of the track. Ellesdon edged up his horse a pace or
two.

'Then time is with us. The militia will be here at eleven.'

'The militia?' All three voices showed surprise. 'From Folkestone?' added King.

'From Folkestone. Captain John Jordan, Extraordinary Ryding
Surveyor, and twenty men. They ride by Old Rumney and Lydd to
beat the alarm. Do you, Mr King, take Chidwick and hold the
road above the Midrips till the horsemen come. But hold fire
when you hear the hooves, lest friends make a mark for you and
our enterprise fail. We stay here to press the owlers into your pistol
range if they are beforehand with us and have a mind to beat the
militia. But when the horsemen come, leave all. They have their
instructions.'

King stood a moment as though disposed to argue. 'I like not this Jordan,' he began. 'I have heard . . . Yet I have heard nothing.' His voice dropped to a mutter and scratched among the sand.

Over against him stood Manley, his composure on wires again and teeth long in his speech. 'He has been twice Mayor of Folkestone, I have heard,' he said, stock-still.

'And may be bailiff of hell hereafter, for all I know,' cut in Ellesdon shortly, with some of the words of his old command. The halt had restored his wits. In the cut of wind and war to come he was an individual again, with a personal cause and the grudge of better knowledge. London and gritting fears were put away. This was the marsh he knew and yonder were the owlers. It was suddenly as simple as that. Manley was not a crushing force but an intruding third party who had so far prevented calculation. The metropolitan was play-acting again, spitting orders and venom. What of it? Good might come even of this trickery if only it were taken up now, in all its clever-leggedness, by a man who knew the marshes. Ellesdon turned away, back with his servants and the obscure loyalty that counted England more than economics and less than a pride of rank.

It was seven minutes at least since the stealthy light swung from the bulwarks of the French shallop had been answered from the shore. Manley and Ellesdon had been long in uneasy position by the road, a hundred yards back towards Lydd, in case the Frenchmen should beat back for the boat. In lying so close they were adding another hazard: if the alarm came too soon and they were forced to reveal their position in order to hold up the retreating French, flanking fire from the boat-guard would probably take them out of time and rid the owlers of them quickly and for all. But it was a risk that had to be taken. The whole plan hinged on the militia. On this open shore four men could do little, save by the merest chance. It was the militia or nothing. Faintly, away across the marsh, the church clock of Lydd was heard striking eleven. The notes came bunched in groups like riders shouldering a lull of wind.

A pistol cracked out, small and far away above the Midrips. King and Chidwick were at work. The Frenchmen must already be well along the sea road, though not a sound had marked their landing. God grant the owlers had no sentries on the Rye side, or King and Chidwick need show their backs but once. A scattered volley answered the first alarm. The landing-party had gone to ground behind the sea-wall. They would test out the opposition before renouncing so important an enterprise and running for the boat. The moon had retired into a cloud as guardedly as she had come and nothing could be seen of the beach further than the few scatterings of foam that came running in obliquely almost under hand. A shot or two obstinately broke the regular roll and crunch of the tide and took cover with the falling pebbles. It was impossible to say how the engagement was going. Manley and Ellesdon stood up and breasted the road, caring little for silence now but moving slowly forward, pistol in hand, knowing that the wind would carry their advance ahead whatever their precautions. The business grew less pleasant every second.

One pair of feet, soft shod, was running not far away. The boat was near then. They were strengthening the boat-guard. King was holding, must be. Manley and Ellesdon halted, anxious not to press the issue too soon. The owlers, altering their own dispositions, had evidently not heard them as yet. Waiting might do better. A pistol cracked again from the wall four hundred yards off. This time the flame could be seen, momentary and desperate. After a second or two came the answer, muffled and indefinite in the distance. To the listeners it seemed only a reflex, without impetus of its own. King too was waiting, as they were, for the end of this phase, for the portent of expected destruction. Even the urgency of the Frenchmen failed to beat up into this ebb of will. The pebbles behind the wall were smooth and slipped unnoticed away with the recession of purpose.

'Hist,' said Manley. 'Towards Lydd. D'ye hear something?' The off-shore wind sent little spurts of white on a late errand over the incoming waves, starting an off-beat in the unceasing repetition. 'The militia,' said Ellesdon, craning above the sedge and staring into the wind. 'They are coming.'

Like a wave of blood to the head they came and drummed on the ear for an instant, reared up in the sight bloodshot and headstrong, and were gone in a broken flurry. The wind whistled after them and the road was suddenly empty with realisation. Amid the crashing of hearts there was no one to notice that the pistols were immediately quiet. But an order rang out, sharp and foreign in intonation. Then oars were heard in the water. On the road itself there was a clash of movement, beating further and clashing more feebly as the seconds passed. There were no voices. The owlers fought in silence, grimly. Once a whip cracked. And again a man screamed, high-pitched and dreadful. The plunging horses were already at a distance. 'The sabres are out,' muttered Manley.

Round the curve of the wall the rout went, fading on the wind. The night and the sea sound roared their repeating scale again when the surprise was over. Within another minute the hasty stroke of oars was lost. It was finished now, for good or ill.

Manley and Ellesdon began to move along the road again, treading heavily and without disguise. At two hundred paces the marks showed, cut and turn and stricken stone. At two hundred and fifty they came upon the body of a militiaman humped against the wall, one arm dragging backwards in the road. King and Chidwick showed a light a few yards ahead, enlarging the pale rim of vision to take in the scudding lines of sea. On the other side of the wall was the moving counterpart of this, the spirit of the stopped shadow, the dancing exit and entry of death, going and coming under the wind. 'Nothing to show this way,' said King as he came up. Manley turned the body over. 'Know him?' he asked.

Ellesdon looked closely at the mottled face. The beard was grey and draggled with dust. He shook his head. Richard King peered over his shoulder, finally bending down to lift off the stones the cold underside of the fallen cheek. 'James Boyd, one-time officer of the landguard,' he said, 'of late schoolmaster in Folkestone. I knew him for a strong man when he was young.'

'He died by sabre-cut,' muttered Ellesdon. The coat over the left shoulder was sodden with blood and cut deep by the collar-bone. 'From behind, a stroke from behind.'

'God's truth! The one true Englishman!' cried King, swinging the lantern in a dangerous excitement.

'What mean you?' . . . 'I mean the one man not of the owling party. That was no Frenchman's work. The blow were impossible from the road.' The force of the discovery carried King into the centre of the little group.

'But the militia . . .' protested Manley, striving for composure and time to think.

'Have driven the owlers into Sir Robert Guilford's haven, whence they may depart unhindered, do what we may,' finished

Ellesdon. 'I would I had been in the Warren with Underwood. He is either dead or without friends or enemies that he need dream of. And this poor soul here would take no dissuasion, doubtless, and is dead for very honesty.' His voice was low and bitter.

'Captain Jordan shall hear something to ill effect,' said Manley, braving the blow with his teeth. His back was straight towards London again, the wall of achievement firm to his heels and the fringing danger fixed with a centrifugal eye. The light no longer beat into his face but seemed to issue from it like a slowly revolving lamp.

Ellesdon turned away, tall and impervious. 'If you find not he has been called to Dover this day on urgent business and the muster-roll be not burned,' he said sarcastically from the darkness. The circle had contracted, leaving only Manley within the lantern's ring, vexedly feeling the shortening arm. King and Ellesdon were visible still as a sort of nearer stiffness among the sedge at the road's verge, harsh as the stones of the kingdom. Chidwick alone was a little forward.

'The Frenchies buy the wool and the men, all who dunna see the light,' he said ingratiatingly.

Out over the sea another lamp winked mockingly twice.

A Night for the Curing

~

It was getting on the end of October. Not that one could readily distinguish that month from any other up there on the moor by Y Gât. When night came down pricked with red, it set tongues about the huddle of woollen mills on the shelve of the land westwards. But more often it picked the grey unfolded blanket off the shoulders of day with a sudden twitch, sending a little flurry through the grasses and bundling everything out of sight with irritable haste. Between these unceremonious visits the moor sprawled dull and hoggish, working a short year for the hands of man and a long year on the soul.

On the nearer edge of this plateau lived a few squatters, left there exhausted by the neap tide of poverty. The moor had collected them, as the last strand might do shells or desperate swimmers. Each survivor in his first grasping moments had built a shack or a cottage and stuck there, limpet like. The buildings stood singly, disarmingly, where the builders had dared to pinch out a yard or two by the discovered roadside. Few of them had more than one storey and fewer still in the years since they had clambered into existence had seen enlarged the little rectangle of tillage around their walls. In them lived labourers from the valley farms, a carpenter or two, even a wheelwright. These men held precariously to the lodgement of their life, and bred without thought or hope. Their thoughts grew out of the soil and wormed back into it again, seeking cover in the few inches above the rock, ashamed and yet constant. Spare and black the squatters were, crying for little once they had parted the teeth of hunger.

To the east, where the moor fell away gradually into broken ground and gorse covered the scarps of forgotten quarries, three cottages had settled humbly upon the same incline, half a field's width from one another. The lane which served them began broadly enough from the high road but lost heart and dwindled into a series of patches in the grass before it reached them. Only the hedges continued past them, acknowledging the further slope and the dull memory of the climb. On this October day a butcher's van was planted stubbornly across the beaten space between the hedge and the low door of the nearest cottage. From somewhere in the rough garden came an agony of squealing. Methusalem Morris was having his pig killed, and Jones the butcher was up from Cwrt Bailey on purpose. It was the custom in that still country, where the least improvident of the squatters kept in their hearts the remembered hospitality of better days, to rear a pig or two against the winter. The ritual of killing was followed, time beyond mind, by the distribution to the neighbouring cottages of pieces of pigmeat, cut from the carcase before curing. It was a custom that only fools and pagans had thought of slighting, and they but once. In that still country it was not good to be alone in spirit, not when a little compliance would make a path across the field and bring a hail or two out of the lengthening dusk. There was the gratitude too, elaborated by generations of practice, when the pigmeat was presented, the fry for supper, and the comfortable providence of future return in kind. No, it was not good to be alone, to throw away the fellowship of poverty. Only a fool or a man with a new knife would be at it.

That was why Jones the butcher was up special, and at a bit of inconvenience too. For him it was always inconvenient. Annoyance was part of his job. People said he had practised getting red in the face so that he could look like a butcher. When he was a boy up at the Hall he was quite pale, they said. But just now he was too busy to show his anger special.

Inside the shed at the back the squealing broke into a last coughing. The stillness came back at the corrugated walls like an arrested wave, and the long grasses stepped stealthily a pace nearer.

'Mr Morris bach, see you let this hang a good long while before cutting it now.'

Morris nodded and clasped and unclasped his hands uncertainly. The butcher was too busy with the entrails to look round. Had he done so none of his experience with dead animals would have helped him greatly in the reading of this live one. For through the motion of the man behind him ran the whole chase of tragedy. He sagged and stiffened, circled and deployed, crooked his neck and reached bolt upright, all in the space of one normal emotion. Execration, anxiety and cunning followed each other over his face like shadows over the stubble. His eyes ran shallow and deep by turns. Within the shed and the narrower limits of the bone he pulled the nerve-ends of tension to him.

Now and again, when the butcher paused to take up the dead pig's grunting, Methy stopped short. In the half-light from the door his face looked dark enough to be the past unveiled. Not an old man yet, he was broad of head and his skin was stretched tight over the cheek-bones. Little had run his way from the stream of life, but what he had seen he had dammed for the sake of the high vein of vanity in his heart. At school he had cheated, not for advancement, but for the fun of outwitting everybody. As a young man he had been taken with a fever in the fields more than once. It was good, he thought, to lie in bed and listen to the anxious wrangling about him on the other side of the wall. In middle life he slipped cleverly out of the shackles of his mother's heart and learned at last how to deceive himself. Then there was no one left. He lived alone with his many selves, unsure of any of them. One part of him was out-tricking another every day, leaving behind a chaos of indecision. He did not know any longer which self was the most machiavellian: every day a file of blunderers overbore each other's plans and passed again, unwanted and irreplaceable. They were parading now, each in the disguise he fancied, but not one of them made the entrance he was looking for.

The knife-blade drew a long line from neck to rump and the butcher paused a moment in approbation. Methy stopped too and tensed his knees. His eyes grew calm and narrow as he came in upon the tack he needed.

'Un bach yw e',' he said. 'He's a very little one.' The butcher looked up, surprised. 'Nage, Mr Morris, not at all. He'll keep you in pigmeat a supper or two and in bacon a good bit of the winter, if you will be careful.'

Methy did not move. 'From by here he do look a very little one, anyway,' he persisted, determined to fight on the ground he had chosen.

The butcher's face hung full-blooded over the carcase. His hands were dyed yellow with its draining. Irascibility beat like a pulse in his head.

'From by where, mun? Don't be talking so daft. From by where you're standing he looks as big as he do by here. All's the same both ways round. He isn't keeping more meat on one side than he is on the other.'

The mounting blood had broken in a froth of wit. Methy was glad of it without caring for its cause and let the wave run back again, light-headedly.

'Ie wir, un bach yw e': gyda bod ei ben e'n dod mae'i gwt e'n dod. As soon as his head appears, his tail comes.' And he laughed, ingratiatingly.

The butcher suddenly put down the knife. His free hand shut tight upon the urge to shout. When he spoke it was after an interval of seconds. His voice was quiet, reasonable. 'Here is as tidy a little pig as anyone could wish, and here you are, moaning away at him. Mr Morris bach, talk some sense.' Do what he would, aggravation had begun to grate like sand in his words. He paused for a new thought to get its hold on him. 'What for all this song now anyway, Mr Morris? Are you not sending for me special all the way from Cwrt Bailey? Is it for me, this bit of complaining? What is it you are after?' His red face lowered onto his shoulders like a shut box. But the mind behind it lay open, waiting.

Methy was suddenly conscious of the other's narrow scrutiny. He had let loose a bungler after all. The trick was not with him. There was no sense in antagonising the butcher. Not for that had he started the game. No indeed. Sudden with anxiety, he stretched out both hands with the ingenuous gesture of a child smoothing the fur of a ruffled animal.

'Mr Jones bach, indeed I am very grateful to you. Don't you be angry now. Don't you be angry. I'll be telling you what is in my mind straight, isn't it?' As the soft speech reached the butcher, Methy drew back the anxiety in his hands and moved nearer the door of the shed. The imperfect light left a dark pool in his cheek. 'A poor man I am, Mr Jones, as you are knowing. A poor man. Now there is Sara Jones Pelican and John Havard Tyisaf, good people both and neighbours of mine, but much better off than me, mun. Much better off. But indeed they will be expecting a bit of my poor little pig, a bit for each of them. And me not able to find enough money to go down these three years past to the sea for Dydd Iau Mawr. Poor I am, Mr Jones, that is it.'

His cheek-bones drew the light out of the failing sky. The whining monotone of poverty quavered a little and sank. The butcher's eyes, straining away from the luminous ridge of the face before him, fixed on the shadowed wall to his right. In the breeze that was springing up a cobweb shivered, hanging by a single thread from the lintel. He watched it intently. It would break at any moment. It must. If not the wind, then Methy Morris's head at that height . . . Yes, it would break. The butcher, unimaginative as he was, heaved with sudden relief. He was too short for it to touch him. The question when it came, as he was sure it would, could not be the same now. It lay in his choice, not the spider's.

The shining ridge of the face was losing some of its light. The strain was gone from the butcher's eyes and the edge from the other's whining. 'Give Sara Jones the head,' he was muttering, 'and Havard Tyisaf the trotters, it will be the last year's fry that I will be tasting for my supper of nights. Yes indeed, the last year's. And me a poor man, Mr Jones, a poor man.'

His head sank like a stone on his breast and lolled sideways a little, oddly. The chance sun of the moor struck him below the cheek-bone, brimming in through the doorway, filling the charlatan's tale with passion. For a moment the cheek was a pool of pig's blood with poor men swimming in it. Then the shaft shut off as suddenly as it had come. The shed seemed cold. The tale of the moor was close to the telling and the question struggled for lips to speak it.

The mind of the butcher knew its shape. He was in earnest to be going. Out of the shed now, with a hand on the door of the van, he was at bay with his answer.

The tale moved on with a new spurt of passion. 'What am I to do then, Mr Jones? What am I to do?' The trick in it was still trapped in the corner of the mouth. 'Will you be saying nothing?'

The butcher slowly got into the driving seat, affecting to consider the point. When he spoke, he had had time to persuade unpleasantness to wait its occasion.

'Well, see here Mr Morris, say you the pig is stolen. My van is here in the lane, plain to see. Mrs Jones Pelican will know I am up. No good to say I was not. Say you the pig is stolen, mun.'

'Stolen?' There was aggrieved surprise in Methy's voice, and the alarm of discovering a fool within the secret. 'But who will be believing it? The pig is in my shed and the pig is stolen. Who will be believing it? Who would be stealing from me here on the moor? The pig might have died with me now, if you had not come, but how can the pig be stolen?' He twisted the handle of the van door to and fro with his words, pressing the metal into his disappointment. 'No no Mr Jones bach. No indeed. Help from you I am needing.'

Across the space of the window glass the secret of the pig found no rest. Its blood stirred on the butcher's hands and beat hidden in his cheek. The patience of his tone had taken guile from the thickening sky.

'Say you the pig is stolen, Mr Morris. Take him indoors by you and hang him from a beam in the bedroom behind a bit of cloth. Leave him in the shed for tonight, to settle a bit first. Then take him in first thing.'

'But how will I be telling Sara Jones Pelican?' Methy protested, his anxiety rising to the top in a bubble of anger. 'She will be laughing. Mister Morris bach, she will say, there's funny you are with your little jokes.' The truth was a scum on his words and clung to the sides of his tale unnoticed. 'She will laugh, I tell you. My pig is stolen, Mrs Jones fach. O darro no. She will be laughing me back to the house again.'

The butcher's words came quietly round the corner into the wind of argument and tacked into it for a moment. The cleaver lay still on the floor of the van. In the red hand was only temptation. 'Look you then, Mr Morris, I will be up in the morning on my way to Carmarthen for the market. If you will be at the end of the lane I will stop the old van. About seven it will be. And then you shall be telling me the tale. See if you look like the pig is stolen, Mr Morris bach. See if you are shouting loud enough.'

The insinuation came up cold under Methy's shaken confidence. He struggled to thrust it down with a denial.

'O I can shout, don't worry. There is a look with me at times like I have lost fifty pigs. But not for Sara Jones. Not for her, no. When I am dead she will be digging me up to see. She will not believe. And there it is, Mr Jones.'

The sun was gone and with it the hope of the pig that died accidental. The butcher spoke with the authority of the coming dark, overwhelming what was before.

'Mr Morris, you must try. Your pig is stolen or you give a piece to Mrs Jones. It is as you wish.' He was in haste to be gone. The discreet blood had suffered the fool enough and its beat was a warning to his guile. 'To Carmarthen I am going tomorrow and if you will be at the lane end I will stop. But say I was not here I will not. Choose you.' He worked the starter. The van roared and began to move.

Methy still gripped the door handle like the scheme of today. It was torn from him before his grip changed. 'Seven o'clock you said, isn't it? Mr Jones, seven o'clock, isn't it?' He was still shouting as the van scattered the gravel fifty yards down the lane. In the droop of his head as he went back through the gate was the unhappiness of a hundred plans all cleverer than this, frustrated and too late. Jones butcher was twp. Stolen, it was hopeless. All the other blunderers shouted that it was. But Jones butcher was gone, with his daft ideas. And with him choice.

In the shed he prodded the hanging carcase with a musing finger. From it a slow drop hung, pendant under the disappointment of the heart. Methy turned to go. In the doorway the wind-blown web swung out from the post, caught in the dark hair and was carried away with its going.

In the night that followed two shadows came over the fields by Gelli and lifted the latch of the shed. Methy Morris, with shut eyes and brain swaying with the infinitesimal to-fro of coming satisfaction as the pig climbed to the curtains of his bed, heard nothing. The engine of the van on the high road was silent. There was only the faint click of the falling latch and the spider thrown down from his latest thread.

Long before six Methy was lighting the fire in his yellow papered kitchen. Early they were then in the country and up before the mist lifted off the coarse grass of the moor or the first dark shadow of the Pelican fell upon the lane hedge eastward. His mind simmered faster than the kettle, with anger for its hob. In his heart an insistent knocking was reminding him of what he had to do that morning. Round the kitchen it went, knocking for an explanation. Knocking. Knocking in his head. He stopped. 'Well, there's sense,' he muttered. 'No no, Methy bach, no explaining. Shout out. Let Sara find out the story after. Mrs Jones fach, indeed I don't know. The pig was in the shed . . . The pig . . . The pig *is* in the shed. Fetch him in, Methy bach, fetch him in. Into the bedroom with him, my boy. Behind the bit of curtain on the beam.' As he crossed the bare patch of ground between the house and the shed the mist lifted a little over the lane. Smoke stood up from the chimney of the Pelican. Sara Jones and her dark finger were beginning their accusation. No time to lose.

He opened the door of the shed and stood bewildered. The empty corrugation wavered across his mind and all but drowned the thought of his coming. Then it flashed again on the next crest. The pig was gone. Methy did not move, grappling with his fear. Had he then, had he then taken it into the bedroom after all? There had been something, yes, above his dreams all night. Something. His body made a sudden dash after the terrified brain, scattering sweat through the kitchen and wasting strength on the curtain beyond the bed. There was no need to stare. The beam was empty. The pig really was gone.

Methy could not think. He could not think. One part of him stood there wide open, aghast. The other tottered in futile persistence between the shed and the bedroom.

All at once they synchronised, mind and body and the other little scurrying selves caught in the vast defeat. They roared in unison, so that the drops were shaken from the morning webs. Out went the wounded spider with no thread but rage unspun. Out went the spider, quick for succour to the hand that broke the heart of his building. Quick to the lane end at seven. The lane end at seven.

It was still nearer six as he ran on, gravel crunching underfoot. The main road was wet like a stream in the increasing light. Mist pressed down on its farther ends and behind them the promise of movement was muffled. Not a sound came to Methy at the lane end, lifting his feet restlessly out of the catching mud. In the house the kettle boiled unheard and blew a fierce spout off the fire of former intentions.

Minutes passed. Hours, it seemed. Methy felt in his brain the worm without end. His features set silently into dolorous cast. The pig, morose and spiteful, trotted from the shed to the bedroom and back. Out and round the Pelican it went. She'll never believe me, won't Sara. But the pig is gone, woman, it is indeed. Here comes Jones butcher now.

'Hey Jones, Mr Jones, the pig is gone.' All Methy's face welled into his eyes. His words were spun thick with misery and caught in the net of his throat. 'The pig is gone,' he wept.

'Good morning, Mr Morris bach.' The butcher was leaning out of the van. The underdone cut of his face rose above a clean collar, bland as Sunday dinner. 'O very good, very good indeed. Mrs Jones Pelican will be sure to believe you. Indeed you are good, Mr Morris bach.'

For a moment there was a stop to sorrow. Methy's face, already swollen, went dark with anger. With his last breath he choked back the tide of swearing. What came out after the struggle into the colder air was small and thin and miserable as before. 'But I tell you the pig is gone, Mr Jones. Not acting for you I am. No, no. The pig is gone. He is stolen. He is gone from the shed.' Methy was swimming for the next word now.

The butcher was leaning out of the driving window, heavy with admiration. 'There, there, Mr Morris bach, steady does it now. You'll be hurting yourself, you will, if you are not careful. Steady now, mun,' he said with authority, as Methy caught at the handle of the door in a frenzy of tears. The pressure of the unyielding metal brought back the folly of yesterday and the two miseries, mingling inextricably in his mind, tripped up his thoughts and stopped him. The butcher's momentary apprehension passed. 'Steady,' he went on in a smoother tone. 'Go you to Mrs Jones Pelican. Now quick, before your face is changing. She will be believing anything you say. She will be that sorry for you, my boy, that it will be cawl and breakfast you are getting. Indeed you are a good one. There's acting for you, duw, duw.'

'I am not acting, Mr Jones. The pig is gone complete,' muttered Methy, unable to find his moment of anger again. The tears had run out of him, and pride too. Only the little struggling clevernesses remained, washed up on the flats of disbelief.

'That will do now, Mr Morris.' The butcher's throat was full-blooded again and the engine roared a little with the opening of the throttle. 'Go you to the Pelican like I am saying. Cawl there will be for you if Sara's heart is not in the quarry. Go on now.'

As the van began the rise towards Carmarthen the blood of the pig went on to sacrifice. On the face of the moor it had dried before dawn.

Methy turned obediently to the lane, still wet with diverging tears. The mist was lifting altogether and lay in wisps, comfortingly, in the trees. In front a small cloud came up with the sun's first fingers. Every minute Methy expected a snout to it, but it came on, flushed and fussy, with ribbons flying from the cap. Its voice was the voice of Sara Jones Pelican and its eyes were credulous. 'Yes indeed, Mr Morris bach, I know. The pig is stolen with you. There's sorry I am.' Methy was suddenly comforted. He walked on more strongly, catching at the ribbons as he went.

The Palace

~

Mr Burstow was a Devon man, though not notably acquainted with the Seven Seas. In fact, almost the only thing he had in common with Drake and Hawkins was the predilection of his detractors for his surname. Somehow it was unthinkable that he should be Jack or Reginald like other men. There was an unalterable meniality about him which permitted the mighty without difficulty to condescend but left him exposed to ridicule as the visible remnant of some sort of suspended hierarchy. It was not very apparent who could be beneath him, and yet his manner desired respect rather than ease or familiarity. His career, needless to say, had not been one of meteoric success.

The best that could be said was that an addiction to overalls had made him look as though he liked work. And so he did, if only to escape his wife. There was a wishfulness about his rolled sleeves and hurrying boots that had carried him into a number of jobs from which his rambling face, mounted unnaturally above a collar, would have debarred him. He had few claims to beauty. They had kept a snack-bar together, his wife and he, as employees of an enterprising Italian, and a great red burn like a dessert-spoon on the back of his left hand, the more obvious because his forearms were consistently bare, was the chief memento of this episode in his career. He had been hospital porter and caretaker at the Constitutional Club, too, in his time, but a certain inability to forget his position or merely to capitalise it had always denied him promotion. Now he had come to the Palace as gatekeeper, after a brief and uncommunicative interview with the Ministry of Works in Bristol.

Mr Burstow had sandy sad-looking hair, interlarded with evidences of his recent employments. The look of dissipation that supported it was one more injustice of which he was quite unconscious. When accosted suddenly or by a superior he blew his nose once like a rather unwarlike trumpet and kept the handkerchief handy. If the occasion merited a continuance of this excitability, his nose disappeared altogether in a cascade of mutterings and the handkerchief remained, a flag of alarm, masking the fall. Only the production of certificates testifying to his undoubted integrity could have convinced the doubtful officials in Bristol that the raddled little man, wearing his coat that day in the manner of a particularly uncooperative clothes-horse, would serve their purpose. Mrs Burstow, who had accompanied him, was small and pallid. Both mind and body were ailing.

When the couple saw the Palace first it was a dank January day, with the leaves sopping under the wheels of the open lorry that carried their few chattels. The long journey into Wales and the lowering sky had kept their hearts down, out of sight of the tips and the chip-shops, down in a kind of grey confinement with the rubberised matting and the angles of the gear-box. They had not spoken to any of the natives of the country, except in a little chocolate-coloured pull-in the other side of Newport, and Mr Burstow was of the opinion that they had still been in England then. Once the driver had leaned out to ask the way. They could not hear the reply, but he had seemed satisfied. Mostly, however, the crossroads were clearly posted and they drove at speed.

A narrow Norman tower rose at them in the dusk like a mute swan and they veered away to the left down a lane closely shadowed by trees and cold with the sound of mud. A few hundred yards and the lane dipped, marshalled itself over a bridge and under what remained of a stone arch, and finally lost all identity in an intercursus of soil and water between a high wall and broken hedges. In front and slightly to the right a noticeboard leaned apologetically on the arm of a projecting wall. 'To the Palace' it indicated from its reclining position and pointed round the angle eastwards. Beside the intercursus two palm-trees, swathed to a height in a frail of decomposing leaves, lived at the top an existence of gesture and abandonment, like muezzins in a strange land, unaware of silence and a soil without response. Everywhere to the right the high wall shut out the light. A few yards around the corner was disclosed a gate, on which a bell on a spring, of the kind which formerly tintinnabulated in the kitchens of great houses, stood upright expectantly. Low outbuildings and part of a yard could be seen. Mr Burstow pushed at the gate gingerly, the bell at once challenging on a high inquisitorial note. 'Here,' he shouted. 'You can bring the lorry up to this gate and back 'er in. There's no turn-round.' The driver already had his sidelights on, and the wheels began to churn in the mud. They had arrived.

Weeks later Mr Burstow came to think of the bell with a degree of equanimity. It did not ring often, during the early days of the week scarcely at all, and on Saturdays at infrequent intervals. Always it maintained the same calculated inquisition, so that he began to look upon it, still perhaps with an element of reserve, but with the increasing approval that a man in authority extends to an efficient underling. Had he been better used to a hierarchy of power whose immediate pinnacle was himself he would have warmed even further towards the bell. But he was not yet sure either of his wish or of its absoluteness. He was accustomed to making reservations, most of all about himself.

There was not really a great deal to do. That was one of the serious disadvantages of the place. 'There's a plan of the buildings on a window-ledge in the Camera,' he told visitors, and discharged any further duties with the sale of a twopenny booklet. Privately he thought the shilling he took per head more than the place was worth. Nobody stayed long, though few expressed any positive disappointment. Possibly they had not expected much. As he looked ruminatively down the list of names pencilled in the gatebook, he could see that few, if any, of the comers had travelled a distance. The Palace was out of the way, almost off the map. And the locals, he knew, had paid their fine for the privilege of looking him up and down as much as for any belated interest they were fostering for an unneighbourly ruin. He did not complain of that. They were harmless enough. Indeed, the burr in their talk was at times not unlike that of his own west-countrymen. No, he did not complain of that. Only that their coming did not occupy, at best, more than half an hour of his day.

Mrs Burstow had insisted, early on, that he buy a cow. The animal had been lodged, regardless of sentiment, in the fallen sacristy whose open gable-end gave on to the field adjoining, and its entry into the main buildings barred by raising a gate across the gap between the chapel and the north wall of the Old Hall.

Milking occupied a little of his time thereafter. It was he, however, who had insisted on digging a patch of the levelled bank across the lane from the gate and calling it a garden. Too late came the realisation that he had made a mistake, a strategic mistake of the first magnitude. The patch was in full view and cry of the kitchen window. Whenever Mrs Burstow tired of her own pity and preferred wrath, the slightest variation, he knew, from the stoop of a man whose mere existence was at her mercy would bring down the window with a clack like a descending guillotine. Often enough, as it was, his posture was insufficient, and a summons to some petty meniality indoors followed. He had chosen badly, of that there was no doubt. The host of seedlings offered no cover and as full broccoli promised none. Always there would be the head and trunk of his offending.

In the days before realisation came he had never really bothered to examine the Palace, except in the most superficial sense. Once he had satisfied himself of the existence of a plan of the buildings, displayed in the greenswarded room called the Camera towards which all visitors were first directed, he troubled no further. Indeed, there was cause for the poor opinion implicit in the offhandedness of departing sightseers. It wasn't much of a place. And what there was of it might have continued a matter of the utmost indifference to him had not the drag of an unusually long quarrel made impossible the mere thought of mulching and hoeing on the bank opposite. His nose began to run dispiritedly. The knifelike drop of the window was hoisted above his torn nerves, a ceremonial of shock through which, inevitably, he would live, the more awful for it. He dared not turn his back. Sidling away from the thought he wandered off, round the sacristy and in at the gate, dully and without intention. Scholarship had never been his, nor History. Drab accounts of sieges and seafights had never made him feel any particular relation to Drake. As he sat down in an embrasure in the Camera he had no more than the faintest sense of comfort afforded by a shield of buildings, whose rooflessness left his heart open to impulses of sun and charity.

For a long time his eyes were fixed moodily on the wall immediately opposite. Unseeing, their gaze dropped to the turreted worm casts climbing among the grass. It was very wet. A great part of the room was beyond the sun's reach. Presently a chill came out of the embrasure and embraced him. He rose, stiffly, to be confronted with the fact of return, with the absolute necessity of the garden on the bank and the window clack dropping on his shoulders. No, not yet. Not yet. Without curiosity, he began to mount a narrow stairway whose foot showed in one corner of his consciousness. Neither floor nor ceiling remained to the chamber which had evidently risen above the original Camera and the gallery which served it had crumbled too. It was not very apparent where the stairs *could* now lead. He mounted, wondering under his oppression at the narrowness of the turning crack and the nimbleness of other days. A wooden ladder of recent date bridged a gap where the masonry had disappeared, and a sharp turn-away from a fallen-in garderobe brought him to the roof-walk, still intact on three of the four sides and protected outwards only by a low castellation. The boy in him raised his head and began to delight, kicking a way through the clumps of valerian that everywhere lifted up the ancientness of the stones, feeling the width of the air about his ears. A couple of smoothed round chimneys, tapering upwards from the Great Hall as from a nether kiln, jumped up ahead to shadow him from the sun. They were old and yet obviously makeshift, grown-up children about the place. He was amused. Deliberately he stopped and peered down into the gaping mouth of another chimney whose pursed stone lips had fallen apart. His whole mood had changed. About him the sun shone, a little punily in the March afternoon and yet confident of growth and health to come. Down in the field the geometrical foundations of old army huts crowded up to the great wall like lesser tombs of the pyramid age, as rased and empty as their purpose. On one of them stood Flower, the black and white Friesian, careless of impropriety. Wider still there was visible a distinct boundary, not always continued in hedge and wall, but shadowed and unchanging: the edge of the old demesne. West-ward the gatehouse stood up challengingly by itself in the meticulous kitchen garden of a nearby mansion. More southerly ran the old wall of the Palace, indented with chutes and garde-robes, following the line of the stream that simpered openly among the trees, losing itself among curious humps of earth-covered building and smiling away into shallows that had been fishponds. There was something curiously satisfying about the prospect. Neglect and disappointment and decay were every-where, and yet under the sun it was March. Buds would break and towers shoot again in a month or two. What the season had stripped was not supplanted for ever but lay alive and indecorous under the soil and in the spawning river. The Palace, the concrete rectangles and Flower had some perfectly right relation to each other, congruous and unaesthetic. Mr Burstow, who was not in the least aesthetic himself, began to feel right too. Stock-still on his roof-walk, he was lost in an inner hierarchy, fixed and intransigent, yet changing by the very day. Suddenly he was very happy.

It would be folly to pretend that this mood persisted indefinitely or even returned to him frequently. And yet it grew dependable. From tiff and trial he made his way towards it, guessing the direction and more readily arriving. On steel-grey days the boundary of the demesne looked from the roof of the Camera as though it had been etched into the earth, separating with inveterate edge the Palace and its ordered relationships from a sprawling world. His garden was outside it, across the outer road. He went there less and less. It began to irk him unspeakably that the outbuilding which was his house and contained his wife should have been permitted within the barrier. It was as though the inquisitorial bell had grievously failed in its duty, shutting the gate after the enemy had come in. But from the Palace roof, in and among the chimneys, he could minimise the error, pinning it down to one toad-like spot on the fringe of existence. As April gleamed fitfully along the southern wall that overlooked the river, the worms in the grass floor were casting busily and the fishponds moved with promise. His heart was in the Camera and, like the secret it was, grew out towards the spring.

Mrs Burstow had begun to weaken. The life in her that leaped only in chiding failed and fell tired increasingly as she saw her husband fixed and impervious. He did not answer back. Indeed, he no longer heard. She did not understand, and her not understanding weighed on her like a tombstone. Coming to the Palace would be the death of her, she said, and still did not understand. At times she crawled out to the garden on the bank and bent over it miserably. Her husband never touched it now. He spent half the day on the roof-walk, shading his eyes and watching the distance. As though watching were his very life.

What worried his wife increasingly, during the shortening periods when her pains let her care what happened, was Mr Burstow's changed demeanour towards visitors. He no longer bothered with twopenny pamphlets. The pile was gathering dust in the house. There was something challenging, too, in his manner of late: he followed each infrequent sing-song of the bell with a hoarse shout and a rush towards the gate. The ridiculous aspect of his slight blue overalled figure was hidden now in stridency and menace. It seemed as though a positive effort of will was required to pocket the shilling and proceed with the brief formalities of instruction. One day he took a man by the throat who did not understand his challenge. A moment later he apologised with the old wealth of nose-blowing and the matter was hushed up. But rumours spread to the village and the bell rang even less frequently.

In May Mrs Burstow died. He followed her coffin to the church with the swan's tower, and rushed back along the greening lane to the intercursus, fierce and quick in his new possession. The palm-trees, newly out of their frail, no longer looked alien, and on the high wall was a dance of sword-frond and sunlight. He banged the gate to and fronted round to it, joyously. The circle was complete.

That same evening, when the copses on the far hill were as motionless in the swaying dusk as a chant that has ended, there was evidence of that completion. For some time past, as dark was falling upon the grasses of late April and early May, he had had a sense of something happening just before, only the barest instant before, he had looked that way. It might have been thought the intrusion of an eyelash only but for the answering bound of blood in him more vital than a thousand eyes. Buds were shooting, the valerian on the wall was bunching out across the void, and the whole Palace was quick with fresh intention. All this had been growing naturally and without command. But this evening, he knew, was different. From the roof-top he caught a glint of metal by the fishponds and the lower wall above the river was chinking with people. He turned to the stairhead and stopped, experiencing no surprise. A man was coming up, at speed. A man with a flat cap and a torn half-tanned jerkin, who shouted at him as he came. Words and accent were strange and yet he understood perfectly. The gatehouse? My Lord of Essex expected? The fellow struck at him as he passed and swore, not very prettily. Mr Barstow, full of contrition, sprang down the steps and ran determinedly past the garderobe and along the gallery above the Camera, making for the wall that would lead him to the gatehouse. The Devereux, like father like son, brooked no idleness in their servants. The sky in the west was a deep orange, and the bars of the night were nearly up.

It was a full day almost before they found him, the weal from the snack-bar urn livid along his outstretched arm, lying face downwards on the sward of the Camera. His overalls showed a congruous blue against the live green of the floor and there was no sign of fear or malice on his face. But for the ceaseless lowing of the Friesian, heavy with milk, he would have lain longer.

'Chap from Devon,' they said. 'Never settled down in these parts. Wife's death must have finished him.'

The church with the swan's tower received him willingly enough, though it was a formality to mourn. Over at the Palace Flower cropped unconcernedly from the sacristy to the concrete foundations opposite and back again. In and about the grass the worms were casting busily, aware of the continuance of the sun.

The Eleven Men of Eppynt

~

Nine days there had been no mails in Eppynt. The drift against Matti Jenkins's cottage had taken a jump overnight: it sat there now like a huge protective child with white arms stealing round the chimney and the black uppers of its boots dirtying the yard. Old Blackbird the mare stood recklessly out on a cliff of snow, the hedge of Cae Coch lost and under contempt. Mistress and servant, so long at ease, had come to look strangely during the last days.

Matti herself was not worried. In her slow purposeful way she had shovelled most of the fall out of her little yard and now stood, like a sack of potatoes in the bottom of a trench, looking solidly at the rest. Lumpish she was, with sloping shoulders and face flat like the pastryboard on which she had kneaded for upwards of forty-nine years, but in look neither frightened nor womanish. The narrow cwm her home, the dockish fields too steep for any tractor yet, and the chilling rain that beat down crop and spirit wiled in the softnesses of summer, these were not answered by grace and tenderness. There had been no help for Matti many years, except an odd day or two from Jack Gunter with the warts on his cheek-bone who came, never before the third time of asking, to scythe the bit of orchard she had. A ready bend to her back there was and a good deal of digging in her past. She was not easily confounded.

None the less, this was a bitter winter. Never before had Cops y Gwdihw sifted up white above the trunks. Never before had Matti seen the bark of the blackthorn in the hedge peeled and nibbled green and yellow-white against the interstices of snow. In the wired garden of Bronheulog not a stalk nor a sprout was above ground. Over the top came the rabbits from their mountain of ice, over the trench Mr Soul, the Commander's gardener, had dug as a last defence, and though every morning there was a slack bundle of fur at the bottom that the dog worried for a moment and then left still, the long enclosure looked as though it had been levelled by some desperate machine.

Down the valley it was the same, they were saying. Llwyniago that stood by itself under a fifty foot drop had disappeared altogether. Soldiers had taken food to the schoolhouse at Erwood, farther east. And on Thursday week, before the road was quite closed, there was the news that the Merthyr train was fast in a drift and three days since it started. O the winter was bitter above the doors and colder than even the old women could remember. In the cwm was a strange shallowness and shapes like buried people. Snow was a beauty and a grave.

In Matti's eyes the clean and the unclean, the mounded trees, the hedge shoring the snowbank, the sopping yard, merged patiently. Long as a siege, or short as the fight of Llewelyn Olaf in the thicket, each danger was fixed in the day, tidied in front of her with a broom and piled firmly in proportion to await her ultimate dealing. So many steps on firm crust, one might say, so many lost to the waist and beside the path, over to the Wern for flour. There, clear enough, was this Saturday's preoccupation. At the Wern, of all places, down on the main road, should be some to spare. So beat the old heart of calculation, unburied in the new dimension.

It was a risk indeed, but not because of the hardship of snow. All Matti's thinking about the Wern was touched with the colour of contempt. And the subject of bread was not one on which she was easy spoken. For bread was baked no longer in the farmhouses of Eppynt. Gone was her grandmother's art, the iron crock of dough hidden in a raked red cavity roofed with wood and ungreyed coals. Crusty yellow bread they all remembered who were of age and tongues made mourning for it. But no hand moved towards its resurrection, not even Matti's, in the years before the snow. It was sufficient to remember and be contemptuous. Bread came now from the town, tougher from the tin and easier to hand, in the black and cream van of Thomas Brothers, 19 Wind Street. But the van had not reached Eppynt since the road was blocked. No farther than Dinas could the bread or the mails come now, and perhaps not as far as that. It was three days since there had been news, and now there was no more bread in Matti's house. The cows' yield was less and less because the feed was so poor. Over to the Wern must go Matti and her doubts, not really believing that Maggie Thomas, her head hanging dimly over Wild West magazines in the winter light, could have laid in the flour when *she* had not. But step down to the main road she must, her doubts going footless over the fields before her. Long before she arrived, breathless and bruised with leaving the path for a shoulder of snow, they had been asking questions of Maggie Thomas, peering in at the larder window, and getting as many answers as rungs there were up to the granary door.

'Jacob was telling me the minister's tree is down, neat as needlework between the house and the garage, not touching either. There's a blessing.'

Any tale, of trees or ministers or steers on the Bar 60, was equally a blessing to Maggie Thomas, her shock head now half out of the shed door, unable to fetch the paraffin she wanted for fear of breaking off the conversation. It needed an event of some sort, and if it were disastrous so much the better, to restore her to Eppynt and bring on a Saturday courage. When this ran down, as a man's memory of a football match runs down, there was no more need of the present or reason for action. Eating and sleeping excepted, of course, and the hour on Monday when she could expect Trevor Stamps with her weekly magazines. Maggie was born to heroism and outside of common sense.

'If there's no flour with you then, what are you going to do?'

Matti was not interested for more than a moment in the minister's escape. The Reverend Arwel Jones was a good and respected man, but plainly from his contours not one who had often called upon manna for his salvation. Nor had his sermon on the loaves and fishes ever seemed up to his best standard.

'How will Sam Evans's baby do with no milk, gel? Things are getting bad, whatever you say. Your brother John, what did he think now when he was in breakfast-time?'

'Oh, nothin' special. Only he was in a temper about three ewes he had dead up on the Mound.'

'Well, Maggie fach, you know I'm not one for worrying. But there's a bit of difference between using brains and just hoping, isn't it? Seems to me your brother John, Isaacs Cefn, and a few more of the young men should get into town before it's too late.'

Out of this germ sprang the journey. To Matti it was merely good sense, to Maggie a half-understood excitement, a rare opportunity for whipping up the boys and measuring them against her recurring appetite for danger. It made her proud to be a woman to see them fall short, and sad to be in Eppynt to see such poor figures of men.

To persuade them now, that was her bit. First her brother John, though first in no other sense than that with him she must begin. Stiff, hair going grey at the temples, good-looking till he opened his mouth, Maggie's brother John looked more like a soldier than a farmer. At least that likeness would need less qualification. Just now the snow had put him sadly out of countenance. Farming was a habit of existence to him, no more, and any unusual event could make his home a strange place as well as any journey.

First Maggie's brother John, first in the asking that is, though in replying he remembered his looks and kept his mouth shut. Then the boy from Pant. Jack Pant he was to everyone but Mr Jones the minister, whose insistence on calling him *Mister Jones* was no more than a point in his campaign for the higher status of the Joneses as a class. Jack Pant. Heavy as a bolster he was in the mornings, when dawn light crossed the cwm from Erwood way and it was a mile or more to the fields of Coygen, but ready for anything bar work by half past twelve. A jiffy, and he would cut you a stick from the stoutest hedge and point it heavily with a joke. Just now he was fit for Maggie's whistling. He could sit up and give the right answer too. A long way from the Bar 60 and only a boy of seventeen, but he was the part of Maggie that would set out through the snow and expect the cheering when he came back.

Maggie's brother John and Jack Pant. Maggie's brother John, Jack Pant and Lewis the Carbuncle. That was the order. Lewis was the third on Maggie's list since he happened up to the Wern for flour a little earlier than most: ordinarily she would not have lifted her head on his coming in. He was a married man with two children over five, but his name and reputation harked back nearly twenty years to his early teens. For, indeed, as carbuncles grow his had been prime, the best in the valley for many a day, handled and criticised by the most experienced judges from Llandefaelog to the last farm above Eppynt. But of this great era the nervous neck-held-high step was all he had kept. His appearance now was a disappointment, certainly among strangers where his name came in first. Thin and sallow, with plenty of skull beneath the skin, he looked what he was, a man worked out in early life, parcelled by will and a lengthening string of muscle.

Maggie's brother John, Jack Pant, Lewis the Carbuncle and Gunter Beili-bach. No connection with warts in this case, Jack Gunter being no nearer than a second cousin. But a big raw fellow with one eye down-dropped and a rumble like a gambo, fresh from waisting it in the upper pasture after his ewes and driven out at last from Beili-bach by a wife harassed about her children's food. That was Gunter. The more you saw of him, the less you knew. Whether his eyelid dropped from weakness or because his eye was like an auger in the wall, it was impossible to say. Wondering about this made his trundling talk go by almost unheard, and half-consciously he took the credit for a mysterious and unreasonable interest in his waistcoat buttons.

Maggie's brother John, Jack Pant, Lewis the Carbuncle, Gunter Beili-bach and Billo the Jumper. Last he should come in any company, whatever start was going. But fair mornings and before eleven o'clock, Billo had the voice of a man and the sound of a man coming. Up to the Wern he had shuffled like the others, the drop on the end of his nose threatening the spectrum and glory twitting the yellow edges of his moustache. A maternal uncle of his, who lived at Goytre, had once had a third in the National Hunt Cup, and since that was the first occasion recorded on which Billo, a week or two let into ankle-stranglers, had opened his teeth to boast, the Jumper he had been ever since. All in the course of justice, however, for his lips had rarely parted for any other purpose since. Billo ran after fame as others do butts, and was caught bending by every bus-stop. Not one sally in ten of his either got or deserved an answer. On this day of all days, however, he had chosen to come Wernwards dressed, ambiguously enough, in an old rusty jersey with a stretched polo collar that served his head like a meagre pig's on a vintner's plate. He looked vaguely cold and tusky.

Maggie's brother John, Jack Pant, Lewis the Carbuncle, Gunter Beili-bach, Billo the Jumper, Harry Evans Coygen, Joe and Ossie Francis the Allt-arnog boys, Trevor Williams the Post Office, Morgan the Agent and Cardi Morgan from Beili-brith. The last six came up in a bunch, looking as though no opinion had stuck to them. And since Maggie thought her best speeches, already tried on Jack Pant and Lewis, would hardly improve from them on, conversation was a bit shorter than under the first dispensation. They had to do the job without being persuaded.

There was a company then, at last. Eleven of them together, shaking their hides like dogs and saying nothing but listening to the women. They were patient and clever enough on the hill-slopes, all except Trevor Stamps and Morgan the Agent that is, but unaccustomed to decisions out of habit and across times.

'What you all standing around for? Time's getting on.' Matti angled her attack from the kitchen window giving on to the yard's east side. Closer tactics served Maggie's ends: she had taken to running in and out among them, worrying them individually, like a championship bitch with the last few seconds to go. She was not sure what sort of heroism she was expecting, that was the trouble. Her own excitement would have been higher if there were to be no bread and no flour at the Wern or anywhere in the valley till the snow cleared. There would be an opportunity to show them. But Matti had finished that with her talk about babies. No answering her flat face. So now it must be John or Jack Pant who had the chance. Her shock head bobbed in and out like an Eskimo's.

'John, John, mind you call at the Dot for some cakes as well. And Mam's medicine from Hope-Evans. Bottle's on the dresser ready. Mind you don't forget it now.'

The men, unsure of themselves, hung about near the kitchen door. Cardi Morgan had begun what looked like a day's work scratching the top of his head. Jack Pant, the only eager one of the lot, was playing with the black and white pup and growing a week nearer experience every time Maggie bobbed out under the bowed door. 'Sled's over by there,' said the Francis boys together. 'Easier to carry the stuff like, we thought,' said Ossie. They both looked very young.

'Don't need that darn thing. I could carry back enough bread for us all for weeks,' said Billo the Jumper, head bouncing off the plate with contempt. Nobody answered him.

Outside, the sun was threequarters round his red circuit already. It was getting on two o'clock. The snow looked dirty and unheroic, a less than worthy adversary here in the yard. But by the copse the swelling was strange and the bounds of knowledge were displaced.

'Did you hear about Llwyniago, mun?' said Trevor Stamps, stepping right through the crust at once and falling on every farmer's secret fear.

'Too much fuss about that, by half,' cut in Cardi Morgan, whose own holding was among the most isolated. 'Let's get on.'

This was the switch of hazel needed. 'Bye, Maggie.' They moved out of the yard. The snow powdered delicately in front of them on that part of the road where a good many had walked, down as far as the barn where the turning is for Coygen. After that it was difficult. The sled bounded on the snow lumps like a live thing, and once in a while caught Ossie, who was hauling it, a playful blow across the heels. He cursed freely. Apart from that, there was not much talking. Only the sniff, sniff of Billo bringing his dewdrop with him and earnest to keep it from the ground.

Three to four miles off they came to the place where Thomas's van had given up and backed out of a drift that lay like a fallen cloud just beyond the last of a line of elms. Four fingers of black ice pointed out of a central crater, in which a minute portion of the road's surface was visible. Half a mile on there was evidence of more vehicles, and the going became easy. Lewis the Carbuncle began to sing. A tune and he could no more than tip caps to each other, but he performed his salutations with tooth-grating zest. He was right through the first verse and chorus of 'Pack up your troubles' before the others realised what was the matter. Then Cardi Morgan, who *could* sing, set up in defence of his ears, and soon they were all at it, Jack Pant, Morgan the Agent, the Francis boys, Harry Evans Coygen, Trevor Stamps, Gunter and Billo the Jumper, Lewis cheerfully making room for them in the same octave. Even Maggie's brother John, forgetting his profile for a moment or thinking that Morgan the Agent, who was next to him, was not looking anyway, parted his lips a little.

And so they came in sight of the mountains, singing. Round a turn and past a hollybush in the high hedge fluffed with snow like the first sight at a children's party, and there were the Beacons hanging like a candelabra of snow lamps out of the sky, flushed with rose from the perfunctory sun. Over the tableland they hung, over the iced farms and stiffly-rutted roads, shadowed and detached from below like mountains in a dream, coming no nearer willingly than the castle of Ysbaddaden Chief Giant which hid Olwen of the White Trefoil. On came the company, a spattering on the white, lacking the magic of Arthur and the tongue of Merlin, but singing. Over the straight-up smoke of Brecon town in the sudden hollow, over against the mountains of enchantment, they came singing. Jack Pant, Lewis the Carbuncle, Gunter Beili-bach, Trevor Stamps, the Francis boys, Maggie's brother John, Harry

Evans Coygen, Morgan the agent, Cardi Morgan and Billo the Jumper, all singing, and the mountains over against them fleeced and shining out of a dream. 'She'll be riding six white horses when she comes' . . . The song was as coarse and lumpish as discarded sacks on the granary floor, and Olwen of the White Track put never a foot in their direction as they came down to Wind Street for bread. The mountain lamps began to go out one by one and the sun went redly on his journey round the Antipodes. The streets were shadowed and for a Saturday there were few people about. Snowflakes began to fall again, dallying on pavement and window-ledge like chickens edging in to roost.

In Thomas Brothers' there was protesting and describing. Outside stood the sled, right up against the black and cream van hackled about the tyres, and on them both were the flakes, soft and apologetic in their settling. Maggie's brother John, roused by the singing, was swinging his mam's medicine bottle like an Indian club because he said it reminded him. Jack Pant was juggling with three loaves and picking them out of the sweepings every time he thought the girl assistant had an eye in his direction. Fast in the arguing crowd was the appointed bargainer, Cardi Morgan, nagging the shillings onto the cold-veined counter like a bad harvest. 'Think I'm payin' for the whole damn lot, do you?' He looked alarmed and aggrieved. Joe and Ossie, both paid up, were sidling out, trying to look old enough for the side bar of The Bell. Lewis the Carbuncle was nowhere to be seen.

An hour later it was almost dark. Up the steep slope by the cathedral they heaved, seven of them, Jack Pant, Gunter, Evans Coygen, Cardi Morgan, Trevor Stamps and Joe and Ossie Francis, who had remembered it was *their* sled. Maggie's brother John had forgotten his mam's medicine after all, and Morgan the Agent had had to go down with him to see he got back. Further back still were Lewis the Carbuncle and Billo the Jumper, talking about one for the road and breeding from it. Up they came in three relays, striking fire and curses from the receding pavements, up into the Norman arch of night and the hummocky fields about Pontwillim. Plateau by day, range and crater after dark, so it was with the road. The darkness had a suggestion of mountains and a feeling of high command, inevitable and sheer. Gone was the white track of Olwen, gone the tune out of every throat. There was only the ridge of ice that carried the sled runners diagonally towards the ditch and rose across the most elementary purpose. Cardi Morgan nagged in a solemn undertone. Once Harry Evans, who was haulier on that stretch, slipped to his knees and the sled carried into him, a couple of loaves squarely boxing his ears and making off along the road. Jack Pant was the only one who laughed. Snow fluffed in between his teeth and the laugh ended in a spit.

Morgan the Agent came up at a great pace pulling Maggie's brother John by the bottle. A light winked in the uplands by Garthbrengy and down on the road towards Llandefaelog Fach the dignity of man took another bounce.

'Billo, Billo, stop it mun.' A vague gaggle of sound rearwards. Lewis and Billo were running. An occasional huff and a silence, followed by raucous laughter, provided a Morse code of their progress, only the dashes were longer. At the last one of Billo's rushes felled Morgan the Agent flat. Whether Billo was over Bechers at the time or going in for rugby no one bothered to find out.

'Little bastard,' said Morgan the Agent.

'Come on Walter Scott,' said Jack Pant, hooking him up by the collar. 'Mush, mush.'

'Get off it, mun.' Harry Evans spat into the wind and wiped it off with his coat-sleeve. 'My old woman saw that one last summer and came home crying. Looked at me as though I had no damn right to be home at all.' He laughed shortly.

The snow was thick now, driving from the front and settling affectionately on the inner edge of the thick scarf Morgan the Agent was wearing. No light was visible from the hill eastwards, and on the road feet broke out of the snow caverns less and less willingly. At every turn someone slipped, usually either Trevor Stamps, whose boots were not up to the job, or Billo and Lewis behind, for whom an occasional hump and ridge were as nothing in a turning world. Both the latter had several purple periods with hands on the moving sled and feet at a quarter to three the length of half a man away. The name of the Almighty was much taken and manifestly in vain. Once or twice the sled toppled altogether, hitting the snowbank in the darkness, and how many loaves were lost in the drifted ditch not one of them could say for certain. Joe Francis alleged he had stepped on one and sent it down to warm, but the light of Ossie's labouring match showed only drift and gash, brown snow and boots innumerable with a fine froth of white climbing the ankle. Every step now felt the snow surface mounting and the more need of a good shove on the sled.

After what seemed hours the van tracks ended. They were back in their own Eppynt country, back and away from bread in tins and the long bricked ovens of Wind Street, back in the old fight of man against the flint and snow of an unwilling circle. Ordinary men, devoid of heroism, but dogged and going home. Home to the clean fight of white and black that is the simpleness of the untowned man, the foreigner outside the mazes of comfort. Home, a limited objective, but enough for strength.

No singing now. Nothing of mountains except a darker fear around the white world's limit. Nothing of Ysbaddaden Chief Giant or of Olwen of the White Track, of whom they had never heard. Nothing of legend or glory or belief between the lot. Only bread, and Mam's medicine in the bottle with Maggie's brother John, and a wash of beer inside Lewis and Billo the Jumper. They had no words or breath for the shortest slogan. It was not what Matti had said, but a sort of compulsion coming out of her, mingling with a dim feeling of rightness that they had left over from long ago, that had made them come. There was nothing now to explain or encourage, much less to help. Jack Pant, cold as a cellar stone, barely remembered what he had thought in Brecon about wishing Maggie would be up to see them come in. To come in, his tired legs said over and over, would be marvellous in itself. The little lines of the cwm, the short range of vision, the solid encounter of hand and foot with difficulty, the desire of the belly for warmth, these were all they had now. Going on was a habit and obstinacy was in it. The habit of going home.

Just short of the turn for Coygen the sled went over full pelt, and Trevor Stamps, Harry Evans and Ossie Francis, who were on the wrong side, went flat down. Everyone was breathing hard, with exhaustion near. No one noticed Jack Pant go down too, ahead of the rest. Only a boy, and dead beat. Cardi Morgan and Morgan the Agent were righting the sled with the uncertainty of men beyond their strength. Joe Francis and Gunter began to pick up the loaves mechanically, one by one, and put them back. No one spoke. Lewis the Carbuncle was down on both knees away from the sled, holding his head and muttering. Over the shoulder of the hill the light of the Wern was showing to a man who was standing upright. But nobody was.

There was not a leader among them, save perhaps Cardi Morgan and he too old. But somehow the sled got going again with a lurch, curving off diagonally and stopping before the same resistance of snow. If Billo had not slipped immediately, within a few yards, and come down in the nearside gully, he would never have seen Jack Pant lying there, head between outstretched arms and moving spasmodically. 'Jack boyo. Up now.' The boy's head yanked urgently against Billo's jerseyed hip, his heels leaving a wide and varying wake in the lane behind. One of Billo's arms went across his chest and under his lower armpit. On they staggered, against rule and noisily unreasonable.

The sled was gaining on them. The pin-point of light from the Wern window swung to and fro, gleaming yellowly off magnificent walls and shooting gloriously into Billo's eyes from every angle. Suddenly he slipped, both feet making down the ridge of ice in the same direction, fast and inseparable. One hip-bone thumped the road centre and slewed. 'Not lie down yet,' he muttered. 'Not home.' He thought ponderously. At last he recovered his feet from the hedged darkness, shifted his grip on Jack's armpit and began the drag again.

Over the field's edge came the light, spreading a net that dragged every corner of Billo's eyes. There was no escape from it. Rut and hummock tripped and staggered him: Jack Pant's heels knocked dully on the mountains over which he had come: but he was pulled on fiercely, unremittingly, by his eyes, contracted and stubborn against the light. They were the only part of him now which could be pulled. The flat omnipresence of the light, pulling from in front, bustling and buffeting from behind, he associated somehow with Matti. *She* had put it on for them. He had always hated her slow appraisal of him and her sorrowful neglect of conversation. He, Billo, was as good as any of them. But *she* had put the light on, no doubt of that. Mother and sister and woman of no sex, she had thought of everything, foreseen everything, waited for everyone. Even for Billo.

A feeble cheer went up ahead. The sled had arrived. Jack Pant broke into a gabble and jerked out of Billo's frozen grip. They both fell, Jack's body trapping and twisting one of Billo's legs. The heap groaned and lay still.

The snow was bathed in light. A miniature world of glacier and alp lay above the straggling forest of Billo's upper lip. The hairs at the back of his neck began to bristle, magnetic in the light. Jack Pant was lying on his back, lips blue and frothy. Billo stared at him for more than a moment, his mind working at quarter pace. Inch by inch he edged around till his face was in shadow, put his hands carefully under Jack Pant's armpits, and kneed his way backwards, rowing them both along with a very short stroke. The light spoke gently in his ear.

A shout nearby. 'Where's Jack?' Then a feminine whimper. 'Where's Jack?' went all round the black crags of the cwm and came back along the hedge-lines to the centre of light. Feet shuffled along the road, throwing off snow and a half-sob. The light came up over his shoulder. He could feel the blind side of the lantern turning against the sky. 'Mam, it's Billo,' shouted Maggie. 'Drunk again. And Jack Pant. There's a pair.'

'There's a man,' said Matti. 'Let me help.'

'No, no,' muttered Billo, still rowing along. His mind was as clear and incandescent as the holly-tree nearby, seeing the heelmarks tap back along the cwm into the far country. Home he was and in his own right. Home they were every one.

Agger Makes Christmas

~

The butt end of wood and hill shutting off the valley bottom was a concealed residential area that as winter dropped into it looked like a lighted forest or a sack tight over a frame of candles. You could take your choice and back your fancy. If you could crawl after it in daylight, you found yourself standing coldly outside the gate of a delightful detached semi-Tudor residence, 4 bed, 3 reception and all usual offices. If still interested, key at Custance and Custance, in the village. Also permission to view.

Agger sat looking out of the prefects' room window at the promise of fog in the December hollow and the sharp tops of the conifers cutting under the last light. He did not fancy the scene or anything about it. But it was preferable to watching Boot, Holland and the rest packing their trunks. Turning, he tipped one of Boot's yellowbacks surreptitiously over the arm of the settee. A man must show wisdom when there are bad days ahead.

'Got a spare stone or two, Agger? Put your great clumping hoof on here, will you?'

'It's a pity you still don't know how to address your betters, Boot. One day, perhaps, you will appreciate the enormity of your offence.' Agger was well aware that speeches of this sort were entirely without effect, particularly on Boot, but an acid dignity was the only contribution he felt able to make to the life of the room. It sometimes stirred the mud in which wit lay.

'Put your blasted hoof on here and shut up. Sitting there on your backside and not doing a damn thing.'

Agger rose and stood delicately on one end of the bursting trunk, while Boot contorted himself over the lock at the other.

'We all know you only stay here over the Christmas vac so that you can get on with your smoking full-time.' This was Holland, a goatlike boy from Bridlington, whose nickname of Zider was still occasionally taken back to its originals in Zee Zider and Zider Zee. It was a familiar jest that he needed a high wind to hold him up.

Agger stood on one leg to concentrate his weight. Either Boot or the trunk continued to rumble volcanically.

'Matron goin' to look after you, Aggy?' said Evans, who was emptying his shelf on the far side of the room. 'Bet you'll go to work on the mistletoe or start a pin-up collection, you dessicated old romantic!'

'Agger doesn't have to take dirty cracks from sub-prefects yet, Evans,' retorted Boot from ground level. 'You pipe down, or I'll see you get more than your share of Table Six next term.' The back of his neck looked red and aggrieved.

The only expression on Agger's face was one of mock dignity. If he had an illusion, it was that he was something of a foil. Out of much girding might come warmth and a companionable spark. So he felt, and cherished the idiosyncrasies of the room like an antiquary. Of souls outside and their methods of contact he knew little. It sometimes seemed to him that a deal of organisation was necessary to get people into touch at any point. For himself, he had nothing to offer. One could only be ready. That was why secretly he cherished the existence of Boot. Good old one-track Boot, Boot of the one joke, the invariable booming tone. Every Sunday when they were all letter-writing, Boot, who never wrote home (though he always went there rapidly enough when the holidays came), stood behind the big central table and waited for their attention.

'D'ye know the noise my grandmother makes when she comes downstairs, boys?'

'No, Boot, of course not. Never 'eard of it.' This was the weekly ritual. They had heard it scores of times.

'Boooo . . . Boooo . . .' went Boot, like a trombone-player taking the solo. His grandmother had flatulans.

'That's how she goes, boys. Boooo . . . Boooo . . .'

'All right, Boot old man. We've all laughed.' It was the privilege of Henniker, the senior prefect, to indicate that the merriment was at end. 'Go into Hell and do your piece.' With the unvarying solemnity of the ritualist Boot went, closing the door of the cubbyhole under the stairs on himself and pulling the saw between his knees to the half-window. 'Annie Laurie' was not everyone's choice, but undoubtedly, like Boot, its determined sentiments had their place.

Yes, good old Boot. Agger felt that a piece of his world was really fixed in position, like one of several stage flats leaning to an uneasy farce, against a background of clouts and throw-outs from earlier and discarded productions. He was not unaffected by other oddities, like the skull that Huddington bought at a fair and burned on the prefects' room fire. One would have had to be lacking in at least four out of the five senses to remain impervious to that, in any case. But few such things, even the odorous ones, were for keeps. Unlike Boot's grandmother, they did not bear repetition. Agger's quiet acid needed the resistance of a piece of rocklike and indigestible mirth in order to throw up a curd or two of phrase and an odd spurt of personal energy. The chemistry of his need was by no means public. His stage was under-peopled and there was only one standby for a character part. It was for that, not for the chivalry of his defence nor for the luminous idiocy of many of his remarks, that Boot was on the bill.

Evans moved over and switched on the lights, his lip curling a little. Agger stepped down from the trunk without looking either at him or at Boot, no sign of enmity or gratitude in his face. Already he was withdrawing from the circle, practising for his future wounds. A cloud like a giant's coat, folded and fleeced, had edged out all but a last seam of light touching the tops of the conifers. Already the Tudor candelabra against the hill was sending points of yellow shooting down the glass sides of vision, and the wintry pane gave back nothing but Holland and Boot and Westgate and Evans and the ceremonial packing of trunks, all in a distortion of black skeltering sadly around the central bulb. The pressure of the season was heavy, inside the room and out. Agger sat still, feeling the change clawing at him.

Some projection of himself went out, across the stone-flagged playroom, where the sound of roller-skates pirouetted groaningly up to the gas-lit dome, visible as glass only where streaks in the grime let through the blue-black of the night sky, on through the cloisters and up the dark corridor to the Staff quarters. Matron would feed him in the Committee Room as usual, he supposed. Dark green baize cloths, a clattering of the few plates to cover the embarrassing lack of contact, Matron in all her bulk standing by on the first day in a perfunctory attempt to create a welcome. The round would be as usual. Dinner with the Old Man on Christmas Day, and perhaps a show in Town later in the week, if the Old Man's car would start. Decent enough but all strained through a tight cloth. He had come to wonder why it was that good intention and even idealism failed so dismally to find its counterpart in another being, when a divergent eccentricity could send a spark through all the points at once. Perhaps indeed there was nothing under the surface of contact that men held in common. What did his father know of the Papuans' souls now after so many years, more than the way they built houses and the frizz of their hair? What was there to know? Why go out into the dark with Christianity or Uno or any other crowd who believed in the oneness of man? To him it was all like the roar of roller skates under a glass dome, cold and thunderous in its beginning, eerie and repetitive and menacing in the upper reaches of its imperfect sky. How much better to be glad of the broken pieces, to welcome the new joke in the repertoire, the fresh oddity by the fire! Christmas was nothing in itself. It had to be saved and distilled out of all the rest of the year.

Agger did not usually consider himself morbid, but self-deprecation had been setting in for some time past. The role of curator grew progressively less worthy. He got up.

'Badger's on duty tonight, Aggy,' said Holland. 'Better watch Bop Jones and that crowd. Remember it was salt in the Staff tea last time.'

Agger nodded. 'How could I forget, O Zider mine?' But he gave not a thought to Bop Jones and his crony The Faggot as he went down into the echoing playroom. A roped trunk or two still stood in the corners and the gas flared gustily as the door opened. Here and there a tyro handed himself desperately along the walls. Agger cut straight out into the circle of skaters monotonously crossing right leg in front of left, lulling like birds in the heart of a storm. The props bowler would serve his purpose, he thought, handing off an approaching wingspan and making like a knife for the dark artery of the cloisters.

Before dawn the ritual of the 7.14 to Town was well begun. From the half-cooked beef sausage in Hall to the joy of shouting unnecessarily in the swirling mist of the valley road it had its establishment and fresh intent in every generation. Besides going home there was the desire to impress that fact on every swathed and bowlered figure caught up in the giant march. Agger heard himself carrying on in high and animated tones which appeared to carry conviction. He also possessed a small attaché case.

His decision to come to the station with Boot and Holland had occasioned mild surprise. But it was not an atmosphere that would let surprise live long. He had to go to Town anyway, he said, to attend at his solicitors' somewhat later in the morning, so why not the 7.14? Why not, indeed? Boot was glad for a moment that he would not have to go to Agger's bed to shake hands. It was always awkward. Not much of a joke really.

'Look here, there's one thing I must explain to you chaps. No, not explain. Just tell you, I mean. I can't travel up in the same compartment with you. Never mind why not. I'll come to that next term. Only don't ask any questions now.'

Boot and Holland looked utterly mystified. 'Got a girl waiting for you or something?' asked Holland.

'I said *don't* ask any questions, Zider. Next term I'll give you the gen. Honestly. O.K.? Or if your disgusting curiosity hurts you too much, one of you – I said one of you – can take a turn past my compartment to make sure there's nothing on my lap or up my sleeves. That satisfy you?'

'I suppose so,' said Holland slowly. He did not look satisfied. Boot was already trying on an expression intended to indicate lack of interest. It was not a success. Suddenly the entrance hall jumped at them out of the mist and stood over them, threatening seven o'clock.

A hundred or more juniors were hither-and-thithering over the nearer end of the platform, and Agger was seized with a fear that it would, after all, be impossible to get out of the GENTS un-observed. Getting there was simple enough, and to produce the props bowler from his case a matter of seconds only. But he stood screened by the door for several minutes before risking the crossing to a carriage, despite the fact that his morning coat and striped trousers were in splendid accord. Possibly the hunched-up rush with which he finally threw open the compartment door was not out of keeping with his pretensions. Heavy breathing, too, was an accepted attribute. At any rate, as he fell back in the corner seat on the corridor side, the compartment's only other occupant took not the smallest notice. The only risk now was that some wretched junior would venture so far forward.

Presently he rose and placed his case with some care on the rack opposite, diagonally away from him and as far in the other corner as possible. Minute after minute crawled away and the risks began to shorten. The motor began its irregular hum. All at once a clutch of overcoats and briefcases was forced in, as though by the whistle's breath, and all the seats were full.

The train jerked off through the osier-like woods. A ginger man with a lot of barrack-square left in his face, who sat opposite, opened the *Daily Herald* very deliberately, running his thumb down the fold. An older man with a sniff and a tic in his near eye, sitting on Agger's left, began nervously to pick ends of cotton off his trouser legs. He was a nuisance, but he was a portent of unease. There was a place for him in the verities.

A seedy Adonis with a rolled umbrella and yellow fingers took down a briefcase stamped S.M. from the rack and began to rummage in it. As the train left Beringley and gathered speed, Agger too stood up and, moving with deliberation among the serried toes, took down his case. He opened it on his lap, face rapt. Slowly and reverently, placing both hands inside, he lifted out a brick and, bending his head, pressed his lips to it. Then he slowly replaced it, closed the case and put it back in the far corner of the rack.

All breathing had stopped. The man with the tic twitched a glance into Agger's lap and looked away. The Adonis sat with both hands inside the briefcase, transfixed. An undercurrent of communication suddenly bubbled in the silence. The ginger man, accustomed to the direct method, put down his paper and stared at Agger. Agger looked out of the corridor window like the keeper of a mausoleum. The ginger man picked up his paper again, shaking it into place with the fierceness of his attention.

'Shortage of Building Materials.' The headline caught Agger's eye. The man with the tic, having dealt with his trousers, and finding them inconveniently near the seat of trouble, was reading it too. The train was singing its high steel song between Orleton and the main line junction at Morse Hill. Agger rose again.

This time there was genuine apprehension in the compartment. All pretence of other interest ended abruptly. Every eye was riveted on him. The ginger man's chin pressed heavily on the *Herald*.

Agger opened his case as before, taking out the brick gravely and placing it across his knees while he fastened down the lid of the case, which was otherwise entirely empty. With constraint white in his face he placed the shut case on the seat behind him and slipped to his knees with the brick poised between his palms. Presently he began to intone over it, slitting his eyes and running through a rule or two from North and Hilliard, the consonants unstressed. His shoulders quivered like the combs of a wave.

The Adonis, shock giving way slowly to ignorant curiosity, nudged his farther neighbour: 'No religion that does that, is there?' The train began to run into the platforms of Morse Hill, its song now no more than a punctuating click or two. Agger's tone rose by contrast. He began to contort himself.

'Here I say,' began the ginger man. The train stopped and jerked backwards. Agger opened his eyes. Suddenly he tossed the brick straight into the ginger man's lap, crowing 'Passed to you, sir,' flicked his case off the seat and leapt out.

As he ran across the platform he had a half-image of the ginger man, all red jaw and anger, with the brick high over his head. There was a crash of glass and confused shouting. Agger rounded the refreshment room and cut back beyond the footbridge to his own platform. Carriage doors were open and he was well screened by a waiting rout of bowlers. A few yards away Holland had his thumbs outside the corridor window. Within, Boot faced away from the engine like a monarch incognito. 'My regards, Zider,' said Agger, setting the props bowler jauntily on Holland's head. 'Bye, bye. Good vac.' The rearward carriages howled as he passed.

Outside the station it was still only half-light. He stopped on the road bridge that crossed the waist of the lines a few yards off. The train was still standing at the UP platform. Not far from the engine was a little knot of people, menacing in its stillness. From the bridge the noise of riot in the rearward half was plainly audible. 'Good old Boot,' he breathed. 'I'm with you.'

The signals made a pattern of lights like the larger presents on a Christmas tree, and over them, higher, above the valley from which he had come, were the quick tongues of little woodland fires as breakfast was eaten in a hundred Tudor-type residences. It was a firm pattern, warm even in its distant points, and in the growing light it took down the grimy glass roof from the sky. The interminable circle of sound was broken, at least until another term. Agger rubbed his hands. This was the best Christmas yet.

Ffynnon Fawr

~

For the last few moments before the car stopped the valley had seemed full of rain. It seethed in the wiry grass that ran from the moorland down to the road's edge. It slanted from above the eyeline angrily into the hazels that bushed out over the last pitch to the valley bottom. There was no plopping sound now, as of drops sniping at the dry, hairy surface of the hazel leaves. The main body of the rain had arrived, ranked and iron-eyed, and the brown patches which high summer had worn on the mountain shoulders were put away against another week.

Ever since the grey Vauxhall, in second gear, had taken the sharp turn above the waterfall, Rendel had had the house in view. Its situation presented no difficulty at all. In the long arc of valley the water of the reservoir pressed the mountain walls hard at all save the nearer, eastern corner where the house stood, right up to the mudded edge, biding its time. There was no mistaking it, the purplish L of the gable and the lean, unhumble look. But for the cottage by the waterfall and a farmhouse a mile or so distant at the foot of a westerly cwm there was no other house in sight. It was not like searching for scraps of identity in a suburb. Ffynnon Fawr was individual enough, even when given up for dead.

To keep it in view, then, was a simple matter. Every twist of the descending road towards the eastern mountain had brought it in full face. But as the first flurry of hazels flicked at the windscreen it became obvious that the road would have nothing to do with the house. Through the rush of leaves an occasional gate promised. But there was no vestige of way for a car. A sudden, swooping hollow showed, in any case, that he was now on the wrong side of a broadening, peaty stream.

Rendel remembered then, even if somewhat belatedly, what his mother had tried to thrust into his heart in Virginia Springs the day she died. He could feel all at once, through the angled strokes of the rain, the tangible heat bouncing into the little box-room from the concrete verandah of the up-country hut. Across the table-top landscape were the hangars of the aerodrome, a little northward the admin buildings where his sister worked as a typist. It was not an edifying scene, not such as he could retail with the right admixture of sentiment to all-comers. There had not even been the gratification of a rough success. His father, a roadman once among the lanes of Caerfanell, but always carrying with him too thin a skin and a cry that his house was too low for justice, had worked for a while as a labourer in a factory making aeroplane parts just over a mile from Virginia Springs. His death seven years ago, so far from bringing an aura of respectability to the name of Morgan, had nailed down his failure underground in an unjourneying coffin. Rendel himself, slight and unremarked, and with less than his father's unease, had become a mechanic at the aerodrome. At least he was hard enough for that. And then had come the day when his mother lay breathless in the heat on her box-bed, her upper lip shining uncannily with the oncoming death-sweat. His main preoccupation at first had been to fix the correct mood in himself, to make the scene indelible in his personal history – the motes drilling in from the window, the line of scrub like a breaking wave beyond tarmac, the old black country skirt over the chair that his mother had never put off till she was taken to her bed for the last time. No, it was not an effective scene, though in his anxious way he had striven to make it so. The last link with Caerfanell breaking. His sister Elsie, born when they were down country at Newcastle, tapping her keys in ignorance half a mile away, part of the hard Australian underbrush on the wrong side of the world. He himself, four and a half years in Caerfanell before his half-ticket was bought by bewildered parents, a meek, undersized emigrant, long since yellowed and drabbled with engine oil. It was not that up to that time he had been unhappy. Nor even particularly sensitive, at least not in the way that mechanics find easy game. No, he could not explain what overtook him during his mother's last illness. It was a horrible excitement separate from and yet connected with the box-bed facing the tarmac. Something important was happening. And he was not sure what it was. Only that when his mother had struggled up on one elbow a bare minute before she died and stayed there, contracted with effort, the foxhole of his own breath was stopped and still with listening. 'Go back,' said the whisper. 'You must go back. Ffynnon Fawr is still there, waiting.' The tongue fell back in her throat, and the last fight was on. 'Promise me, Rendel. Promise.' He nodded, gripping her. And then she was flat on her back, thinner than all the lost years and drained of expectation. There was no need to call Elsie. She would not understand.

What his mother had said earlier, scattered over the weeks of perpetual dust, gradually coalesced in his mind. The reservoir, yes. Something about the reservoir. The valley filled with water since their day. But the house still there, alone, unchanged, in front of it the cypress his father had planted the day he was born. The road down to the Drinkwaters' and the Lawrences' under water now. And a new motor road on the other side of the valley, careering by, serving no family that they had known. But the house still there, water right up to the garden bank and muddying the lawn's edge when the mood turned. For a time one of the reservoir workmen had lived there, but the hearth was cold long since. All this from the letters of Mrs Evans, Tyle-Clydach. But she had died too, a few months before his mother. It was a new world he was entering, as well as an old. There were none here to know him, with his savings of three years and the car hired in London. Only a thunder in his blood told him that he had ever set foot before on the green arc of Caerfanell. That, and the thunderous, familiar rain.

Presently he could see that the road was abreast of the lakehead, visible for a few yards against a slough of red mud spiked with occasional blades of coarse grass. The house, then, must be directly in line, though he could not see it. The slanting rain, hardly noticeable now against the water-pall, dug a series of quick heels into the surface of the lake and spattered away from the shallows out of sight. There was no point in going further. The new road plainly, as Mrs Evans had said, had nothing to do with the house and to go on would merely bring the reservoir between him and it. Driving on to the uneven grass verge, therefore, at a point where a three-strand fence closed a gap in the hazels, he buttoned his mac collar to the throat and stepped out. For a moment he stood looking at the back of the grey Vauxhall, neutral and solid against the pressure of earth and sky. CGW647.

Haphazard figures. The car itself was a chance, its part soon to run out. A thing of movement, and yet the most recent rest he had known. Calmness at knowing he was on the way. Peace, and a hired car.

That was in coming. But what in arriving? All at once he did not know. To have driven past was unthinkable, but now that the grey chassis was drawn in upon the grass, its tried solidity held him, held him solemnly in the affection he could feel for all things of which he had the mastery. Typewriters, aeroplane parts, steering wheels of cars, for him they had long been aids to unconcern, swings and pressures that he could call up at will to supersede a shock too sudden or too long sustained. But in coming to this point he must renounce such mastery and venture, unregulated, softly into the valley whose challenge he was too young to remember, venture too without understanding fully wherein his father and mother had failed. It was a moment for hesitation.

He turned and ducked under the wire into the rank grass that ran down to the water's edge. A few steps brought him to the stream, swollen with recent decision but jumpable some fifty yards back where the channel was deep and the banks were undercut. From there on the going was increasingly wet. His fawn sportex trousers, bought in London, were soon sopped to the knee by the springback of the rushes and the occasional little swords of water that came out of the mossy mêlée. Ruefully he hesitated, shrugged and went on again. Halfway across the lakehead it became apparent that there was a raised way running parallel with his course and some yards nearer the water, though where the beginning of this had been he could not judge. A minute's splashing brought him to it, a solid grassy track still concealing only partly the cartwide stone foundation. A few wildfowl beat out of the reeds before his breathless advance, stretched their necks into the shortening pall and were gone. He was startled. The reddish eddies quietly curled back around the roots and the water resumed its finicky, irregular slapping.

Rendel quickened his pace along the made way. Presently he stepped gingerly over long stones balanced across a muddy inlet and saw above him the outline of trees. The path divided into two, and after momentary hesitation he took the right-hand one, which climbed diagonally and suddenly into overhanging shadow. The hissing of the rain was now a more distant sound. He had a child's feeling of comfort at it, as though there were warmth here, warmth as of a bed with the rain beyond the window striking in vain for him among the cowering grasses. But he was not long in comfort. With something akin to shock he knew all at once that the house was near, over his left shoulder and along the low plateau whose top he had reached. Eyes still screwed up in the shadow, he knew too that the house had seen him first and that no subsequent guise would serve. It was a slender advantage, but perhaps enough.

There was little about the sight that he could recount afterwards. A red, almost purplish, sandstone wall, a few rain-bent shrubs meagrely against it, and high, coarse grass, bladed with overbearing drops, between it and the trees under which he stood. Discouragement marked him down. For the first time he asked himself why he had chosen to visit the house in the middle of a rainstorm. And peering over the welter in his mind's front was the head of another question. What did he intend to do by visiting it at all? Buy it? Rent it for a time? From whom? It came to him then that he had neglected all reasonable precautions. He did not know what he meant to do. He had made no enquiries, except of the way. Only in the recess of his stomach beat the unanswerable nerve which drove him on and which created its own area of devastation and unsettlement in front of him as he went. He had not been able to eat a solid meal since he landed. A peck or two for dinner and no breakfast. He had struggled with this absurdity, but without reward. Excitement came in shivers, regarding neither convenience nor company. Twice he had dreamed of his mother's black skirt, thrown with difficulty over a chair the day before she died. What power this had it was impossible to say. It was evocative neither of his life in Virginia Springs (he never remembered noticing it particularly before that day) nor in any special sense of Caerfanell. It was a black skirt, that was all: his mother had worn no other. Since his two dreams, however, he had been assailed by a cold unmanageable fear that he would not see Ffynnon Fawr because he had left the skirt in Australia – as though he and it were the only two entities above ground that had known the house before and neither could return alone. It was all part of the fever that was on him, of course: but it was some indication of the virtual stoppage of a part of his intelligence that he had arrived at the house with no notion of what he intended to do.

It was almost five-thirty and the rain showed no sign of slackening. The roof of the house, near as it was, had its edges fogged like an unsatisfactory photograph. The grass was full of movement. Innumerable drops, overweighting at last the hairs to which they clung, ran down the blades like quicksilver and fled among the sobbing tops. The bushes hissed miserably and gathered themselves to the wall. The whole plateau garden was like the source of a great river, whose gathering force could be heard but not seen. He wondered feebly how far away the car really was, and why he did not go back to it.

Neither of his questions turned themselves round to answer. Every visible projection of life seemed fully engaged, isolating his hesitation. Minutes passed. There was no change in the sky. The rain still jumped and muttered down towards the reservoir. Unable any longer to resist the natural order of commitment, he suddenly broke from under the trees towards the wall, feeling the casements of the windows in a blind haste.

There was no give in the flaked wood, now streaming with water, though the frames appeared less fastened than stuck. But he was in no mood to work on them. Excitement, together with his recent doubts, had put him in a sort of feeble impatience. He moved on round an angle, stumbling over the wet tussocks. In a recessed part of the wall he came upon a window that was partly open, a pantry window by the look of it, and narrow. He tugged it wider with both hands, but it did not move. Wet and exasperated, he stood away, considering the existing aperture. The first heave-up was not successful. But a second, a minute or so's careful negotiation of the frame, which squeezed his hollowed chest unlovingly, and he was inside, with no more hurt than a sorry mixture of lead rust and water on the palms of his hands.

There was nothing in the room but a stone slab running the length of one side and an empty half-tub under it. Beyond there was a passage at right angles, with windows giving on to a genteel area of grass, oppressed of late by troops of feather-tops and plantains. He was in the toe of the L, small dairies and out-rooms opening off the passage on either side of the room from which he had come. A step or two to the left brought him to the interior angle in which the front door was set, the framework strong and diagonal. The door stood wide open, and a hopeful river had made several yards among the knots and shallows of the wooden floor.

He did not smile at the folly of his precipitate entry. Instead, he felt more than a little afraid.

With his back to the wall, he could see from the doorway that the grass sloped sharply at its farther end to a gate, beside which stood a half-grown cypress. Beyond was the water of the reservoir, puddled from right to left by the rain and slatting the earth bank with appreciable noise. Beyond that again was the rain-pall, falling like a cotton-wool sky into the lake. Rendel had a feeling of being bound, at least for the present, to the house and its destiny, of which the open door seemed both the beginning and symbol. His fear left him, and he gazed unmoving at the pelt-marks in the water for several minutes before bothering to explore the house further. There was no hurry after all. There might be a lifetime.

All the rooms on the ground floor were scattered with sheep-droppings. The kitchen, distempered a powerful rose at some comparatively late date in its occupation, was especially foul. Rendel looked up at the empty hooks in the ceiling-beam and was nauseated. The notion of the animal misplaced touched off his imagination and even the history of persons was defiled by it. The place of reminiscence was intolerably usurped.

Upstairs the floor was clear. In the largest bedroom a boot, obese with the pressure of bones and mud, stood by itself before the fireplace. Someone had lit a fire and the ends of the sticks had fallen away to the sides of the basket unburned, leaving in the middle a pile of light grey ash. How long ago match had been set to it there was no telling. Rendel was now thoroughly ill-at-ease and unhappy, all his urge to come drained away. He turned and stumbled out, missing the narrow stairhead in his haste.

It was a smaller room into which he blundered. Small and square, the one window looking out at the riot of tall grass by which he had come, the other innocently at the green side of the mountain, as though expecting, by mere attention, to see the heart beat in the ribs of rock. There was nothing about the room at all. And yet he did not retreat within the second as he had intended. It was a secure little room, in a way that the bigger, with its burned-out fire, was not. It was bare, but boxed and firm above the grassy seas like the light on the Bishop Rock. Rendel sat down, although a moment before nothing had been further from his mind.

It was hard to say why he sat down. He did not expect to be comfortable on the worn boards. Neither had he any real intention of staying. Periodically he still remembered the car and muttered to himself. But he had not resolved his intention, and action could hardly run before it. Running, in any case, even walking, seemed far from this room. It was a room for sitting down. Even, unreasonably enough, lying down.

The anxious hubble-bubble of the rain in the grass-roots went on. Day slowly relaxed its pretence and grew tired. Rendel lay on his arm and dozed, entirely content. As in the years when he never had to care for these things, he did not remember when he fell asleep or if, in fact, he did sleep.

When he awoke it was quite dark. The rain seemed to have stopped. Or, if it had not, its thin streams were thrust aside by the forward wave of footsteps splashing along the sodden road between the window and the mountain. A group of people, four or five it sounded like, shouting and arguing. Under the window there was a crescendo of noise, a drunken speech and intermittent clapping. But it was not this in which Rendel was suddenly caught up, the hairs at his nape bristling like the moonlight spines on Twrch Trwyth swimming for his life. It was another sound. And yet not a sound, but rather an impression of sound, caught in closed gurgles and chesty eddies from confine to confine. It was in the room with him, near, very near. Neck rigid, not daring to move, he lay where he was, powerless by the wall. The soundlessness of the air's suck in and out exhausted him, as though the tight bones of his chest had to open to equal, by some physical law, the space outside it and stretching to the four walls. In all the room there was no shadow but himself as the soundless crying went on.

All at once the weight was lifted and the air came back, sorry and more comfortable. He felt himself carried to the window, which creaked open before him as he stared. Immediately the outer noise reasserted itself, a puddle of laughter and splashing in which the moon joined. One of the men was leaning against the dairy window, his cheeks puffed out over the knob of a walking-stick, short as a drummer in the middle of his mime. Gusts of merriment blew out to him from under the farther hedge. The fingers on the stick were cold and moonstruck, plying up and down in the pool like growths on a taper root. All about the upper window, however, there was resistance. A voice in Rendel's ear hung downwards like a stalactite, threatening but not reaching the ground. 'Edwin Drinkwater, take yourself off. And the whole damn lot of you. Sharp too. Dowlais Fair is all very well, but you've waked the child. You'll not get in his way, as you've done in mine, damn you. Get off home, man. Go on, all of you.'

The window frame banged to. Realisation spread like a hunter's pressure on the ear. That eager, youthful, undignified breathy tone – his father's voice! Seven years dead, and yet alive in the hulk of Ffynnon Fawr, still speaking for him as he had always done. Hoping and caring for his growth, like the cypress by the front gate that grew with him. And here, now, still expectant, still watchful, looking for the times that were greater than his!

Back in his place by the wall he felt as though his heart would burst. Moveless of body as he was again, he knew the tears filling his eyes were not from the understanding of a child. There was stillness, and yet no peace. The black procession of the air marched by him, disposing itself horribly towards eternity. Latterly he supposed he slept, chiefly through weakness, and was not deterred by dawn.

It was broad daylight when he rose, stiff and damp in the joints in the bare room. The window was still open. He hobbled to it and looked out. The lane outside was streaked with the red mud carried down from the hill, and at the water's edge, where the reservoir came round the cape of lawn and stopped it, a few green stalks coated with red stood up in the cloudy to-fro of the water. No one had gone down to the lake for a long time.

He had not really expected it. The house was empty and a strange reservoir slatting against its mound. And no road any more.

The morning had a grey, hard look after the night's rain, with the wind flattening the sedge and moving the clouds around brusquely. Rendel did not look back at the house till his hand was on the door of the hired Vauxhall. It made no motion now to him nor he to it. The mound of trees, the open door under the swarming green hill, the reed-beds in which the lake died, were etched-in in hard lines after the washing of the night's streams. The young cypress faced the water stubbornly, giving nothing away. Heart had been lost somewhere between rainset and dawn.

He stood with his hand on the car door, realisation growing. Yesterday he had not known what he meant to do. Now that pulse in him which beat him half across the world had stopped, and in the unexpected stillness he could hear failure forming in his breath. He was too timid for Ffynnon Fawr, too timid to make a future where the generations cried out on him in their sleep. He had not known that life had gone on here, raining and shining and stirring and, above all, waiting. He had thought to bring such of it with him as he wanted, like family bric-a-brac, and that he himself would be enough, unsure even of what hopes had lived. Elsie with a guess and a memory, that's all he was. And his guess had been wrong.

As he put the car into first gear a long ray of sun, dipping under the clouds, tipped the reeds at the lakehead like so many spear-points. The cypress was upswept momentarily in a ruffle of strength. What he had been and was not and now could never be clutched at him. Caerfanell had come again too late.

The gears of the Vauxhall were morose, but simple enough. The length of the reservoir, back to London, over sea to Virginia Springs, and slowly towards the next night, it was all one road.

Match

~

The night had been uncertain of rain or moon and the grass in the longer patches on the slope towards the pill showed silver and green impartially, as though it had been dewed and combed then, roughly and to and fro. It would be a wet ball for a while, no doubt of that. On the lower touch three boys in wellingtons who had completed their office with the flags were beginning to chase each other, ducking under the grabs that went for tackles. Up the hill there was whistling and a workman or two behind the rising walls of the craft block, Saturday-happy and lost. Apart from these, Wynford Hughes was the first on hand. From where he stood the farther posts, barely safe from a sudden fall-away of ground to the thorn bushes at the pill bottom, masted into the full grey waters of the reach. Tide was up, and the calm envelope of morning seemed at pressure.

A hubbub at the field gate told of the arrival of the bus, and as the players, hooped with black and yellow and blue and gold, spread like a hot breath outward on the slope, Wynford knew that he needed to come to a sort of understanding, and that with himself. He had made the effort, he had come out early deliberately in the hope of being cheered up. It would be nonsense now to be girding round and round upon his bitterness when for an hour at least he could be caught up in a fight not his own. No, not his own narrowly. But he had always accustomed himself to loyalty, to being inside the skin of the bodies he belonged to, to enthusing when his enthusiasm was asked for and expected. Some members of the staffroom, he knew very well, regarded this weakness of his with silent pity. Others were not so silent. 'Adolescent,' Garro Davies would no doubt remark if he had the chance. His intentionally audible asides from Intellectual Corner had been a trial for years. Adolescent. Well, what of it? He was a member of the School. Why not shout for it? It was just this self-regarding falsity, this lofty absence of loyalty, that so infuriated him in every walk. Was it only boys, working in a house system without houses, playing for a team ideal that was talked up too much, who would undertake to suffer inconvenience, exhaustion and injury? Who cared if the ideals didn't go much beyond the physical? It was something to have an ideal, wasn't it, and to work towards it? Damn Garro and all his spawning superiors! His very being at Bush this morning was his answer. To hell with them! He couldn't help it and why should he? He was born to enthusiasm as the heart pumps faster. To hell with Garro!

But this was the very thing he had come out not to do, to get bitter again. Look at the game, Wynford boy. Whistle blowing now. Its shrill peep ran round the edge of the plantations, sounded warningly against the quarry, and came back in a huff from the reach, where the morning still waited for a wind. The mud-flats were well covered. It was surely high tide.

When Wynford switched back from long sight he was still in time to see Gethin standing, hands on hips before the referee, watching the quick ceremony of the toss. Gethin, small, black, barely five foot two and smiling the more because of it. Gethin Du he would have been in the Welsh parts. But here just Gethin. Or Geth. Or even Wait, or Weight (no one would care to produce a definitive spelling), presumably from some half-forgotten Middle School joke about Geth your Weight. Possibly too a tribute to the bulging muscles of Gethin's thighs and the thickening pillar of his neck. None of his friends and equals called him Weight. Only perpetual up-and-comers like Ceffyl Collett, who was just the sort of feeble Middle School crackpot to have stuck together such a joke in the first place. Ceffyl Collett. A silly name Ceffyl. But he had been one of those who for rugby's sake had wanted to learn Welsh, and the sound of it had been for him the noise of his zeal. 'Ceffyl, ceffyl, ceffyl a horse,' he went when older boys were about. And Ceffyl he had become and went on becoming, the great sandy mane and twitching ears growing a hand or two higher every time one looked. Running the line today was Ceffyl, an expert whose own play, some rearing and bucking in the tight excepted, rarely went beyond whinnying the side from a yard or two back. No peace on the field if Ceffyl had the flag and wind left.

Well, there it was, Wynford reflected. Ceffyl on the lower touch meant peace, comparatively, till half-time. Ah, there was Sam Toogood of the Staff in sight now, pegging along at speed, afraid of missing a minute. He would be no trouble. The world was well lost to Sam once the game started. A column of mist, barely distinguished at its base from the plinth of wood and misted hill beyond the quarry, stood up like the morning-sign of prophecy over Monkton Cave. In that half-world of heights and shapes it seemed no great step from the hyena bones under the rock and the middens of the gnawed-at ages. Perhaps only additional physique and a stripier jersey.

But to attend. Gethin had kicked off, downhill towards the reach. The fresh hide of the ball as it flew was lost for a moment in the stealing water greys behind. A clean catch from one of the Gwendraeth lumps in the second row, and a boot to touch. Regulation so far. A deal of rucking and mauling followed, all on the lower side over against Ceffyl, whose voice made raucous encouragement. But it soon appeared that of the two packs that of Gwendraeth was much the heavier and harder. Ben Thomas, their captain, muscles squared-off and head shaven, was worth two men at close quarters, and his up-shouldered, angular form came through again and again like an auger through lath. Once he ran clear and was pulled down more by luck than judgement. Then a stoppage. And out. Out it came, the ball thudding from hand to hand. Roberts, the tall red-headed centre, went streaming out into the open spaces beyond the hands of Ogley and Russ in the middle of the home line. The long stride lengthened, short-cut red-gold hair seeming to balance and helmet the figure as it ran. Roberts was away. But no. No. Gethin Du was coming. Across, across, short thick black legs cutting into the arc of danger. The full-back challenged. Roberts thought to dummy and did not, feeling Gethin's breath. Out went the ball to the wingman, left, up the hill. Out, up the hill came the short legs, quick steps calculated, converging on the wingman running blind, head back, for the line. A sudden bulge of spectators shut Wynford out of view. There was a thud and a cheer. 'Good boy, Weight,' came clear across the field from Ceffyl. The ball was now passing high over Wynford's head at an angle into touch. Gethin was up already, had played the ball and cleared. As the spectators stood back, the wing was slowly getting up.

Exaltation shuddered up Wynford's spine. He was involved and fully, as he had not been for more than odd minutes in the past year. 'School!' His voice tingled out from the top of the spine with a primitive volition of its own. He *was* the black and yellow, jersey and man and heart.

And yet the moment ebbed. Mauling had begun again on the far touchline. The tickling seconds when he had *been* Gethin Du, calculating and heroic, had slipped away. Back and fore slopped his spirit now, in the sump of the game, and over the slug and beat and repeat he could see again the look that he had come here to forget – the look of Kathy's head against the reddened edges of his anger. It was not, by this time, a tearful visitation. Neither was it a vision changeable or topic for argument. Kathy's head, how well he knew it! – black and fit and curled as for a medallion, tidy and composed and short of conversation, yet tearing grouts in his composure day in, day out. Heaven knew he had tried to be dispassionate. Iorwerth was not a bad fellow, he supposed. There were points about him, that cool ability to dissect and analyse, for instance, which impelled both respect and dislike, that more charming Garro-ishness which left one tamping and without a cause. Not difficult to understand that Kathy's ordered mind should prefer Iorwerth to his own moody evasions and wayward enthusiasms. Mind, ordered mind? What had that to do with it? He could have borne Iorwerth's mental superiority and agreed that Kathy should admire it. But who knew that it stopped there? Mind, bah! There was no mind about it. Just a damned dirty intrigue, growing and growing ever since Iorwerth came to lodge with them. What a fool he had been to believe that such an arrangement *could* work! All in the cause of kindness. All towards the end of a world.

Where were they now, while he worked out his stupid enthusiasms? God, wouldn't it be something to die in a moment of complete, honest, spiny engagement, not knowing or caring for anything but the reach of arm and heart and the blessed cry of battle about the head? Wouldn't it? Ceffyl was shouting. That was it. That was the nearness he had in the ears. Ceffyl was shouting, at full stretch, hoarse. Ceffyl was shouting. God, the noise! What about, for heaven's sake? He looked. There was a heap near the lower touch. Something had just happened. Scurlock, perhaps, in a scrap again. Still shouting. No. Out came the ball. Gwendraeth,

Gwendraeth. On to Evans, on to Roberts. And Roberts was away again, pushing off from Ogley's chin and cutting left. Roberts with his red-gold Mercury-head and his long stride was beautiful, beautiful. And he kicked. This time he kicked. Short and neat over the full-back's head. He's in, he must be. No, no. What's that? What is it? What's happening? Gethin again! Doubling back on the far side and under the ball first after all. Down on one knee and Roberts flat out over the top! Up and away now, Gethin, running forward again and pointing the ball high and long towards the lower touch.

No matter. It could not last. Wynford's identification with the School had ebbed entirely. Something about Roberts obsessed him. The red-gold helmet of his head. The purity in the lines of his body. The determination, the severity, the will to conquer. The will to pierce clean through and wound, wound, wound. To strike here, there, anywhere. To ward off with arms like flails that little black figure, that composed little black figure, to upset his calculations and trample him and leap over him and go on, on. So far, oh yes, so far, those little tricks had held out. That composed manner, the black hair still in place. But it would not be so much longer. No, he would go through, and through, and through. Hit 'em again, boy. And again. Let there never be any answer, any come-back. Ever again.

Roberts drew Wynford's eyes magnetically all over the field. Monkton Cave and its flanking woods had thrown off their hieratic mist and the slate-smooth of the sea-reach was no more than a mirror for the nearer action. No outside portent now would sway the issue. The battle was here. The sun threatened presently from behind an aqueous pall, but for the moment withheld.

Half-time came and went, with no more effect on Wynford's trance of vengeance than the barest registration of a temporary stillness. It was a time for girding on, for red-gold preparation, for sharpening the shaft of righteousness. It was a time too that brought Ceffyl up from the lower touch. Ceffyl, a little hoarse and glassy with exhaustion. But Wynford cared nothing for him now. He might screech as he wished, sweat as he wished for School, for the dark ranks of obstinacy, for man and his puny endeavours, for the trickiness of sin. Bellow, boy, bellow! Much good may it do. Shout! The grace is departed and the glory with it. To your tents, O Israel. God shall smite you with his red-gold shaft and thereafter there shall be no truth that you can bear that cannot I. No meddling truth that can touch me. Not of Kathy or Iorwerth or Garro or any damned infidel among you. Go back, back. Because you must. Must.

'Hir,' said Ben Thomas suddenly from near at hand. Gwendraeth were throwing in from touch. 'Watch the long, boys,' yelled Ceffyl in a translator's ecstasy. 'Watch the long! – O Connie, get your man, for God's sake get your man.' But Gwendraeth were boring through, punching holes with every moment of possession. Ben Thomas, angular and shaven, was talking away, first on one side, then on the other, working every trick he knew. Ogley went down to a rush and sagged over the shoulders of those who helped him up, his head fixed in one direction and eyes staring, unlidded, like those of a lizard caught in the open. Gethin picked up off Ben Thomas's toes and aimed a neat punt at Ceffyl. But it was no good. The forces of Wynford's vengeance were pressing on. Back, back went the School, back against the sea, and no wind stirred to their aid. Up in the air, down on the ground, Gwendraeth were the masters. Of all save Gethin. Gethin, unsmiling now and breaking his usual rule. 'Cover, boys, cover,' he shouted in the distance, crossing and crossing again like the pattern of darkness. Cover? Cover what? And with what? Wynford's thoughts moved in eagerly. There is no cover for you, my boys. You'll be pierced through and through and behind that line you'll know what I've put up with and lived. No time so long as the time behind the line. You'll know.

Here it comes. Roberts, away again. Away on the left. Red-gold head moving against the grey of the sea, not quite distinct in the lower field corner, but moving in, practised as an arrow. Out to Devonald on the wing. Full-back takes him. In to Roberts again. Oh this is it! He must be in, must be! Wynford screwed up his eyes in a haze of conviction. His red-gold, righteous victory . . . – Suddenly Ceffyl, fifteen yards off, whinnied himself several hands higher than usual. 'Weight, O Weight, well done boyo! Ruddy marvellous!' From the lower touch there was a deeper roar. Through a momentary lane left by the fast-gathering forwards Wynford, not believing, saw Roberts, arms outstretched for the line, lying flat on his face, and nearer, lower, a black form leeching his ankles. It could not be. It could not. There was nothing they could say against his cause, was there?

But it went on. Minute after minute and still no score. Gethin, the outhalf of darkness, was under every ball that Gwendraeth kicked and thudding into every man who came through. Back and across and back and kick and across. How dare he pit his rotten cause against the stride of vengeance? How dare he? Back and across and back and into touch. And Russ. Russ was backing him now. And Scurlock, there, catching Roberts in the open for the first time. Black hearts, how can you? Know you not justice and the meaning of wounds? Ben Thomas talking now, cursing under breath, trying every trick that forward dominance could manage. Evans and Roberts switching and scissoring. Devonald cutting inside. On, on. Time yet. On. No. Russ challenging. Taking Devonald high and hard. Ball loose. On, on. Roberts following. No, Gethin coming in with a swoop and picking off his feet and twisting, down – caught! Caught at last by Ben Thomas and two others. Caught in possession. Down on the ground. Now, now for it. On the line itself. No – no, godfathers no, Gethin up and playing the ball and twisting again. Back and fore, weaving, held by his jersey. Touch, screw kick to touch. And the whistle! The whistle!

Wynford could not believe it. The rest of the morning passed bitterly through his mind. A drawn match. So much right and so much power on one side . . . All of the game, the very rules themselves, on one side. And a drawn match. Intricate the manner of darkness, and the effrontery, the effrontery of those that should be cast away . . . He stopped suddenly and looked.

Gethin was passing, overhung with Ceffyl and the gamut of words. 'Boy O boy, didn't the School play well?' Ceffyl was stuttering. 'Didn't they just?'

Gethin said nothing. His face, grimed with sweat, was composed. He looked at Wynford as though about to say something, and then neither smiled nor spoke. Presently he had passed on up to the gate.

The world was turning, turned. The sun, where was it? Right overhead, and it was noon. High noon unrealised. Shafts everywhere. Among the trees, the grasses. Neither for nor against. Light upon the unshadowed, emptying field and the sky windless. Was it always a draw if one had enough courage?

Looking up to the gate, Wynford could just see Ceffyl's mane hanging over the last incomers to the bus, jogging and demonstrating still. Against all his feelings of an hour he stared, and heard the blood run back to his heart. Ceffyl, voluble, idiotic enthusiast, beyond reason and beyond bitterness! The School play well, did he claim? Man alive, there had been no team but Gethin! And no fight but in that composed black courage. But *the School* played well. So said Ceffyl in his folly. Could it be that so many collective feeblenesses, so many miseries, so many downright sins of commission could be retrieved in part by playing on to the end with nothing but courage? And did not that courage speak to him now against the heat of blood, against conviction of right, against the very wounds dealt and not paid for? To play on to the end, hiding regret and only learning the rules too late to win. But never too late to draw.

With a shift of shoulder he settled his heart in place. So his medallion head might fight a draw against all odds and remain silent, the same but unrecognised. The sea's reach was shorter now and the tide less full. Copper of beech and yellow of lesser trees ringed the field's southern edge where the quarry lay. The hyena bones were at one remove in their cave. 'Kathy!' he cried for only himself to hear, and turned to face the hill.

The Only Road Open

~

'Bye now.' The two women, deposited at last on the roadside where the snow-ridge broke for a moment, dropped their fuss with the driver and, raising a hand for farewell, turned to walk up the grey smudged cart-track between the frozen banks that led to the farm they lived in. It was one of many such stops. The bus began its answer, ground wretchedly at what was no more than a slight gradient, and stopped again. The engine roared. Back wheels turned furiously and the bus wriggled sideways a little before settling down to begin its crawl up the hill. What a townee the driver looked, thought Alun. White hair that had been fair once brushed long over the ears and round in two wings over the back of the head. Not angel's wings either. One of them seemed shorter: it had developed an arrogant little kink before it tucked in and disappeared. But the face was kind enough, smooth and unlined as a clerk's, if quite unfit to front such a mountain of weather. A clerk he was anyway, conductor as well as driver: he had been as cool against the press up the steps at the town stop as though he were safe behind glass. Not so cool, though, out here, balancing his bus on the road's crown and keeping it away from those browned-over ice-packs that edged out of the ditch. A townee playing pioneer on the only road open, and the depot behind him.

Alun began to take stock of the passengers who were left, the very few of all the clamberers in town. Opposite him was a boy of sixteen or seventeen, a countryman he seemed from the square of his boots and hands, but an incomer none the less. His replies to one of the women who had just alighted, quizzing him about a parcel his mother had promised, had been genteel, controlled, Welsh neither in tone nor warmth. He was no farm boy. The only other person remaining was directly in front of Alun, though two seats away, a vast-bosomed woman in a violet coat, a travelling mountain of colour in a pale and diminished world. The coat drew what was left of light into itself: from time to time it shuddered, shivered probably with cold, and a violet glint ran off it to the slopes beyond the river and back again. On another day, on a day of sun or spring, it would have been a horrible coat, a coat with long individual hairs on it as though an orang-utan had been caught, dyed and trained to sit in a bus going tentatively through the snow, and to sit in it with a positively human patience. But now it was a mountain, it was the moving pole of a world. The light shaped up to it and flickered back again to the bare fields opposite, hummocking silently under a weight of cloud.

Certainly it was no ordinary day. As the bus ran now, skeltering uneasily on the ups and downs of road, the river gleamed occasionally like a detected snake, twisting among the shoals of snow. The driver glanced right more than once, as though its pursuit startled him. Of the mountains beyond only the lower slopes could be seen, fields picked out where a tree or two plotted the hedges, a cotton-wool sky pressed ceilinglike on the few uneasy dots of sheep. It was a world contained, cut-off, a portion of time and space in a country Alun had not seen for many months and now could scarcely squeeze himself into. He had followed this road many times before, but never with this feeling of strangeness and deprivation. He was unhappier than this journey had made him for a very long time.

'Put me down at Scethrog,' said Violet-Coat suddenly. The mountain's movement broke into Alun's reverie. 'Road'll be no better than the lane in weather like this. No sense in goin' the long way round.'

The driver nodded. 'Pritchard Maescar came down it this morning. All right, he said. Except that it wore 'im out. You should manage.' He grinned, visualising the sweat and the battle, the vastness of Violet-Coat and the immovable monument of snow. Perhaps he was not such a townee after all, Alun realised.

The driver was winking now at the boy opposite, as much as to indicate what a wealth of wit had to be sacrificed for courtesy's sake. And, of course, for the sake of bus schedules. The boy smiled amiably and said nothing. As the bus jerked forward again, the last sight of Violet-Coat was a splurge of colour that the black, overhanging branches of the lane took and held for a second as a cave might hold some imperial animal in a denuded and silent domain.

Some of this conversation had been lost on Alun. He was oppressed with a misery and uneasiness that he did not fully understand. Only last night he had enjoyed coming this way in the dark. He had promised his mother he would come, and there was a tinge of excitement, even for one whose boyhood was far behind, about picking up the last bus, after four hours' travelling, on the only road westwards that was still open. As he had eaten his sausages and chips in Abergavenny among bearded and gritty-eyed long-distance drivers he had slipped for a moment into the camaraderie of danger. It was coming home, yes, and getting through.

This morning, of course, was *leaving* home, and he had never achieved this yet without a pang, without indeed those homesick reckonings of the distance travelled in miles and yards – always with the absurd supposition behind them that he could jump out at the next station or the next bus-stop and slog it back again. He had never done this, never really come near to doing it. It was just a hurt, childish thing there at the back of his heart, to be pulled out, as a stopper is pulled out, if the pain got too bad. But this afternoon his calculations had already become intermittent: the terrible lastness of seeing with which he was accustomed to greet every landmark on an occasion like this had had to be remembered, to be whipped up, as though it were a convention only. No, it was not that he was growing out of it. Nor even that many of the landmarks could not be seen on this January day, though this did make forgetting easier. He was suddenly aware, without being able momentarily to explain it, that the source of his uneasiness was ahead, not behind. As soon as he recognised the direction of the pull, however, he could no longer mistake. His mind fixed on his father, dead since the summer and buried in the little chapelyard on the slope of Glyn Collwn, with the Wenallt facing him and the Morgans, his wife's people, at his back. Nothing to see this afternoon of the defile his thoughts conjured up, nothing more than the leg that the Wenallt thrust out into the wider valley. A line of white cloud, rolled and hitched at the edge like a stage curtain, had been lowered across the opening. Presently the river turned and shot a silver tongue searchingly at it. But nothing else moved in that direction. Nothing. Certainly not the bus, which was shaking along the main road, making up its mind to cross Collwn's front at a safe distance. Alun was swept with an almost uncontrollable sense of strangeness and grief. There was no way in, no way in at all. Still in the land of his birth and his remembering, he was shut out from the secret centre of being. He was outside, outside for ever and rapidly moving away. His hands gripped the rail of the seat in front. Unconscious of all else, he stood up.

Desperately he tried to force himself into that narrow cleft, to pull away the snow curtain and bring back summer. It had been July when his father was buried, a day of sun on the high shoulders opposite. The grass in the chapelyard had been cut in his honour, and even when the scatter of red earth greeted the coffin it had been possible to believe that nothing would really be lost. Not a thought, not a memory. Only a worn-out body that had to be shed. And there, in Collwn of the years past, even that would be at home. Higher up, where the edge of the reservoir came now, was the isolated farmhouse where he, Alun, had been born. Behind the chapel, a few hundred feet up the course of one of the many streams which came off the mountain, was the cottage where his mother had lived in the days of courtship. Opposite them both, in full view of the chapel ground, ran the track on which the Merthyr train, its endless conversation reassuring, thumped every day up the gradient to the last long tunnel above Torpantau. It was an enclave, that narrow valley, scarcely inhabited now and a place of preservation. In the July sun, even in the high noon of grief, he had believed in its power to keep what was committed to it, whatever of love and happy memory should be needed against a day when the wanderers came back.

'Still got something to do,' the driver observed. He had looked back and seen Alun standing. The strained fixity of the latter's gaze had made him turn his attention riverwards too. Near the bank an engine was blowing steam. 'Can't give up playing with trucks all at once, you know.' He savoured his wit for a second and then turned to watching the road again.

Alun had not moved. He had made nothing of the interlude. Trucks? He looked again at the jet of steam from behind one of the engine sheds which was all that could now be seen. Then for a moment his everyday mind came back. The line was closed, had been since last week. One of Beeching's cuts. It was a second or two before this swelled to a personal significance and burst in to add to the terrible pressure of his recurring thought. No trains up the Glyn any more! The curtain he could see was inviolable. Never, in nature, could he go that way again. Only the way the bus went, away over the bwlch in the other direction. He shivered incessantly, as though seized with an ague. Pictures of his father jerked unsteadily before his eyes, old browning prints, thumbed across one by one. The young dark italianate face, cap on the back of head, the streets of Llanelly etched in behind it: the tricky, tireless out-half, tasselled cap on one finger; the veteran student, still young but bulging learnedly over his butterfly collar. No, these were no more than paper strength, they were second-hand memories that he had been building up since last July. Even as he shivered they were torn apart. What he felt now rather than saw was a wisp of body, a leaf merely, a thin sliver of bone, imprisoned trembling under the snow, alone and conscious of its aloneness, with brown liquid eyes – it was all leaf and eyes, as a squirrel might be – looking fearfully, agonisingly at the fallen curtain, at the blank face of the mountain opposite, at the unpeopled wilderness that Collwn had become. That other self of mine, that man I am but for age, is up there, caught, imprisoned, Alun said but without voice. When they sprinkled earth on his coffin I never knew it. When the sun was high and the red soil in their hands was part of our living I never knew it. But now I know it. I am there and here, trapped and yet free, if free only to ride away. There are two of me, and one of us must die.

He had never known such a moment of agony and constraint. He saw, and did not see, the boy of seventeen, his only fellow-passenger, alight on the slope beyond the church and turn back down towards the river and the Wenallt. It is hard to recognise the past in what looks like the future.

It was turmoil, darkness. A darkness of snow and cloud. What the bus did Alun did not know. It ran down the other side of the bwlch with increasing speed, the driver risking it a bit with so many empty seats behind him. Slumped now in his seat Alun saw nothing. Or if he did he had never been that way before. Fields, mountains, banks of snow, the dirty brown of the road curving round woods and down pitches, it was all one. It was a way of going. A way of leaving all that he had known and loved. The cloud curtain hitched itself up higher on the mountain as the road dropped, the river came back frowning from a dark visit to Llangynidr, and Alun rode on, unseeing, the traveller who no longer cares enough to complain or speak. Gliffaes. Even Crickhowell. Still no passengers. And then, yes, one. A man in a black alpaca coat, a minister. Alun stared at him vaguely. He had a thin sallow face, with cheek-lines deeply marked. A face that was totally unfamiliar to him. The minister nodded to him as he reached the top step, but said nothing. He pulled out his money, passed it to the driver with the bus already under way, and seemed concerned only to watch the road.

Alun did not look at him after the first few seconds. But his thoughts, if the black torrent within could be so described, had been diverted. That face? He had never seen it before. What was this prick of recognition? Nothing, nothing. The merest nonsense. In Wales one always thinks one recognises everybody.

But there again was the road running between snowbanks, dark brown and twisting to and fro along the floor of the valley towards the distant plain. He recognised it at last. It was the only road open.

A View of the Estuary

~

It was a narrow cul-de-sac set at an angle upwards, with a mere pretence of a turn-round at the top, and I made a poor job of parking, shuttling to and fro feebly for more than a minute and bringing the car only very slowly to point downhill. For once Celia wasn't there to get worked up about it and my nylon shirt collar didn't get as sticky as it usually does. Mair sat quite still. And when the gear-pushing was over and the wheel was turned in against the curb, I sat too and looked.

Over against us, and seen haphazardly rather than clearly through the old fly-spots and the oily residue on the windscreen, was a reach of grey water, river broadening indistinguishably into sea. Behind it was the long black shore of Gower, cliffed just high enough to cut off any view of sea eastwards and beyond. The stacks on the nearer shore tipped and barred the water like organ-pipes, dropping to trebles and sizes smaller, it seemed at first sight, as the water broadened away above them in the distance. At an angle lower was the scurry of roofs, slate-grey and slithering after the recent shower. It was a scene not meant to charm. It was full of the commonness of man, rugged, makeshift, tricky, work-stained, attaining any sort of peace only insofar as it avoided self-justification. There was sea if one cared to notice it, but a sea of silted-up harbours and derelict tramp ships. A sea which was neither pleasure nor profit, into which rivers poured themselves and were forgotten. A sea which was one with the red waters of the tropics only in the sense that there are different months in the same year, and a different moon in each of them. I dwelt on the scene for some minutes, neither expecting beauty nor finding it. The pull was one of verity, of life lived. It was years since I had seen the Llwchwr, as many years as would carry me back to boyhood, and yet there was nothing to wax sentimental about. 'How've you been, mun?' was the brusque greeting it gave me. And I to it. The question was unanswerable, anyway. 'Working,' I might have said. 'Working' might have been its nod too. Times were easier but we had long memories: my working day would long be over before the river, in its turn, could show a face that made believe that it, too, had forgotten.

What impression this scene and the odd silence that accompanied it made on Mair I did not enquire. She had been born away and outside the generations of rigour and needed no excuse to continue sitting. At my signal we got out and opened the gate from which paths splayed to both halves of the bungalow which presented its length above. There was a dilapidated terrace with posts and roofing that had not been painted for years, and the door into the leftward half looked little used. On one of the posts to its right it was possible to make out the name GLANABER in a spidery Sunday black, two of the letters weathered away but easy enough to guess. I knocked at the door once: then again after an interval.

'Uncle's very deaf these days,' I said. 'Or else he's out in the garden.' I knocked again, louder and more insistently.

Round the corner of the right-hand bungalow and up onto the covered terrace came a woman on the young side of middle age, plump, bespectacled and a little short of breath.

'Mr Evans is shaving,' she said. 'Besides, he never hears anyone at the door nowadays. You should go round the back.'

She stopped, taking in my rumpled but obviously formal suit. 'Wait a minute.' She thought while I could have counted three. 'I'll tell 'im.' Still puffing slightly, she disappeared the way she had come.

After what seemed an infinitely longer count, the woodwork opposite us began to shudder and give inwards at the top. The shuddering increased in dimension: there were sounds of heaving inside. Then the door was flung open with a violence its obstinacy had deserved, and in the gap, half-carried away by his own impetus, stood my uncle, one cheek-bone shaved but soap still adhering strenuously to all other portions of his face. Over his left arm was a towel which he had obviously meant to apply before the priorities got confused. He was wearing three pullovers, the longest of which left a couple of inches of greyish woolly vest showing above the dark-blue suit trousers, which had wide out-of-date bottoms and were frayed in several places. His braces hung down from the sweat-darkened turned-back tops.

'Well, well. Couldn't think *who* it could be. Dewch i mewn!' And again, 'Well, well.'

He stood, towel now in hand, overcome by the crisis. His hand went up as though to wipe his face, but another thought got there first. He smiled with his eyes and forgot about the soap.

'Who's this then, bachan? Which of your daughters is this? Mair, did you say? *Mair.*' He rolled the 'r' around his tongue and savoured the name as though it were a new word. 'Never seen you before, have I, Mair? No? I like to be sure.'

He remained standing on the threshold, looking at us, his perfunctory invitation to enter forgotten. 'Well, well,' he said again, using the towel now to dab at his eyes. 'Your aunt will be surprised. She will indeed. Sara,' he shouted turning at last and disappearing down the passage. 'Sara, look who's here!'

Left to ourselves, we made our way into the dark little kitchen, which was plainly the hub of the confined life of Glanaber. 'I was just getting your aunt up when you came,' Uncle Ben shouted from the next room.

'I thought you were shaving,' I said with an amused face that I knew he could not see.

'Eh, what's that?' he asked, coming out. 'What's that? What did you say?' He was watching my face. 'Oh, chipping me, is it? I always had to watch you, didn't I? Always up to something you were. I remember! Not changed a bit, have you?' His dark face, topped with greying scalp-curls as tightly rolled as an African's and fronted by the great nose that looked as though it had grown up too ambitious for its station, was crinkled with laughing. The flecked brown eyes, which all six brothers (my father amongst them) had had in common, were liquid and friendly. Just to catch a glimpse of them turned the years back and made me a child again.

He remembered the towel at last and rubbed off most of the soap from the unshaven cheek and jowl, forgetting that he hadn't really finished the other side. 'Eisteddwch i lawr,' he said. 'Sit down, sit down.' His hands and arms were dark, tanned in the way holiday-makers dream of, but there had been little sun and leisure in his past. His fingers were thick and clumsy now, the joints stiffened and the thumbnails broadened and turned in towards the quick.

'You mustn't mind me,' he went on. 'I'm a bit slow now. Don't hear very well either. So Auntie and me, we don't do a lot of talking. Can't be helped, though, can't be helped. But I'm glad to see you, bachan, indeed I am.'

Mair was sitting quite still, waiting to understand. She had never really known her own grandparents, who had died long ago, outside the first unthinking decade of her life. This was the first time she had been really close to an old age that was linked to her in blood. Sensing a little constraint, I stood up to close the gap and rally Ben a bit. I peered in the glass beside him.

'The older generation of Evanses may not have been handsome, but they were certainly distinctive,' I said. It was true. Six brothers and three sisters, some round-headed and some long-, three of the brothers and one of the sisters dark as Spaniards, and all of them with the haughty, sometimes digressive, nose that looked as though it were a child's attempt at distinguishing a Roman patrician. Ben's nose was the best of all, the most digressive and outrageous, achieving by stature what it lacked in accuracy. And it was the only one alive too.

'Should have some value as a museum-piece, shouldn't I?' he queried, amusement leaping from crag to crag of his face. 'Scarcity value. Very hot on that these days, I'm told. Eighty years old and a craftsman's job. Nothing like it round here now.'

'Mair,' he said, turning, 'don't take any notice. Your father's always rude to me.'

'I don't,' she said. 'He's always rude to me too.'

'Well, well,' he murmured, recovering his grasp of routine. 'Time to get Auntie out.' With that he disappeared into the adjoining bedroom. I had been in the bungalow just long enough to notice how cold it was, and trying to suppress a first shiver in action, I got up to see whether I could help. At the door of the bedroom I stopped: Ben was already coming towards me with a bundle in his arms. There was condensation on the top panes of the only window.

'Take her a minute, will you, while I get the chair ready.' I caught my aunt under the armpits and held the poor four stone of her, clothes flouncing and dangling, nothing visible except the head lolling against my chest. From this burden came up a foetid smell, the smell of incontinence, of clothes lived in like a burrow. I was sickened momentarily, revolted. I tried desperately to hold my breath. Then Ben was taking the burden from me and tucking it down in the chair. On what looked like a child's face, pink and white and unlined, was a feeble smile, made of parted lips and something, just something, in the eyes.

'There, Sara. You didn't believe me, did you? But here's Gerwyn, as I said. And Mair. You've not seen Mair before, but I've told you about her, haven't I? You remember. She's at University now.' Mair and I in turn felt for the limp fingers hidden in the end of the long woollen sleeve.

'How are you, Auntie?' I asked, my voice sounding louder than necessary. The lips moved, but no sound was detectable at the range of formality. Bending down, I picked up the burden of the whisper as it was repeated. 'All right, boy. All right but for this ol' complaint.'

'Good, good. That's it, that's the way.' I followed with other meaningless heartinesses, of which I was ashamed even in the saying. I did not know the end, let alone the way. And to have known something of the beginning seemed at that moment of very little help. It was a mercy that these dishonesties elicited no further reply beyond the barest parting of the lips.

But my uncle was not one to leave me in difficulties for long. Never getting any answers, or none that he could hear, he had long been accustomed to a rhetoric of his own devising, which bounded forward at quick, irregular intervals, as though, having played his ball onto a wall or an angle of his private fives court, he had to jump in and slash it back, or missing, take it another way on the rebound. He appeared to know that he could afford a second or two for plain inattention, but must then make some immediate, possibly violent, move.

'How's Celia, then, bachan?' He did not wait for an answer, his dark face animated. 'Our Rhian's won a scholarship, did you know? To University, yes. Clever girl, she is. There's not many can say they've got a grand-daughter that's won a University scholarship, now is there?'

'When . . .' I began. 'When . . .' But my thought had already been distracted by a movement that I sensed rather than saw. I was conscious of some urgency in the doll-like figure in the chair. Looking more closely, I realised that the lips were moving.

'Photograph.' The word formed slowly and whisperingly. 'Ben, show them the photograph.'

Ben was talking hard, rallying Mair now and pushing her shoulder back with the blunt ends of his extended fingers. He had taken no notice of my attempted question, let alone his wife's tiny excision of her envelope of silence.

'Uncle,' I said. '*Uncle!* I see I shall have to do some bullying too.' He looked at me in surprise half-thinking I resented his familiarity with Mair. 'The photograph. Auntie says what about the photograph.'

For a second or two he still looked at me blankly. Then, realising and turning almost concurrently, he disappeared into the front room and came back with it in his hand. 'There,' he said triumphantly. 'Isn't she a fine girl, our Rhian?'

I looked at the photograph carefully. There were the features again, unmistakeable. The dark, handsome, almost negroid face with the distended nostrils and the mass of little scalp-curls. Idwal to the life, all but the squint she had against the brightness of the light. A fine-looking girl, by any standards.

'Taken in Adelaide?' I was trying hard to avoid the real questions.

'Yes, Adelaide. That's the University in the background.' It was a slab of white wall. It could have been anywhere, provided anywhere was sunny enough.

He took the photograph back slowly, keeping his eyes on it as though there were something about it that he had not really seen before. Then, turning away, he put his arm round Mair's shoulders with sudden boisterousness. 'Come on, merch fach i, let me show you the bungalow. Great place we've got here, you know. Extensive. Room for twice as many.' His voice swept down the passage and into the front room. I was at a loss. The invitation had not seemed to include me: indeed, I had some sort of sense that it was important to Uncle Ben that I should not tag along. 'At all costs,' said a cowardly urge, 'don't get left here, mun. Don't be left with Auntie. What will you say?' I went down the passage far enough to be out of sight of the invalid chair and stood still. Uncle was talking photographs in the room beyond, pointing out each individual face. Mair was mute, probably muddled by the many names she did not know and afraid to reveal her ignorance. They wouldn't be out for a minute or two yet. I stood in this transit-place, aware that I had deliberately walked out of life and all ears not to be caught doing it. I stood with both palms against the clammy wall and thought.

That photograph. Shaking really, that anybody could be so like. The past living again, but in Australia. Something about that transplanting was a wound, even to me. It was an end and a cutting-off, whatever life there was in it.

I found myself pressing against the wall, for no reason that I could name. Perhaps I had walked out of time too. I was possessed by that utterly alien feeling that one has only in childhood, that sense of seeing and understanding and not being at home. I was back forty years and the wall was cold behind me. Uncle Ben was an ironmonger then and Aunt Sara, in her cold, composed way, was queening it among the locals. An inexorable social aspirant, Sara. Her good looks, broad brow and closely curling hair didn't hold the attention long. The hardness came out like a ratchet to fix one exactly in one's place, and it had to be a very special occasion for me not to be conscious of being pinned down, not so much intimidated as powerless to escape the measuring-tape with which her square hands were so constantly occupied.

Whatever Ben and she were did not so much matter. It was for Idwal, her son, that she planned and drove. Ben must work harder, make all possible. Ben must immolate himself on the altar. Ben must not question the unspoken contract she had with the greatness of her son's image. It was a hard, cumulative story that had cracked now as iron cracks. It was all so old, and unbelievable. And yet it had produced Idwal, if only for a time. Idwal was in some ways a replica of his mother, only handsomer, with black, curly hair and dark, almost negroid features with wide-spreading nostrils. How poor Ben, with his digressive nose, could have had a part in such symmetry was at first hard to see. But he had given the boy his colour and the black scalp-curls too.

I remembered going down to the river at Llanybyther once to find Idwal. He was about twelve then, bare feet and jampot for tiddlers and all, and I was two years younger. I went to the river because I had been sent. The truth was that I was a bit afraid of Idwal: he was tougher than I, more confident as well as older. Not at all prissy and sensitive like I was. Idwal laughed when I arrived and showed me off to a lot of other kids. 'My cousin, look,' he said. '*My cousin*. Down from the Valleys.' He laughed again, as though daring any comment. I quivered inwardly, wishing myself anywhere else in the world, knowing that the next step would be a dare. Across the river by way of the stones, many of them awash. What would my mother say? And my best shoes too!

Later, more than five years later, Idwal proposed to follow a course in medicine at a London hospital. Ben, at Sara's bidding, sold his ironmonger's shop and bought a dairy business in Cricklewood at a price that crippled him financially – just to save lodging money for Idwal and to keep him in Sara's sight. We met occasionally in the next few years, Idwal and I – I was a clerk in the Aldgate branch of Lloyd's Bank for my first permanent appointment – and once in a while we foregathered at Stewart's or Pritchard's in Oxford Street or at Hyde Park Corner. These meetings would be on Sunday nights when I had come across for the service at King's Cross Chapel, whether for my cousin's sake or to hear Elvet Lewis I never quite knew. Idwal had the same confidently jovial manner then as that day by the river, but enlarged as perhaps only London could enlarge it. He slapped me on the back and patronised me happily to his fellow-students. 'Our banking member,' he called me. I didn't feel much larger on these occasions than if he had dared me to wet my shoes again. Rotund, earnest and vulnerable, I reserved my wit for those I was sure of, meaning too often, I suppose, those who were a bit slower than I was. I knew I cut no figure beside Idwal's broad shoulders and dark, authoritative head.

Once or twice, too, I visited the dairy at Cricklewood looking for my cousin. Uncle was always dead beat with work, cycling the last rounds himself in plimsolls with a few bottles on the tray of his bike. Up at four in the morning, working sixteen hours a day at least and grey in the face with fatigue. My aunt kept a prim house behind the shop and welcomed me with only the briefest of smiles. She regarded me as a hanger-on, an amiable nobody who could not, even if he would, help her son in any way. I didn't like facing her on my own. Give Idwal his due, when he was there he brushed past all this, jollied his way in and out. And then even my uncle would joke for a minute or two, till his arm dropped off my shoulder with weariness.

Idwal failed his exams a couple of times, but the power behind him was inexorable. In the end he passed. Six years – or was it seven? He could hardly do anything else. And then he suddenly said he wanted to join the Army, become a doctor in the RAMC. I say 'suddenly' because I'd never heard of it until it happened. I was over at the dairy one night after the results of his examinations were known – this was not the celebration: we had had our junketings at Stewart's and in The Coal Hole and other places too many to remember – and I sat down at the piano to play for Idwal to sing. He was no singer but he liked to have a bawl now and again, a concession to the Welshness of his youth, and Sara approved my pianistic skills (which didn't really go much beyond knocking out a tune by ear) because they were a means for Idwal to make more noise than I did. She sat in the background, a faint smile on her face, intervening only to suggest that we might drop some of those ol' Welsh hymns and sing something a bit more refined. Ben came in once, in his plimsolls, and joined in a verse or two, singing in a resonant voice that was nearer the note than Idwal's. But Sara was impatient, waving him away. 'Get finished, Ben, before coming in here. You know very well it'll be ten o'clock before you've finished with those bottles. Go on.' Almost as the door closed, Idwal switched his bawl to the sort of conversational tone that he thought wouldn't ding my ear in. 'You know I've decided to try the Army, don't you?' In my astonishment – partly at the news and partly at the unnecessary drama of the decibel-drop – I let fall my hands on the keyboard in an unspeakable disharmony of sound. Sara's patience with me, always thin, broke at that, and it was no more than a perfunctory few minutes before I was on my way out. I didn't really need to work for my bank exam – I'd been at it both the nights previous – but it was the quickest thing to say.

It was some months before I heard the news and many years before I understood that I should never see Idwal again. The rigorous medical examination he had been given by the Army Board had revealed a kidney complaint at a stage already advanced: he had, in the doctors' opinion, six months at most to live. It was suggested to him, however, that his life might be prolonged if he could make up the salt deficiency somehow, perhaps by going on board ship and crusting it in by wave or wind all hours of the day and night. The hope was not much but he seized it; he signed on as a ship's doctor and, war breaking out within the next few months, sailed back and fore to the Far East in troopships – at least till Singapore fell, and after that on voyages more devious but always fresh with the winds of continuance. So nearly eight years passed: the war was over, and Idwal, still journeying back with the repatriated and out with the emigrant hopeful, strengthened his hold on life. So much so that he ventured on marriage to Margaret, a nurse of Welsh descent who had been brought up in Australia (where her mother still was), and steeled himself to take a post ashore. For nearly a year the omens held: Rhian was born of the union, Idwal managed as a houseman in a Liverpool hospital. Then the end came, and suddenly: he went blind and was dead within the month, prescribing for himself with full medical competence at each deteriorating and terrible stage of the disease. It was an exercise in doggedness, the tight-lipped parries of a man who had counted out his days for more than a quarter of his life.

It was the end, all this, of more than Sara's hope in Idwal. Margaret went back to Australia to her mother, taking Rhian with her: later she married a schoolmaster named Robertson, a colleague of hers in the boarding school where she served as matron. So all that was left of this flesh and blood was in the Antipodes, a slip of a girl with an Australian accent and a name that her acquaintances would most certainly mishandle. And that photograph! - the likeness was uncanny. The hatpeg nose would die with Ben, but his colouring and the curled wool of his hair had been transplanted successfully. A whole culture off and yet a biological survival.

It would be ridiculous to suppose that all this flashed through my mind's maze as I stood with my back to the wall in the passage of the bungalow. And yet it was all there, coiled, uneasy in my consciousness. It had been collected from letters, the chatter of an ageing female cousin, and just two visits, the last one more than ten years ago. Truth to tell, I hadn't wanted to see Sara. Why should he survive, I could imagine her saying: why should he survive who never had anything about him, when Idwal, with twice the presence, could not? An aircraftman, that's all I'd been, and a pretty poor one at that. And if I was a bank manager now, was it due to much more than a ready smile and a terrible fear of doing the wrong thing, socially and financially? But there was really no need any longer for this reluctance of mine to visit Ben. Sara had had Parkinson's for upwards of six years and for the last three or four she had said nothing. Nothing that was readily audible, anyway. And yet I couldn't face her, couldn't produce tenderness for one who had needed fear of old. And pity? I was suddenly uncertain of my motive for coming at all, though I had thought it a matter of conscience that had been nagging me for months, years.

It was at this uneasy moment, when I had begun to lose myself as well as time and place, that I heard Ben's voice growing louder. He had been the round of the photographs and was shepherding Mair back to the kitchen. I had no time for a new posture: all I could do was to advance with an air of happening to be on my way to look for them and to meet them in the doorway.

'Nice bungalow we've got here, haven't we, Mair?' Ben said when he saw me. 'Too big for us really. You must come and stay some time. Leave your old Dada. He doesn't appreciate you. Only thing he cares about is counting the coppers. He won't notice you're gone even.'

Unease or no unease, I couldn't help rising to this. The Evanses could always spark off the present, whatever past or future might say. 'Go on, uncle. You set too much store by that unique beauty of yours. Unrepeatable value and so on. There's something to be said for bank managers, you know.'

'Something, but not much,' said Uncle Ben, his eyes wrinkling with a friendliness that took all the sting out of the words. 'Come and look at the garden,' he added, fumbling with the back door, which had a piece of sacking nailed to the bottom to keep out the draught. An overlapping piece was stuffed down the side, too, and it was this which made necessary what looked like furious efforts on my uncle's part. 'All these damn doors stick,' he muttered, suddenly flushed about the temples. The garden, when it finally came into view, was a large kite-shaped patch with the length of it dragged steeply uphill to a point where two other gardens nipped it with brick walls and shrubbery and held it there, immovable. In the middle distance were some old brussels sprout stalks, bare to the palm-plumes at the top. Nearer were one or two lumps of squitch and a great deal of groundsel. 'Too much for me now,' Ben said heavily. 'Good soil, too. But it can't be helped.'

Goodbyes came a few minutes later, despite Ben's unwillingness to let us go. Tea was something he could manage, part of the old code of hospitality. 'You could stay long enough for that, bachan,' he said wistfully. 'Auntie would like it. Wouldn't you, Sara?' I couldn't be sure whether the shapeless little doll in the chair moved or not. Perhaps there was something minutely different about the expression. I tried hard to think so as I took the power-less hand and came for a moment again within the foetid arc. 'Goodbye, Auntie! Look after yourself.' The ridiculous words came out before I could stop them. I rushed out after the others, fearful that Mair might have heard. I knew Ben would not.

But they were standing by the gate looking at a small yew cut like a bear. It had an empty tomato tin upturned on one paw. 'His honey pot,' said Ben, simply and without excuse. 'Who did it? You?' I asked breathlessly, anxious to purge myself by saying anything, anything. 'Yes,' he said, waving a hand as though expansively. 'I can't draw any more, but I still like to make things.'

'You'll come again, Mair, won't you?' he asked. 'You're not too far away, half an hour on the bus at most. Never mind what your Dada says. He can't stop you from where he is. Come now.' His grip on the girl's arm was urgent and his face serious.

'Yes, I'll come,' she said. We got into the car and slid away quietly down the cul-de-sac. I could see Ben in my mirror: he was standing outside the gate with one arm upraised, motionless. The stacks against the Llwchwr dropped quickly out of sight, and the sea's dull grey was lost behind the rising angle of roofs. What elevation there had been, and it was just enough for us to see the river as it debouched, had disappeared, and near-sightedness, the care of the crowded road, took over again.

Siams

~

Icould see, through the glass panes in the upper half of the door, that someone, a woman, was up on the steps with a paint brush. That made me pause. Was this the right house? Across the road were the grassed-up dunes that the sea had dumped there at some time long past: further along, on the seaward side but where the road cut inland for a few hundred yards, was a bizarrely modern structure that proclaimed itself a church. I knew, because I'd been up there and back again, scanning the gateways. But a step or two towards town, where I had parked the car, there were a few houses set back on a little sweep of by-road, and then came these four together, of which 'Y Gilfach' should be the first. But there was no name either on door or gate. I was momentarily flummoxed. As an additional check, I walked down the path again and in through the next gate. No, that was 'Aysgarth', delineated clearly enough. I must have been right the first time. But the woman? Who could that be? Domestics didn't wield paint brushes, or only very unusually. And I had thought Uncle Aaron lived alone.

He wasn't really my uncle. In fact, he was my father's second cousin, the only child of a much older first cousin by a second wife. It would all seem pretty complicated set out in black and white. But in the old Carmarthenshire days they had lived close, the whole poverty-stricken cousinage, until my grandfather got work in Llanelli and moved his immediate descendants away. I had never seen this old man because he too had left the Rhos, had gone away to Scotland to be an exciseman, and by the time I, as a child, had accompanied my father in the rediscovery of his cousinage amongst the squatters dotted over the sour uplands of that backward region, Aaron Aaron was a name no more than occasionally heard of. But my father, when he mentioned him, always said that he was 'sharp'. He meant intelligent. Not an academic, but intelligent beyond the expectations of any son of a one-cow-place such as he was. And there hadn't been room there for another carpenter, not even when my grandfather left. So he went away. And now he was in his eighties, only a year or two retired from reporting for a whole bunch of north Wales newspapers, a job he'd taken up when his time in the excise service came to an end. Oh yes, he was sharp enough. But now that I was close to meeting him, I wasn't sure why I had taken the trouble to come. Except that he was one of only two left from the oldest generation of the family. And, after all, I *had* had time between meetings to drive across and back. But what did I know of him? Only that his name had been first on the list of subscribers to the *Blaid* for more than a couple of decades. Impressive, perhaps? Not when you considered how hard it would be to beat a name like Aaron Aaron for precedence. No, it might not mean much.

It was a cold, blowy morning and I was beginning to reproach myself for being so hesitant and cowardly. Had I really driven twenty-five miles to be balked now? I went back to the gate and the short gravel path I had first traversed.

The doorbell gave one of those reluctant rings that indicate a battery just about to lie down and die. But it was enough to get the woman off her steps. After an interval (for she had first disappeared down the passage) the door opened. A slender woman she was, with still-fair hair, the remains of a delicate prettiness lingering about the cheek-bones and mouth. She waited for me to speak.

Yes, Mr Aaron lived there. Would I come in? He wasn't fully dressed yet, but would be ready shortly. The room at the end of the passage, the kitchen-living-room, had a cheerful open fire. I stood about uneasily, my academic bonhomie sadly out of place. It was the not knowing who this woman was that bothered me. She, for her part, made no attempt at conversation. After glancing at me with some uncertainty for a moment and parrying my trite remark about the weather with a monosyllable, she went upstairs. I could imagine her getting the old man up quickly, bundling him into trousers, shirt and tie. A series of irregular bumps seemed to indicate haste and a lack of co-ordination between force and the subject to which it was applied.

At last he came slowly down the stairs, along the passage and into view. It was the face of a man who had not long begun to look old, still capable of total illumination, as I was to find. Dark, long-nosed like all my father's people, the hair thin like that of all the cousinage but not yet white, he shuffled in a way the head belied. His face was not a forceful one, rather clerkish and humorous, with a frequent gleam in the corners of the brown eyes. But the voice at first speaking was slack, uninterested, almost a trifle resentful, as though he had been hurried for nothing. It turned out later that he was expecting some chapel business that he was less than pleased about. The woman had not asked my name and there were reasons, as I realised later, why she would not have known a chapel messenger unless he were one of Aaron's cronies.

All the same, as he was speaking his first words, the tone changed. He looked at me closely as he held out a hand. Obviously I was nobody from the chapel.

'Walter Aaron,' I said. 'I've written to you a couple of times over the years. Do you remember?'

'Wel, bachan,' he said, his eyes lighting up. 'Wel, wel. Family after all this long time. Wel, wel. Mawredd, I'm glad to see you.' He went on holding my hand without shaking it. 'Didn't think to see you ever, though I've got some of your books. Didn't think any of the family would come so far north as to pay me a visit.'

'There is the great modern invention of the motor-car,' I said, trying to take a little of the emotion out of it. 'I was in Aber anyway. It's not really so far.'

'Family,' he said again musingly, ignoring the tone of my intervention. 'Not so much of it left, is there? Tell me' – and here he lifted a forefinger between his face and mine – 'tell me, that chap on television, the quizmaster fellow, he's one of ours, isn't he?'

'There are quite a lot of Aarons about,' I replied, obfuscating to improve what I was to say next. 'But this one's my son. You guessed from the name Tyssul, didn't you?'

'No,' he said, 'No.' He fingered his cheek-bone for a moment. 'James Tyssul Aaron. It was the face. I knew it had to be one of ours.'

'But sit down, sit down. I want to hear everything. Do you ever see Siams?' He used the old Carmarthenshire form. 'Siams and I, we were very close in the old days. Now we're the only two alive.

They're all gone, the others, your dad, Ben, Dafi, Ifan, all of them.'

Siams was another cousin of my father's. It was a sort of triangle, with long-dead Aarons at the crossing points. I hadn't seen Siams for years, though the news was that he was still interrogating former pupils amongst the back-to-back terraces of Dafen, where he had been for decades headmaster of the local secondary school. Truth to tell, I'd never wanted to see him much since I was about ten years of age. Whenever we'd called in at Dafen (it was no great distance and my father had been a great caller-in on his relatives) Siams had me cornered within minutes. 'You're a bright boy, they tell me. Now do this simple little sum for me.' And out would come some mathematical problem whose only point was that there was a catch in the answer. I was never any good at arithmetic and most oral questions about it would have flummoxed me. But Siams's deliberate enunciation, a kind of gravelled country accent cut off from a drawl by the persistent clipping of final consonants, and the gleaming expectation in his eye that he was going to put me down yet again, made my young mind an immediate maelstrom. I would begin to perspire within the minute. Even then I knew enough in another way to imagine him saying to himself: 'Clever boy, is he? Who says so? His school? Dewch ymlaen, Siams, let's show him he wouldn't get into Dafen Intermediate, shall we?' He was immensely competitive, was Siams, but with a kind of perfection in view. Years later I heard that he asked himself questions too, and often. Oh yes, Siams was sharp. They had been a sharp lot down there on the steep slope above Saron. But it was a sharpness that as a boy I hadn't been able to bear. I wondered, even as Aaron was speaking, whether *he* had been like Siams when he was younger.

Even the mention of Siams's name had sent me into total juvenile recall. Those humiliations were never far from the surface, though they rose less frequently now. But for Aaron the connotations were radically different: he had been talking of boyish exploits and was about to launch himself on a more detailed narrative when he perhaps noticed that my eye was dull and inward-looking. Whatever the reason, he was restored to a consciousness of his duties as a host. For the five or six minutes I had been there the faded-looking woman had been fidgeting behind the settee, not knowing whether to stay or go. Aaron must have been partly conscious of her because he had so far spoken only in English. But now he looked across at her and waved his hand.

'My daughter Marjorie,' he said. 'Looks after me now. Been with me nearly twenty years, ever since I came back from Manchester.' There was a faint air about him, not of pride exactly but of some sort of achievement.

I offered a hand. It seemed the best way to cover the slight awkwardness. The woman smiled faintly, her hand limp in mine.

'I'll get you some coffee,' she said quickly. 'I'm sure you'd like some after coming so far.' She disappeared to the scullery at the back without waiting even for a nod from me.

'Siams.' The last half-minute had barely interrupted an irresistible train of thought. The old man was back at his remembering, his guest entirely out of mind. But suddenly he returned to the present, leaned forward in his chair and spoke to me in Welsh.

'You know,' he said, 'Siams was always on at me to take care. The few times I saw him after he went away to College, he always told me, *take care*. Women, he said, they're too smart for the likes of you, boy. Too smart by half. You want to watch who you go with. Or one of them'll make a fool of you, sure enough. It's all in the head, he'd say. All in the head. You want to take care.'

I had an immediate vision of a watchful Siams, younger and less gravelled, saying this out of the high stiff collar I'd seen in his photograph. He'd been an usher in the school at Saron before getting a Queen's Scholarship. And there he was, forever on the piano in the front room in my old home in Marble Hall Road, looking cocky and contained – those long ears with a noticeable point at the top had given a face that even in youth was long-nosed and fleshy enough an indescribably puckish look – separated entirely from the bringer of terror I had encountered later. I suppose you could say that the priggish-sharpness carried over from the first memory to the second, but the duality was something I hadn't thought about for years. The devil of it was he had been right. Right in the cases I knew of, anyway. Right in the case of his own son – his only son Huw – who had married a London hospital nurse too quickly and less than well. I recalled my own shock one morning years ago when, having settled into a seat on the London train I had boarded at Neath, I had heard that unmistakable boxed-gravel voice coming up the corridor, getting closer with every exhortation. I never found out whom he was travelling with. The fact was that at sight of me he sat down at once in the seat on my right, the compartment being empty but for one other person, and raved all the way to London (if one can rave in a voice that continually clips its natural excesses) about Huw and his being a slave to sexual passion. Huw had been at school with me in the County, a nervous, highly-strung boy who ran round and round the narrow vegetable plot we had at the back screaming either with excitement or fear whenever he was chased. It depended who was chasing him. He wasn't afraid of me. I was a nervous kid myself but I had found him an embarrassment. This raving of Siams's opened an even more awful vista, another narrow plot with screaming in it, the note in it changing all the time. Even with what I remembered I found it hard to believe. But Siams had been right. The marriage had lasted a few years and produced a daughter or two, with the woman revealing herself as coarse, unbearable and prone to scream herself when the rage was on her. Huw had gone off on his own, out of sight for a while. And Siams had not spoken one word to him until the break came. Yes, I could see that young usher in the high collar telling Aaron to take care. And I could see Aaron the disciple, sharp of nose and eye, admiring, listening to the world as it spoke through one who knew it. Perhaps he had had a high collar too. I'd never seen him caught and framed in any of the family front rooms.

Aaron was watching me carefully, trying to gauge my reaction to Siams's warning. What my expression was I find it difficult to recall. Memory had overcome me and no doubt my face showed it. But Aaron went on, evidently under compulsion.

'You know, Siams hasn't spoken or written to me for nearly sixty years,' he said. 'And now that we're the only two of the old generation left, it seems a pity. I've offended him, I'm sure. I must have. He would have written else.' His manner was eager but I sensed that he was equivocating a little.

'Have *you* written to him?' I asked. 'Or been to see him?'

'No,' he admitted uneasily. 'No.'

'Then why should you think he's quarrelled with you?' I pressed the point a little by leaning forward. 'Have you quarrelled with him?'

Again that uneasy 'no' and a slight spreading of the hands.

I didn't like to press the point too hard. After all, I didn't know him really and I had been brought up to respect those older than myself. In the family, anyway. Outside I'd go for greybeards like the rest.

'Well then . . .' I began, but he interrupted me. There was an urgent, surprising tone to his voice.

'I'd like it very much if you'd go to see Siams for me,' he said. 'Or write to him and say you've seen me.'

This was ridiculous. Dafen was right off my normal track now that we'd sold the house in Marble Hall Road. Anyway, I had no desire at all to find myself a small boy again in Siams's presence. I began to demur, using the arguments of commonsense. Why didn't he write himself?

But he took no notice of what I said. He continued to plead with me. 'Write to him for me,' he urged. 'Tell him I'll be glad and grateful to have a word from him.'

I was baffled. It was all so nonsensical. What good was I as an intermediary, anyway? But I could see I should have to agree. He was becoming emotional about it.

Then the door opened and Marjorie came in with the coffee. Aaron changed the subject immediately, composing his features as he did so. Sitting back in his chair, and with some of the observant gleam I had noticed at first, he began asking me about the study of economic history, pointing out that he had at least one of my books on the shelf above my head. But he couldn't take this far and I felt it was inappropriate to enlarge. We fell to sipping politely and talking about the family. But I was uneasy about Marjorie. Not because of anything about her demeanour, though that was reserved enough. But because I was trying to dredge from my memory what I'd once heard. It was all so vague and long ago. She'd been married, to an artist with an Irish name – Shaughnessy or something like that – and divorced. Of why I knew nothing and couldn't possibly ask. But no doubt that was why she was here, living with her father. Aaron, for his part, seemed determined that I should know something about his daughter, if not the nub of the matter. He insisted, with an air of gaiety, on her telling me about her children. There were two, it seemed, both married: a son living in Arfon and a daughter in Australia. And there were six grand-children so far. It sounded good, good enough for a smile from Marjorie and an expansive sentence or two. But she spoke flatly, with no lightening of the eye, and in an accent, I was curious to note, that seemed devoid of even the smallest Welsh intonation. As the conversation went on, she fell out of it, listening patiently but with no great interest as I described my branch of the family. It was Aaron who pushed the enquiry into every corner, persisting till he uncovered the last great-nephew. No, that's an exaggeration: it didn't take long to work out those who still bore the family name, and that's what he seemed to be interested in.

'Only you and Tyssul, your brother William and his son Roy, you say, and Siams and Huw. That's all,' he said musingly. 'Not many when you remember the tribe at Saron.'

'Ah, but wonderful quality,' I replied jokingly. 'Few but beautiful.' He looked at me as though I hadn't spoken.

'Huw's at stop,' he said. 'That leaves Tyssul and Roy. And both of them in England.' He went into a gloomy silence.

Marjorie saw her moment to collect the coffee-cups and make her exit, which she did with a kind of stealth, as though too obvious a movement might set Aaron off again. But no sooner was the door closed than the old man sat up in his chair again and beckoned me over to the nearer one which Marjorie had occupied. He leaned over and began to whisper rapidly in Welsh.

'I want you to know this,' he said. 'Listen carefully. When I was in the excise service as a young man I was stationed at Grantown-on-Spey in Scotland, and there I met my wife. Fay Donaldson her name was and beautiful fair hair she had then. But she diddled me. Oh yes, she diddled me. Marjorie doesn't know it, but she's not *my* daughter. Fay didn't tell me until after we were married and then I couldn't bring myself to go near her, not from then on. She's been dead, Fay has, these many years, but I can't forget. My grandchildren, you see, none of them family. None of them really Aarons. I want you to know because the ones who are left must be certain about this. It would be a greater shame not to tell.'

It was Siams he was telling, I knew that. The disciple was on stop too, had never really started. All that eager beavering around, all that sharp-nosed respect for academic success, all that high-collared savvy, this is what it had brought the pair of them. Two well-scrubbed young men, ascetic in their country boots, they had come out of the customs of poverty with an inbred suspicion of the world outside. But it hadn't been enough. They hadn't managed to carry the line they meant to. A is for Aaron, W for Wales. Very nearly Z.

I was conscious of not making an adequate response. This was the message. To me, and through me. And Aaron was willing it into me, his eyes bulging slightly around that sharp brownness, knowing that the door would open again at any moment. And for his purposes, within his lifetime, that is (bearing in mind how many years it had taken me to get to 'Y Gilfach' at all), knowing that it might never close again. I nodded a little feebly and began to gesture words that were in need of more force than I could give them. The opening of the door saved me. Marjorie was there again, her faded delicacy a little brightened by the knowledge that she had discharged her duty as a hostess.

The tale was over. There was really nothing that I could add, not from economic history or any other discipline. Perhaps there had been too much discipline already. I got up to go.

Aaron did not dissuade me, but continued to look into my face with a kind of silent pleading. I promised to visit him again, not knowing how far I meant it. In the passage was a smell of paint. Marjorie warned me not to go for the door handle myself, but to wait for her. I saw that she had smoothed the passage walls and the inside of the door with a battleship grey.

Outside the wind was still gusting, the salt in it noticeable after the warm kitchen odour. Over those dunes somewhere was the sea, and down the road the continuing life that I supposed I was part of. Did I feel a slight shrinking from it, as though I had been ashore on a half-forgotten family sandbank? Aaron had not come to the door: Marjorie waved me neutrally off, her hair blowing in the wind and her face lost in shadow.

I made for the car. Somewhere out there were Tyssul and Roy and my brother William. And Huw. And yes, I would go and see Siams. I might satisfy him as a proxy if not in my own right.

Notes

~

Introduction

p.xxiv '*For M.A.H.*': published in *Break In Harvest* (1946).

p.xxiv '*The rows at Tew . . . Lucius Cary*': i.e. rows of trees in Great Tew Park, about five miles north of Enstone. For a while, Lucius Cary, second Viscount Falkland (1610?–43), lived and entertained at the manor house there. Among the friends who enjoyed his hospitality were Ben Jonson, Edward Hyde, earl of Clarendon and Thomas Hobbes. In the period leading up to and during the Civil War, Cary was active in politics in the royalist cause. He became secretary of state to Charles I and, in 1641, was sent by the King to negotiate with Parliament. Despairing of peace, he threw away his life at the first battle of Newbury, September 1643.

p.xxiv *Hampden . . . Chiselhampton*: John Hampden (1594–1643) was the most prominent of those MPs who opposed the king's tax-raising policies in the period leading up to the Civil War, and a great leader and political strategist. In June 1643, he took a hastily gathered small body of parliamentarian troops to harry a larger force led by Prince Rupert returning to its quarters at Chiselhampton. They met at Chalgrove Field, where Hampden courageously led the charge but was mortally wounded.

p.xxxvi '*They Have Not Survived*': published in *Absalom in the Tree* (1971).

p.xxxvi *cenedl*: usually translated 'nation', but the word also means 'kind' or 'kin'. The writer's English synonym is 'cousinhood'.

p.xxxvi *tallut*: a dialect word used in the west of England and south Wales, meaning 'loft', especially the loft formed by laying boards on joists over a stable.

p.xxxviii '*A Letter*': published in *The Roses of Tretower* (1952).

p.xxxviii '*Indictment*': published in *Absalom in the Tree* (1971).

Saturday Night

p.1 '*Call him louder*': these words come from the recitative, 'Call him [i.e. Baal] louder! he heareth not. With knives and lancets cut yourselves after your manner: leap upon the altar ye have made: call him, and prophesy! Not a voice will answer you', which is Elijah's response to the chorus 'Baal, we cry to thee . . . Hear us, Baal!', from Mendelssohn's *Elijah*.

p.1 *the stained blanket*: the prophet Elijah wears a mantle. At the end of his story, when a chariot of fire appears and he ascends 'by a whirlwind into heaven', the mantle falls on Elisha (II Kings 2). The way in which Elijah 'troubled' the wayward Israel of King Ahab and his Queen Jezebel is told in I Kings 17–22.

p.1 '*Is not His word like a fire*': the opening words of an air from Mendelssohn's *Elijah*, 'Is not His word like a fire and like a hammer that breaketh the rock? For God is angry with the wicked ev'ry day! And if the wicked turn not, the Lord will whet His sword.'

p.2 *finger-stalls*: a covering of leather or some other material, used to protect an injured finger.

p.2 *a cloud like a man's hand*: from I Kings 18: 44: 'Behold, there ariseth a little cloud out of the sea, like a man's hand.' It presages a storm for King Ahab.

p.2 '*Arise, Elijah, for thou hast a journey before thee*': recitative from *Elijah* by Mendelssohn: 'Arise, Elijah, for thou hast a long journey before thee. Forty days and forty nights shalt thou go to Horeb, the mount of God.'

p.2 *Great he was in Carmel*: Mount Carmel is the scene of the confrontation above, between Elijah and the priests of Baal. In *Elijah*, it is introduced by the recitative and chorus, 'Now send and gather to me the whole of Israel unto Mount Carmel; there summon the prophets of Baal, and also the prophets of the groves who are feasted at Jezebel's table. Then, then we shall see whose God is Lord.'

A Duty to the Community

p.4 *the Rhos*: Rhos Llangeler (*rhos* = moor), the original home in Carmarthenshire of the writer's father, Evan Mathias, and his numerous kin.

p.4 *the Waun*: *gwaun* is grazing land, moor or meadow, here the name of a smallholding added to identify the person referred to.

p.4 *mun*: equivalent to 'man', frequently used in south Wales English, usually as a friendly or cajoling addition to expression, and applied indiscriminately to both sexes.

p.4 *butties*: 'friends' or 'workmates' in the south Wales vernacular.

p.4 *Glaspant*: *glas* = green; *pant* = valley or hollow; therefore literally 'green hollow', used like 'the Waun' above.

p.5 *Dafi Bach*: *bach* = little; *Dafi* is an abbreviation of Dafydd.

p.6 *Mari Penfforddnewydd*: *pen* = end or top; *ffordd* = road; *newydd* = new; therefore literally 'at the end of the new road', used to identify Mari, like 'the Waun' above.

p.6 *Pwllgloyw*: *pwll* = pool (or pit); *gloyw* = shining, bright; therefore literally 'bright pool', again used like 'the Waun' above.

p.6 *O Mawredd*: a gentle expletive; *mawredd* = greatness, majesty, a synonym for God.

p.7 *bachan*: derivative of 'bach', roughly equivalent to 'little one', more commonly used affectionately or, as here, patronizingly.

p.7 *Blaenllain*: *blaen* = front or in front of; *llain* = a narrow strip of land; the name of a place or holding.

p.7 *twp*: stupid, usually adjectival, but here employed as a noun.

Jonesy and the Duke

p.8 *the [Iron] Duke*: Sir Arthur Wellesley, the duke of Wellington (1769–1842).

p.8 *Cwmmwd Coch*: fictional town name; *cwmwd* = commote, a small administrative division of land; *coch* = red.

p.8 *a tidy man*: one who is sensible, solvent, worthy of respect. In the vernacular of south Wales, 'tidy' has a host of generally favourable meanings depending upon context. It is applied here with more than a hint of irony.

p.8 *And if business takes him to the Mandrill Arms of a Sunday ... thirsty*: Cwmmwd Coch is evidently close to the border with England, where the licensing laws of the time permitted drinking in public houses on Sundays, as distinct from Wales, where they did not.

p.9 *Labour Officer*: official in the 'Labour Exchange', which had the task of finding work for the unemployed.

p.9 *Quarter Brass and the thin red line*: 'Quarter Brass' is military vernacular for Quatre Bras, penultimate encounter of the Napoleonic Wars, where Wellington intervened in an action between the French and the Prussian forces. Two days later, 18 June 1815, Napoleon was defeated at Waterloo.

The 'thin red line' was a term applied to the British force that held its ground against the numerically superior French and finally won the day.

The Roses of Tretower

This story appears in draft in the writer's 1941–3 Notebook under the title 'The Roses of Cwmdu'. The text differs in only minor respects from the subsequent typed version which is printed in this volume.

p.12 *the Cross Keys*: a public house.
p.12 *Parcylan . . . Bwlch . . . Cwmdu*: villages a little to the south of Brecon.
p.12 *tidy*: see the note for p.8, 'Jonesy and the Duke', above.
p.12 *Cynghordy*: the name of a farm, which the author may have borrowed from a village near Llandovery, just outside the Brecon Beacons national park, but in Carmarthenshire.
p.12 *Talgarth . . . Crickhowell*: small market towns in Breconshire (now Powys), the former a little to the east of Brecon, the latter about ten miles to the south.
p.12 *the Vaughans . . . the court*: Tretower Court, a medieval manor house near Crickhowell, given by William Herbert, earl of Pembroke in the mid-fifteenth century, to his half-brother, Sir Roger Vaughan, who enlarged it. The Vaughans remained a prominent Breconshire family for some 300 years, were involved in the Wars of the Roses and other violent disputes at home and in France, and include among their generations the poet Henry Vaughan (1621–95). The manor house is still in a good state of preservation and its garden has been re-created in recent times.
p.13 *cwtch*: south Wales vernacular for a small, snug, hidden or hiding place, often the cupboard under the stairs. Also used as a verb, roughly equivalent to 'cuddle'.

Joking with Arthur

The MS draft of this story is contained in the writer's 1941–3 Notebook. The text there differs little from the subsequent typed version which appears in this volume.

p.15 *Tredomen*: a hamlet a few miles north-east of Brecon.

p.15 *maldod*: dandle (children).

p.16 *bara ceirch*: oatcakes.

p.17 *Darro*: euphemistically modified mild expletive = 'Dammo' or 'Damn'.

p.17 *saltpetre*: potassium nitrate, a white crystalline substance used in preserving meat (and in the manufacture of gunpowder).

Take Hold on Hell

p.19 *the big seat*: the place in chapel reserved for the deacons.

p.19 Ben Gunn: character in R. L. Stevenson's *Treasure Island*. In *The Eleven Men of Eppynt* 'Gunn' is spelt 'Gun', a typographical error.

p.20 *Duw!*: a mild expletive = 'God'.

p.20 *Solomon*: Old Testament King of Israel, celebrated for his wisdom.

p.21 *darro*: see note for p.17, 'Joking with Arthur', above.

p.21 *the Pentre*: (= the village) a common place-name.

p.21 *Isaac Williams the Bryn . . . JP*: – a justice of the peace (an unpaid lay magistrate) who lives at a house called 'The Bryn' (= the hill).

p.21 *the Watton*: a street in Brecon.

p.22 *Bobol annwyl*: literally 'Dear people', an idiomatic expression of delight, surprise, concern, despair etc., depending upon circumstance. In *The Eleven Men of Eppynt* 'annwyl' is spelt with a single 'n'.

p.23 *Mr Roderick the Vro [Fro]*: another, like Mr Williams the Bryn, with some local influence. 'Fro', the mutated form of 'bro' following the definite article = district or land, especially low land.

p.23 *the undeb*: literally 'the union', here a trade union.

Incident in Majorca

The MS draft appears in the 1941–3 Notebook as 'Majorcan Story'. Though the structure of the story remains the same in the published version, few sentences were allowed to stand without some editorial amendment. Notably, the final words of Dr Mallinson were changed. In the draft, Sampson, one of the boys who accompany the Head in his final hours, reports: 'And he mumbled something just before he went out . . . it sounded like "I'm done for: he's beaten me at last. Tell Emily he's beaten me at last"'. The narrative tells how the merry dance his stepson, Littlejohn, leads him into the gorge of Torrente del Pareys precipitates

Mallinson's collapse and the reader needs no confirmation of this. His reported last words in the published version (p.34) instead open up new possibilities of interpretation as they recall the relief when the party that has pursued Littlejohn reaches the coast and the forces of darkness seem, for a moment, to be repelled by those of light. Escorca, still no more than a scattering of dwellings, is the usual starting point for a descent into the gorge of Torrente del Pareys ('river of the twins'), which reaches the sea on the north-west coast of Majorca. It is considered an arduous expedition for tourists.

p.25 *peerless Baedeker*: travellers' guidebook; one of the many published by the firm founded by Karl Baedeker at Coblenz in 1839. The guides had a worldwide reputation for reliability; in this context 'peerless' is used ironically.

p.26 *little poop*: someone who is a nuisance, or of no account, or both, derived from the term for the built-up stern part of a ship and applied vulgarly to the human rear end.

p.27 *wisp*: a small boy.

p.27 *whippers-in*: a term from hunting, designating the huntsman employed to manage hounds, but here applied to the young men whose task it is to keep the party of boys together.

p.27 *twirp(s)*: [also twerp] term of contempt.

p.27 *baited*: [also bate] put someone in a rage.

p.28 *high-hat stuff*: overbearing treatment.

p.28 *Ol' Moke*: 'moke' is slang for 'donkey'; here it is a schoolboy pejorative for the headmaster, alternative to 'Old Man' and 'the Boss', used elsewhere in the story.

p.28 *plus-fours*: baggy trousers reaching to the knees, worn with long, usually tartan, socks, formerly much affected by golfers.

p.29 *bruit*: outcry.

p.29 *corpse-warming world*: metaphoric description of the general tendency to analyse past events.

p.29 *called over the coals*: [also *haul* over the coals] scold.

p.29 *Oxted*: a town in Surrey a few miles south-east of Caterham.

p.29 *Cullingham*: fictional name of a school.

p.29 *Halewood's*: a house for boarders in a public school.

p.33 *young blister*: a nuisance; someone whose presence is a pain to others.

One Bell Tolling

The draft of this story, under the title 'Small Bells Tolling', appears in the 1941–3 Notebook. A good many minor changes were introduced in preparing the published version. Some of the editorial deletions make the story less predictable and add a touch of mystery to the sense of foreboding that accompanies the climax of the story. In the draft, for example, we learn that Uncle Jack has a tubercular hip, while the terror that grips Hedley is clearly explained:

> He knew. That was the trouble. He knew now. It would never be the same again. He had met it. Yes, met Death. All at once the air was not warm, it was foetid. Heavy with clutching breath. That was why. He shook. That was why she was so slow. She was giving all her time to breathing. Death was overtaking her bit by bit . . . It was irresistible; not triumphant but certain and cold . . . But death could only catch him in a small place like this. Only if he couldn't move. Duw, out, out, he must get out. He started to his feet.

The change of title in the published text, evoking more clearly Donne's 'It tolls for thee', is the exchange for this loss of the explicit.

p.35 *Boadicea*: [or *Boudicca*] widow queen who, c. AD 61, raised a revolt of her tribe, the Iceni, against the Romans. She famously led her forces from a horse-drawn war chariot, without benefit of pneumatic tyres.

p.36 *slivered*: an adjective formed from the noun 'sliver', a piece of material cut or broken off lengthwise.

p.36 *Upper Boat . . . Llanbradach . . . Sirhowy*: the barest outline of a route from the Vale of Glamorgan, east and northwards via the Taff Valley, through Trefforest, to Llanbradach in the Rhymni Valley, and on again to the valley of the Sirhowy, which has its source in the mountains above Tredegar, not far from Beaufort/Garnlydan, where a branch of Roland Mathias's mother's family had its roots.

p.37 *frivols*: trifling behaviour.

p.37 *Blaen Onneu*: [Blaen *Onnau* = the upper reaches of the valley of the River Onnau] another location a few miles across the mountains, north of Beaufort, on a crest overlooking the Usk valley, near Crickhowell.

p.37 *The Rhiw*: [Pen Rhiw = top of the hill] another location a mile or so due east of Blaen Onneu, above Llangattock, which faces Crickhowell across the River Usk.

p.38 *Dam, O dammo*: a mild expletive, 'damn'.

p.38 *Mamgu*: common south Wales equivalent of 'Gran' or 'Granny'.

p.39 *John bach*: 'bach' = little, but here it is also applied as a term of endearment to a child.

p.39 *Tyisha*: the name of a farm, literally 'lower house' from 'tŷ isaf'; a variant of 'Tyisaf' as used in 'A Night for the Curing'.

Cassie Thomas

This story appears untitled in the 1941–3 Notebook, but a good deal of astute editing occurred in readying the text for publication. For example, the moment when the delinquent evacuee takes the cane from Cassie was omitted – 'Alf took the cane out of the dummy's hand with a contemptuous look and walked back to his seat with it' – though the retrieval of the cane remained – 'The cane was recovered from Alf by stratagem before many minutes were up'. The effect of the omission is to reinforce the dislocation of sense suffered by Cassie as her other self, the schoolteacher 'dummy', fails to react to the crisis in the classroom.

p.43 *Trebanog*: village in Glamorgan at the top of a hill above Porth in the Rhondda Valley.

p.44 *merch Tom Thomas*: daughter of Tom Thomas.

p.44 *the miners' lodge*: i.e. union lodge.

p.44 *coll*: abbreviation for 'college'.

p.44 *Trefriw*: village in the Conwy Valley near Llanrwst.

p.44 *Pontlottyn*: village in the Rhymni Valley close to the town of Rhymni.

p.44 *Peterchurch-on-Arrow*: fictional location. The River Arrow rises in the hills of Powys not far from Kington and flows east through Herefordshire to join the River Lugg just south of Leominster. There is a village named Peterchurch on the River Dore (and the B4347) in the Golden Valley, Herefordshire.

p.45 *evacuees*: children evacuated to country districts from London and other large towns targeted by the German bombing campaign early in the Second World War.

p.45 *Cwrt y Cadno*: hamlet on the River Cothi in Carmarthenshire, about midway between Llanwrtyd and Lampeter.

p.45 *V sign*: i.e. V-shaped, but the 'V sign' had a particular significance during the Second World War as a Churchillian symbol of defiance and promise of ultimate victory.

Block-System

Comparison with the MS draft in the 1941–3 Notebook shows that a number of changes were introduced in preparing the text for publication. Notably, two daughters in the original are reduced to one, Beryl. The draft lines 'Misery they were now, the English words, once round and skinned with beauty . . . he was too old to work at them again' become in the published version '. . . Welsh words, round and skinned with magic. Now they were cinders to him', but the former are closer to the writer's father's account of acquiring his first English words in school – which is also the source of the recollection of the toy horse and the word 'horse' that names it.

p.49 *Paiforce*: administrative section of the army, the 'pay-corps'.

p.50 *machgeni*: colloquial abbreviation of 'fy machgen i' = my boy, here a wife's familiar form of address to her husband.

p.51 *Rhos Meurig*: fictional variant on Rhos Llangeler, original home of the family of Evan Mathias, the author's father.

p.51 *Horsa*: joint leader of the first successful Saxon invaders of Britain, AD 449. Etymologically, a connection exists between 'Horsa' and 'horse': hence the link between the historical imposition of the Saxon language on the Celtic Britons of Kent and the infant Ben learning his first word in English.

p.53 *Pontwillim*: fictional home in rural west Wales ('Llanelly', in the Notebook draft).

p.53 *this time ten years*: ten years ago.

p.54 *Plasdu Estate*: fictional version of Stepney Estate, Llanelli, where Evan Mathias's father brought his family and made a living as a carpenter.

p.55 *Jack Saer*: 'saer' = carpenter; the word can be a surname but here identifies 'Jack' by his trade.

p.55 *Ben Davies, Cefen*: here Ben is identified by the name of his family home. 'Cefen' [*cefn*] could name a village (Cefncoedycymer near Merthyr Tydfil is one of several in south Wales), or a dwelling.

Digression into Miracle

The MS draft of this story is included in the 1941–3 Notebook under the title 'Mine Country: Digression into Miracle'. The narrative is identical to that in *The Eleven Men of Eppynt*, reproduced in this volume, but the two versions differ considerably in matters of detail as the editing concentrated on increasing the tautness of the story. In particular, the varying accents of the workmen at the mine are distinguished more clearly and consistently in the printed text. The following paragraph of historical background in the draft was omitted:

> Thomas Bushell in London was uneasy. Of what use, he pondered, was the grant of mines in Wales, the grant which had sprung from his display of engineering at Enstone Rock, if he were prevented from mining them? Charles was not likely to give endless audience to his virtuoso pleas. He had granted him already the unheard-of right to mint the silver at Aberystwyth, but where was the silver to be minted?

p.56 *Thomas Bushell*: (1594–1674) page and protégé of Francis Bacon (Lord Chancellor, Baron Verulam), and loyal supporter of the monarchy. In 1636, Charles I visited the walks and fountains he created at Enstone, Oxfordshire, and granted him rights to work the royal mines in Wales. In 1637 he was appointed Master of the Mint at Aberystwyth.

p.56 *St Stephen's Chapel*: the building in the Palace of Westminster where the House of Commons formerly sat. It was destroyed by fire in 1834.

p.56 *Enstone*: village in rural Oxfordshire, historically connected with Thomas Bushell and Charles I, and also the original home of Molly Mathias, the writer's wife.

p.56 *Secretary of State Windebank*: Sir Francis Windebank (1582–1646), joint secretary of state to Charles I, and engaged by the king in secret negotiations about the unification of the Anglican and the Roman Catholic Church.

p.56 *Lord Bacon*: see the note on Thomas Bushell above.

p.56 *Talybont*: a village about five miles north-east of Aberystwyth.

p.56 *Sir Richard Pryse of Gogerddan*: (died 1651) scion of a notable Welsh family, landowners in north Cardiganshire from the sixteenth century. His first marriage was to Hester, the daughter of Sir Hugh Myddleton (see below). Plas Gogerddan is a few miles from Aberystwyth, just south of Bow Street.

p.56 *charke*: charcoal used in smelting.

p.57 *Agricola*: Georgius Agricola, latinized version of the name of Georg Bauer (1494–1555), German mineralogist, metallurgist and author of works on these subjects that earned him a reputation as the father of mineralogy.

p.57 *Myddleton*: Sir Hugh Myddleton (1560–1631), entrepreneur and goldsmith in the city of London. In 1609 he financed the New River project to improve London's water supply. His lease of the Cardiganshire lead and silver mines in 1617 brought him large profits.

p.57 *feeder*: a tributary stream, useful for washing minerals brought to the surface.

p.57 *deads*: mined material of no worth and so discarded, spoil.

p.57 *adit*: more or less horizontal or gradually sloping shaft into a mine.

p.57 *forefield*: the furthest point reached in mine workings, the face.

p.57 *Strata Florida*: a ruined abbey in Cardiganshire some fifteen miles south-east of Aberystwyth.

p.58 *Goginan*: a village a few miles east of Aberystwyth.

p.58 *whimsy*: more usually 'whim', a machine consisting of a vertical shaft with radiating arms, turned by a horse, for raising ore from a mine.

p.58 *Cwmsymlog . . . Cwmystwyth*: locations near Aberystwyth, the former about five miles east, the latter some twelve miles south-east.

p.59 *Big Tom*: Thomas Bushell.

p.59 *Gwely*: bed.

p.59 *Jawch*: euphemistic variant of the mild expletive 'diawl' = devil.

p.59 *bellon*: lead-colic.

p.61 *devil*: work as an apprentice.

p.62 *cwtch*: see note for p.13, 'The Roses of Tretower', above.

p.62 *diallin' be none so good*: a dial in this context is a compass for surveying in a mine.

p.62 *a piece*: a piece of ordnance, a cannon.

The Rhine Tugs

Although the narrative is the same, the story as it appears in this volume is much changed from the draft entitled 'Tugs on the Rhine' in the 1941–3 Notebook. Editing excised the name of the narrator ('Richard') and his meditation on degeneracy, of the Isherwoodish kind in Germany before the war, and in Britain under the influence of American culture after. On the other hand, the psychology of the introspective narrator and details of his recollections were augmented. The reference to Wordsworth (see below) was changed from the draft's 'Should he, like Wordsworth, almost quarrel with a blameless spectacle for lingering, an image on the mind?' The shift from the unhappy present to the distant childhood past is clarified in the published version, but identification of Hugo Stinnes ('ex-capitalist and mine owner, co-founder of Nazi power') was dropped, because it is extraneous to the development of the story. Refinement of the draft, often subtle, affected most sentences.

p.64 *platz*: German equivalent of 'place' or 'square', an open space surrounded by buildings in a town or city.

p.64 *Hohenzollern bridge*: bridge over the Rhine at Cologne named after a German noble family.

p.65 *Mulheim*: a quarter of Cologne on the opposite bank of the Rhine.

p.65 *clicked heels*: heel-clicking was incorporated into the style of saluting favoured by the Nazis. The phrase therefore signifies a military presence.

p.65 *The Dom*: the cathedral.

p.66 *Blindgasse*: a street in Cologne.

p.66 *pogrom*: organized massacre of Jews.

p.66 *Judenhetze*: literally 'Jew-baiting', the systematic persecution of Jews in Nazi Germany.

p.68 *Harpies*: predatory monsters of classical mythology that live in filth and contaminate all they touch.

p.68 *Master Gerhardt*: Paul Gerhardt (1607–76), German poet and Lutheran pastor, famed for his preaching and hymn-writing. In *The Eleven Men of Eppynt*, this was spelt 'Gerhard'.

p.69 *Wordsworth almost cursing his memories of Arras for the sake of Robespierre*: in 1791–2, Wordsworth spent a year in France. He became a strong supporter of the French Revolution, but disillusionment followed when, in 1793, Robespierre instituted the 'Reign of Terror'. More specifically, this is a reference to *The Prelude*, Book X, lines 449ff., in which he recalls these experiences:

> We walked, a pair of weary travellers,
> Along the town of Arras – a place from which
> Issued that Robespierre, who afterwards
> Wielded the sceptre of the atheist crew.
> When calamity spread far and wide.

The 1941–3 Notebook contains the opening 600 words or so of an essay on Wordsworth, which were clearly written about the same time as the story. At the outset, the writer admits that he has just read *The Prelude* for the first time and then passes quickly to Wordsworth's politics: 'If in the end he contrives to pass on something of his domineering sincerity, he owes it chiefly to his account of his political changes of front, of his early Jacobinism, his subsequent disgust both with the England that declared war on the revolution and the France of the Terror.'

p.69 *Hugo Stinnes*: see the introductory paragraph on pp.187–8 above; Stinnes was a leading German industrialist at the time of the First World War.

pp.70–1 *Hugo Stinnes VIII . . . Brunhilde . . . Albert Ballin . . . Hugo Grotius*: the actual, well-remembered names of tugs observed by the writer as a child. *Brunhilde* is the legendary queen of the Siegfried saga; the *Albert Ballin* was named after a shipping magnate of the turn of the nineteenth century; *Hugo Grotius* is the Latinized name of Huig de Groot (1583–1645), Dutch statesman and author of a book acknowledged as the foundation of international law.

p.71 *schloss*: the German word for 'castle'.

p.71 *Andernach*: town on the Rhine, south of Cologne, near Coblenz.

p.72 *Domplatz*: cathedral square.

p.72 *Riehl*: suburb of Cologne, where the family of Evan Mathias had their first home.

p.73 *Ehrenbreitstein*: another tug, named after a small town, now virtually a suburb of Cologne.

p.74 *Marienburg*: a small town in Nordrhein Westfallen, south-east of Cologne.

p.75 *He gave a little wave of the hand that was pitifully like a gesture of drowning*: a curious foreshadowing of Stevie Smith's 'Not Waving But Drowning' (1957).

The Neutral Shore

A close knowledge of the historical background is not necessary to an appreciation of this atmospheric story. Nevertheless, it is firmly grounded in the history of trade between England and France in the second half of the seventeenth century and especially the 1690s. In the course of his Oxford research Roland Mathias uncovered many details of the 'war' between customs officers on the south coast of England and those combined French and English interests determined to export raw wool to France. This was strongly opposed by the Council of Trade (part of whose remit was 'to consider some proper methods for setting on worke and imploying the Poor'), because it restricted the creation of employment opportunities in woollen manufacture in England. With only a few exceptions, the characters in the story are part of that history.

p.76 *council-chamber*: a private meeting room at an inn.

p.78 *[Robert] Hudson*: testified to the Board in 1696 about his incarceration in Calais and reported that he had heard the French 'would have wool, do what we could, for they had friends here, which we did not think of'. Hudson was literate; he submitted a written report to the Commissioners. This emerges in the story when Manley shows him written instructions (p.79).

p.78 *Calliss*: Calais.

p.80 *Isaac Manley*: sent by the Commissioners for Customs late in 1696 to superintend the work of local customs officers. He later reported to the Board about a battle at Folkestone Warren between the French and three officers (of whom he was one). The militia sent to their assistance were, with the exception of a single man, all themselves owlers.

p.80 *Owlers*: English engaged in smuggling wool to France.

p.81 *the Folkestone Warren*: a location, not identifiable on modern maps, adjacent to the town of Folkestone.

p.81 *Captain John Ellesdon*: in command of the three customs officers posted to Lydd. There were only thirteen officers for the whole coastline described in the story. Ellesdon was fortunate to have two of his own servants as additional aides.

p.82 *Commissioners of Customs*: government-appointed commissioners to oversee the implementation of laws imposing duties on goods imported or exported. Excise collection, introduced in 1643, was taken under direct control of the government in 1683. Excises were exploited to finance wars following the 'Glorious Revolution' of 1688–9, which led to James II being replaced by William III and Mary II. This is the period in which the story is set.

p.82 *John Sansom*: secretary to the Commissioners of Customs.

pp.82ff. *Lydd . . . Dymchurch . . . New Rumney [Romney] . . . Hythe . . . Shorncliffe*: towns, villages and, in the case of the last named, a beach on or near the coast in Kent between Folkestone and Dungeness.

p.84 *O generation of vipers*: Matthew III: 7: 'But when he saw many of the Pharisees and Sadducees come to his baptism, he said unto them, O generation of vipers, who hath warned you to flee from the wrath to come?'

p.85 *William Carter*: clothier and the author of *A Summary of Certain Papers about Wooll, as the interest of England is concerned with it* (1685). In 1668, and again in 1684–5, he was appointed to command coastal preventive guards at the instigation of clothiers of Exeter and London respectively, who were concerned that little had been done to enforce the Act of 1660 forbidding the export of wool. On both occasions the French interest at the court of James II brought these efforts to an abrupt end. In 1696, with the support of clothiers in Colchester and Leeds, he tried to persuade the Commissioners to appoint him director of anti-smuggling operations. Part of Carter's proposed strategy was to intercept the French vessels at sea, as he had attempted (with notable lack of success) in 1685.

p.85 *Admiral Allen*: commissioned to take the battle to the smugglers on sea. The effort was doomed, in part because of the influence at court of the French, who protested that innocent fishing vessels were being harrassed.

p.85 *shallop*: a small, two-masted sailing ship.

p.85 *Lille and Tournay*: neighbouring industrial towns about fifty miles south-east of Calais, Lille in France and Tournay [Tournai] now in Belgium.

p.85 *Mounseer Colbert*: Jean-Baptiste Colbert (1619–83), Louis XIV's great finance minister. He introduced major reforms in the financial system and, as 'minister of marine', created a powerful French navy. Among many other activities of far-reaching influence, he founded the academies of science, of architecture and of inscriptions, and instigated the construction of the Canal du Midi, which was inaugurated in 1681.

p.86 *Commissioners for Trade and Plantations*: members of the Council of Trade, a body revived in 1696 to oversee trade and notably that of cash crops such as tobacco and sugar from plantations in North America and the West Indies involving the use of African slaves.

p.86 *John Pollexfen*: fl. 1675–97, merchant and writer on economics; member of the Council of Trade.

p.86 *old Sir Philip Meadows*: Sir Philip Meadows (1626–1718) had been appointed Latin secretary to Cromwell's council in 1653 to relieve Milton. A notable diplomat, he was also a member of the Council of Trade.

p.86 *His Papistical Majesty*: James II (1633–1701). Soon after succeeding to the throne in 1685, following the death of his brother, Charles II, he declared himself a Catholic. He sought alliance with France and escaped to France at the 'Glorious Revolution' in 1688. After his defeat at the battle of the Boyne in 1690, he spent the rest of his life in France.

p.86 *Master John Locke*: the philosopher (1632–1704), who, among many other public and private roles, was secretary to the Council of Trade 1673–5 under Charles II, and a member of the new Council of Trade 1696–1700.

p.87 *Lillibullero*: an anti-Catholic ballad written by Thomas Wharton, the first marquess of Wharton (1648–1715), a strong supporter of William

III. It has continued popular as a military marching tune and remains the call sign of the BBC World Service.

p.89 *Denge Marsh*: marshland immediately to the north-west of Dungeness.

p.89 *East Guldeford*: village close to Rye, to the west of Dungeness.

p.89 *the Midrips*: another location between Folkestone and Lydd no longer identified on modern maps.

p.89 *Thomas Chidwick*: one of the officers serving under Ellesdon at Lydd. A reformed owler, he was considered a useful man. His salary was a paltry £20 per year.

A Night for the Curing

p.95 *Y Gât*: the scene described is Gât Bwlch-Clawdd, Rhos Llangeler, Carmarthenshire, where the family of the writer's father had its roots.

p.96 *Cwrt Bailey*: literally 'Bailey's Court', a fictional location.

p.97 *Un bach yw e*: 'He's a little one.' Here as elsewhere in the story, Welsh expressions are followed by their translation.

p.98 *Tyisaf*: the name of a farm, literally 'lower house', from 'tŷ isaf'.

p.98 *Dydd Iau Mawr*: literally 'Big Thursday', the day of the annual outing for the farmers and smallholders of a district.

p.100 *darro*: see note for p.17, 'Joking with Arthur', above.

p.101 *twp*: see note for p.7, 'A Duty to the Community', above.

p.101 *Gelli*: more properly 'Y Gelli' = 'The Grove, a fictional location.

p.103 *cawl*: soup or stew, traditionally made with lamb, leeks and other vegetables.

The Palace

p.105 *Drake and Hawkins*: Sir Francis Drake (1540?–96) and Sir John Hawkins (1532–95), famed seafarers of Plymouth, Devon.

p.105 *The Palace*: Lamphey Palace; the ruins of this ancient seat of the Devereux family are to be found about five miles south-east of Pembroke Dock. The writer's interest focused particularly on Sir Robert Devereux, second earl of Essex (1566–1601), a favourite of Elizabeth I, who became embroiled in disputes with other powerful courtiers. He was later found guilty of plotting against the queen's counsellors and executed.

p.106 *intercursus*: a patch of land running between two features.

p.107 *the Camera*: the name given to one of the chambers, a 'green-swarded room', in the ruined palace.

p.107 *the burr in their talk*: the distinctive south Pembrokeshire accent, which resembles that of the rural west country in England.

p.109 *garderobe*: a privy set in the wall.

p.109 *valerian*: a plant with small white or pinkish flowers.

p.109 *demesne*: the land surrounding and belonging to an ancient dwelling.

The Eleven Men of Eppynt

p.113 *Eppynt*: Mynydd Eppynt: mountainous area in Powys, between Brecon and Builth/Llangamarch, occupied by the army during the Second World War and subsequently.

p.113 *Cae Coch*: literally 'Red Field', a fictitious location.

p.113 *Cops y Gwdihw*: 'Owl's Copse'.

p.113 *the bark of the blackthorn in the hedge peeled and nibbled green*: i.e. nibbled by rabbits desperate for food and put within reach of the hedges by the packed snow, a phenomenon remarked in the press in the winter of 1947–8.

p.113 *Bronheulog*: 'Sunny breast' i.e. of a hill; a fictitious dwelling.

p.114 *Llwyniago*: 'Iago's Grove', fictitious location; Iago = James.

p.114 *Erwood*: a village about twelve miles south of Builth.

p.114 *cwm*: valley.

p.114 *short as the fight of Llewelyn Olaf in the thicket*: Llywelyn ap Gruffudd, also known as Llywelyn Olaf (Llewelyn the Last), Prince of Wales, was murdered on 11 December 1282 by a marauding band of English knights on the banks of the Irfon, near Builth.

p.114 *the Wern*: 'the marsh', a fictitious location.

p.114 *Dinas*: literally 'city', though the name is borne by a few small villages: a fictitious location.

p.115 *steers on the Bar 60*: the kind of tale Maggie Thomas reads avidly in her weekly Wild West magazines.

p.115 *Isaacs Cefn*: see note for p.9, 'Block-System', above.

p.116 *Jack Pant*: Y Pant = the hollow, the name given to a fictitious dwelling and attached as an identifier to its occupants.

p.116 *Coygen*: a fictitious dwelling.

p.116 *Llandefaelog [Fach]*: hamlet a little way north of Brecon on the B4520 road to Upper Chapel and, eventually, Builth.

p.117 *Beili-bach*: literally 'small bailey' (i.e. yard or court), another fictitious dwelling.

p.117 *gambo*: heavy farm wagon.

p.117 *Goytre*: [Goetre] literally 'house in the wood', a village in Monmouthshire some twenty miles south of Brecon.

p.117 *ankle-stranglers*: workmen's puttees.

p.117 *butts*: discarded cigarette ends.

p.117 *Allt-arnog*: another fictitious dwelling; the name is a colloquial abbreviation of 'Allt-ysgyfarnog' = hare's hillside.

p.117 *Morgan the Agent*: the agent who deals with tenant farmers on behalf of the landowner.

p.117 *Cardi Morgan*: a man who came originally from Cardiganshire.

p.117 *Beili-brith*: literally 'speckled bailey'; another fictitious dwelling.

p.118 *like a championship bitch*: i.e. as a sheepdog harries the sheep in a competition.

p.118 *the Dot*: familar abbreviation of 'The Dorothy', a café and confectioners' in Brecon.

p.119 *the mountains . . . the Beacons*: a mountainous area, more extensive and higher than Mynydd Eppynt, to the south of Brecon.

p.119 *Ysbaddaden Chief Giant . . . Olwen of the White Trefoil*: Olwen is the daughter of Ysbaddaden in the tale of Culhwch and Olwen from *The Mabinogion*. As the result of a witch's curse, Culhwch is fated to marry Olwen or no one. With the help of six heroes from King Arthur's court, he eventually overcomes all the obstacles Ysbaddaden places in his path, kills the giant and takes the hand of Olwen (= 'white track'), one of whose attributes is that four white trefoils spring up behind her wherever she walks.

p.119 *Arthur . . . Merlin*: Arthur was a fifth/sixth-century military leader against the Saxons, who became the hero of a great body of folk tale and romance; Merlin, a poet and prophet, was his legendary counsellor and companion.

p.121 *Garthbrengy*: a hamlet a little to the east of the B4520.

p.121 *Bechers*: 'Beechers Brook' is a notorious jump on the Grand National steeplechase course.

p.121 *Walter Scott*: Jack Pant has confused the novelist with Robert Falcon Scott, who was the subject of the popular film *Scott of the Antarctic*, released in 1948, the year after the snowfall which is the inspiration of the story.

Agger Makes Christmas

p.125 *yellowbacks*: cheap, popular novels in a uniform yellow binding.

p.126 *Zider Zee*: schoolboy wit; the reference is to the Zuider Zee in the Netherlands, formerly an inlet of the North Sea, now largely reclaimed land sealed off in 1932 by the construction of a dam.

p.126 *Table Six*: prefects' duties include taking meals with pupils to maintain order; 'Table Six' is difficult to control.

p.126 *flatulans*: Caterham Latin: flatulence.

p.126 *the saw between his knees*: a musical saw.

p.126 *Annie Laurie*: poem by William Douglas (1672–1748) which became a well-known song.

p.128 *Uno*: anachronistic reference to the United Nations Organization.

p.129 *his morning coat and striped trousers were in splendid accord*: the bowler hat Agger has assumed complements his school uniform, transforming him into a typical commuting employee in the City.

p.130 *osier-like woods*: the bare branches of the trees resemble the willow twigs used in basket-making.

p.130 *Beringley . . . Morse Hill*: fictitious names.

p.131 *North and Hilliard*: well-known Latin textbook.

Ffynnon Fawr

p.133 *Caerfanell*: a river that rises in the Brecon Beacons between Craig y Fan Las and Craig y Fan Du and once flowed through Glyn Collwn to join the Usk near Llansanffraid. Glyn Collwn was flooded to create the Talybont Reservoir. In this story, the writer uses 'Ffynnon Fawr', the actual name of his birthplace, but for Glyn Collwn, the name of the valley in which the farm once stood, he substitutes 'Caerfanell'.

p.134 *Tyle-Clydach*: the farm first occupied by Joseph Morgan and his wife, grandparents of the writer, when they came to the area. Clydach is the name of the stream that runs beside the farm, which is also mentioned in the poems 'The Tyle' and 'On Newport Reservoir'.

p.135 *fawn sportex trousers*: a fashionable garment, unsuitable for the conditions of Ffynnon Fawr, foreshadowing Rendel's own unsuitability.

p.138 *a half-grown cypress*: reference to the tree planted by the writer's grandfather when he was born and, now fully grown, still marking where the farm once stood.

p.138 *the light on Bishop Rock*: a famous lighthouse on a lone rock off the Isles of Scilly.

p.139 *Twrch Trwyth*: legendary boar in the tale of Culhwch and Olwen, between whose ears are lodged the only comb and shears that Ysbaddaden will accept to dress his own hair. The boar is hunted across south Wales and into Cornwall before it finally yields its tonsorial equipment.

Match

p.142 *the pill*: from the Welsh 'pwll' which can mean a pit or a pool, not uncommonly applied to low-lying land where there is, or once was, a pool in a river or estuary. Applied here to a land dipping down towards the sea at Pembroke Dock.

p.143 *a house system without houses*: the usual case with schools in the maintained sector. In public schools, the houses to which pupils belong are separate buildings.

p.143 *Bush*: in 1955, Pembroke Dock Grammar School became a grammar-technical school offering the opportunity for pupils to specialize in agriculture. With this extended remit the school moved to new premises at Bush, near Pembroke.

p.143 *Gethin Du he would have been in the Welsh parts*: north Pembrokeshire still has a sizeable Welsh-speaking population, in contrast to the south of the county, which has been English-speaking for centuries. 'Du' = black, a reference to his dark hair and swarthy appearance.

p.143 *Ceffyl*: 'horse'.

p.144 *Monkton Cave*: a coastal cave in south Pembrokeshire where prehistoric remains were discovered.

p.145 *tamping*: very angry.

p.146 *To your tents, O Israel*: 'To your tents, O Israel: now see to thine own house, David', I Kings 12: 16. Completion of the quotation is pertinent to Wynford's predicament.

p.147 *Hir*: (=long); the pack leader's instruction to the wing-threequarter (whose role it then was) to throw the ball to the back of the line-out.

The Only Road Open

p.151 *Scethrog*: hamlet about five miles south of Brecon on the A40.

p.151 *Pritchard Maescar*: as in several of the stories, individuals are identified by their surnames and the name of their farm, or their place of origin.

p.152 *the little chapelyard on the slope of Glyn Collwn*: the chapel at Aber, a village near Talybont-on-Usk, just below the Talybont Reservoir, where the writer's father and mother and members of his mother's family are buried.

p.152 *the Wenallt*: literally 'white hillside', the name of the mountain ridge facing Aber across the valley.

p.153 *the cottage where his mother had lived*: the dwelling known as 'Tyle-Clydach' (= Clydach Hill; Clydach brook runs down it) – see note for p.134, 'Ffynnon Fawr', above.

p.153 *Torpantau*: area in the Brecon Beacons about six miles north of Merthyr Tydfil and a little to the east of the Neuadd Reservoirs.

p.154 *One of Beeching's cuts*: Richard Beeching, later Baron Beeching (1913–85); as chairman of British Railways, he instituted in 1963 the notorious rail closure programme known as the 'Beeching Axe'.

p.154 *the bwlch*: a pass or gap. The village of Bwlch is some ten miles south of Brecon on the A40.

p.154 *Llanelly*: conventional spelling of the name of the west Wales industrial town in the 1960s when the story was written. It has since been changed to 'Llanelli', the form that appears in the later story 'Siams' (1978).

p.154 *the unpeopled wilderness that Collwn had become*: the valley was depopulated to make way for the reservoir – see note for p.133, 'Ffynnon Fawr', above.

p.155 *Llangynidr*: a village on the south bank of the Usk, below Talybont-on-Usk, about two miles from Bwlch.

p.155 *Gliffaes*: a mansion house, now a hotel, overlooking the Usk, just off the A40 near Crickhowell.

p.155 *Crickhowell*: a small town beside the Usk on the A40, about ten miles from Abergavenny.

A View of the Estuary

p.156 *the Llwchwr*: a river rising in the Black Mountains of Carmarthenshire and entering the sea via a long tongue of estuary that separates Llanelli, to the north, from the town of Loughor and the Gower peninsula to the south.

p.158 *Dewch i mewn*: 'Come in'.

p.158 *bachan*: literally 'little one', a term of affection, used as often familiarly between adults as to children.

p.158 *Eisteddwch i lawr*: 'Sit down'.

p.160 *fives court*: the enclosed area of a game similar to squash but played with bats (or the hands); the writer played fives at Caterham.

p.161 *merch fach i*: [fy merch fach i] = my little girl, again an expression of affection.

p.162 *Llanybyther*: [Llanybydder] village on the A485 in Carmarthenshire near Lampeter, and within a dozen miles or so of Rhos Llangeler.

p.162 *the Valleys*: the industrial valleys of old Glamorgan.

p.163 *Elvet Lewis*: Howell Elvet Lewis (1860–1953), well-known preacher and hymn-writer.

p.166 *squitch . . . and groundsel*: couch grass and a plant with small yellow flowers considered a garden weed.

Siams

p.168 *Y Gilfach*: here a house name, literally 'Little nook'.

p.169 *the Blaid*: Plaid Cymru, the nationalist 'Party of Wales'.

p.170 *bachan*: see note for p.158, 'A View of the Estuary', above.

p.170 *Wel, wel*: the common expression of wonderment given Welsh orthography.

p.170 *Mawredd*: see note for p.6, 'A Duty to the Community', above.

p.170 *Aber*: common abbreviation of Aberystwyth.

p.171 *Dafen*: a suburb of Llanelli.

p.171 *Dewch ymlaen*: 'Come on'.

p.171 *Saron*: village in Carmarthenshire about three miles from Rhos Llangeler.

p.174 *Arfon*: that part of north Wales mostly to the south and east of Caernarfon, corresponding roughly to Snowdonia.